Arturo Santos Jr.

PRINCE ADINOR
Days of Distinction

STRATTON
—PRESS—
Publishing Life

Prince Adinor: Days of Distinction
Copyright © 2021 **Arturo Santos Jr.**

All rights reserved. No part of this book may be used or reproduced by any means, graphic, electronic, or mechanical, including photocopying, recording, taping or by information storage and retrieval system without the written permission of the author except in the case of brief quotations embodied in critical articles and reviews.

Stratton Press Publishing
831 N Tatnall Street Suite M #188,
Wilmington, DE 19801
www.stratton-press.com
1-888-323-7009

Because of the dynamic nature of the Internet, any web addresses or links contained in this book may have changed since publication and may no longer be valid. The views expressed in the work are solely those of the author and do not necessarily reflect the views of the publisher, and the publisher hereby disclaims any responsibility for them.

ISBN (Paperback): 978-1-64895-398-9
ISBN (Ebook): 978-1-64895-399-6

Printed in the United States of America

PRINCE ADINOR
DAYS OF DISTINCTION

For my mom.

ACKNOWLEDGMENTS

Thankfully, this process was not done in a vacuum; as such, I'd like to recognize a few instrumental people in the process.

I'd like to thank everyone at Stratton Press for the hard work and patience in dealing with me. I'd like to recognize Kobe Williams, Tatianna Gray, and Hope Edwards for their organization, communication, edits, and diligence in the process. Their patience with my constant demands and questions is tremendously appreciated.

I'd also like to thank my favorite English teacher of all time, Mrs. Nancy Dicharry. Remembering back to my middle school days, specifically, her reading my stories out loud in class was perhaps the highlight of my elementary school experience, and it continues to be a wonderful treasure of mine to this day. Thank you for lifting me up with your gift of recognition and guidance.

I'd like to thank my Viki (Vedrana). 2020 was a difficult year, but you were the biggest blessing throughout it. You'll never know how much strength and fuel to keep moving forward you give me with a solitary word of encouragement or belief.

Lastly, though gone from this earth, my mom, Patty Galdamez (2016), will forever be my source of inspiration, guidance, miracles, and mother-bear-like love. God's greatest gift was my mom. She was so unendingly caring and helpful to my sister and I. The first mentions of this book I shared with you years ago, and as always, you encouraged me to "use your gifts." You always believed in me. I hope I keep making you proud. I love you forever, Mom.

Chapter 1

"I trust you'll stop the attacks in Pionard that have killed dozens of our people without trouble, Bolios," said the King.

Bolios knelt down and replied, "Yes, my lord."

King Ralphus took another step and reached out his hand, touching the shoulder of the teenage boy standing next to Bolios. Dwarfed by the size of Bolios, the boy remained covered in the behemoth's shadow.

"And do make sure my only son gets back to us safe. It's his first quest, and though he's Prince of Mastada, he doesn't know combat like you and I."

Bolios was silent as Prince Adinor continued to sweat. Bolios rose and shook King Ralphus' hand and walked out of the throne room and headed straight for the armory. Prince Adinor remained behind with his father. The young Prince took two steps forward, extending both arms, and was soon enveloped by the embrace of his father.

"Make us proud," said the King.

"I will try, Father," replied Prince Adinor.

* * *

Inside the armory the King's foremost military leader, Bolios began preparing his group for their newly assigned mission. In the middle of a black stone room stood the giant of a man, twice the size of any other soldier. His hair, long and thick, fell down to his broad shoulders. His caramel-brown skin rippled with muscles as he gripped the axes and swords placed carefully on the racks overhead. Rumors throughout Mastada said that he wasn't human at all, but those closest to him knew of his upbringing and the many tears he shed during it.

"Travel light, we go to the western edge of the kingdom," said Bolios while grabbing his sword and spear.

"Do we go to the forest, my lord?" asked Theodonus, Bolios' captain and second in command of the warrior company.

"Of course not, you fool," replied Bolios, "you know well that is forbidden. We go only to the village nearby. One in need of our help."

"With all due respect, sire, why do we take the Prince?" asked Dolamite, a round and burly soldier with bright red hair and a bushy mustache with practically no neck. "He will only slow us down in our travels. He is just a boy."

He concluded and drained the remaining wine from the skin pouch he gripped mercilessly in his large palm. The drops of red wine collected on his mustache, a source of amusement for the rest of the soldiers standing nearby. Nine in total, all proven warriors experienced in battle from campaigns in foreign lands and from crushing unrest within the kingdom as well. Dolamite continued ripping apart the chicken leg he held in his other hand, for he chose to finish his meal rather than arm himself like the others. The warriors walked around him, choosing their weapons carefully and ignoring Dolamite's obsessive appetite. A common practice, for when Dolamite ate, nothing could take away his attention from the meal before him, a source of aggravation for his wife.

The armory was a familiar place for warriors, always the starting point for the quests required of them. The same couldn't be said, however, for the young Prince Adinor who aimlessly walked the halls of the warrior command center. Already late, the Prince hurried through the quiet halls only to arrive at the wrong chamber. He stepped inside and entered a massive open room featuring strange symbols carved of wood hanging high on the walls. He looked, and all around the outsides were spears, but some were made of wood like those he practiced with in his triped training. There was no one there, so he ventured back into the network of halls, hoping to find the armory this time. It was difficult enough to find his way for it was early morning and the sun was just beginning to rise. The Prince ran toward some light ahead and entered another room. After looking inside, he kicked the ground. It was also empty. His heart was pounding partly from the running, mostly because he was supposed to meet the company of warriors at daybreak. His palms were wet. He was late.

He ran back into the labyrinth of halls and raced through them once again. The warriors all remained in the armory waiting for the Prince, the sole reason for their delayed departure.

"Perhaps he's decided not to come," said Ecclesias, one of the tallest of the group.

"It's better if he doesn't," said Malchomite. "I don't have the patience for them."

"Patience for what?" asked Litovic, the youngest of the warriors.

"For children," replied Malchomite.

The warriors continued expressing their disdain for the Prince's need to join them.

"Let's just keep him out altogether, Bolios," said Theodonus. "The men have a point."

Prince Adinor turned a corner near the armory entrance and almost passed it, but for the warriors conversing.

"He's not ready," said Marcus.

"My brother is right," replied Salazar.

The two most trusted archers in the group stood side by side as the other warriors continued to pile on the Prince. Hearing the conversation from just outside the armory entrance, Prince Adinor chose instead to wait and continued to listen to all the comments. He pressed his face against the cold stone wall separating him from the warriors just on the other side and closed his eyes. He crouched down and hid his face in his hands. The warriors continued talking and soon erupted in laughter from the mocking of Prince Adinor. Bolios couldn't help but smile at some of the amusing comments. As the warriors continued the revelry, Bolios walked toward a steel shield resting carefully on the wall near the armory's entrance. He soon noticed the Prince crouched just outside through the reflection of the shield. He was crying. The louder the warriors laughed, the more the young Prince was bothered. Bolios turned to his company of warriors, his jaw clenched.

"You asked me, Dolamite," said Bolios, "why take the boy? Was there not one day that even you were also a young warrior incapable of holding up your very own sword?"

Dolamite's laughs gradually slowed.

"And you two," continued Bolios, pointing to Salazar and Marcus, "I remember a day neither of you could stomach a full day's ride without complaint. Don't tell me I have to remind you of the episode you put us all through a few winters ago."

The warriors all laughed. The jokes about one another continued. Outside the armory, Prince Adinor's hands were now covered with his salty tears. He hurried to dry them on his clothes and rose quickly. The Prince pressed his face on his sleeve, dabbing away any remaining, as he smelled the perfumes of the royal palace. Already it seemed so far away. He closed his eyes once. His hands began to shake. The thought of having to face the warriors that had ridiculed him made him sweat.

"Will you join us?" said a voice.

The Prince opened his eyes, and standing in front of him was Bolios.

"Thank you," replied Prince Adinor. They both entered the armory.

All nine sets of eyes stared at the Prince. His remained fixed on the ground just ahead of his feet. The only light came from two small cracks in the walls to either side, making seeing the warriors more difficult. The armory was void of the previous laughter; only the steady drip of water falling from the corner of the room could be heard. No one moved. The warriors looked on at the meager teenaged Prince before them. They observed his hands, unblemished and soft, different than their calloused and bloodied fists. Bolios, in particular, saw the Prince's gentle face as a painful reminder when he'd been a boy who was only expected to milk cows and tease the neighborhood girl…a time he could barely remember.

The Prince's clothes, free of tears and cuts, were different than the tattered rags the warriors wore. Even the Prince's eyes reeked of innocence. The drops of water continued. Bolios walked from behind the Prince and stood directly in front of him.

"My Prince, we are ready for the task before us. Have you all that you need?"

"Yes, I believe so," replied the Prince. "When do we leave?"

"Now," replied Bolios.

The warriors and Prince Adinor, led by Bolios, walked out of the labyrinth of halls inside the warrior compound and stepped onto the dirt grounds of one of the outdoor training areas. In front of them were hundreds of other warriors practicing fight skills. The yells filled the air as blows from fists and kicks alike met their intended targets. Bolios and his men walked through the training as many stopped to greet him and the others behind. The trainees curiously stared at the Prince who was unrecognizable beneath the armor and battle garbs. Prince Adinor looked on through the tiny slit in his helmet which kept falling as he mistakenly grabbed one size to large. The warriors continued fighting, grabbing one another and throwing each other to the ground. Others punched and kicked, drawing large amounts of blood from their opponents' faces.

"It's not for the faint of heart," said Bolios.

Ecclesias and a couple of the warriors smiled as Prince Adinor sheepishly watched. Another fight nearby pitted a single warrior against three others. An average-sized man stood in the middle, surrounded by three men twice his size. The three men ran toward the lone combatant in the center and struck him repeatedly.

"Those were the days," said Dolamite, laughing.

Bolios led the group out from the fifty foot tall wood gate of the warrior grounds, the sole entrance into the compound. The arched wooden planks fastened with black iron slowly closed behind them. Dozens of large men standing near a chain system of pulleys and gears patted large oxen on as two ropes closed the gate completely. The warrior company walked toward the city center stables located between the Royal Palace and the northern wall of the warrior grounds. The Prince smiled at the familiar sight of the Royal Garden. The southern entrance to the Royal Palace, to their left, was a more enjoyable sight to him, for he'd often played in it as a child and still walked it frequently with his mother and father.

The distinct smell of animal feces and musk came upon them even before they arrived at the stables. Inside were hundreds of horses, carefully housed in numerous wooden stalls. Bolios walked to the end of a long aisle covered in straw as the warriors each wandered through the different sections, searching for their preferred one. Prince Adinor stood in the center of the stable, surrounded by all of the horses neighing and the strong odor of dew covered hay and horse feed. His stomach tightened, and a vile taste filled his mouth. He was covered in cold sweats. The warriors and Bolios were all gone. Prince Adinor bent over, grabbing his weak knees as he stared down at the ground. He stood and moved one step backward toward the stable entrance, and then another. The heat from underneath his armor was suffocating. In a flash, he was in a full speed run out of there. He sprinted toward the large fountain directly in the center of the three capitol stalwarts; the monk temple, the royal palace, and the warrior grounds. The sounds and smells of the stable faded behind him. He threw off his helmet and breathed in deep full breaths and gradually the bile-like taste in his mouth dispensed. Arriving at the fountain, he reached down and scooped up some the clear water and splashed it on his face. The drops ran down his neck and through his hair. His stomach loosened.

"No one is allowed to drink this water," said a figure standing nearby.

The Prince lifted his head and noticed the distinct dark robe of a monk.

"I'm very sorry, Prince Adinor," replied the monk, "I didn't realize it was you. Are you all right?"

The Prince rose and brushed his hair back behind his ears. The water continued to drip from his head.

"Yes, I'm fine," replied the Prince.

The monk turned and walked toward the temple, leaving the Prince alone at the fountain. The Prince looked toward the arching main entrance of the city center and noticed the vast open lands of Mastada in the backdrop. Its rolling hills, snow covered mountain peaks, and rich agricultural lands seemed never ending. He thought of the many trips he'd taken with his mother and father to visit the farming guilds and villages nearby. Small plumes from those same villages rose into the skyline. Sometimes upon returning, they would wander in the markets at the foot of the city center road that led back up to the spot he now stood on. He would soon pass through those very same markets, but this time was vastly different. Pounding on the dirt ground and rumbling sound announced horses approaching. Bolios and the warriors rode toward him. For the first time, he thought, *maybe the warriors were right. He was unfit for this journey.* Seated atop their horses, Prince Adinor recognized in each of the warriors' grizzled faces filled with scratches and battle scars. Each had damaged looks from harsh winters and long summers. The task of leading these men was an impossible one.

"Prince Adinor, it's a long journey, sire," said Bolios. "I wouldn't recommend it on foot. Malchomite brought your horse."

"Here, Prince Adinor," said Malcomite as he threw some reins down to the Prince.

"Thank you," said Prince Adinor. "Bolios, perhaps—"

"We ride."

A quick push on the horse's head and Bolios was at full speed, followed closely by the others. Prince Adinor grabbed his helmet and climbed upon his horse. He hurried to catch up. He raced through the cloud of dust trailing the warriors and was soon alongside the last rider, Malchomite. The group made their way down the steep city center road and trodded through the market below as they galloped onto the western edge road. It would take them in the direction of Pionard. Prince Adinor strained his eyes to keep a close watch of the warriors, for their armor reflected so boldly that it was difficult to look directly at them.

CHAPTER 2

They arrived at a small lake. The heat was stifling. The warriors all filled their containers with water as the Prince instead walked toward the open lands. Rolling hills and plains of corn and wheat fields seemed to go on forever.

The Prince turned in every direction as the high thick stalks of corn waved in the wind. The golden wheat seemed to dance as a delicate breeze passed over them. A group of trees not too far from the lake fluttered as large birds flew from their branches. As the Prince walked toward them, he noticed movement beneath them. A small set of bushes began to shake. The Prince looked back at the lake and warriors. He was more than a hundred yards from them. Out of the bushes, a figure appeared. It seemed to be approaching. Prince Adinor raised both hands to his brow, trying to shield his eyes from the glare. He hoped to see what came out of the bushes, but he couldn't. The Prince looked back hoping to signal the warriors, but they were resting under the shade of some banyan trees near their horses. He lowered himself in the wheat and looked toward the bushes as the figure in the distance quickened its pace. It was now coming directly toward him.

Its pace quickened as the dark figure neared. The Prince's heart raced as he became covered in sweat once again. He felt anxious. The smoldering heat made the air thick around him. It was difficult to breath. How he wished he would have drank from the lake as Bolios had instructed him to. As the Prince looked up again, the figure coming toward him became clear. It was no man at all.

"It's a minotaur," said the Prince. "It can't be. They haven't been seen in years."

The Prince strained his eyes once again. Then all the colors of the wheat and corn blended together. The sky above and ground below seemed upside down. He felt cold and weak. His palms were wet, and just as he reached for his sword, he collapsed to the ground and lost consciousness.

* * *

"This is supposed to be our king."

The Prince opened his eyes slowly. He was lying on his back atop soft crushed wheat.

"Mind your tongue, Salazar," said Bolios.

The Prince began to regain his strength.

"The figure," said the Prince, "I saw horns like that of a bull and it was tall. I've only heard of them in tales, is it true? Was it a minotaur?"

Bolios handed the Prince a jug of water. The Prince snatched it from his hands, wrapping his lips around the jug's narrow spout spilling some onto his clothes. Then suddenly, a giant shadow was cast over them both and there before the Prince appeared the figure he had just seen.

"It would be wise for you to drink slowly, young Prince," said the figure. "Haste makes waste."

"Elmahigh, it is unnecesary for you to accompany us on this journey," said Bolios. "Surely, you have better things to do."

"My dear friend, some days I do what I want," replied Elmahigh, "today, I do what is asked of me."

"You're not a minotaur," said the Prince.

"Not even on my worst days, young Prince," responded Elmahigh as he chuckled.

Elmahigh reached down to the Prince and helped him up. The Mastadan soldiers walked back toward the horses near the road. They shook their heads in disappointment and left Elmahigh and Prince Adinor behind in the wheat field.

"From a distance, you seemed different," said the Prince.

"Well, I'm sure it's not often you've seen monks," replied Elmahigh, "let alone one on horse. Truthfully, most in my order do not ride at all."

The Prince stood alongside Elmahigh and noticed far different attire than any monk he ever saw. All monks in the temples near the Royal Palace wore simple brown wool tunics with ropes for belts and never carried weapons. Elmahigh wore a white hooded tunic made of cotton. His sword, a large blade with a silver handle, hung from his leather belt. He also donned an incredibly large cross made of silver. It shone much like the warrior's armor.

"Why don't you dress like others in your order?" asked the Prince.

"There are not set rules we must abide by young Prince," replied Elmahigh, "the monks you are most familiar with choose a strict adherence to our order's message, opting for the life of a student and teacher within our order. They are the keepers of all things historical and informational. Their purpose is peaceful practice of our order. They do charitable works often helping those in need like the sick, dying, or helpless. They also serve as a resource to the leaders in our kingdom."

"What do you practice, Elmahigh?"

"All in due time, young Prince," responded Elmahigh, as he mounted his horse. "Perhaps you should gather your things and rejoin the group. It is time."

Elmahigh walked his horse in the direction of the warriors waiting at the road. Prince Adinor stumbled behind him and made his way to his horse still tied to the tree where he left it. As the Prince passed alongside the lake, he noticed his reflection out of the corner of his eye. He couldn't face it. He was embarrassed.

"We ride until we reach Pionard and will stay there for this evening," said Bolios. "We will not stop again. Make sure you consume your share of water for we have a long distance ahead."

A couple of warriors' faces wrinkled from previous snickering. Dolamite began to laugh aloud. They joked among themselves about Prince Adinor's fainting spell.

"Whatever is so amusing can entertain you further, Salazar, for you will stay with the Prince throughout the ride, making sure he's safe," said Bolios.

Prince Adinor removed a small leather jug from the pouch on his horse. He ran to the lake as the warriors rode off. Bolios and Elmahigh led. Prince Adinor reached down into the water and dunked the jug below the surface. Small bubbles formed at the top of the spout of the jug as water filled inside. The Prince looked at the lake, observing its stillness. He remembered his episode at the fountain in the city center courtyard and hung his head, breathing a long sigh for twice now, he showed his inexperience. The bubbles stopped. He pulled out the jug and covered it, running back to his horse where Salazar still waited for him. The Prince tucked the jug back into the pouch and jumped on his horse when he first noticed Salazar's blank stare

"Are you ready, Prince Adinor?"

"Yes," replied the Prince.

The two of them took off. Having soon reached the warriors, the Prince smiled as their travels through rolling hills covered in lush green grass and high fields of wheat and corn calmed him. In addition, he saw a variety of animals like fat cows and wild mustangs roaming the landscape. The Prince noticed elk and deer startled by the sounds of the men on horseback. Herds of bison and buffalo grazed on the rich grasslands. As the ride toward Pionard continued, the brothers were the first to break silence. Salazar and Marcus riding toward the rear of the group took to telling the Prince stories. He leaned forward with his eyebrows raised and listened.

"Prince, it wasn't until we removed the lion's mane that the spell of the wicked death dweller was undone," finished Marcus.

"Stop your twisted lies," said Dolamite.

"What's a death dweller?" asked the Prince.

"That's not important right now, young Prince," said Dolamite, "these two are getting the story all wrong."

"I sayest no lies," said Marcus. "Tell them Salazar."

"Me brother's right," said Salazar, nodding, "we had to remove the lion's mane just to make sure the bleeding thing was finished. And not until a moment before was the task over. I will tell ye that magician was satisfied with our success. I promise you."

The two brothers smiled.

It was then the Prince noticed the striking resemblance. The siblings' wrinkled foreheads and their pronounced cheekbones were identical. Until that moment, the Prince struggled to see the similarity at all. One brother wore his hair braided while the other had it messy. Salazar used a thin beard and the other thick. They both had the same coarse red hair, but with a slight variance, for Salazar's were darker than Marcus.

"Prince Adinor, be sure to listen to these fools with only one ear," said Dolamite, "because you can only believe half of what they tell you."

Dolamite reached inside his pocket and pulled out a small pebble. He studied it and launched it toward Marcus, hitting him on the shoulder. Salazar responded in kind, sending a similar-sized pebble at Dolamite. The three laughed together. Prince Adinor sat atop his horse unsure of whether to join in the amusement or remain quiet. He chose the safer option. Dolamite joined in the conversation with the brothers and engaged in a heated competition of who could impress the Prince with the greatest tale of heroism. The Prince smiled and listened to every detail of each story. He was oblivious to anything else around him.

Toward the front of the riders, the conversation was different between Bolios and Elmahigh.

"What do you think of him?" asked Bolios.

Elmahigh turned back, looking toward the rear of the group and saw Prince Adinor smiling together with a few of the others as their laughs increased.

"A yearling's born. A rabbit romps. A dove's among the sky and all do try. As days turn nights, theirs is supply," answered Elmahigh.

"You speak in riddles, Elmahigh," said Bolios. His stern gaze was directed at the monk instantly, "I trust my instincts and my senses."

"And what do they point to you, my friend?" asked Elmahigh.

Bolios turned and studied the Prince. He looked on at the teenager and studied his eyes and laughs. He noticed the way he rode and how he held the reins. He turned back forward and said, "I'm not sure yet."

Elmahigh smiled.

The group soon arrived at the Canyon of Maldoon. Bolios rode to its edge and was joined by Elmahigh and the others. They saw the massive chasm three miles below. Its steep walls on either side were made of dry brown rock. They rose vertically from the wide valley. At the bottom was a small creek flowing in the middle. It was fifty yards wide.

"There is a narrow bridge where we'll cross further along," said Elmahigh.

"I will lead in front," said Bolios, "and everyone follow behind in a single line. Elmahigh, bring up the rear. Prince Adinor follows behind me."

The group rode south as Elmahigh directed toward the bridge. No one spoke. The jovial conversations were over. The Prince rode behind Bolios. The rest of the soldiers followed him single file.

"There," said Elmahigh, "just behind the bushes is where we must begin."

Bolios circled his horse and directed it toward the wooden bridge. Its large planks below were several feet wide and half as long, the round thick vines tied to the ends connected up to two equal round ropes stretching from one side of the gorge to the other. As the horse approached, its eyes widened. It reared up on its back legs and stopped just shy of the first plank. The warriors and Prince Adinor behind him all circled around, moving back away from the edge. Bolios brushed his horse with his massive hands and patted its small fine hairs. The horse relaxed as Bolios spoke to it. Again, Bolios moved into position and this time succeeded in getting the horse to go onto the bridge. The animal stepped forward, placing each hoof on the planks below. The only sound heard were the creeks coming from the dry wood under its feet. Bolios noticed no margin for error. He glanced over his right shoulder and saw the direct drop down. The slightest mistake would cost someone his life. His horse moved forward as he turned back to see the Prince following behind. While the rest of the group began to cross the bridge, Friedrich spoke, "What is taking so long?"

Elmahigh glanced over to Friedrich and the two other soldiers still waiting at the top of the gorge yet to cross. Then he looked up at the sun as he calculated the amount of daylight left. He rode to the edge of the gorge.

"Patience," he said.

With Bolios and Prince Adinor across the bridge and the others more than halfway, Malchomite, Ecclesias, and Friedrich began to cross.

"Careful, gentlemen," Elmahigh said.

"I hate heights," said Ecclesias.

"Calm your nerves," suggested Elmahigh.

"I'm calm," said Friedrich. "I don't know if the same can be said for Ecclesias."

Ecclesias, drenched in sweat, clenched his eyes shut as his horse continued forward following Malchomite's toward the awaiting Mastadans on the opposite side. Elmahigh smiled as he brought up the rear.

In moments, they were all across. They all gathered away from the bridge near a large tree. Bolios and Elmahigh studied their options. Prince Adinor noticed a few of the warriors shaking Ecclesias' hand and patting him on the back. The color returned to his face as his sweat dissipated. Bolios rode toward a dry dirt path and Elmahigh followed. The rest did the same.

As they continued riding the sun began to set. They were blanketed in darkness, increasing their desire for rest. Prince Adinor's eyes were heavy. At first, the occasional conversation from the warriors helped keep him awake, but the slow pace of the horses walking and the cool breeze sweeping his face swooned him. As the trip continued, he heard the faint conversations of the warriors mixed with the footsteps of the horses and occasional sounds of an animal nearby. The crisp air around him chilled his bones. His breath formed small puffed clouds as he exhaled. The Prince adjusted himself on the horse and shook his head from side to side to stay awake. Despite the efforts, the breeze in his face and cold air wore on him. He struggled to grip the reins and hunched forward as he fell asleep on the horse. Only the feeling of falling off his horse would startle him awake, renewing the battle against his own fatigue. It continued on like that in the obscure darkness. The howl of wild wolves or chirps from birds and bugs revealed the nightlife around them. The bats overhead flapped as they flew in search of food in the darkness. Prince Adinor's thoughts drifted to his home and his family.

He dreamed of one of his father's gatherings. The occasion involved a neighboring kingdom's food shortages, a result of a long harsh winter and a drought thereafter. The lack of rains contributed to terrible harvests and people were starving. An emissary was sent to ask King Dolamaic for help. It was only a few years ago.

The emissary walked with the king accompanied by the music of pipes and drums. The jesters entertained as all the court danced. The men wore large plush hats as the woman donned long yellow and red dresses. Some even wore masks. It was a grand party and pleasant atmosphere. Despite the fun, the emissary stopped King Dolamaic with the point of his finger. He stepped another foot closer to the king and said, "We are prepared to take if what our people need is not given. I come here to make absolute certain that in the event our demands are not met, we will strike your perfect kingdom. Even the great King Dolamaic in his prestigious Mastada can't live like fattened pigs forever."

The Prince was hiding behind a large stone column just a couple of paces away from the encounter. Although young, he felt his skin become hot as the words from the emissary concluded. The Prince's hands began to shake. He twisted his head just barely around the column, but enough to observe his father's response. King Dolamaic stopped walking. His father gripped his left hand with his right and moved closer to the emissary. He then reached out his hand, touching the messenger's shoulder. Prince Adinor stepped further out from behind the column and heard his father say.

"Look around you. You have come into my kingdom. I have received you as my guest. I have offered you a place at my table to better understand your troubles. I know your king well and your people are my neighbors. As King, I know of the importance of peace throughout the kingdoms, but make no mistake, threats will win you no support in our kingdom or any."

"Sire," said the emissary, "our people starve. With every passing day, more and more of our brothers and sisters die. I have seen your abundance, and your people have plenty. It's unheard of."

At that moment, the Prince, who extended himself too far past the column, fell and landed a few feet from his father and the emissary. Both the emissary and King Ralphus Dolamaic turned. The secret plot to overhear was compromised. King Ralphus' dour gaze frightened the Prince, for he'd seen it just before the King slapped a thief who'd been found guilty of defrauding the royal treasury. The King lifted his hand as the Prince tucked his legs into his chest and pressed his head down onto his knees in preparation for a blow, but received only a gentle caress from his father's large hand. Surprised, the Prince opened his eyes as his father bent down toward him and lifted him up by the arm.

"You rotten boy," said the King with a smile.

Prince Adinor looked across at the emissary who remained silent. The weight of the King's massive paws on Adinor's shoulders bent the Prince forward. Looking back up as his dad, the Prince noticed his father's thick beard. He wondered if he would have one someday.

Then King Ralphus again spoke.

"You are correct, messenger," he said, "our kingdom is fortunate. We have abundance, but it comes at a price."

The emissary's head shook as he said, "Do you plan on giving us nothing? Our people are despa—"

"Silence," yelled the King.

All music and dancing stopped.

Prince Adinor shook as his father's words reverberated through his entire body.

The king continued, "As I was saying our people understand that the abundance we have comes at a price. The price is the responsibility and our long-documented understanding of helping others in need. I have your answer, emissary. I will do everything in my power to help your king. Rest assured, you will return home fattened, rested, and cared for as a symbol of what we will do for your people."

"Thank you, great king," said the emissary. He bowed repeatedly.

"As I will do everything in my power to help your people," said King Ralphus, "you must be sure to tell your king only this."

"Anything, great king," he replied, "anything."

The messenger was still bowing.

King Ralphus placed his massive hand upon Prince Adinor's head.

The Prince tried looking up to his father, but the weight of the hand was too great to overcome. He stood still and chose to look at the emissary instead.

His father said, "One day, my son will reign over this kingdom. And just as I have extended our kingdom's help in friendship to your people in a time of need, if the day should come in which my son is in need of favor from your King, then he must do the same. As a token of friendship, your people must forever remember this day and this act of service by the people of Mastada. If my son one day calls upon that friendship, your people must serve accordingly."

The emissary continued bowing and said, "Yes, my lord, I will see to it."

The Prince felt his father's massive hands move him. The king stepped closer to the emissary and whispered, "For if your people do not, I will haunt you and for all the days of your people's existence. The famine you experience now will pale in comparison to the vengeance I will inflict on you. Whether living or dead, I will terrorize you forever."

Prince Adinor's eyes widened, and his mouth opened wide. He looked at the emissary who looked equally concerned.

"It shall be done, King Ralphus," he said.

Laughter filled the rest of the evening. The King and the messenger ate and drank. The court members danced inside the banquet hall. The dozens of tables featured roasted meats, fresh fruits, and wines and beers from all over the kingdom. Both the Queen and King eventually pulled the Prince from the wooden table they all sat at and dragged him onto the large dance floor. Everyone began to clap as the pipes and drums played the King's favorite tune. The entire court circled around them as only the royal family danced. Adinor's mother and father laughed and smiled as they lifted him high into the air. The Prince beamed with happiness. They spun around the dance floor, following the pounding drums.

* * *

"We've arrived, young Prince," said Elmahigh.

The Prince struggled to wake up. He felt the soft hairs of his horse rubbing against his nose. The Prince wiped the sleep from both eyes as the image before him became clear. A torch flickered ahead. They finally made it. They arrived at Pionard.

The inn was nearby. They tied their horses to a long oak post and entered. The warmth of a log burning fire instantly hit their faces. Inside were three large tables with accompanying wooden stools tucked under. In the corner a young boy played a flute. The smell of hot stew filled the place. A four-foot tall heavy bald man approached them, carrying three overflowing glasses of maltsenhop. All of the warrior's mouths watered at the sight of the delicious frothy beverage, a Mastadan treat. Dolamite barged through the group, grabbing one of the glasses from the innkeeper, drinking it hand over fist before even a word was uttered.

"I'll just take those two as well," he said. He grabbed the other two glasses, pouring one of the frothy fruit and alcohol concoction down his throat. Its perfect blend of sweet strawberry aroma and earthy taste delighted Dolamite. He drank the third just as quickly. Bolios, Elmahigh, the Prince and all of the soldiers just looked at one another and began to laugh.

The warriors sat near the fire and listened to the young boy's music. The group drank repeated mugs of maltsenhop and ate hot stew filled with roasted meat and large chunks of potatoes. The group enticed the Prince to have a drink. Only Elmahigh and Bolios escaped the occasion and sought out the innkeeper instead. After several rounds of drinks, the warriors began to dance and even managed to coax the Prince into participating. They began to fall over one another and burst into laughter as the fast-paced rhythm from the music of the traditional dance played by the boy confused them all. They poked fun at the Prince and relished the evening.

CHAPTER 3

Prince Adinor's face remained smushed on the bed, his hand still clutching a mug of maltsenhop. He couldn't remember how he'd made it to his room. Light crept in from the small window and the sounds of all the warriors stirring meant they were up, though some struggled more than others.

Theodonus and the two brothers, Salazar and Marcus, prepared the horses just outside the inn and packed provisions for the day ahead. Dolamite strolled about the inn, eating whatever scraps were spared from the previous night.

"That was sitting out," said Friedrich as Dolamite bit into what appeared to be a cold chicken leg.

"That's right," said Dolamite. "I can't believe I didn't eat it then, so I sure wouldn't see it wasted now."

Friedrich could only muster a chuckle as he sat on a stool and watched the appetite of Dolamite at work. The innkeeper brought out hot bread and seasoned beef as well as venison. Pounding footsteps announced the emmergence of Ecclesias and the three other soldiers from above. They said nothing and walked through the inn, heading straight for the well in the middle of the street to fill all the containers with water.

"Why so serious?" asked Friedrich.

"Maybe they're hungry," said Dolamite who nibbled on the last few pieces of chicken leg and started on the hot bread and seasoned beef. He devoured some of the food as others joined him when he said, "But they won't get any of mine."

Small pieces of food flew out of his mouth, hitting one of the warriors in front of him. Prince Adinor entered the dining hall and sat at the table alongside Dolamite. The Prince folded his arms on the table and buried his head in them.

A long winding creak was heard as the wooden door at the inn's entrance opened. They strained their eyes. It was Bolios. His face was stone like.

"It's time to leave," he said.

They stood and remained in attention.

"Yes, sire," they all answered.

Prince Adinor slowly wiped his face as the feeling returned to his hands. He raised his head and saw the warriors all walk toward the inn's entrance. The taste of maltsenhop remained in his mouth, only now it was bitter and acidic. He rose from the table and stumbled toward the entrance, exiting the inn. The ground under him seemed unstable. Outside, the others walked around their horses to the large fountain with no such problems. The streets were empty. Prince Adinor felt cold once again and wrapped his own hands around his arms, desperate to rub off the winter chill. As his vision improved, he saw only dark grey and blacok skies above. The Prince walked over to his horse still struggling to find his legs. The saddle was wet from the heavy fog covering all of Pionard. A few of the warriors laughed as they observed the Prince mounting his horse. The reins didn't seem to cooperate with him and his head was pounding. Marcus walked over to the Prince and helped. The Prince smiled as Marcus also handed him a piece of beef wrapped in piping hot bread.

Theodonus, Bolios' second in command, walked toward Bolios and asked, "How serious of a situation are we dealing with, sire?"

Bolios looked at his captain and remained silent. He whipped his horse, rattling the chain metal, and galloped toward the others still amused by their Prince's condition. The warriors stopped talking. Bolios paced in front of all of them as they formed a single row and sat in attention.

"Last night, while you fools were enjoying yourself with perhaps more maltsenhops than I can count," he said.

The warriors laughed.

Then Bolios continued, "In all seriousness, men, I have spoken to the innkeeper. And what he shared with Elmahigh and me is of real concern."

The warriors and the Prince looked around. It hadn't occurred to them that one in their party was missing.

"Where is Elmahigh?" asked Prince Adinor.

"Elmahigh departed this morning to seek out more information and will meet with us later," replied Bolios.

The warriors began to stir and the chatter increased.

"Quiet down and listen," said Bolios. "The innkeeper has spoken of some events in detail that are true horrors of madness the likes of which have not been witnessed here. It is important for you all to know what has happened so you are ready for what we will face. For the past few weeks, dozens of villagers have gone missing."

"My father spoke only of thieves," said Prince Adinor.

"Yes," replied Bolios, "initially minor thefts were the first reported issues. It has escalated since the first reports sent to your father. While an emissary was dispatched to the city center, a band of men here organized a party to search for the missing members of the village. A thorough search of all Pionard took place and strict inquiries of travelers passing through were made. After a search of a few days, nothing was found. The most recent disappearance of a villager was just two nights ago. It is unclear who would be daring enough to commit such acts, for in doing so would guarantee confinement under the laws of our kingdom."

"Sire, is there any particular pattern to those taken?" asked Theodonus.

"There was none," replied Bolios. "Those taken varied between male and female as well as roles here, within the village. The attacks seem to be completely random."

Then Malchomite inquired further, "Bolios, my lord, how many missing in total?"

"Factoring in the attacks from just two days ago… the total has now reached thirty-two?" he replied.

Prince Adinor's stomach tightened as it did at the stables. He began to sweat and felt a chill running down his spine. Prince Adinor knew the small village of Pionard numbering a couple of hundred Mastadans was in danger.

"There's more," continued Bolios, "two nights ago, the night of the last attack. A young boy, perched atop the roof of his father's bakery, witnessed a woman and her young daughter's abduction. The boy we go to now is the only person who has actually seen the attackers. Since the night, the boy has not uttered a word. Perhaps we will be fortunate enough to get some much needed information from him."

The warriors had little time to think as Bolios turned and led the soldiers down the fog-filled streets of Pionard in the direction of the bakery. As they arrived at the boy's home, dozens of villagers stood outside. Men carried farming tools and small daggers and the women clutched their children in their hands. They all turned as the warriors arrived. They grabbed one another and crouched down to the ground. Bolios waved to his soldiers and had them wait farther away from the home. He dismounted his horse and began toward the crowd. Prince Adinor did the same. They walked past the group of pale frightened villagers and stepped quietly into the baker's home.

Several scared faces inside turned toward Bolios and Prince Adinor. They were surprised and happy at the sight of helps from the capitol.

"Will you find them my Lords?" one said.

"Are there more of you," asked another.

Bolios didn't answer and only gestured with both hands in a plea for calm. He and Prince Adinor approached the crying man doning an apron who was crouched near a small dark-haired child below him. They stood just behind the baker and waited. The baker let go of his son's hand and placed his wife beside the boy. The baker stood and greeted Bolios.

"Has anything at all been mentioned by him since that evening?" asked Bolios.

"No, sire," said the baker, "not a word."

Prince Adinor left the conversation and made his way toward the boy who was lying on some straw. The boy's eyes opened and remained fixed on the ceiling overhead. As Prince Adinor got closer, the boy's mother gave a delicate bow of her head. Tears flowed down her face dropping onto the boy's pant leg. She gripped the boy's hand. Prince Adinor looked on and felt the cold chill down his spine again. It was hard to look at a young boy in such troubling condition. The Prince felt his chest tighten. He left the mother and the child and stepped outside the home. He struggled for air as his chest tightened. His palms were sweaty as he felt the ground beneath him uneasy. He pulled at his shirt collar and wiped his face with his fingers. Bolios walked up from behind him.

"The boy's father says the child doesn't speak," said Bolios, "not a word. He hasn't eaten or drank anything."

Prince Adinor remained silent. His face was pale and he continued to perspire.

"Are you all right?" asked Bolios.

"He's only a boy," said Prince Adinor.

"Four years old," said Bolios, "the youngest of the family. There's nothing that child can offer us."

Bolios began to walk away from the Prince when they were surprised to hear a familiar voice.

"Let a different set of eyes see if there's something yet to discover here, my good friend," said Elmahigh.

CHAPTER 4

"Where have you been?" asked the Prince. Elmahigh walked toward them. He reached into a small sack he carried at his side.

"I rode through the village," said Elmahigh, "hoping for any signs of the attackers, but to my initial disappointment, there was none. However, nothing worth finding is ultimately easily revealed."

"So you found something?" asked Bolios.

"Indeed," responded Elmahigh, "I sat atop a rooftop, settled my mind, and simply was."

"Stop with your games, monk, what did you find?" replied Bolios.

"Oftentimes, our eyes deceive us," said Elmahigh. "Things must be revealed to us another way. And so, I collected myself and performed chautruce."

"What is that?" asked the Prince

"Nonsense, Prince Adinor," said Bolios, "an absolute waste of time. It's too early in the day for foolishness, Elmahigh."

Bolios began walking toward the warriors but stopped as Elmahigh once again began to speak.

"Chautruce, my Prince, is an ancient tool used by my order. It is the process of connecting oneself to the environment around you by silencing your thoughts and shutting out everything except the deepest most profound sense of being. In doing so, one connects with energies and frequencies of nature and all existence around you. It helps in revealing visions or glimpses into the past or even perhaps the future. Do you understand, my Prince?"

"Madness," said Bolios. "It's pure madness."

"I've never heard of that before," responded the Prince.

"Of course not," said Bolios. "No one talks about it because it would be a waste of time. Elmahigh, you said you found something, well, come out with it, man, what was it?"

Elmahigh removed a small purple plant from his bag. Its soft petals were indigo and the center yellow. Its delicate smell was well balanced and enjoyable. Its sweet aroma captivated them. Bolios took a step back toward Elmahigh and Prince Adinor as the monk pulled apart each petal, placing the flowers in one hand and discarding the rest on the ground.

"Follow me," said Elmahigh.

They walked back into the boy's home and stood next to the young child. Elmahigh placed the petals on the boy's chest and reached over to a nearby candle. The boy's parents reached out to their child out of concern, but Bolios grabbed them both. They began to cry as Elmahigh lit the petals on fire. The petals burned and a citrus aroma filled the home as purple smoke emitted from the flower. Prince Adinor looked on as Elmahigh covered the smoke with both of his hands, trapping it underneath. The smoke poured out from either side as Elmahigh moved his hands toward the boy's face. He propped the boy up and funneled the smoke to the boy's nose, forcing more in.

"What are you doing to my son?" yelled the boy's father.

Bolios and the Prince bent down to get a closer look. The boy's pale color began to change. His blank look began to cease. Then he blinked. The natural light brown color returned to his skin. His parents embraced one another and smiled. The boy's mother began to cry as she realized that her son was getting better. The boy looked at Elmahigh with a ear to ear smile as his parents ran through Bolios' grip, embracing their child.

"What I discovered on that rooftop while in my chautruce," said Elmahigh, "was that this boy was exposed to something. The energy I felt on that roof was far different than anything I've experienced before."

Prince Adinor looked at Bolios. The blank expression on his face showed his disbelief about what just occurred. Elmahigh began to speak with the child as Prince Adinor observed from behind the monk. The boy revealed all the details that he could remember. The attackers wore black armor. The boy mentioned they were all male and on horse. When asked about the attackers' size, Prince Adinor began to laugh as the boy pointed toward Bolios and said they were even bigger than him. The mysterious riders rode directly into the direction of the woman and her young child and plucked them right off the ground. The boy only remembered up to the point of the taking of the woman and her child. The details thereafter were ambiguous. Elmahigh's additional questions were ignored as the boy became more focused on the wooden toy nearby. Frustrated, Elmahigh and Bolios rose and began to walk out. Just before they exited the home, Bolios turned back to the boy and said, "You've been a brave little soldier."

The boy smiled as his parents squeezed him.

"Do you recall the direction the men rode to?"

The boy continued playing with the wooden carved toys on the ground. Elmahigh, Bolios, and the Prince shook hands with a couple of villagers standing near the door, and as they walked out, the child responded, "They went into the forest."

CHAPTER 5

They stepped out into the street, speechless. The rest of the warriors meandered nearby. Realizing their leader returned, they walked back to their horses in anticipation of his commands.

"Finally we can get going," said Ecclesias. "I'm excited to see something different."

"You won't be once you find out where we're going," mumbled the Prince.

"What did you say?" asked Ecclesias.

"Nothing, I..."

"Gather the men," said Bolios, "there's something I need to tell them."

"Yes, sire," replied Ecclesias. He rode off to grab the few men wandering nearby.

While Bolios, the Prince, and Elmahigh waited for their return, they looked at one another but said nothing. Bolios shook his head. Elmahigh sighed at looked at Prince Adinor.

"What do we tell them?" asked the Prince.

"We tell them the truth, my Prince," responded Bolios.

"But no one can enter the forest," said Prince Adinor. "It's forbidden."

"That's right, my Prince," replied Bolios, "but someone has deliberately violated the laws of our great kingdom. More importantly, they have taken innocent people. There are families, husbands, wives, and parents now in mourning for the lives of their missing loved ones. I see no other option."

Elmahigh listened and stared off in the direction of the forest. He seemed vexed. Just then, the men returned.

"Everyone is here, sire," said Theodonus, "the men are at your command. Where would you have us go?"

"We have been most fortunate," Bolios began to explain. "The boy spoke."

He paused briefly and looked toward the Prince and Elmahigh. Both were just as attentive as the others.

"The boy shared the path the attackers departed to," said Bolios, "and so we will pursue them there."

All of the men were eager for battle and, in unison, began to yell.

"Well, it's about bloody time," responded Dolamite. "I was starting to think we'd have to stay around here and eat some more of this terrible food."

The brothers, Marcus and Salazar, began laughing uncontrollably as they knew all too well of Dolamite's unprejudiced appetite. Then Malchomite inquired, "Bolios, where are we going?"

The warriors' laughs subsided, and they focused back on Bolios.

"We go into the Petruchani Forest."

Large black buzzards flew overhead. Only their shrieks were heard. The fog moved in around them.

Prince Adinor looked on as Elmahigh grasped his staff alongside Bolios.

None spoke.

"How can that be?" asked Friedrich. "No one enters the Petruchani Forest. It is forbidden."

"Illegal isn't the biggest concern," said Ecclesias.

"It's a place filled with the most dangerous animals," said Salazar.

"And poisonous plants," continued Marcus, "the stories of the horrors in that place are far too grim for anyone to set foot inside. I've heard rumors of gargoyles that fly and eat the flesh of man."

"As a child, I heard tales of the dragons that live deep inside the forest," said Malchomite. "When angered, their mouths breathe fire hotter than lava from Mount Citerac... hotter than the surface of the sun."

"It doesn't matter what dragons you could run into," said Marcus, "the most deadly thing encountered are the enchantresses of the forest."

"That's right," continued his brother Salazar, "the magical fairies that are capable of mesmerizing any man with any words uttered from their lips. Once under their spells, you're enslaved for life."

The Prince began to sweat for just when he thought he had heard the scariest evil another soldier would outdo the last. Bolios had enough. He raised his hand. In a moment, he had their attention once again. They struggled to look directly at him and hung their heads.

Bolios threw the reins of his horse over its side and walked in front of all of them. He removed his helmet and looked up toward the sun and back as his men. They all sat on their horses tortured by Bolios' silence. He crouched. His black boots dug into the soft dirt below. He reached down as his massive hand dug into the soil beneath him. His fingers closed as he squeezed tightly crunching some small pebbles into fine dust.

"The stories you all speak of I too have heard," said Bolios, "the stories you've shared are known to us all. They've been passed down before I was born, and they'll be passed down after we're all gone when we become dirt once again."

Bolios rose to his feet as every warrior's eyes followed him. He pointed toward the forest. "What truly lies inside that forest is unknown to me. The stories about that place's contents are just that, stories. What I know is that my fellow countrymen have been taken against their will. Women, children, and men alike have been taken but to what end... I'm uncertain. I go into that forest, so they know there are those that wouldn't stand idly as the evil of others goes unpunished. I will scour the entire forest and face whatever creatures, dragons, or fairies may exist because with my sword in my hand and my brothers at my side, there is nothing I cannot defeat."

The warriors sat up straighter. Their jaws clenched.

Bolios mounted his horse and reached for his helmet, placing it on his head. The others did the same. He drew his sword from its sheath as the massive steel blade reflected in his hand. He raised it toward his men and said, "Let us go and find our missing brothers and sisters. May we be the new stories that are passed down from generation to generation."

The warriors raised their swords together and yelled, "Yes."

Bolios and Elmahigh whipped their horses and began. They raced past the baker's home and weaved between the Pionard streets, cutting through the fog as they all rode toward the Petruchani Forest. As the group rode beyond the narrow dirt streets lined with Pionard homes, they approached a small creek ahead. Bolios continued forward as the first trees of the Petruchani Forest were now in sight. The horses flew into the creek, splashing its shallow waters onto the warriors. As they crossed the creek, Prince Adinor looked back and saw the fading homes of Pionard disappear in the thick fog. Bolios continued forward as Elmahigh rode alongside him, taking the first few paces into the Petruchani Forest. The massive trees surrounding the group swallowed them. Elmahigh was the first to speak once inside.

"Bolios, there is something I should share with you."

The Prince listened in as the fog increased. Even Bolios and Elmahigh began to fade. He could only hear their words.

"What is it you foolish priest?" replied Bolios.

"I should tell you the chautruce that I performed on the roof as well as the time spent with the boy at his home have revealed something," said Elmahigh.

"Is that right?" said Bolios. "Well, monk, this would be a good time to share."

"The boy was not frightened," said Elmahigh.

"Then why wouldn't he speak?" asked Bolios.

"He was under a spell," replied Elmahigh.

Bolios looked at Elmahigh, but Elmahigh only continued looking forward as they all continued further into the fog deeper into the forest.

"You speak of spells," said Bolios, "but those are lies buried in old scrolls you and your kind keep."

"Even the unlikely is still possible my friend," said Elmahigh.

"I rely on what I see, not figments of my imagination," said Bolios. "Now tell me how do you know?"

"I can't be completely sure yet," said Elmahigh, "but consider this. While in chautruce, I felt energies coming from where we eventually learned the boy witnessed the attacks. It was pure evil. I felt something dark and cold. An evil not born within man alone, but rather, something mysterious. Something not of nature."

Prince Adinor moved closer to their voices. He could no longer see even his own horse's head.

"Go on," said Bolios.

"When I use chautruce, I see flashes, visions of events that take place nearby," said Elmahigh, "never have I experienced a time when I see nothing."

"Well, there are firsts for everything," said Bolios.

"True, there are," said Elmahigh, "but the energies that I felt and the fact that I was blocked from seeing the soldiers are perhaps two coincidences, but there's more…at the boy's home, did you see how I used the plant to help the boy?"

"Yes," replied Bolios.

"I didn't say to spare his parents added concern, but that plant used in such a high concentration was used long ago for possessed souls."

"Possessed?"

"Yes," said Elmahigh, "the boy wasn't in shock. The young child was possessed. Were it not for the plant and its effect on him, I believe a prolonged exposure would have caused further undesired consequences."

"Elmahigh, wait," said Bolios.

They both stopped and permitted the others to catch up.

"The boy was put under a spell," said Elmahigh. "The reason I couldn't see a clear vision of the attackers and the reason I couldn't see the boy's experience when I visited with him in his home is because something or someone made certain I couldn't."

The Prince arrived, and Bolios turned to look at him, struggling to hide his concern.

"Is it possible the legends are true?" asked the Prince. "Is everything the others said true?"

"Of all the stories passed down, I'm unsure," said Elmahigh, "however, there is sorcery at use here evident in my inability to see and the boy's condition. Of that, I am certain. I believe what we seek is not merely just missing villagers and perhaps not even crazed vigilantes, but rather something more diabolical."

Bolios stared back at Elmahigh as the rest of the group began to surround them. They all gathered as the fog burned up in the rising sun. The large trees around them were covered in moss. Small bushes nearby were thick with thorns and sharp branches. They all studied the forest for the first time. After looking around, it occurred to one.

"Where's Litovic?" asked Theodonus.

CHAPTER 6

The men looked around as they spun atop their horses. The last of the eleven showed no signs of appearing.

"Litovic!" yelled Dolamite.

"Litovic, over here," shouted Theodonus.

Elmahigh and Bolios rode around in circles looking everywhere. The other warriors began to do the same.

Everyone was frenzied.

"He was just behind me," said Malchomite, "how can this be?"

Far off in the distance was a rumbling from deep inside the forest. A massive thud came from a different direction. The warriors turned and pulled out their swords. Adinor looked toward both Bolios and Elmahigh when suddenly shrieks and howls sounded behind them.

"What's out there?" asked Dolamite.

"Quiet," replied Bolios.

"But, sire…" said Friedrich.

"I said silence!"

Prince Adinor noticed as Bolios' jaw clenched. Bolios' massive hand tightened its grip around the sword and every muscle in his arm flexed. Friedrich began to shake, his face was pale white. The Prince and the two brothers, Marcus and Salazar, began to sweat. The shrieks and howls grew louder. They were coming closer.

"What animal is that?" asked Theodonus.

"That is no animal," replied Elmahigh.

The noise grew stronger and became higher in pitch. The men struggled to cover their ears and protect from the noise. All the horses became restless and began leaping around and standing on their back legs. Prince Adinor and the two brothers, Marcus and Salazar, failed to control their horses and were thrown to the ground. The noise continued piercing their ears. Chaos ensued as the others tried to assist the fallen warriors, but they too struggled from the dreadful noise. The sound was approaching and continued to get louder. The Prince, Marcus, and Salazar were still on the ground. They rolled in the dirt, clutching their ears, grimacing as the sharp pain increased. They reached for the swords and swung them in the air, hitting nothing. Even Bolios struggled. He clutched his ears and looked on as his men were reduced to wild behavior.

Elmahigh struggled too. The noise continued approaching. Sensing more trouble, he galloped a dozen yards to Bolios' position. Elmahigh yelled at him, but Bolios did not respond.

The source of the noise now closer than ever, the pain began to spread to the rest of their bodies. Desperate, Elmahigh reached over and punched Bolios on the shoulder and finally gained his attention. Bolios looked over at Elmahigh as they both grimaced.

"We must flee from here," he shouted.

Bolios nodded in agreement as Elmahigh grabbed the leather reins of his horse, leading it to a nearby dirt path as he headed deeper into the woods. Bolios followed shoving some of his men as he passed, pointing to the path nearby. He stopped where Marcus and Salazar stood and said, "Get Prince Adinor back on that horse."

The Prince stumbled to his feet several yards away.

One by one, the warriors fled behind Elmahigh. Bolios took off, leaving only three, Marcus, Salazar, and Prince Adinor. The two brothers managed to remount their horses and were almost away, but looked back only to discover the Prince motionless on the ground. They looked at one another as the pain in their ears continued. With no further consideration, they jumped off their horses and ran to the Prince. The moment they did, Salazar's horse fled as did the Prince's. The brothers picked up the Prince. His head hung lifeless as Marcus and Salazar each held him from opposite ends.

Marcus pointed at his chest, and with that, Salazar helped carry him over to his brother's horse. They struggled to lift the Prince overhead, but managed to get him onto the horse. Marcus mounted it and looked back down at his brother, Salazar, who looked scared. They both nodded as a tear rolled down Marcus' face. With that, he took off behind the rest of the group. Marcus raced through the woods carrying the Prince, putting as much distance between him and the noise as possible.

Salazar clutched his ears and watched as his brother move farther off into the distance. Salazar reached down to wrap his fingers around his sword and removed it from the sheath. His back was to the noise and when he could no longer see his brother or the Prince, he turned around to face it. The noise stopped. Salazar walked around where his fellow warriors—his friends—had just been. He gripped his sword. His knuckles turned red. A small bead of sweat collected on his forehead. His eyes wandered back and forth bouncing between the trees in search of movement, but there was nothing. He ventured in the direction where the sound was coming from and found more dense forest. He lowered his sword, turned to where the group was gathered moments ago, and noticed the Prince's large white horse had returned.

"Well, I'll be," said Salazar, "I thought we surely lost you, girl."

He walked toward the horse as it ate from a bush several yards away. He grabbed the reins. He steadied himself and leapt.

"Well, you'll just have to do since I've gone and lost my horse," he said.

He turned the horse in the direction to which everyone had departed.

"See, beautiful, that wasn't too bad, was it."

He smiled, but felt peering eyes upon him. He stopped the horse and reached for his sword. As he drew it, he felt an immediate burst from his back then into his chest. He fell right off the horse and collapsed to the ground. He writhed in pain. His eyes watered and he struggled to find his sword. He lay helpless on his side. Desperate for breath, he looked down toward his chest and found an arrow lodged deep in the middle of it. His vision started to fade as the light of day became dark. His breathing slowed ever more. He looked around and found his sword under some leaves a few paces away. He struggled for air and reached out his hand toward it. A sudden pain shot through his hand. Salazar looked and atop his hand was a giant black boot crushing it, blocking the view of his sword. He faded. Salazar was dead.

Chapter 7

Elmahigh raced through the forest, avoiding the large moss-covered branches twisting and turning along the way. His horse leapt over a couple of fallen trunks as he continued to hold on for safety. Bolios and the others followed, leaving the noise far behind. Ahead, Elmahigh spotted a clearing. He rode to it and found comfort in the sun's rays shining through the tree line.

"Keep moving," he said.

He hurdled over thorn bushes and arrived at a grass-covered bank and a gentle creek. All the warriors followed. For the first time, he noticed the absence of noise. The large trees hanging overhead bathed him in shade as the horses ate the rich green grass below. Near the creek were brilliant red and pink colored flowers. Elmahigh dismounted. Bolios arrived next, immediately taking his horse to the creek for water. He dismounted and walked toward Elmahigh.

"What just happened?" asked Bolios.

Elmahigh stared at the water deep in thought.

"Elmahigh," said Bolios.

Elmahigh turned toward Bolios, looked directly at him, but said nothing. The rest of the men began to arrive one by one. Each ran to the creek splashing water into their faces and drinking mouthfuls at a time.

Malchomite and Ecclesias walked over to a fallen tree trunk and rested against it. They clutched their helmets in hand. The others talked among themselves as everyone tried to understand what took place. Bolios counted the men and figured three were still missing..

"Did anyone see the brothers or the boy?" asked Bolios.

All of the men raised their heads, realizing three of their friends were still unaccounted for. With Litovic's disappearance, four were now lost. Worst of all, one unaccounted for was the Prince.

Elmahigh and Bolios mounted their horses, but just as they were about to ride back towards where they had just left, Marcus arrived with the Prince thrown across his horse.

"What happened to him?" asked Elmahigh.

"He was collapsed on the ground," said Marcus. "We did as best we could to get him to his feet but he didn't wake. We threw him on my horse and I left."

Bolios walked over to the Prince and examined him for injuries. He placed a finger just below the Prince's nose and felt hot soft breaths.

"He's breathing," said Bolios, "barely."

"Marcus," Elmahigh said, "where is your brother?"

Marcus looked back from where he had just left and did not respond.

"We never should have left," said Bolios. "That is my responsibility. It was stupid of us to leave."

"We had no choice," replied Elmahigh

"Yes, we did have a choice. We could have stayed and fought whatever it was that attacked us," responded Bolios.

"We have no idea what we're facing. This is a far greater problem than we anticipated."

He turned away from the group.

Bolios and stepped closer to the creek. He kneeled near the bank's edge drinking some water from his outstretched hand.

"My blocked chautruce on the rooftop," said Elmahigh, "the child back at village in a trance-like state, and now this. I've never encountered whatever it is we're dealing with."

"I am missing two men," said Bolios.

"That noise was torture," said Friedrich.

"Was it an animal?" asked Dolamite.

"No animal I've ever seen or heard of makes noises like that," replied Ecclesias.

Marcus ignored the conversation and stared at the path leading to where his brother was left behind. He finally spoke, "I'm going back for him."

Bolios walked over and grabbed the reins of his horse, saying, "We'll all go together."

"We cannot move the boy," said Elmahigh.

"What do we do about Salazar?" askeds Bolios. "I won't leave him."

And just as he finished his words, another noise came toward them from the river.

"Not again," remarked Dolamite.

The men all armed themselves, grabbing swords, axes and shields. The sound grew stronger and came closer.

"It's coming from the water," said Theodonus.

"Get ready," said Bolios.

They all steadied themselves standing between the Prince and the noise. A couple aimed their bow and arrows ready for deployment.

"No, wait," said Elmahigh.

"Whatever comes out of that water will surely meet our wrath," said Bolios.

"No, do nothing," responded Elmahigh.

"Are you mad?" said Ecclesias.

"Don't you realize?" said Elmahigh. "The noise…it's not painful."

Unconvinced, they held their weapons and remained vigilant.

"Lower your weapons," said Elmahigh.

"Truly you have lost all reason," replied Malchomite. "Bolios, he can't be serious?"

Bolios thought about Elmahigh's words. This noise was different. There were no searing pains in their ears and they heard each other speak. This noise was calm and peaceful.

"Lower your weapons, it's nearly here," said Elmahigh.

All of the soldiers came together around the Prince and formed a human shield. The Prince remained motionless on the ground. They put their weapons away as Elmahigh requested, as the sound grew louder.

The water became turbid as small waves built up alongside the banks of the creek splashing the grass and flowers. The volume of the waves increased, and the swell sprayed a mist onto the men's faces. The sound went on, and they all looked at one another puzzled at the strange course of events.

The music rose to a powerful pitch, but it was pleasant. The waters grew to two yards high and continued to pour onto the bank in front of them when out from the water exploded three beings the likes of which they had never seen.

Standing before them were three creatures. They had skin similar to scales on a fish. They were bright blue like the color of the creek. As the water droplets fell from their bodies, the color of the scales began to change. The creatures looked more human. They had bare feet, but in place of separate toes theirs were webbed connections like a frog or reptile. The three creatures were equal in stature to Bolios, large and powerful. The creatures had gills where ears would be on humans. The one in front was female.

"What are these things?" asked Dolamite.

"They are the water Nymphs we all heard stories about in our youth," responded Elmahigh.

"That's impossible," replied Bolios.

"Today, my dear friend, have you not learned that the very impossible is interestingly enough likely," replied Elmahigh.

Bolios gave Elmahigh a side long glance and then focused his attention back toward the Nymphs. He noticed something peculiar.

"Whatever they are and however unbelievable it is that they exist, they are armed nonetheless," continued Bolios. "Look there on their waists. They have small blades."

Elmahigh simply looked at him and back toward the Nymphs, remaining silent.

"Be ready, men," whispered Bolios, "there's no sign of their intentions."

"There weapons are not out," said Elmahigh, "and so we must do the same. Come, let us greet our friends."

Elmahigh walked slowly toward the Nymphs as they too stepped closer. Bolios followed closely. The men remained behind to protect Adinor.

"Well, this is a first," said Dolamite, "I wonder if they have any food."

Elmahigh now stood in front of the Nymphs who were even larger up close than at first glance. One of them spoke.

"I am Isilmoire of the water Nymph kingdom," she said. "I am in command of the river patrols and its mission of defense of these arteries of water stemming from the great ocean far from here."

"But you're a woman," said Bolios.

Elmahigh glared at Bolios.

Isilmoire smirked. "And you're just a man," she said as she stepped forward. "My men behind me mean you no harm. We come in peace. Teinmar to your left and Lautner to your right are two of my best warriors and alerted me of your situation."

"My name is Elmahigh and this is Bolios." Isilmoire smiled as Elmahigh continued, "We hail from the kingdom of Mastada under the rule of King Ralphus Dolamaic."

Then the soldier introduced as Lautner began speaking to Teinmar in a language unlike anything Bolios or Elmahigh had ever heard before. It was a soft melodic sound similar to that from the water just moments before the Nymphs presented themselves.

"It was you," Elmahigh said.

"I'm sorry," replied the Nymph commander Isilmoire.

"We heard sounds like those but louder before you appeared," said Elmahigh.

"It's the way we communicate," said Isilmoire, "you would say it's our language."

"How do you know ours?" asked Elmahigh. "How can you speak like mankind?"

"I will explain," She replied, "for now, let us attend to the boy."

Isilmoire took another step and Bolios drew his sword, stepping in front of the Nymph. The Nymph smiled, but all the Mastadans stood alongside their leader stern and resolute.

"You will not step toward him again," said Bolios.

Isilmoire's hands fell behind her back. Teinmar and Lautner flanked her on both sides. Bolios' soldiers steadied themselves, drawing their swords and their arrows. Elmahigh shook his head and rubbed his chin.

"Please understand, Isilmoire," said Elmahigh, "the boy is very important to us. He is the Prince of our Kingdom, the King's only child. We have traveled a great distances and have faced unforeseen trouble."

Teinmar and Lautner removed their blades, waving them from side to side. Bolios and the others noticed for the first time how small in size the blades were, made from animal bone. Isilmoire spoke in her native language, and the two warriors stepped back one step. Then she said, "Why are you here, human?"

"A small village just on the outskirts of our kingdom was attacked by a group unknown to us," replied Bolios. "They have taken innocent people. We were dispatched by our King to end the attacks and we intend to fulfill his command."

Isilmoire gazed upon the warriors over Bolios' shoulders and then back at Bolios. She said something in the Nymph language and then both Lautner and Teinmar put away their weapons and retreated toward the river's edge.

"What you seek is why we patrol these waters," she said, "oddly enough what seems like more and more often. For what begins first as a small creek can become a raging river, and raging rivers flow into endless waters…" She paused and looked toward the river once again. "There's an evil breeding in these woods."

"And you and your people must be part of it," said Bolios.

"Bolios," said Elmahigh sharply.

"So small a mind," said Isilmoire, "so petty the thoughts that come from it."

"Forgive us, Isilmoire, we have already lost two men," replied Elmahigh. "One of our soldiers vanished amid our travels into the forest. Moments ago, we've misplaced another of our party. We go now to find him."

"You will only find death for his life has been taken."

Marcus gripped his sword and ran toward the Nymphs enraged, but was stopped by Theodonus and Dolamite.

"Lies!" shouted Marcus.

"I'm sorry," said Isilmoire, "I understand the loss of a soldier is difficult, but we know it to be true. I'll gladly explain as much as I can, but it's important you all come with us now. The boy needs help."

Bolios pointed his sword toward Isilmoire, saying, "We're not going anywhere with you. We'll stick together, far from your kind, She-Nymph. We must find our fellow soldiers."

"Bolios, their intentions seem noble," said Elmahigh, "they also know more about what we are facing. Clearly, we need to seek their wisdom. The enemy we face can only be weakened by the extra knowledge we gain from hearing them out."

As Bolios and Elmahigh continued to debate, Lautner bent down toward the ground, rubbing his hand on the grass and dirt below. He again yelled to Isilmoire in their Nymph language. Isilmoire leapt toward Bolios and Elmahigh, grabbing their arms and said, "There's no time. The dark army approaches once again. Lautner has detected their movement and it's coming toward us. What they bring has already defeated you moments ago. We cannot help you here. If you value your Prince's safety, you must come with us."

"What do you suggest?" Elmahigh asked.

"Not far from here is a grotto where my people have a stronghold. There you can rest. We'll attend to the boy and we can talk further of this danger."

Elmahigh and Bolios looked at one another and then back at the men. Just as they looked back, they heard the faint beginnings of the piercing painful noise they just ran from. The warriors began to cover their ears with both their hands as their faces strained.

"We must leave now," said Isilmoire.

"Very well," replied Bolios.

"I'll take the boy," said Elmahigh.

They all ran toward their horses, mounting them in haste. A couple began to panic struggling to store their weapons. One fell off his horse, missing a foothold from his saddle. The painful noise was getting closer.

"How do we get to your grotto?" yelled Elmahigh.

"Follow the river," she replied, "ride hard and fast along this bank, stay true to the river's curve. Go west and I will meet you where the river breaks at the foot of a giant cascade. Under the cascade is the grotto. There you will have more answers. You will be safe as will your Prince."

"And you?" asked Bolios. "How will you keep pace on foot?"

Isilmoire walked away from them and stepped closer to the river's edge. Her scales began to change to blue as she neared the water. She turned back toward the group, smiled, and said, "I wouldn't worry about that." She jumped into the waters disappearing from sight.

Bolios and Elmahigh rode west as Isilmoire instructed. The river narrowed and widened as they traveled. Massive rocks found in the middle of the water caused bubbling white foam to collect around them. The Mastadans maintained a vigilant eye on the tree line to their left, as the threat of danger loomed. The Prince remained unconscious. Theodonus rode close to Bolios and expressed his concern.

"My lord, we know nothing of these things," he said, "why do we ascribe to their instruction? What about Salazar and Litovic?"

"We have no other choice," replied Bolios, "the She-Nymph knows something and we need to find out what. We stood no chance of fighting that noise. What we're dealing with is beyond us. I couldn't risk losing the Prince in a confrontation."

The warriors slowed the frenzied pace to a walk and continued along the river as the Nymphs instructed. A few hours had passed since they first met the Nymphs, but they had not reached the grotto.

"We'll stop for food ahead," said Bolios.

The warriors dismounted behind their leader who chose a well-hidden area covered by high grass and the shade of trees a couple of dozen yards in height.

"Be on guard," said Bolios, "Marcus and Dolamite have first watch while the others eat. Ecclesias and Malchomite will relieve them upon finishing their meal. I'll stay with Prince Adinor."

The air cooled as they sat. The warriors ate, ever mindful of the strange surroundings.

"Have you heard noise like that before, Bolios?" asked Friedrich.

Bolios lifted his head and slapped the back of his neck, crushing a large insect beneath his hand.

"No my friend," said Bolios, "never."

Friedrich and Theodonus held their food without taking a bite. Their eyes peeled as they looked on with their blank stares.

"Eat, friends," said Bolios, "you'll need your strength."

A couple of yards behind them, Theodonus wrapped the Prince's head with a wet rag. Elmahigh touched the Prince's forehead. Bolios joined them.

"He has a temperature," said Elmahigh, "it's concerning for I know not of the distance remaining to arrive at the Nymph grotto."

Bolios shook his head in displeasure and studied the river and the trees of the forest.

"We're too far from the village," he said, "and the noise stands between us and the village if we did decide to return to Pionard." He tore a blade of grass with his fingers and threw it, saying, "We keep going."

The warriors finished their meals and continued on. They rode for another few hours and Prince Adinor's condition worsened. Elmahigh and Theodonus continued to stop wrapping the Prince's forehead and arms in wet rags from the river, to help reduce the fever.

The sun began to set in the distance and still no sign of a grotto. Bolios rode alongside Elmahigh. Theodonus followed just behind them. The warriors observed as thousands of stars appeared overhead. The sound of the flowing river alongside them was the only accompaniment.

"Do you hear that?" asked Bolios.

Elmahigh and Theodonus' wrinkled their brows and focused. The group picked up speed, following Bolios' lead. Ahead was the roaring tumult of crashing water.

"I hear it too," said Elmahigh.

The noise grew stronger as too did the warriors' excitement. Then the river's flowing waters over rocks blended together with a louder noise of surging tons of water being dumped upon it. The warriors approached a mist-covered area. The Mastadans rode closer and welcomed the familiar sound of the recently discovered Nymph language coming from up ahead. They had arrived.

CHAPTER 8

Four Nymph soldiers leaped from the waters and another six approached on foot. Considering the other Nymph warriors aiming their arrows from the trees above, Bolios' men were completely outnumbered. The Mastadans were surrounded.

"Arms," said Bolios.

"No, you fool," replied Elmahigh as he reached toward Bolios' sword. "Lower it."

"Stand down, men," a voice shouted from behind the Nymphs—it was Isilmoire.

All of the Nymph soldiers lowered their weapons and retreated into the water and their hiding position in the trees.

"My apologies, my friends," said Isilmoire, "with the recent developments in the forest, we are on high alert. There is much to speak of. Come, please join us."

Isilmoire walked them toward the cascade ahead. The Mastadans followed as five Nymphs grabbed the Mastadans' horses and led them away for safekeeping. It was at this moment that Bolios and the rest of the warriors noticed all the Nymphs seemed equally large. They were no less than Bolios' height, six feet five inches in height, but a couple even taller. Indeed, they were made for the water for their wide frames in their shoulders and narrow hips seemed an ideal build, it helped them knife through. Their legs were made up of pure muscle and perhaps contributed to good running speed as well.

As the Mastadans followed Isilmoire, they noticed she was the only female among the rest of the Nymph warriors. A couple of the Mastadans found her attractive regardless of her different look. They all looked on in awe of the beautiful sight of the waterfall. The moonlight shone upon the flowing water creating thousands of dancing crystals. Around the pool below the falls and hidden behind it were white rocks jutting out. Both the rocks and the calm dark blue waters reflected the Mastadans' faces as they passed. The white glistening patches on the water resembled the etched painted glass in the great temple of Mastada. Thousands of the multicolored shards came together in a single striking way. The Nymph soldiers conversed in their language, a pleasing sound to the Mastadans. Their voices were soothing.

"As you see, not all is as it seems," said Isilmoire as she pointed up toward the top of the rushing river flowing over the edge of a cliff. There were dozens of soldiers stationed invisible to non-Nymphs, camouflaged by the water's color.

They walked alongside the river bank and arrived at a steep rock formation, which led up into the mountain. The rocks were slippery, covered in water and algae.

"Follow me," said Isilmoire.

Bolios carried the Prince on his shoulder, checking him often along the way. They reached the top and were now behind the falls. The Mastadans reached their hands out and touched the cold waters evoking smiles. Isilmoire paused and then let out a sharp command. A response from inside the mountain startled them. A rumble from within the mountain revealed a hidden mechanism then a large boulder in front of them began to move.

"Come," said Isilmoire, "this way."

The group walked a narrow path. Two Nymphs greeted them inside. The glowing fire from torches hanging alongside the damp walls provided just enough light for them to navigate the hidden path beneath the waterfall. They soon discovered a massive collection of tunnels and paths that led deep into the mountain.

"This place was made by our people," said Isilmoire, "to serve as an outpost for our armies. It was meant to be an extension of support from our kingdom to yours. Long ago, it was responsible for a few of our legions, but now is mostly abandoned. As a result of the latest developments, we have moved a small group of soldiers back, to make certain the witch has no intentions of bringing harm to our people."

"A witch?" asked Bolios.

"By the grace of all things holy," said Elmahigh, "my heart is heavy."

"What do you speak of, Nymph?" asked Bolios. "Come out with it."

"You will have your answers soon enough," replied Isilmoire.

They approached a bright hue of color. The tunnel seemed to open up just in front of them. As they neared, a bright purple light grew stronger. They took the final few steps and entered a great opening. Each Mastadan walked out of the tunnel onto a small ledge. Isilmoire extended her hand, pointing toward the waters and rock formations below their position and said, "Behold the Nymph Grotto."

It was enchanting. The water was turquoise revealing the coral reefs deep below the surface. The corals were yellow and green as well as bright pink and orange. The abundance of fish was magnificent as both small and large could be seen swimming. In every direction the men looked were the flickering torches placed throughout the grotto. They shone down on the water and rock grounds creating dancing shadows. They reminded the Mastadans of sputter bugs from the farm country of their lands which glowed at night. High above their heads was the underbelly of the water cave, which included thousands of bright and unrecognizable crystals. The Mastadans froze at the sight of it. The radiance emitted from them was spectacular. Thousands of purple rubies above remained entrenched in the rock as though both rock and ruby were one and the same. The rubies seemed to glow as the light from the torches reflected. It was magnificent.

Two Nymphs approached. They moved toward Bolios and began to grab the Prince. Just as they did, Bolios said, "Let him go. I'll be happy to remove that hand of yours from Prince Adinor's shoulder with just a quick strike from my sword."

The Nymphs looked back at Isilmoire, confused and fearful. Their gills opened and closed as they awaited commands.

"My friends, your Prince is in need of attention," said Isilmoire, "my people will care for him. Please, let us help you, there is little time."

Elmahigh looked over to Bolios, nodding in agreement.

"Very well," replied Bolios, "Friedrich, Malchomite, and Ecclesias, go with the Prince. The rest of you, stay with us."

"Yes, sire," responded the company.

Isilmoire signaled to the Nymphs, and within moments, they took the Prince toward a different tunnel nearby and were soon out of sight. Friedrich, Malchomite and Ecclesias followed closely behind.

"Come," said Isilmoire, "now to the answers you seek."

Isilmoire led the remaining Mastadans down steps, taking them closer to the water fifty feet below. The beauty of the reflecting purple rubies continued to amaze them. They reached the bottom of the grotto, just alongside the calm pool of water reflecting the torches. Isilmoire walked further. The Mastadans followed her around the clear water, passing Nymph guards holding bone spears seven feet long. The Nymphs maintained watchful eyes on the strange visitors.

The Mastadans neared the largest collection of torches. It formed a narrow path rising from the water's edge up toward a higher platform of the grotto's rock floor. Isilmoire walked between the rows of torches as they culminated at a semi-circular collection at the top of the steps. The group walked up and noticed more Nymph guards flanked the torches in perfect attention. As the Mastadan gazes rose, they observed a large barnacle throne adorned with beads and assorted pearls in the middle of the ring. Two more guards stood by it.

"Just ahead," said Isilmoire.

They stopped in front of the throne.

She uttered some words in her Nymph language and the two Nymph guards disappeared. The Mastadans and Isilmoire stood near the Nymph throne.

"I wished Lord Gillium could be here to receive you, but perhaps he is attending to dire matters back at our home," Isilmoire said.

"Lord Gillium is ruler of the Nymph kingdom?" Elmahigh asked.

Isilmoire touched the throne and shook her head.

"No," she replied solemnly. "Lord Gillium is not our king." She clenched her sword and stared at the throne. "Lord Gillium is steward of the Nymph throne, but we have no king or queen."

She touched the arm rest of the throne and turned back to face the Mastadans.

"I've lost two of my best men," replied Bolios. "Where are your answers?"

"Yes, losses are never easy," replied Isilmoire, "but there will be even greater losses if you should fail."

"My friend, what is it?" asked Elmahigh.

"The bandits you seek are no bandits. They were men like you. Now their veins are poisoned with darkness. They are now shadows of man. They have succumbed to a temptation the likes of which have been unseen for a very long time."

The Mastadans looked confused.

"What follies do you speak of?" asked Bolios

"The dark arts," replied Isilmoire. "Black sorcery has returned to the lands of Mastada. It was said that this black sorcery was vanquished long ago, before any of your time. Even before my time. The killing of the villagers in your kingdom reveals the enemy's growing strength."

"The taking of our people is not growth but rather a suicide announcement," said Bolios, "for the decision to kill innocent people or hold them as captives will bring imminent death to all those party to it."

"Your people are not captive," replied Isilmoire. "They have now become part of the problem. The darkness is spreading. The villagers you seek are now part of the threat."

"This is nothing but more old wives' tales," said Dolamite.

Isilmoire's scaled skin began to change.

The two guards returned carrying a body.

"The black sorcery stems from one person," continued Isilmoire. "This one practitioner has learned of the sorcery's secret powers and is now the root of its continued growth. She—"

"She, who is this she?" said Bolios.

"The Black Witch," replied Elmahigh.

"You have sensed it as well, have you not?" asked Isilmoire.

"There was no way to be sure," replied Elmahigh, "but my chautruce was clouded before. I suspected something, but couldn't confirm it. At the time, it seemed impossible."

"The Black Witch is the source of turning mortal men into servants of evil," continued Isilmoire. "She casts a spell on the weakest of men by preying on their fear, using that to a seduce them. I believe the spell she casts preys on the mortality of men and promises an escape."

"There is no escape," said Theodonus.

"No, there is not," said Elmahigh.

"Not of the natural world," said Isilmoire, "but the witch found a way to replace death with immortality. It comes at a price. To gain immortality, they give up their very souls. These men become something else. They lose the desire to eat, sleep, and reason. They lose the ability to dream, love, or think. They abandon all morality. They seek only to serve the witch and follow her commands. She seeks to raise an army. The villagers you've lost now serve her."

The Nymph soldiers spoke.

Isilmoire nodded.

They placed the body in front of the Mastadans. A wretched smell followed.

"Impossible," replied Bolios.

"Look closely at it," said Isilmoire.

The Mastadans covered their mouths to avoid the stench. Their eyes opened wide as they crouched near the carcass.

"Beneath the armor, you will recognize the clothes fashioned by your artisans," said Isilmoire. "Look beyond the dirt and mud covering the skin. It is the flesh of a man."

The Mastadans were silent.

Isilmoire approached and knelt down on the body. She reached her hand toward the corpse's eyelids, pulling them back, revealing a telling factor.

"Do you see anything amiss?" she asked.

"The eyes are black," replied Theodonus.

"This thing you see before you was a man like each of you. It was seduced by the witch's black sorcery. One of my scouting troops encountered it in the forest. Unprovoked, it attacked for no reason. They were forced to kill it." She stepped away from the corpse.

The Mastadans examined the body more. Its skin was oily. The dried blood from its wounds was black. The corpse had little hair on its head, apart from a few interspersed strands.

"They do not reason," said Isilmoire, "they do not hear words anymore. Their sole purpose is dictated only by the desires of the Black Witch and her sorcery. They destroy anything that stands against her wishes. This is the result of her treachery."

"The dark arts have returned," said Elmahigh who closed his eyes and dropped his head.

"You have come to the outer edges of your kingdom in search of a small group of attackers scaring villagers," said Isilmoire, "but what you sought does not compare to what you have uncovered. But there is time," she continued, "and the time is now. The Black Witch is vulnerable. She has no army. It is for that reason she sought out weak villagers. You have come at a most opportune moment. To prevent her strength from growing, you must seek her out and rid the kingdom of the black sorcery once and for all."

Isilmoire stood over the body and said, "If you fail, this sickness will spread far beyond the edges of the forest and grow into an uncontrollable evil."

"How do we kill these things?" asked Dolamite.

"Clearly, they can be killed," replied Isilmoire. "Do you think yourself less than Nymphs?"

Dolamite reached for his sword and said, "Why I oughta…"

"Enough!" replied Elmahigh. "This is no time for childish behavior. An evil witch, master of black sorcery, seeks to infect her poison throughout the lives of innocent beings. Something must be done."

"Why have you helped us?" asked Bolios.

The Nymph leader looked at all her Nymph soldiers and out toward the grotto's ceiling. The purple rubies shone from above casting brilliant hues down toward them. She was melancholic. Then she smiled and looked back toward Bolios and the company of men, and in an instant, her smile disappeared.

"My people used to exist in great numbers," replied Isilmoire, "our kingdom deep within the bowels of the ocean is not as large as it once was. We have lost a great many warriors throughout our time. The evil this black sorcery represents, if it were to grow, will spread throughout your lands. Eventually, it will spread to ours as well. Just as the rubies entrenched in the rock above are connected, so too are your kingdom and mine. For all our sakes, I hope you will not fail."

"To where do we go?" asked Elmahigh. "Where can we find the witch?"

"The Nymph people stand together with you in the quest ahead. Together, we will seek her out and snuff out the threat for good."

"Well then, what are we waiting for?" said Dolamite.

Man and Nymph alike walked toward the tunnel where the Nymphs and other Mastadans carried the Prince off to earlier.

CHAPTER 9

Isilmoire led the men toward the treatment area where they found the Prince awake. He was seated on a small boulder carved into a seat in the middle of a cave dripping water from a fault line above. He was speaking with Friedrich, Malchomite, and Ecclesias together with the two Nymphs that attended to his ailment.

"Well, glad to see you're all right, lad," said Dolamite.

Theodonus walked toward the Prince and examined him and punched the Prince's shoulder, saying, "He seems in one piece."

"Of course he is," said Elmahigh. "Did you doubt young Prince Adinor's convictions? It's good to see you well, my lord."

Bolios stood in the corner silent. His arms folded across his chest, he leaned on the damp rock wall behind him. The Prince braced himself on the rock and began to stand as the Nymphs helped him on both sides. The Mastadans reached out their hands, preparing to catch him, but he didn't fall. He looked and noticed Bolios' serious face. The Prince scanned the room and asked one of the Mastadans for his weapons.

"Perhaps it is best you remain here, my Prince," said Bolios.

Theodonus, Dolamite, and Marcus looked back toward Bolios. Their smiles disappeared. Elmahigh observed the Prince's reaction.

"I can have my finest soldiers accompany him to the edge of the forest, ensuring his safe return to the main road back to your capitol city," said Isilmoire.

The Mastadans agreed, shaking their heads in acceptance.

Prince Adinor remained in the middle of them all.

"What did you speak about in my absence?" asked the Prince.

"My lord, we've just been given most concerning information which changes the nature of our task," replied Bolios. "As such, it's best you return to Mastada."

"What did you speak about?" replied the Prince.

Isilmoire began, "I—"

"It would be an unnecessary risk for you to continue with us," said Bolios. "Your unfit condition prevents it."

Isilmoire somewhat reluctantly understood the Mastadan's concern and remained silent.

"Tell me," Prince Adinor.

Dolamite and Theodonus explained little by little, each filling in details where the other left off. Bolios and Elmahigh said nothing, choosing to observe the Prince's reaction.

The Prince raised his hand and the men stopped. He looked over at the Nymphs who had cared for him and walked to them.

The two Nymphs knelt as the Prince approached, and he touched them on the shoulders, lifting them up from the ground.

"Thank you for your kindness," he said. "Were it not for your care and strengthening elixir, I may not have lived and our company would be returning to Mastada to bury a Prince. As a result, I can continue…"

"But, sire," replied Bolios.

"Bolios," said Prince Adinor, "Mastadans are under attack. What kind of son of Mastada would I be if I were to abandon their cause? My father knows not of the terror explained to us at this moment. I will not leave you all in the most needed moment."

Bolios and Elmahigh looked at one another.

Isilmoire beamed.

"Please, Bolios," said Prince Adinor, "I will not be a burden to you."

Elmahigh smiled in appreciation of the Prince's newly found bravery. All of the others slapped the Prince on his back and encouraged Bolios with shouts and cheers in support of the Prince.

"Very well," said Bolios, "Isilmoire will lead us to the witch. We leave in the morning. We'll rest here today."

Men and Nymph alike applauded in excitement.

* * *

That evening, the men were invited to dine. They ate the finest Nymph cuisine. The offerings consisted of ocean foods served with spices and delicious flavors. There were large lobsters with bright red shells served with seaweed. Massive shrimp the size of Bolios' hands were grilled over fire to succulent perfection. Aside from that, giant salty squid was served with wine. A few Nymph warriors gathered together and formed a makeshift musical quartet. One plucked a multi-stringed bow with strange modifications. Another Nymph used a wooden flute and maneuvered his fingers atop its several different-sized holes to fabricating delicate sounds. The anoter seated beside him clapped with his hands and pounded the rock like a drum. The fourth sang in the Nymph language, blending harmoniously with the sounds of the others. The Mastadan warriors ate and drank, taking full advantage of the gathering.

The Prince left the table by the water and walked toward Isilmoire and Elmahigh. The two looked on as the Nymph musicians played. Everyone stared into the fire they encircled and listened to the peaceful tunes. Elmahigh and Isilmoire puffed on a carved Nymph pipe filled with dried sea grass. Prince Adinor stood alongside them and watched as the musicians continued thir ditty. The music grew louder and the fire grew stronger.

"What are they singing, Elmahigh?" asked the Prince.

Elmahigh ignored the Prince briefly for he was in meditation, but Isilmoire glanced over to the Prince for an instant and then looked back toward the fire.

"It's a song in honor of those lost in battle, young Prince," said Elmahigh, who blew another mouthful of smoke out the Nymph pipe.

The song continued as it became more tranquil.

"Before a king ruled over Mastada," said Isilmoire, "the entire kingdom recognized no one ruling group and warring among the different communities found throughout Mastada often occurred. During these battles, my people developed song as a way to honor the fallen and also inspire those destined to take their place. The words in the song's second verse speak of it clearly, 'March on for the souls resting beneath you, for your blade honors their beaten will. For your people need peace and protecting, so forge on.'"

The Prince listened to the blissful music as Elmahigh and Isilmoire continued smoking and gazing into the fire. They each reflected while the fire began to sputter and change colors. It turned into a bright white instead of red and yellow. The Nymphs continued playing; the pace of the music quickened. As the music sped up, the fire's color also changed more. It went from white to a translucent glow. Inside the fire appeared small figures that seemed alive.

"What's happening?" asked the Prince.

Elmahigh didn't respond; fixated, he watched on as the figures in the fire continued to dance to the Nymph music. The pace quickened. Isilmoire joined the quartet of Nymphs and began singing as well, clapping in unison with the others. Elmahigh continued studying the dancing fire.

The Prince turned back to the fire and could now distinguish the figures within. They were yellow and resembled men. The Prince couldn't believe his eyes. The fire was coming alive. The heat increased and the smoke from the Nymph pipe was dizzying. Clearly, three men made of yellow flame were inside the translucent fire and then suddenly in front of the men appeared a black figure as well. It was different than the yellow men, too difficult to discern. It wasn't quite human or beast.

Elmahigh and Isilmoire concentrated more as the Prince continued gazing on. His heart raced.

The three yellow-flamed men charged toward the black figure as it charged toward them in response. The beat of the Nymph music was extremely fast paced. No words were sung. The thumping of the rock and pulling of the strings continued and so too did the soft whistle of the flute. Prince Adinor placed his hand on his chest, hoping it wouldn't explode. Isilmoire and the other Nymph clapped faster as the yellow figures in the fire seemed to slam against the black shadow before them. Then one of the yellow figures raised its hands and ran into the black shadow, and then all the figures vanished. The fire settled back to the normal yellow and red. The Nymphs played more tranquil music than before. Elmahigh and Isilmoire began to talk about the vision they had just seen as Prince Adinor sat on a nearby rock sweating. He still held his chest. He attempted to clench his shirt tight, but felt weak and was unable to grip it between his fingers. He struggled to be free of the burning sensation in his eyes and blinked them several times.

"It's the witch," said Isilmoire.

"Too difficult to say," responded Elmahigh.

"It has to be," said Isilmoire. "What else could it be?"

The Prince rubbed both his eyes. The figures were there just a moment ago.

"The black sorcery grows stronger," replied Elmahigh. "Its influence clouds everything."

"Those were men fighting darkness," said Prince Adinor.

"Yes, my Prince," said Elmahigh, "but what that darkness was… is the question."

"I don't understand," replied Prince Adinor, "we already know it's the witch."

Just then, Bolios approached the group gathered by the fire.

"We are sure it was the witch," replied Elmahigh, "but what form will she take?"

"It is said black sorcery can grant the usurper of it unnatural abilities," said Isilmoire. "The abilities manifest themselves through skills like potion making, mind control, spells, and perhaps even extraordinary control of the elements."

"It's not possible," replied the Prince.

"It's clear now we were near her in the forest," said Elmahigh. "The noise leaving us debilitated was likely her work. It's not dissimilar from some of the rumored abilities spread over the ages since black sorcery's last presence."

"It's been said another of her potential ability is to change form," continued Isilmoire.

"What?" responded Prince Adinor.

"That is why it is important to discern the shape the witch will take," replied Elmahigh.

"The vision is still unclear," said Isilmoire. "She may very well be a tree, a dragon, or perhaps her female self."

"Knowing this could prove crucial to our success," replied Elmahigh. "This sorcery is a wicked foe indeed. In the end, we need to know what we are fighting."

"Enough," said Bolios. "Prince, come with me." Bolios took a few steps, but stopped and turned back to the Prince, who left his sword on the ground. Bolios pointed to it and said, "You'll need that."

It was late. Thunder rattled through the cave walls as the Prince followed Bolios. They ascended up toward the entrance of the Nymph grotto. They walked through the cave tunnels as Prince Adinor reflected on the fire image.

They reached the secret grotto entrance and were once again behind the waterfall. They stepped down the steps toward the grass knoll at the bottom of the wet rock steps. Several Nymph warriors surprised at their sudden appearance armed themselves. They did not expect anyone to leave the grotto so late, thinking of them intruders. Bolios paid no attention and continued toward the side of the mountain not covered by the waterfall. He looked up toward the top of the ridge above, reached out, and began to climb.

"Bolios, where are you going?" asked the Prince.

"Climb," replied Bolios, as he ascended the mountain.

The waters raged alongside them. Prince Adinor struggled to grip the wet rocks. The moisture of the nearby onrushing waters made climbing difficult. The poor vision didn't help and finding proper footholds and rocks to grip was nearly impossible. Bolios neared the top of the mountain and hoisted himself up and over the ledge onto the rocky terrain atop the Nymph hideaway. He looked down toward the Prince who was climbing far slower. The Prince struggled, but made progress nonetheless. Bolios grew impatient.

"Come, my Prince, quickly," he said, "we have work to do."

The Prince reached up and gripped the protruding rock over head and lifted himself up. While laboring closer to Bolios' position, suddenly, a piece broke off. He slipped and fell several feet, losing a dagger he carried on his waist. He crashed atop a large boulder sitting on a ridge of the mountain. His abdomen burned, and he felt a stinging sensation on his side. Lifting his shirt, he noticed blood from a large scrape on his side. His stomach began to bruise. The throbbing pain was terrible. He was winded and out of breath. His ribs were also bruised.

"Bolios, help," the Prince gasped, "I've slipped."

Overcome with terror, he clutched the boulder fighting to avoid tumbling down to the base of the mountain below. A drop from here would kill him.

"Bolios," said the Prince once more, but still no response. "*Where did he go?*"

The Prince found a different position for his foot and relieved some of the weight from his upper body allowing him to relax.

"How do I get out of this?"

A large jutting rock was just outside his arm's reach. He located a round rock above his foot. In one quick motion, he jumped, launching himself toward the other new spot. He landed on the round rock and held on to the jutting crag above, smashing his face against the mountain.

"That hurt," he said.

He reached up once again grabbing hold of the next jutting rock and pulled himself up. The drops of water spraying from the falls wet his face and hands. He picked up his foot and again moved higher. He was a few feet from where he fell and continued climbing. His muscle tightened as every bit of energy was needed for the final part. He sensed the top edge near. He extended his hand brushing the ledge with his fingertips. The cool dirt beneath his nails gripped the flat surface. His left hand joined his right as he clutched the edge and pulled up. Revlieved, his knee landed on the rocky terrain securing his weight over the edge. He collapsed having conquered the mountain. Dirt cooled his back cool and relieved his gashes and cuts from the fall. He looked up and saw thousands of stars in the evening sky. A drop fell on his forehead. He laughed and let it drip down around his face. Then another fell and another. A storm poured down rain. He stood up gathered himself and looked around for Bolios.

"Bolios," he yelled.

No response.

"Bolios, where are you?" he said again.

There was no reply. He stood next to the river as it flowed toward the edge of the mountain and crashed down below. He walked toward the edge he just climbed and stood far enough over to see the Nymph guards stationed at the bottom.

Suddenly, he heard a distinct noise. The rain was hitting against something nearby. It sounded like it was bouncing against metal. It was getting closer. The rain continued pounding down; he began to shake as the cold rain drenched him. The Prince moved his hand toward his waist and slowly pulled out his sword. He lifted it and faced toward the direction of the noise.

"Who goes there?" asked the Prince. "Reveal yourself,"

Suddenly, the figure showed itself. A tall shadow in the distance began to move. It picked up speed, splashing the puddles of water as it approached. It was coming right at him. The Prince steadied himself, planting one foot forward and the other slightly behind as he learned in the triped training. He gripped his sword firmly, his breath quickened. He felt a rush of adrenaline as senses were heightened, giving him added strength and warming him. The figure was almost in front of him, so he readied himself for a kill strike. The rain continued pummeling the ground, and suddenly there was a yell from the figure approaching him.

"Aggghh, defend yourself!"

The Prince quickly swung his sword, aiming for the shadow's head hoping to kill it, but was not fortunate enough, for it found instead the sword of his enemy. The mysterious figure was revealed.

CHAPTER 10

"**B**olios," said the Prince.

The Prince breathed a sigh of relief and relaxed. He lowered his sword.

"That is unwise of you, my Prince," said Bolios who walked behind the Prince, pressing the tip of his sword upon the Prince's lower back, "had I been an enemy, your father and our kingdom would be without an heir to the throne."

"Thank you for the reminder," said the Prince.

"You may not thank me at the end of this," replied Bolios.

The Prince turned and faced Bolios.

"Defend yourself!" yelled Bolios as he raised his sword again and prepared to attack.

"Bolios, I nearly died moments ago," said Prince Adinor. "I was dangling from the mountain. I'm weak."

Bolios seemed to transform before the Prince. His eyes became larger and his teeth clenched as his jaw tightened. All his muscles tensed as he shuffled his feet, carefully gripping the ground under them. He raised his sword in preparation for an attack. He gripped the handle tightly and jumped toward the Prince, swinging the sword violently down at him. The Prince raised his sword quickly in defense just in time. The crashing sound of steel upon steel was loud and seemed to ripple through the Prince as he fell down on one knee. He fought hard just to fend off Bolios' strike. Bolios continued pushing his weight down on the Prince, now holding his sword with both hands. With a small shift in Bolios' weight, he dominated the Prince further. The Prince was almost all the way to the ground.

"That's it, sire, fight," he said.

The Prince was able to swing Bolios sword away from his body just as he rolled away from its edge, leaving the tip of the sword buried in the ground. He rolled to safety. The rain weighed him down. Every falling drop punished the Prince and left him lying on his back.

"Surely someone finishing top of his class in the triped can do better," said Bolios.

Bolios tossed his sword from one hand to another.

"I understand what you're trying to do," replied the Prince.

"Do you?" replied Bolios, who again gripped his sword and steadied himself, preparing for another charge at the Prince. Bolios raised his sword overhead and struck down toward the Prince who leapt to his feet and jumped away from the blow, leaving Bolios' blade striking nothing but dirt.

The Prince smiled and said, "You're testing me."

Bolios removed the sword from the dirt and cleaned it with his boot, staring up at the moon high above.

"No my Prince, the test comes much later."

Bolios charged at Prince Adinor who backed up a few paces and raised his sword in preparation for battle yet again. Back and forth they went as the steel clashed under the rain soaked night.

"You've learned quite well," said Bolios.

"You see," said the Prince, "can we continue another day?"

Their blades were both clenched tightly against each other as they jostled for an advantage. The friction between the metal caused sparks to fly. Bolios pushed the Prince back.

"Battles and wars are not fought on convenience," said Bolios.

The Prince began to massage his right arm as the skirmish was taking its toll. Bolios was stronger and more experienced.

"You may have been special among your peers, boy, but this is war," said Bolios, kicking some water at the Prince's face, temporarily blinding him. Without notice, Bolios was raining blows upon the Prince. The fists felt heavy, overwhelming the teenaged Adinor. The sharp pain came first on his face, then on his stomach. Everywhere Bolios hit him was followed by popped blood vessels beneath his skin.

"What will you do?" asked Bolios.

The Prince collapsed from the beating and fell to the ground.

"Our enemy will not have mercy," continued Bolios.

The Prince was face down in a small pool of water as the rain continued. He looked on as the drops of water hit the puddles nearby.

"I've seen many men in battle, young Prince," said Bolios, "men of all ages and experiences. Despite what they thought before stepping foot on the battlefield, one thing they all discover at the moment they finally do. They would rather be anywhere but there. You don't have to be part of this battle. I know you've thought of it. Perhaps it's best you go home and leave this to us."

The Prince struggled to his hands and knees. His arms shook. The words rattled through the Prince's mind, and he found himself thinking again of his mother and father. He thought about the safety of his royal palace and the comforts waiting for him. He shut his eyes, and there in the darkness underneath the rainstorm, he remembered back to his triped trial celebration. His mother and father were overjoyed and eager to recognize him for completing his training. His father surprised him with a special gift on the day of the celebration. He recalled the King's words.

"Come, my son."

The two walked from the great hall of kings as the royal court's celebration continued. The Prince's mother remained behind, dancing and visiting with the royal guests. Father and son weaved through the various chambers of the castle, and the King again spoke to his son.

"Are you proud, my son?"

"Yes, Father," he replied, "perhaps I'm most happy of beating everyone in my class so easily."

"And why is that?" he asked, as the two walked toward the armory.

"I was better than all the others," answered the Prince.

The King paused and turned toward his son, placing both his hands atop Prince Adinor's shoulders. He bent down and stared the Prince directly in his eyes.

"Superiority over another man is meaningless," his father said.

"But, Father, you are king. You are the most powerful man in the entire kingdom."

The two were standing just outside the entrance of the royal armory. The king stepped inside as his son followed. They walked toward a glass case directly in the center of the room. The case was intricate made of carvings, symbols, and gold designs of high quality. They seemed familiar to the Prince. He'd seen them before.

"Whether superiority of strength, weapons, military, treasure, or even authority and power," said his father, "despite superiority of sheer force, nothing compares to courage. You must never forget this, my son."

As the king finished, Prince Adinor looked into the case and saw inside the most exquisite sword in the entire kingdom.

"This sword I give to you my only son and future king of Mastada," said his father. "It's fashioned from the strongest steel in the entire kingdom and forged by the most knowledgeable swordsmiths found near the Mountains of Citerac. Its handle is wrapped with sewn red boar skin and the rubies on the gold base are the precious stones of our beloved kingdom, hammersmede, idorac, tactocite, and zinfeld. It is light and effective. I had it made for you in honor not of your success in your triped trails, but rather as a reminder, my son. "

Prince Adinor marveled.

"Ruling as king is not about my superiority over any one man or woman I rule," King Ralphus said, "a noble and great king is courageous for all those he leads through his service to them. Every king and every leader must discover how they are called to serve his people in a unique way at a unique time."

* * *

The Prince opened his eyes, remembering his father's last words. Shinning under the moonlight half buried was the sword his father presented him on that day.

"Perhaps its best we continue on without you, young Prince," said Bolios, standing with his arms folded in disgust.

The Prince was hit with a sharp pain deep in his chest. It was not from a blow from battle. He recalled his father's words and listened as Bolios echoed the Prince's own internal doubts. The pain was unlike any that he had ever felt. Without notice, he was crying. First one tear, slow and lazy, then another out of the other eye, and soon it was continuous. The sword given to him by his father remained on the ground. He thought back to his father's words that day.

"Courage for all those he leads," he said.

"What did you say?" asked Bolios.

The Prince clenched his fist, not bothering to wipe his tears. He crawled, opened his hand, and grabbed his sword. He examined all the rubies and the bright red handle covered in mud. He lifted his foot and planted it firmly on the ground and was on one knee. He steadied himself and stabbed the sword into the ground and launched himself up. He stood before Bolios as the rain continued to fall. He gripped his sword tightly with his right hand, his left hand clenched at his side. He stared at Bolios.

Bolios looked him up and down confused. The Prince seemed a different person. They stood in silence for a moment, and the Prince spoke.

"I know you don't believe in me," said the Prince, "you shouldn't. I've done nothing to deserve your favor. But by the end of this, you'll think differently of me. I am staying."

Bolios half-smiled, but then was serious again.

"Very well, Prince Adinor," said Bolios.

The Prince smiled as did Bolios.

They continued training throughout the night.

CHAPTER 11

"A glorious morning, is it not, my Prince?" said Elmahigh.

The Prince rubbed his arms from the previous night and didn't share Elmahigh's enthusiasm. His entire body ached.

"You're moving awfully slow this morning," continued Elmahigh.

Prince Adinor gave Elmahigh only a sidelong glance, opting instead to walk to his horse in silence. The other Mastadans fastened their belongings and prepared their horses, packing food and provisions given to them by the Nymphs.

"We need to leave now, Elmahigh," said Bolios, "the daylight will become scarce."

"Agreed," replied Elmahigh, "we should head north toward the higher grounds of the forest."

"There are some things better left for others," said Bolios, "leave directions to me. We go back to where we first encountered the noise."

"That's madness," said Elmahigh, "they may expect us. We should therefore attempt to go an alternate way."

The arguing continued.

"Sooner or later, Elmahigh, you and I are going to have a serious disagreement and I'm not sure I'll be able to stop myself from hurting you," said Bolios

"Teinmar and Lautner have already searched the area you left," said Isilmoire, "there's nothing there for us to find."

"How, when?" replied Bolios, "I don't believe you. Perhaps there are traces of the enemy… "

"Nothing," replied Isilmoire, "they went in the cover of the night. They retraced your route exactly from where we first found you. They looked for clues or a track but found none."

"How can they be sure?" asked Bolios.

"I've trained them well, they would not be mistaken. I trust these men to protect our people and I put my own life in their hands. If they say there's nothing, there is nothing," responded Isilmoire.

Lautner spoke to Isilmoire in Nymph.

"What is it?" asked Elmahigh.

"He found a man," said Isilmoire, "but he was already dead."

Bolios walked towards Isilmoire and said, "What did he look like?"

Isilmoire spoke in Nymph once again to Lautner and translated the response so Bolios and all the other Mastadans could hear. Marcus crumbled to the ground and wept. The description of the fallen soldier was of his brother, Salazar. Prince Adinor ran over to Marcus placing a hand on his shoulder. Elmahigh's head drooped down as the other Mastadans joined the Prince and surrounded Marcus.

"They didn't bury the body to avoid having their presence known," whispered Isilmoire to Bolios and Elmahigh, "I suggest you do the same."

"So what options do we have?" said Bolios. "Where do we go?"

"The Nymph Sea," replied Isilmoire. "It gives us an advantage on two important levels. We can provide you superior support while on it. Our strongest military force will be closer in the unfortunate event we need it. By taking the path of the sea, we can go around the witch's position, avoiding any defenses she may have setup and arrive there sooner. She's believed to be in the northern section of the forest in the Furion

Wastelands given what little information my scouts have gathered north of our grotto."

"How far to the wastelands?" asked Elmahigh.

"By horse, it would take at least a dozen days," replied Isilmoire.

"You don't know that, she-Nymph," said Bolios. "Perhaps it's better if you let us decide how we—"

"From here," continued Isilmoire, "you're only a day's ride to sea. At sea, you'll save at least half the days we would need to travel through the forest on foot."

Bolios grimaced and stepped toward Isilmoire. They were eye to eye. All the others looked on.

"Very well, but I have another small concern," replied Bolios, "we don't have a ship."

"Not to worry, my friend," replied Isilmoire as she smiled.

"Well, all right then," replied Bolios. "Lead the way, Nymph."

"We'll take the river back toward the sea ahead of you," said Isilmoire. "It will give us the necessary time to stock the ship with supplies and food. We'll meet you there. Go west."

They mounted their horses and said their goodbyes to the Nymph soldiers they befriended at the grotto and rode off.

The ride was silent as they mourned the death of one of their own. Though the fate of Salazar was determined, they pondered other uncertainties. Where was Litovic? Prince Adinor remained quiet, though his mind raced. He realized the initial task given to them had evolved to a far greater responsibility than any of them anticipated. The challenges encountered tested their resolve and surprised even their greatest of warriors, Elmahigh and Bolios. What would that mean for him and the little experience he had?

Chapter 12

They traveled all morning, leaving the grotto far behind them. As they moved closer to the sea and deeper into the unknowns of the Petruchani Forest, the plant life around them changed. They entered an area filled of trees bigger than any seen before. The smallest of the trees had trunks over two dozen feet wide. Around the trunks were thick blue and green vines wrapped from the base of the trees twisting all the way up the trunks.

Everywhere bright-colored fruits hung from the vines. The various shapes and sizes of exotic plants and its yields were different than anything grown in the Mastadan farmlands. There were large round purple ones and narrow bright yellow flute-shaped ones. Ahead were bell-shaped green and black ones next to white and orange ones. They found berries of all types.

"Could we make maltsenhop," said Dolamite.

All of the men laughed and gazed, still in awe of the magnificence of the place.

"Where are we?" asked the Prince.

"I'm not sure, my Prince," responded Bolios.

"Surely, we're close to the sea," answered Elmahigh.

Apart from the fruits and trees were all sorts of plants and flowers. Everywhere were bright fresh white ones with long narrow petals and pretty bright pink ones with fat round petals. Millions of small yellow flowers with red centers and bright red roses the size of Bolios surrounded the Mastadans. There were blue roses too. Tall bright green plants stood next to the trees, seemingly waving back and forth in the breeze as the warriors passed. Down below those were also small tiny bunches of indigo flowers that seemed to also move.

"Did you see that?" asked the Prince.

"What?" replied Ecclesias.

"The plants seem alive," replied Prince Adinor.

Theodonus shook his head. "I hope you're not losing your reason, young Prince."

"No, he's right, I saw it too," said Bolios.

It happened again. Then the little creatures that at first glance were indigo-colored plants began leaping off the tall green plants and moved below their horses. The green stems were actually legs and the violet petals their hats, revealing small heads beneath them. They were no larger than a finger's length. To their surprise they approached their horses. They made all sorts of chirping and buzzing noises but weren't harmful. Hundreds of them crawled up the horses and jumped onto a couple of the Mastadans.

"It's incredible," said Prince Adinor. "I've never seen anything like it."

"Nor have I," replied Elmahigh.

Dolamite was covered in the small purple flower creatures. Other small exotic creatures neared as insects with two small heads appeared and birds of all colors flew overhead.

"I think they're quite fond of you, Dolamite," said Elmahigh.

"Well, somebody tell them I'm not fond of them," replied Dolamite who continued to brush them off.

The Mastadan swatted at them, but the more he tried, the more they flocked toward him. He was covered and seemed more plant than human. Dolamite shifted his weight from side to side on his horse, trying to rid himself of the small creatures. He twisted and turned, but began to lose his balance. He waved his hands in the air, swatting at the little creatures, and fell off his horse. All of the men laughed. Dolamite joined the others in laughter, choosing to give up his fight against the tiny harmless plant creatures.

"Well, you're lucky I don't eat you," he said.

All of the soldiers laughed again.

"Bolios, could we stop for a bit?" asked Theodonus. "Maybe even rest and eat."

"Please, Bolios, we could even try some of the fruit," said Malchomite.

"We'd be careful and it wouldn't be long at all," added Ecclesias.

Elmahigh relished the torture of anticipation the men underwent. He gripped his neck and smiled while the Mastadans waited for an answer. They all began to grumble.

"Silence," said Bolios.ND, they continued riding again, but then Bolios spoke once more, "Let's see just how well trained your eyes are for picking."

All smiles, the men leapt off their horses in delight and ran through the great garden, plucking the best-looking ones. Ecclesias reached for the bell-shaped ones as Malchomite grabbed the large violet-colored ones. Dolamite was still lying on the ground as the little flower creatures continued hopping all over him.

They savored fruits and vegetables and threw each other samples of their favorites. They debated which was more savory or sweet. The Prince even contributed, picking some himself.

"See you would want to stay away from this particular one," he said. "You can tell it's not for eating because of the bright maroon shade, you'd want something a bit darker. At least that's what they taught us to look for in my triped trials."

Elmahigh laughed as they all ate. Even Bolios made his way to a neighboring bush with large oranges, a familiar item. He grabbed a couple and threw one to Elmahigh.

"Thank you, my friend," said Elmahigh.

"It's nothing," replied Bolios, "you've done quite a lot more for me on many occasions."

"Are you referring to that time I helped you defeat the water snake that killed many Mastadans at the trident of the rivers of Ire?" asked Elmahigh.

"Well no, but—"

"Or are you possibly talking about the moment I was able to rescue you from being turned into a pig by the drunken wizard on the mountains of Citerac?" added Elmahigh.

"Well, that was a completely different situation altogether," said Bolios.

"As I recall, you were to only investigate the missing ore that was not being turned in by the miners. Instead, you took it upon yourself to pursue reported tales of a wizard from the Red Mountains traveling through our lands."

"Well, in the end, I was right to do it," replied Bolios.

"You were both right and wrong," said Elmahigh, "the wizard did exist, but hunting it him by yourself was the wrong decision."

"Well, I didn't foresee the wizard being that powerful," said Bolios.

"A bit of restraint never hurt anyone in certain circumstances. In particular, one like that."

"That wizard sure was problems."

"Indeed," replied Elmahigh.

They both laughed and shook their heads. Prince Adinor came up to both of them and offered them some of the limotates he just picked.

"Would either of you care for one?" he asked.

Bolios and Elmahigh were still laughing and hadn't noticed the Prince's offer.

"What's so funny?" The Prince asked.

"Oh, just a couple of fools thanking the stars for our fortunes," replied Elmahigh.

"Would you like a limotate, Elmahigh? I've just picked them, they're tart."

"Thank you, my dear boy," replied Elmahigh. "I'll enjoy a couple."

"I'll get the men," said Bolios. "It's time to leave."

"Yes, I fear we still have some distance to reach the Nymph Sea," replied Elmahigh, "and evening approaches."

And so the men gathered what fruit they could carry and sojourned on toward the Nymph Sea. They all rode single file as Bolios led the group forward, always alert to sudden movements, surprises, or unknown along the way. Elmahigh and Prince Adinor followed just behind him. Friedrich, Ecclesias, and Malchomite rode behind them, followed by the grieving Marcus. Stricken by the loss of his brother, he rode in the middle of them all. Void of any zeal following the news at the grotto, Bolios thought it best to protect him. Behind him rode Dolamite as Theodonus brought up the rear. The path through the great garden ended as they approached wild dense jungle with no easy way through.

"Are we lost, Elmahigh?" asked Prince Adinor.

"Difficult to say," replied Elmahigh, "after all, we don't know where we are going."

Prince Adinor continued looking around the expanse of land, amazed at just how much new things surrounded him.

"I wish my father were here," he said.

Elmahigh smiled and asked, "What would you tell him if he were?"

"Well, I don't know, I guess I'm not sure," replied the Prince, "I just thought—"

"Precisely," replied Elmahigh, "sometimes that's enough."

"I'm not sure what you mean Elmahigh."

"It matters not, young Prince, of the why or the how or even the when of things in many occasions," said Elmahigh, "sometimes the only thing that matters is *the what* of it."

"Well, I don't know who, what, when, how, or why of anything you've said," replied the Prince.

"Look out toward the vastness of the fields and trees and birds and animals," said Elmahigh, "see as far out as your eyes permit."

"I see many things," replied the Prince.

"As you look, there are birds of all types flying in the air, horses and cows and deer and buffalo grazing in the fields, water flowing in the stream, and tall grass waving in winds. Trees dance, clouds move, and all in concert."

"Well, I see all of it, the trees, the water, and everything else, but what does that have to do with what I said?"

"We're all interconnected," replied Elmahigh, "all these creatures, all the plants, all the waters, all the Nymphs we head toward, all of us here together, even your father far away and even you here without him. You had a thought of him, a random one, a sentiment."

"Yes," replied the Prince.

"And that very thought, as insignificant as it may seem, can bridge the distance between both of you with a speed greater than anything in our great land. Instantly, he is here before you."

"But he's not here," replied the Prince.

"Oh, but he is, young Prince," responded Elmahigh, "just not out there where you look."

Elmahigh rode past the Prince and arrived alongside Bolios as the Prince pondered his words and thought on their meaning.

"We've been riding for far too long since we last stopped for fruit, this can't be right," said Dolamite.

"Oh, shut up, you're just hungry again," said Ecclesias.

"No, I'm always hungry," replied Dolamite, "we're lost."

"Just keep moving forward," replied Theodonus, "we're almost there."

They continued riding west, but the frustrations did not subside.

"It does seem as though we should have been there by now," said Malchomite.

"Well, we're not, so just keep moving forward," replied Theodonus.

They kept riding, but even the horses tired. They inched forward. Then a cool sensation came from the direction they were riding toward. There was decrease in temperature of several degrees and a refreshing mist hit their faces.

"What is that?" asked Dolamite.

Ahead was an impassible wall of trees, bushes, and long thick grass. Bolios neared it and leaped from his horse and removed his sword, slashing and ripping the thick tall grass as he swung. The massive blade tore into overgrowth clearing a path for himself as well as the others behind him. He kept hacking away at the jungle and began to see white on the other side. He turned around and ran back toward the others who remained atop their horses.

"It's too difficult on horse, we'll have to go on foot from here," said Bolios, "Grab everything you can carry and set the horses free."

The Mastadans each dismounted. They grabbed swords, bows, quivers of arrows, and the fresh pickings from the garden, as well as plants for medicine given by the Nymphs at the grotto, and whatever food they had left. Bolios led them through the clearing, continuing to cut through the dense jungle where he left off before.

Left to right, the fierce sword shredded as Bolios walked through the last bit of grass and stepped onto the sands of a beach. Each Mastadan joined him standing single file, shoulder to shoulder, as they looked on in amazement. Prince Adinor and Dolamite reached down and squeezed the perfect white powdery grains between their fingers. They both smiled as the soft sensation between their fingers were calming.

Prince Adinor looked out into the vast expanse of blue, which seemed to blanket the entire world from where they stood. Everywhere was clear water. Bolios lead them closer to the small trails of foam, as waves flowed onto the shore. Their eyes remained fixed on the sea floor, easily seen from where they stood. The rumbling of the waves crashed against the rocks protruding out from the shoreline in the distance as walls of the sea spit up thousands of drops into the air. Salt water engulfed their noses and the breeze bounced off the water, relieving them of any fatigue.

"Look," said Prince Adinor pointing north, "over there."

Sitting atop the blue waters was a ship and walking toward them along the beach were three Nymphs. It was Teinmar, Lautner, and Isilmoire. They had reached the Nymph Sea.

CHAPTER 13

"Did trouble find you?" asked Isilmoire.

"No, not at all," replied Elmahigh.

"We stopped longer than we should have," said Bolios as he looked over to Dolamite, "some have greater appetites than others."

"You found the Sacred Lilliet Garden," said Isilmoire.

"I beg your pardon, we meant no insult or harm in our intrusion of it," said Elmahigh, "the fruit was ripe and well…it was a perfect respite for us."

"No harm or insult comes of your decision, for it was the right one," replied Isilmoire. "We are grateful to have shared it with you. The Sacred Lilliet Garden was the concept of the Nymph Queen, Lilliet. She was the first Nymph to violate a long-standing law of our kingdom. Then, Nymphs were forbidden to leave the seas. As the story goes, Queen Lilliet saw in man a potential ally and thought it wise to befriend them instead of fighting them. She went against her own husband, King Nemus, ruler of entire Nymph Kingdom, who believed man was by nature evil and therefore were not to be interacted with. Queen Lilliet organized a secret group that would leave from the Nymph kingdom deep below at the sea's ocean bottom in order to plant the special garden you came upon. Legend has it that Queen Lilliet was not only the first to step foot on dry land, but also the one to plant the very first seeds in the garden. It now yields the abundance of delicious fruits you enjoyed. Some believe the goodness of her actions is the cause of the continued produce even today, hundreds of years later."

"We are most grateful for her wisdom," replied Elmahigh.

"As are we," replied Isilmoire, "let us continue what she began. Take only what you can carry, your ship awaits."

They walked toward the ship, enjoying the breeze and calming sensation of the sea. Prince Adinor, Dolamite, and Ecclesias kicked and threw water at one another.

"Getting old isn't a choice, but growing up surely is," said Elmahigh.

"Indeed," replied Bolios, "and some clearly never do."

"Here it is," said Isilmoire. "The *Mercurial*. Built by man and Nymph, the *Mercurial* was a collaboration toward the joint exploration of Mastadan lands and seas. The ship was the vision of the four sons and daughters of King Nemus and Queen Lilliet together with your ancestors, Prince Adinor."

"My ancestors?" asked Prince Adinor.

"Yes," replied Isilmoire, "your great-great-grandfather, King Pontius assigned his best carpenters and engineers to assist in the undertaking. The venture yielded many great discoveries. One of the many results from those explorations included the mapping of Mastada, a feat that continues to be invaluable to us all. I wouldn't doubt a copy is buried somewhere deep in your order's ancient documents, Elmahigh."

Prince Adinor sighed and said, "Why don't I know any of this?"

Elmahigh stepped toward the Prince and placed his right hand on the Prince's shoulder, saying, "There are some that forget the importance of the past. Over time, you've seen this manifest itself in the decree preventing Mastadans from entering the Petruchani Forest and other arcane laws. Perhaps it's time that's remedied."

"Will this relic even make the journey?" asked Bolios.

"It's a shadow of the ship it once was, but it will suffice nonetheless," replied Isilmoire.

"This ship seems better suited for scrap wood for pit cooks in the royal court's kitchens than sailing," said Ecclesias.

"Ha," said Dolamite.

"What?" asked Theodonus.

"Well, I wasn't the first to mention food is all," replied Dolamite.

They all laughed.

"What do you make of it, Elmahigh?" asked Bolios.

Elmahigh looked at the ship and pondered the options.

"Every moment becomes increasingly pressing," he replied, "The Witch continues her black sorcery and all the while her armies grow. If we turn back and journey on horse and ride north, we stand to lose too much time. We also can't risk the straightforward approach. Her wickedness is spreading. She may have eyes in the forest we are unaware of."

"The ship will serve you well, I give you my word," said Isilmoire. "My people have continued maintaining it long since it was abandoned. Many of the most important parts have been replaced. You can't see it from here, but the holes and damaged areas have all been addressed."

"Very well," replied Bolios, "we sail."

"Excellent," said Isilmoire. "Teinmar and Lautner will bring the smaller boarding boat and we'll begin bringing everyone aboard. We've already stocked it with provisions for the journey. Apart from what your men bring, everything else is aboard. We should be able to sail as soon as your men are on deck."

"Very well," replied Bolios, "let's get on it with it."

Teinmar and Lautner shuttled the men, and after two trips, they were all aboard the ship. Though the ship seemed to be of concern from afar, upon closer examination, the concerns were misplaced. The ship's sails were patched in several places. Large chunks of the masts were also repaired with supporting wood. The bow of the ship was worn. The deck creaked with every step placed upon it, a natural result of age. The rear of the ship had a raised platform, making navigating from it easy for the captain. Atop the platform was the large wooden wheel. It was worn and old, but sufficient for the journey. A few of them proceeded down below deck and found two small cabin-rooms with beds.

"Perfect," said Dolamite, "I'll be sleeping here tonight."

"The hell you will, that's mine all right," replied Ecclesias.

As they continued arguing, others continued exploring the ship, walking past them, proceeding to next room. Marcus, Malchomite, and Friedrich stepped inside and grabbed and touched all the items and trinkets found within. Malchomite lifted a small empty tin covered in a hardened liquid. He put his nose to it and asked, "When was the last time anyone used this ship?"

Friedrich shrugged his soldiers and concerned himself more with the compass he found covered in dust on the floor of the room.

"Found something, did you?" asked Malchomite.

"Don't start," said Theodonus, "if anything in here is of use, be sure to let Bolios or I know. Nothing in here is for your possession. Remember, this isn't our ship and we'll need everything that can help us."

"All right, we know," replied Ecclesias.

Theodonus stopped in the storage area. The Nymphs had meats, cheeses, and fish along with barrels of wine and beer in one corner. In another area, apart from the food, were weapons of all sorts. There were long metal spears topped with sharp tips. Long swords and short daggers of different metals fashioned with various handles were secured on the wall. There were axes and mallets. Additionally, there were nets hanging overhead, plus armor and corresponding helmets. Next to the armor, Theodonus found three large brown sacks, which piqued his curiosity. He moved closer to it and examined it more closely.

"What have we here?" he said.

"Don't touch that," said Lautner.

"What is it?" asked Theodonus.

"It's a very special powder we've formulated from a wild shrub that grows in marsh areas," said Lautner. "It's made through a delicate process involving pulling it out by its root and then drying it on land. After a couple of weeks of baking in the sun, it shrinks a bit which means it's ready. We cut the ends of the root, but only the very tips and grind it into a fine powder. We store it until the finely ground powder hardens into what you know see. When set to fire, it makes for a dangerous weapon."

"If it's so dangerous, why bring it at all?" asked Theodonus.

"For the reasons we can't imagine," replied Isilmoire who walked in with Bolios and Elmahigh. "Lautner, be sure to move that far enough from the furnace."

Lautner responded in Nymph and proceeded to relocate the sacks elsewhere in the space.

"This is a useful area for gathering, eating, or preparing for battles," said Isilmoire. "I trust the furnace will provide warmth. And for what the furnace can't supply, the wine and beer suffices."

Elmahigh and Bolios smiled and nodded in agreement. Prince Adinor remained above, strolling the deck of the ship. He walked about the ship, touching the wooden railings, poking at the various replacement sails rolled on deck. He continued pacing throughout the ship and even noticed writing carved into it. They were small letters, some were names and others messages. He traced them with his finger and read many of them. Bored, he walked to the edge of the ship's starboard side, where they boarded and looked down toward the clear blue water below as the quiet Nymph Teinmar continued loading the remaining items.

"Do you need help?" asked Prince Adinor.

Teinmar didn't answer. He instead waved his hand back and forth, which the Prince took as a no. The Prince then walked up the steps leading toward the raised deck. He gripped the worn wheel with his hands and imagined himself directing the ship to its destination and stared out into the Nymph Sea in awe. As he looked out toward the horizon, his thoughts were of the uncertainty that awaited him and his friends. He stepped back as the floor continued to give just enough under him enough to make him nervous. He followed the wooden banister toward the stairs he just used, but instead of descending, he stopped. He turned and walked back toward the high wood wall behind the wheel and jumped. Not able to reach the top alone, he looked for a something. Nearby was an empty barrel propped in the corner, perfect for what he intended. He grabbed the barrel and placed it in front of the wooden wall before him and climbed on top of it. Maintaining his balance, he pulled himself up onto the narrow wooden shelf directly behind the ship's wheel, giving him a perfect vantage point of the rear of the ship. Below him was a straight drop with nothing but water to hit if he fell. His legs shook for he didn't anticipate the height and bent down. He grabbed tightly to the narrow flat area he was perched on and steadied his legs beneath him and rose to his feet. There he stood atop the shelf and gazed back toward the beach and the Petruchani Forrest's western edge. With both hands at his brow, he searched for any hint of the rising tower of the Mastada city center capitol in the distance, but found nothing. All he found instead were massive tropical trees from the Lilliet Garden and the thousands of trees blanketing the Petruchani Forest.

"It would be a shame to have to explain to your parents that we lost you over a silly fall, young Prince," said Elmahigh.

Prince Adinor turned and looked down at Elmahigh leaning on the wheel of the ship, staring back up toward him.

"I can't see home," replied Prince Adinor. "I thought I could see it from here."

"Oh, don't worry, Prince Adinor. Our home is exactly where we've left it."

"I didn't realize we were so far away," replied the Prince.

"The first steps away from home and the familiar are always the most difficult, young Prince. But with each added step away from the customary, you move toward the new. You'll find it becomes easier over time."

"I'm not sure I ever want it to be easy to be away from my home, Elmahigh," said the Prince.

"Well, that may prove difficult for you to accept now," said Elmahigh, "but it will happen one day."

The Prince continued to stare out into the distance. He thought about Elmahigh's words, enjoyed one last look at the land he would be leaving behind, and then jumped down.

"No, it won't," said the Prince.

"Oh, and how is that?" asked Elmahigh.

"It's the wanting to be home that will make sure I always return," said the Prince.

Elmahigh smiled, patted the Prince on his shoulder, and bent down toward him, saying, "In saying that, Prince Adinor, you now move closer to returning home than you have this entire time. You will need that spirit. Do not forget it. That resolve will indeed be tested. For now, let's get you one step closer to home. Get Bolios and the men from down below, let's head for the witch."

The Prince walked down the stairs and then below deck. Elmahigh stared up toward the sky as it turned black. Large grey clouds approached from every direction and the darkness of nightfall crept in. The water began to stir and the surf increased, causing the ship to sway. The wind howled and rattled the ropes and sails of the ship and the trees danced back and forth on the shoreline.

"And so it begins," said Elmahigh.

CHAPTER 14

The seas were rough. Back and forth, the *Mercurial* went, as its passengers were tossed about by the fierce waves.

"Keep your wits about you, men," said Bolios.

Malchomite and Ecclesias worked to secure the thick ropes of the sails with the help of Isilmoire and Teinmar. Lautner went down below deck to secure the supplies. The massive waves pounded them as they crashed over the ship dumping water on the deck, inundating it.

"Friedrich, another one has come loose," said Bolios, "there on the port side."

Friedrich ran to the rope flailing in the wind as the sail came undone. He jumped repeatedly trying to catch it, but the wind prevented it. Several yards away, Dolamite and Elmahigh continued holding the rope with all their strength. The friction from the weight of Prince Adinor, dangling at the end, burned their hands. They held on as the Prince continued swinging over the edge of the ship. The fierce wind sent him away from the ship's wall, then back toward it, banging him hard.

"Hold on," said Elmahigh as he worked with Prince Adinor and Dolamite to release the iron anchor stuck in the raised position. They all hoped releasing it would help stabilize the ship as it teetered in the rough sea.

"I can't see where it is," said Prince Adinor.

"There just beyond your right hand," replied Elmahigh, "reach a little further and you'll find the secondary release in the small alcove. You must cut the rope inside the alcove to release the anchor. The Prince reached out once again.

"A bit further, Prince," said Elmahigh.

The darkness and heavy rains made it impossible to see. Prince Adinor relied only on his touch during the small instances he was by the ship.

"I'm almost there," said Price Adinor.

His fingertips grazed the rope, confirming it was near. His hand flailed around as the strong winds overwhelmed him.

"I can almost reach it," he said.

"We have you," said Elmahigh.

The large waves engulfed Prince Adinor. He disappeared in the water for an instant but resurfaced as the ship rose to the peak of the wave.

"Go on, Prince," said Dolamite.

The rope was just beyond his reach. The Prince stretched again, more intent on reaching it this time.

"I found it," said Prince Adinor, "hold me, I've reached it."

"Excellent, my Prince," said Elmahigh, "release the anchor."

The Prince tried to cut the hidden secondary rope.

"There's far too much tension. It's not working," he said.

Suddenly, a giant wave of water came and again slammed the Prince against the side of the ship.

"Hold on, Prince Adinor," said Elmahigh.

The Prince grabbed hold of the rope and spit out water as he fought for air. Between the rain and waves, it was too much.

"I can't do anything, it will not release," said Prince Adinor.

"So be it," said Elmahigh. "Dolamite, pull. We're bringing him back up."

"Okay," replied Dolamite.

They pulled with the little strength they had left as Prince Adinor fought against the swelling waters and rain. He coughed, swallowing water.

"Hang on, Prince Adinor," said Dolamite, "you're nearly there."

The Prince reached overhead as the ship's deck was within reach. As they pulled him closer, he gripped the deck and helped by hauling himself up. His arms shook as he hoisted himself up and over the railing as Dolamite and Elmahigh grabbed him. They flung him over and they all collapsed.

"Well, that didn't work," said Dolamite.

The men below deck evaded the weapons being flung about. The ship's armory had become a death trap.

"Look out," said Theodonus.

An ax flew from one side of the ship to the other, landing in the support beam, just over Marcus' bent body.

"That was closer than I'd like," said Marcus.

"Quickly," said Theodonus, "we must tie all of the weapons and secure them once again."

Marcus and Theodonus tried to shield their eyes from the fierce winds, struggling to see as they worked. Thankfully, Teinmar helped finish the task. Back above, Bolios and the rest of the men ran to repair damaged parts of the ship as Lautner repaired a torn sail. Isilmoire fought with the wheel and struggled to control its course.

"Bolios," she said, "come quickly."

The high seas seemed to engulf the entire ship. Bolios arrived at the wheel and tried helping her, but to no avail.

"We've done all we can," said Isilmoire.

"What do you mean?" asked Bolios.

"I have to take my men and go underwater," she said.

"Well, that's terrific," replied Bolios, "my men and I don't have that option."

"That's why we need to go," said Isilmoire.

"Coward!"

"There's no sense in continuing to endanger my men if we have a way to stay safe," said Isilmoire, "this way, it ensures one of our group survives."

Elmahigh approached and asked, "What is it?"

"This coward has led us to our doom," said Bolios.

"You barbarian!" yelled Isilmoire.

They began fighting. Punches and kicks flew between them.

Elmahigh ran and grabbed the spinning wheel. "Enough," he yelled.

He held up his hand and stunned them both with a bright light that shot out of his outstretched fingers.

They were both temporarily blinded.

"She's right, Bolios," said Elmahigh, "there is nothing she can do for us. We are at the mercy of the seas. If we fail to survive, Isilmoire can take Teinmar and Lautner to the Nymph kingdom and request an audience with Lord Gillium. Perhaps, upon hearing of the original plan's failure, Isilmoire can convince Lord Gillium to send his forces to attack the dark witch."

Bolios and Isilmoire stared at each other still angry from the skirmish. Then suddenly, a lightning bolt ripped through the sky, illuminating the violent night. The thunder made them all shudder as more lightning rained down from the sky above.

"We don't have much time, the conditions are worsening," said Elmahigh.

"I wouldn't abandon you if there was a better way," said Isilmoire.

Bolios looked over at the ship's deck, his men and Prince Adinor continued working, oblivious to the impending Nymph departure.

"I have no other choice," replied Bolios, "but be sure to return as soon as the storm passes. We will survive this."

Isilmoire smiled. She turned and began to walk toward the steps descending from the wheel and found her two soldiers informing them of the news. Teinmar and Lautner appealed. Angered by the decision, they yelled in their Nymph language. There was a brief discussion, but they recognized the good they could do if the Mastadans did not live.

"Say your goodbyes," said Isilmoire.

The two Nymphs shook hands with the Mastadan warriors and embraced their confused friends. They ran and jumped overboard, disappearing into the dark waters below.

"Well what the blazes was that all about?" asked Dolamite.

"I'm not sure," replied Prince Adinor.

Bolios continued fighting to maintain some direction on the wheel as the storm continued. Elmahigh gathered the men together and explained the decision.

"Cowards," said Ecclesias.

"We should have killed them when we had the chance," said Malchomite.

"Didn't you hear what Elmahigh said?" asked Prince Adinor. "It's the only way we assure someone survives. We can't let the Witch escape. This guarantees at least a fight."

The Mastadans focused on the ship's repairs, but struggled with a smaller crew.

"Theodonus," said Bolios.

"Yes, sire," he replied.

"Come grab the wheel," said Bolios.

They exchanged places, and Bolios jumped down from the platform to help his men on deck.

"If the Nymphs abandoned ship, we won't survive the night," said Ecclesias.

"Hold your tongue, man," said Bolios.

"We shouldn't even be here," said Malchomite, "we should have gone back to the capitol and gotten the full army."

All the Mastadans gathered around and began to shout ideas.

"Silence," said Bolios, "all of you quiet down. We've done exactly what we've needed to do. I've always asked much of you. You've always given everything you could. Don't you stop giving me your all now."

The lightning continued crashing as the thunder followed the bright flashes in the sky.

"We can't control this weather any more than I can tell you we'll survive it," he said, "but what we can do is try with everything we've got. With each other's help, we'll give this storm our best fight. In the end, no matter what at least we've done that. I sure as hell can't swim underwater like a Nymph, but I can fight like a Mastadan."

"Yeah!" they all yelled in unison.

"We're going to need everyone above deck," said Bolios. "I will be at the wheel. Elmahigh will be on deck working together with all of you. Theodonus will be responsible for replacing any sails that tear.

"Yes, sire," said Theodonus.

"Dolamite will help provide materials Theodonus requires."

"You can count on me, Bolios," said Dolamite.

"Ecclesias, get all of the rope we can spare from down below, we may need it," said Bolios.

"Right," said Ecclesias as he disappeared below deck.

"We've made some distance even through the storm," said Bolios, "I'm going to need someone up at the top of the lookout mast to help find land. It's dangerous, so if no one volunteers, I'll do it myself."

The remaining men were quiet.

"I'll do it," said Marcus.

Elmahigh smiled and nodded toward Marcus in encouragement.

"Are you certain you're feeling up to it, Marcus?" replied Bolios. "You've lost more than any of us. I wouldn't hesitate in taking your place."

"My brother is gone," said Marcus. "If there is something I can do to help us find those responsible for taking him from me, I'm the better for it."

A few of the men patted him on the back in support.

"Very well," said Bolios, "the rest of you stay close by. Elmahigh and Theodonus will direct you where to go as needs arise. Prince Adinor, you come up to the wheel with me. Take your positions."

"Yes sir," they all yelled.

They all assumed their places. Some worked on replacing damaged ropes. The waves increased in size, spilling more water onto the ship's deck. The lightning even seemed closer.

"Hold on," yelled Bolios.

A massive wave crashed over them, knocking down all of the men.

"Is everyone still aboard?" asked Bolios.

"Yes, everyone is still here," replied Elmahigh. "Theodonus, there beside you, grab that end."

Elmahigh helped him as the two made their way toward the front of the ship, carrying with them a large wooden plank. They secured it over the cracked mast, needing only to tie it. Every single one of them fought the weather.

"Help him," said Ecclesias.

"You got it," said Malchomite.

The two men aided Dolamite to his feet. The three worked together and were successful.

"I see something," yelled Marcus from up above.

"What?" asked Theodonus.

"I see something," he repeated, "it's close."

"Can it be?" asked Elmahigh.

Elmahigh strained his eyes, hoping to see ahead. The darkness made it impossible.

"There I see something," said Marcus again.

The ship continued directly toward it. The *Mercurial* went up and down and side to side. The continual punishment seemed destined to tear the ship apart. The men were tossed around like children.

"Bolios, we've spotted something," said Malchomite.

"What direction?" asked Bolios.

"Stay on this heading," replied Malchomite.

"We're going to make it, Bolios," said Prince Adinor.

Bolios glanced over toward the young Prince and then grimaced as he fought the wheel.

"It looks like a mountain," said Marcus.

"We've found land again," said Ecclesias.

"We're going to make it," said Dolamite.

Theodonus smiled and relaxed as the news sunk in.

"We're nearly there," said Marcus loudly.

Elmahigh continued staring into the distance as he observed the sky above desperate for a clue. He looked over both sides of the ship and found nothing. As he continued searching, he heard a faint noise overhead.

"What is that?" he said aloud.

None of the men paid attention they would be on land soon. Elmahigh again glanced toward the direction ahead as the lighting continued once again.

"There, did you see it?" he said.

"No, Elmahigh, I didn't see anything," replied Theodonus.

The two looked forward, trying to catch what Elmahigh spoke of.

Crash, another lightning strike not far from the ship and the sky was lit once more. In the brief moments of it, Elmahigh saw the supposed mountain Marcus spoke of, but it looked odd.

"Do you see it, Elmahigh?" asked Marcus. "What is it?"

"Not quite," replied Elmahigh.

Another thunderbolt ripped through the skyline. Again there was more lightning.

"There, there it is," said Elmahigh.

"Where, Elmahigh?" asked Theodonus.

"Just there ahead of us."

Another lightning strike followed by two more behind it in quick succession, and as the sky lit up, Elmahigh finally saw the figure ahead.

"That's not a mountain," said Elmahigh. "It's something else. We must turn around."

"What?" said Theodonus.

The deafening thunder and high winds made it impossible to hear each other despite being close.

Elmahigh grabbed Theodonus by the arm. "See to it that Marcus gets down."

"I will," said Theodonus, "but I don't understand."

"Do it," said Elmahigh.

"Okay."

Elmahigh raced toward the rear of the ship, warning all of the men to brace themselves as he sped toward Bolios.

"What did he say?" asked Malchomite.

Elmahigh continued toward the wheel.

"Bolios! Bolios!" he yelled.

"Yes, what is it?"

"Turn the ship around at once."

"Why?" said Bolios.

Elmahigh stopped and heard more of the faint noise, which was stronger. Prince Adinor heard it to.

"What is that?" said Prince Adinor.

"Sounds like birds," said Bolios.

"It's not birds," said Elmahigh, "it's her."

"What?" responded Bolios.

"And it's not a mountain ahead," replied Elmahigh, "it's unlike anything I've ever seen."

Then suddenly, there was complete silence. The sails stopped flapping and the ship was steady.

"It's too late," said Elmahigh.

Without notice, a giant funnel of water that seemed to stretch from the sea up to the dark clouds overhead came right at the ship. The Mastadans all yelled. In a swift knifing action, the massive water spout split the ship in two. Hundreds of pieces of wood splintered and were sent into the sea. The *Mercurial* was ripped apart. In moments, both halves of the ship began sinking into the dark deep below.

The winds died down. The rain subsided. The seas became tranquil once again. There were only scarce lightning strikes thereafter. The storm passed, but the destruction was complete. It would be daylight soon. The sea was littered with pieces of wood and remnants from the destroyed ship, but there was no sign of any of the warriors.

CHAPTER 15

Isilmoire approached the round gold entrance of the Nymph throne room and signaled to the guards to open it. The entire Nymph kingdom was on alert as word arrived of the growing treachery in the Petruchani Forest. The horrors of the dark witch were spreading and stories of good men turned to demon warriors resulted in widespread panic even for those under the sea.

"I need to see Lord Gillium," said Isilmoire.

"Very well," replied the royal guard.

Isilmoire entered the royal throne room and swam straight toward Lord Gillium. His head was buried behind both his hands.

"Ah, Isilmoire, what news do you bring?" asked Lord Gillium.

"The rumors are true," replied Isilmoire. "There is an evil brewing in forest. A witch has begun attacking a Mastadan village and poisoning men, turning them into demon monsters bent on only serving her will."

"How can that be?" replied Lord Gillium. "I foresaw a different report from you."

Isilmoire rolled her eyes.

"Perhaps you saw wrong, sire," replied Isilmoire. "There's more. We've met a group of Mastadans—"

"Mastadans?" replied Lord Gillium. "I thought those foolish people never ventured to the forest anymore."

"Mastadans are in the forest and we were on route to the Furion Wastelands where my scouts believed the witch to be," said Isilmoire. "With the threat of the witch building her forces, the Mastadans and I agreed the prudent choice was to immediately pursue. But we were hit by a terrible storm. I explained to them I would travel here to get your approval to send the entire Nymphian force to support them or defeat the witch ourselves if they didn't survive."

Lord Gillium leaned back in his throne resting on one side of the coral chair. He gazed out at all of the monuments and busts of the different kings that ruled the Nymph kingdom, all his predecessors. He looked over to the famed reef lance. A modest weapon at first glance. Its dulled coral and seaweed construction would appear to be the last weapon of choice when battling a giant sea serpent.

"Do you know the legend of that weapon, Isilmoire?"

"Yes, my lord," answered Isilmoire, "all Nymphs do."

"So you're familiar then with the sea serpent responsible for the death of many Nymph warriors which almost destroyed the Nymph kingdom many years ago," said Lord Gillium.

"Yes, my lord," replied Isilmoire.

"Long ago our people enjoyed times of glory, but no longer is that so. We are but place holders in time."

"Lord Gillium. With respect, you know why I am here."

"Yes, Isilmoire, I know. You would have me give you command of what little army we have left to pursue this brooding evil which threatens everything good left in this world."

"Then dispense with the history, sire, and let it be so," she said.

"That, I cannot do."

"Why, sire," said Isilmoire, "it's a mistake for you to—"

"Isilmoire," said Lord Gillium, "what you must realize is that perhaps long ago we had the luxury of engaging enemies in combat. Perhaps long ago, we could send our bravest into battle, but we are a small people now. We cannot waste the little resources we have. The times of defeating sea serpents, fighting wars, and overcoming odds is over. Those are the ways of the past. We must make decisions of certainty."

"I told those Mastadan men we would support their efforts," said Isilmoire.

"You told them you would. All I can offer is a few soldiers, specifically, you and your choice of a few warriors, no more. You promised too much, Isilmoire. I am not to blame for that. I cannot think of merely the opinions of a few, when my responsibility lies with the entire Nymph people."

"Lord Gillium…"

"Look around you. The greatness of our people is gone, Isilmoire. The actions you propose are delusions of fantasy, and it simply is not possible. You mistake yourself to believe otherwise. You are foolish to believe taking our army would make any difference. You said Mastadans go to battle the witch, yet we know nothing of the size of her force at this moment, what if her forces have grown? What if her powers have grown? If indeed your scouts have found nothing, then perhaps she's left the forest and the Mastadan warriors are merely on a fool's errand. If they do find her, perhaps they'll be dead soon enough. When King Ralphus discovers his warriors have failed, he will rally his army and seek out the source of their demise himself. It is not our place to do more than provide what little support I grant you now."

"How could we so easily send those men to do what you now fail to do yourself?" asked Isilmoire.

"Simple," said Lord Gillium "they have the resources to do it. We do not."

"We must act, Lord Gillium," said Isilmoire.

"This is not a discussion. If you came to ask me for the Nymph army, you cannot have it."

"Then I will fight for the cause of our friends without it," replied Isilmoire.

She turned disappointed. Before she exited, she said, "Lord Gillium."

The Nymph steward raised his head as it was buried in his hands. He replied, "Yes, Isilmoire. What is it?"

"Greatness isn't defined in the results of the action, but rather in the decision to act itself. I think our people still have much greatness in us. If only they are lead."

Lord Gillium looked on as Isilmoire swam out of the royal throne room. She dove deeper into the clear sea, which darkened as the depth increased. Isilmoire approached a small light near a cave opening. Several Nymph warriors swam ahead of her toward the same light. A school of large fish gathered above their location. Inside the cave were dozens of Nymph warriors organizing themselves into small fighting squads. Teinmar and Lautner met their leader at the cave's entrance as the continued chaos ensued. Isilmoire looked on as her Nymph companions readied themselves for a battle that would not take place. The dozens of warriors grabbed spears, tridents, and swords alongside the cave's walls.

"I have spoken to Lord Gillium," said Isilmoire, "it has been decided that only a few soldiers will accompany me to try and find our Mastadan friends."

The Nymph warriors all discontinued their preparations and gathered around their commander. The long faces revealed their disappointment.

Isilmoire spoke again, "Nevertheless, we will press on and find the Black Witch. Considering the circumstances that we face, I understand if you hold apprehension in wanting to go. That is why I only take Teinmar and Lautner with me, leaving everyone else here to help defend our kingdom. Many of you have families. It's best to enjoy your time with them now. If we should fail, my hope is that this brooding evil never reaches our kingdom. In the event it does, you will give thanks for these last enjoyed moments."

"We want to fight alongside you, Isilmoire," said one Nymph.

"We go with you, Isilmoire," said a younger Nymph warrior.

"Our place is with you for the honor of the Nymph people," shouted another from deep inside the cave. All the others joined in speaking Nymph, praising Isilmoire's courage.

"I am grateful for your enthusiasm," she said. "It does not surprise me, but ultimately, Lord Gillium has decided. It is best only a couple of warriors make the journey with me. I am pleased in your exuberance, remember it, should you need it later. We leave for the northern shores, where I hope to reconvene with the Mastadans. Maintain high alert and communicate to all warriors throughout the Nymph Sea. Should you need everyone back in defense, you know what to do. There are not many of us left, but what forces we do have should prove difficult for anything that dares attack us."

The Nymphs shouted once more and embraced Isilmoire one last time. Then she swam away accompanied by Lautner and Teinmar. Nymphs were swimming in and out of caves at the ocean's floor, carrying tools and food. The entire kingdom was in action over the recent news from the forest. Isilmoire noticed the anxiousness in the frantic behavior of her people. They neared the main entrance of the shining clear crystal kingdom they called home.

They swam in the direction of the northwestern coast of the Petruchani Forest. Having left the entrance of their domain, they began swimming at full speed, passing up dolphins, sharks, and whales along the way. They emitted Nymph sound waves, coaxing the sea creatures to stay out from their path, giving them freedom to go full speed with ease. Isilmoire, Lautner, and Teinmar swam over the great underwater canyons of the Nymph Sea. They didn't speak and instead enjoyed the contrasting black and phosphorescent colors from the undulations of the canyon. Now in open waters, the Nymphs traveled for a few hours before surfacing near the beach of the northwestern edge of the Petruchani Forest.

The waves of the Nymph Sea rolled onto the rocky beach of the coast. The white wash of the salty waters sprayed the shore as the rumbling of the waters continued. The Nymphs arrived at the beach and searched for their friends who were supposed to wait for them there. A few hours had passed and still no sign of the Mastadans.

"Keep looking," said Isilmoire.

Lautner and Teinmar scoured the rocky shore, hoping to find clues of their missing friends. They examined any discernible oddity and obsessed over every detail. As they spread out, it became apparent that it would be difficult to locate them. The area of their last known whereabouts stretched beyond what the eye could see.

"There's nothing here, Isilmoire," said Lautner, "any clue has been washed away by the sea."

Teinmar looked up and down the beach. He glanced left, then right. He looked south then north and there it was again. He stopped, and then all of a sudden, it appeared once more. Without notice, Teinmar ran toward the water, leaving a trail of footsteps behind.

"Are you okay, Teinmar?" yelled Lautner in Nymph as Teinmar ran away.

Now knee deep in water, Teinmar paused, looked down toward the water, and then vanished below as he dove in. Lautner and Isilmoire abandoned their own searches and ran to the spot Teinmar was just at. They stood and waited for their friend to return, looking in all directions, hoping to spot him. They looked at each other perplexed, and then suddenly, Teinmar emerged from the water, fifty yards farther down from them. He swam toward the beach, the Nymph Sea still covering his scaly skin as the reflection of the sun shone over it. Something was different.

"He has something," said Lautner.

"Indeed, but I can't see what it is, the sun is too bright," replied Isilmoire.

Teinmar was out of the water and walked toward them. Isilmoire and Lautner met him on the beach.

"What did you find?" asked Lautner in Nymph.

Teinmar extended his hand, and in it was the newly discovered item. Isilmoire reached both hand out as he grabbed an elegant sword. It was large and sharp. It was adorned with four large rubies and its handle was wrapped with a bright red boar skin, tight and easy to grasp.

"A fine instrument," said Isilmoire, "truly light…an excellent weapon indeed."

"It was the boy's," replied Lautner.

It was the Falanx.

"The sea has washed away their steps," said Lautner, "surely, they have survived Isilmoire."

Isilmoire gripped the sword as she stared out into the sea and then back toward the forest. Their travels from the Nymph Sea and their search on the beach had exhausted the better part of the day. The sun began to set. Teinmar darted into the forest. Lautner and Isilmoire looked at each other, smiled, and ran after him.

They now walked through the northern end of the Petruchani Forest. Short steps took minutes as they moved forward with caution.

"It's never a welcomed experience to be in this dreadful place, despite the numerous times we visit it," said Lautner.

Small animals off in the distance bellowed as shouts of horror echoed through the night.

"The trees seem distraught with sadness and all things alive within the forest give the air of mourning," said Lautner.

"Indeed," replied Isilmoire, "darkness shrouds everything here. I fear the Black Witch's work is spreading."

The Nymphs continued walking through the diseased forest. Signs of the poison were everywhere. Giant spiders crawled along their long and thick webs high above in the trees and also in the bushes and grass below. Small yellow sets of eyes stared back at them as they walked through the forest as bats, rats, snakes, and other creatures studied their movements.

"Is this wise, Isilmoire?" asked Lautner. "Should we not travel by day instead for we have no idea of where the Mastadans are? The Witch and her forces could be near?"

"No, we've lost much time," replied Isilmoire, "we go on."

Teinmar made a motion with his hand, indicating silence.

"Look there," said Lautner.

Isilmoire and Teinmar noticed harvingers sitting atop the tree branches high above them. A flesh-eating creature, the size of most Nymphs, these detestable nuisances were often the cause of disappearances of Nymph and human children alike. They had large powerful wings allowing them to fly for long distances at high speeds and altitudes. Their bodies were covered with slimy fur, often a sign of its most recent meal. Its sharp claws dangling below its bodies helped provide an excellent weapon for damaging its prey or holding heavy objects. They were detestable.

"We must proceed carefully," said Isilmoire, "we are without a bowman."

"Yes, it would be difficult to take them without one," said Lautner

They stepped forward desperate to avoid detection as the path narrowed ahead. They were now below the harvingers. The sound of their sharp beaks tearing the flesh of its prey could be heard. They ravished the corpse. The large trees created some distance between the Nymphs and the harvingers, but they still remained in a precarious situation.

"Careful here, there are large tree roots ahead," said Isilmoire in Nymph.

The two trailing Nymphs looked down at the ground, trying to distinguish between tree, dirt, and foliage; it was impossible in the darkness.

"Isilmoire, because of the thick brush and large roots around us, it's as though we've been traveling for days," said Lautner in Nymph, "we won't last long at this pace."

"It is not the first time you have gone without rest or food, Lautner," replied Isilmoire.

"Yes, but something is different, he said, "it's as though this forest adds to our ailments, as if it worsens our injuries."

"Is it possible?" asked Isilmoire.

A crunching sound on the ground, not far from their location, startled them. The three Nymphs drew their weapons. They then heard a crack of dried branches being stepped on. Teinmar pointed in a westward direction. He narrowed the source of the noise.

"I agree," said Lautner.

Another crack.

"They'll alert the harvingers," said Lautner.

Teinmar nodded in agreement.

"What should we do, Isilmoire?" asked Lautner.

Isilmoire looked over her shoulder toward the harvingers who were still feasting on their prey. She turned forward towards the source of the noise. The Nymphs were between two threats. The noise continued as the branches and bushes ahead moved.

"Hold your position," said Isilmoire, "it moves toward us."

The heavy steps approached, but the source remained impossible to see in the darkness.

"Teinmar to my left," said Isilmoire, "Lautner the right."

The Nymphs found their positions and prepared for a fight. Isilmoire looked back in the direction of the harvingers high atop the trees overhead, but something was different. She saw nothing.

"They're not there," said Isilmoire.

"What?" said Lautner.

"The harvingers," said Isilmoire, "they're not there anymore." She readied her shield and sword. "They're going to attack."

They looked up toward the sky, hoping to see any sign of the flying filth above. At the same time, they heard another crunch from behind. They turned toward it, still poised for battle.

"We cannot fight the Witch's forces and the harvingers," said Lautner.

Isilmoire concentrated toward the harvingers behind them.

"Lautner and Teinmar focus on whatever comes on the ground," she said, "leave the harvingers to me."

"There are too many of them," responded Lautner.

Another crunch on the ground, and this time it sounded familiar.

"That's the boot of a man," said Lautner.

A large deafening shriek specific to only one creature thundered throughout the forest as the unmistakable sound of the harvingers descended upon them. The trio came closer together, as the vile black creatures began multiplying overhead, waiting for an opportunity to strike.

"Stay low," said Isilmoire.

"Right," replied Lautner.

The harvingers began to fly lower as their speed increased and the shrieks and noises continued.

"Their fur is least prominent at the neck, just below their beak," said Isilmoire, "strike there if possible."

"I can't see," replied Lautner, "there's only darkness."

"Listen for the sound their wings make as they approach," replied Isilmoire.

Then suddenly, two harvingers dove straight down for them with speed and power. Their massive claws opened as they now hunted the Nymphs.

"Move!" said Isilmoire.

The three dove out of the way, rolling from the attack. The harvingers grabbed only dirt. They unleashed deep loud shrieks, announcing their displeasure to the others overhead.

"Is everyone all right?" asked Isilmoire.

"Yes," replied Lautner.

Too many harvingers to count flew overhead. Then they heard flapping coming from behind.

"Ruuuuun!"

The Nymphs sprang forward as fast as possible just ahead of the harvinger behind them. It shrieked and chomped with its beak, trying to bite them. Diving behind a couple of trees, the Nymphs once again evaded capture.

The harvinger flew up and gathered together with the rest of the flock. The shrieks and chomping became more prominent as the excitement of another meal gathered more to the hunt. Then, just as the Nymphs rose to their feet, another attack from the harvingers.

"Get down," said Isilmoire.

The three Nymphs dove to the ground, trying to evade another attack from the wretched creatures, but only two were successful. Isilmoire heard one of her men scream for help, calling on her.

"Isilmoire, help me!" said Lautner, but there was nothing that she or Teinmar could do.

"No!" yelled Isilmoire, "Lautner, hold on!"

Teinmar and Isilmoire got up from the ground and ran as fast as they could behind the harvinger, trying to keep pace, as the beast clutched Lautner in its massive talons high above them. Despite their efforts, the distance between they and the harvinger increased. The creature was almost out of sight. But to their surprise, the harvinger changed direction and turned back toward them as it still held Lautner. Isilmoire and Teinmar continued running, closing the distance between they and the creature. The harvinger neared, but their attentions shifted toward a noise in the distance.

"Did you hear that?" asked Isilmoire.

Isilmoire stopped and listened again.

"Light them," a voice yelled from afar.

Several distinct flames sprang from numerous positions on Teinmar and Isilmoire's right and left.

"Attack!"

Fire arrows flew from the scattered positions near them, unleashing a barrage upon the harvinger carrying Lautner overhead. A few struck the beast, lighting it on fire, forcing it to drop the Nymph down onto the thick dense brush below.

"Come on," said Isilmoire.

The Nymph captain and Teinmar ran toward Lautner's position, hoping to find him alive. Other harvingers now swooped down toward the flames, trying to attack those responsible for the death of one of their kind. Shrieks and chomping beaks echoed throughout the forest as the burning arrows flew through the air finding their intended targets.

"Again," said the voice off in the distance.

Flaming arrows continued to fly through the air as Teinmar and Isilmoire arrived at Lautner.

"I'm fine," said Lautner.

"Good to have you back," said Isilmoire.

The three Nymphs observed the harvingers' attempts to evade the attacks, some were successful and others not.

"They're being hunted," said Isilmoire.

"Whoever is hunting them is doing well," said Lautner. "I'm alive thanks to them."

The bushes moved as something approached fast.

"Arm yourselves," commanded Isilmoire.

Teinmar and Lautner steadied their weapons. The footsteps were upon them, and then suddenly a person jumped out of the bush, directly in front of them.

"Isilmoire, it's good to see you," said Prince Adinor.

CHAPTER 16

"Prince Adinor," replied Isilmoire.

Teinmar embraced the Prince.

"It is good to see you too," said Isilmoire.

"I think everyone will share the same sentiment upon seeing all of you as well," replied Prince Adinor.

"Everyone?" asked Lautner, "we thought…"

"We didn't know what happened," said Isilmoire.

"It is understandable," replied Prince Adinor, "let's join the others. Come. This way."

The Nymphs followed the Prince through the dense thicket. They walked toward several torches ahead where the battle raged. The harvingers continued attacking the Mastadans, hidden beneath palm trees close to the torches. The shrieks and yells of the harvingers continued as commands from Bolios and Elmahigh matched their every move.

The Nymph trio and Prince Adinor neared the first torch. Prince Adinor stopped, knelt down, and pulled out a small dagger. The Nymphs crowded behind the Prince, when Adinor began to pound the blade against the small rock he carried.

"Come on then," replied a voice.

"Okay, let's go," said Prince Adinor.

And so the three Nymphs and Prince Adinor again rose and proceeded toward the first camouflaged outpost. The identity of the voice was revealed as Ecclesias once again spoke, saying, "So it was them."

"Yes," replied the Prince.

"Elmahigh was right," replied Ecclesias, "I'm doing okay here, but if you could spare someone, send him my way."

"We're indebted to you all," said Isilmoire, "If you can use Teinmar or Lautner, they're yours."

"It may not be a bad idea," replied Prince Adinor. "We've got something planned for the rest of the harvingers sticking around.

"Lautner will stay with Ecclesias then," said Isilmoire.

"Wouldn't you know, I've got a spare bow to boot," said Ecclesias as he handed Lautner a bow and a quiver of arrows.

"I'm looking forward to getting some retribution," replied Lautner.

"Let's go," said Prince Adinor. Teinmar and Isilmoire again rose and tiptoed behind the Prince to another torch position just ahead, where Theodonus and Malchomite were taking turns lighting arrows as they fired high toward the harvinger nest overhead. They struck it repeatedly and set it ablaze. The remaining harvingers flew in unison and attacked one of the outlying torches, destroying it and everything near. They dug their claws deep into the torch, throwing it and breaking it into pieces. They flapped their giant wings, sending dust and dirt everywhere. Prince Adinor, Isilmoire, and Teinmar arrived at Theodonus and Malchomite's position.

"Good to have you back, young Prince," said Theodonus. "You've brought company."

"Did Marcus and Dolamite make it out of their post before the harvinger attacked?" asked Prince Adinor.

"Yes, they rotated to the other position as planned," replied Theodonus. "There are only a few left."

"All right," said Prince Adinor, "I will take Isilmoire and Teinmar to Bolios."

"No Prince," replied Theodonus, "perhaps its best you remain here. The smoke rises from Bolios' position. It's time."

"Well spotted, Theodonus," replied Prince Adinor, "my bow."

"Here, sire," replied Malchomite.

The three men lit their arrows and pulled back on their bows, aiming up toward the remaining harvingers. The smoke from Bolios' position stopped. Then they heard a loud yell from the voice familiar to them all; it was Elmahigh standing high above, atop a giant tree branch. He wielded his sword and staff as he conjured an ancient prayer in a loud voice. Suddenly, there was a bright light streaming from his staff and sword, stunning the harvingers. Dazed, they remained hovering in the same position, central to all the torches below.

"Now!" yelled Bolios.

Every soldier sent wave upon wave of arrows, hitting most of the giant harvingers overhead. The demon creatures shrieked and fell from the sky, plummeting to their death. The others, lucky enough to survive, flew away, quelling their charred hair with the repeated flap of their wings. Yells of victory broke out from all of the Mastadans as their plan worked. Bolios gathered them all together as Elmahigh made his way down from the tree. The soldiers embraced and smiled.

"Well done, Prince Adinor," said Bolios. "I see you've found our long lost Nymphs."

"You've fared well, I see," replied Isilmoire.

"It seems to be getting easier as we go," replied Bolios.

Isilmoire nodded.

"Don't let him fool you," said Elmahigh, "this forest and the darkness within it is evil. None of us should feel comforted by—"

"Well, we were doing fine on our own is simply what I am saying," said Bolios.

Elmahigh walked toward the three Nymph soldiers and shook his head at Bolios.

"Our friends have come looking for us, and it is welcomed," said Elmahigh. "Tonight was a terrific victory, but lest we forget what we are meant to do. We're getting closer, and the Black Witch knows it. With every step taken toward her, the tests will be harder. You've come at a most important time, Isilmoire. You will be needed."

"How did you come to this place?" asked Isilmoire. "How did you survive the storm?"

Elmahigh, Bolios, Prince Adinor, and the rest of them looked at one another and smiled.

"It's a tale worth sharing," replied Elmahigh.

"But not before we get some food," said Dolamite.

"Agreed," responded Lautner.

The Mastadans led the Nymphs on a half-hour long walk toward a small camp, set up by Prince Adinor and Marcus, just a night prior. They all sat around a large fire. Prince Adinor continued feeding it with large tree branches and tinder from the stockpile they collected earlier. Traps set during the day produced a small catch, a rabbit and one fat boar. They gathered some herbs, the little carrot and potato they still had, and made a stew worthy of the finest king's palate. Even Bolios made certain to encourage his men to enjoy, for now.

"Any day culminated in victory is a good day," he said.

There were shouts of agreement and yells of encouragement.

"We are still here," continued Bolios, "each moment we breathe, the Black Witch draws closer to enjoying her last."

"Right you are," said Malcomite.

"Yes," said Ecclesias.

Isilmoire walked around the fire and made her way toward Elmahigh.

"You're still surprised we've come this far, are you not?" asked Elmahigh.

"In large part yes," replied Isilmoire, "dreadful stories of the Witch's killings spread to my people."

"I can imagine you're surprised to see us then," replied Elmahigh.

The Mastadans danced around the large fire. Dolamite swung Prince Adinor around, grabbing him by the arms and lifting him repeatedly.

"I didn't want to believe it," replied Isilmoire, "but some made you out to be dead. How?"

"How what, my friend?" replied Elmahigh.

"How did you…every one of you, survive?" asked Isilmoire.

Elmahigh rose and began to walk away from the fire. Isilmoire followed. Dolamite and Theodonus began lifting Prince Adinor up high in the air and throwing him into the sky. The other soldiers continued encouraging it, prompting them to continue. Even the two Nymph warriors laughed and partook in the zeal of the evening as well. Then, they suddenly looked at each other. Teinmar pulled out the Falanx. The two walked over to Dolamite and Theodonus.

"Do you want a chance to throw him?" asked Dolamite.

The Nymphs gestured toward the Prince's sword. All smiles faded and the Prince was lowered to the ground. Adinor looked up at the Nymphs as a massive smile came across his face.

"Thank you," said the Prince.

The Nymphs knelt.

He touched them on the shoulder.

Dolamite stopped and said, "Where is the maltsenhop?"

All of them broke into a boisterous laugh. The group continued on entertaining one another while Isilmoire and Elmahigh increased the distance between themselves and the group.

"If you must know, Isilmoire," said Elmahigh, "it was not by our doing at all."

"What do you mean?" replied Isilmoire.

"Some things are not to be explained for their complexities are too much of a responsibility for any one man or Nymph to understand," replied Elmahigh.

Isilmoire stood next to a dry rotted tree trunk as Elmahigh sat on a stump. They were far enough away from the group to prevent being heard.

"You see high in the sky above us," said Elmahigh.

"To what do you refer, the blackness of night?" replied Isilmoire.

"No," said Elmahigh, "do you see the bright lights the flashing bits of light high above us both?"

"Yes I do," said Isilmoire, "but what importance is it to how all of you managed to survive?"

At that moment, Bolios arrived and stood alongside Isilmoire.

"Are you hoping to count them all tonight, Elmahigh?" asked Bolios.

Elmahigh ignored Bolios' question and remained fixated on the sky above.

"I was just explaining to our friend how it was that we survived," replied Elmahigh.

"Allow me to give you the short version," replied Bolios, "we swam."

Isilmoire smiled and shook her head.

"As you recall, we were aboard the *Mercurial*, good friend," said Elmahigh.

"Just before you decided to abandon us to our death, Isilmoire," said Bolios.

Elmahigh stood up and walked toward Bolios. Sensing Elmahigh's anger, he avoided eye contact all together.

"Go on, I won't interrupt again," said Bolios.

"Yes," replied Isilmoire, "we left you as you continued north into open water. We proceeded to our kingdom to speak to Lord Gillium."

"That's right," said Elmahigh, "not long after, the storm became overwhelming. The high seas poured onto the ship, nearly drowning us. The strong winds twisted our sails, tearing some of the smaller ones and wrecking our chances to make the destination. We spun around."

"So the ship crashed?" asked Isilmoire.

"It may have been more beneficial had it, but our fate was a different one," replied Elmahigh, "just as we thought the conditions couldn't worsen, we heard what seemed to be birds of some sort."

"Farrowers?" asked Isilmoire.

"No, no, it wasn't anything pleasant like that," replied Elmahigh, "seeing those beautiful creatures would have been a welcomed sight."

"Then what?" asked Isilmoire.

"It was her, the Black Witch," said Elmahigh.

"If it even is a her," said Bolios, "didn't your song and dance with the Nymphs reveal the incarnation could take almost any form?"

"The spirit fire did reveal that much," said Isilmoire, "but too clouded to know for sure how it will manifest itself."

"I'm certain it has already manifested itself and I'm certain the evil is the Witch," said Elmahigh.

"There's no way to be certain," replied Isilmoire.

"For once, I agree with you, she-Nymph," said Bolios.

"I didn't finish the rest of the story," said Elmahigh.

The two warriors were silent. Bolios returned to stargazing and simply shook his head in disagreement.

"Very well" he said.

"There was anger buried within the screams of the wind," said Elmahigh, "It was subtle, but I felt her presence. It was persistent that night. The sounds of birds were actually her sorcery. The storm itself was her conjuring. Her powers have grown. She had dominion over elements for the Witch's conjuring that night revealed itself in the faint hint of her own voice in the wind."

"I don't understand how you *feeling* her presence lends any proof to your theory," said Bolios. "It was a storm. No person can control natural forces, despite all the stories told. It's impossible."

"It is for that reason why I believe it to be true," said Elmahigh.

"My people pass along stories dating back years that support Elmahigh's position," said Isilmoire.

"Evil that powerful would be unstoppable," replied Bolios.

"Which is why I believe we were spared," said Elmahigh.

"What?" asked Bolios. "We were thrown into the water, nearly drowned, climbed onto floating wood, and made our way to shore.

Elmahigh and Isilmoire were silent.

Bolios continued, "We survived because we swam."

"We survived because powers greater than any one man made it so," said Elmahigh.

"Absurd," said Bolios, "we are alone. It is by the hands of one another we have come this far and it is by those same hands we will destroy this evil."

Elmahigh looked back up toward the stars above. He then noticed a blinking star.

"Why do you find it so hard to believe?" asked Elmahigh.

"How can you find it so easy?" asked Bolios.

"Goodness and unselfishness are my allies," said Elmahigh, "and although courage and strength are mighty, nothing compares to the capacity of the root of all these qualities."

"Is that right," said Bolios, "well, what might you say then, oh grand and wise sage, would the root of those qualities be then?"

"Love," said Elmahigh.

"Well, you be sure to remember to use love against the evil that seeks to destroy us all," said Bolios, "which has already begun to kill our men, take our women and children, harm the innocent, and heaven only knows what else."

Bolios wildly slashed the dead dry bush with his sword and kicked over several rocks nearby. He walked away from both Isilmoire and Elmahigh, opting to join the others at the fire.

"I intend to," answered Elmahigh.

Isilmoire reflected as she and Elmahigh stayed away longer. After some exchanges and laughs, they too returned to the group.

"Elmahigh, you missed the fun," said Prince Adinor.

"Is that so?" replied Elmahigh.

"We all wagered on how many times Dolamite could jump over the fire without burning himself," said Prince Adinor.

Elmahigh laughed as Prince Adinor explained the specific rules and retold the story.

"So the bet was honored," said Elmahigh.

"It was," said Prince Adinor, "best of all we have a reminder of it for good."

Prince Adinor pointed to Dolamite who was sleeping. Upon careful examination, Elmahigh noticed a discernible large black char on

Dolamite's bottom. Both the Prince and Elmahigh laughed and joined the others in an attempt to rest.

"Elmahigh," said Prince Adinor

"Yes, Prince Adinor," he replied.

"Bolios arrived just ahead of you and Isilmoire's return. He was angry. Is everything all right?" asked the Prince.

"Yes," he replied, "he was just trying to arrive at an answer."

"Will he find it?" asked the Prince.

"Time will tell for us all," replied Elmahigh.

CHAPTER 17

Bolios strode back into the encampment as a couple of the soldiers were still sleeping. The light emerged through the dense trees overhead.

"Wake the Prince and Ecclesias, it's time to go," said Bolios. "We make our way east now through the rest of this forest until we find the Witch."

"Bolios, and what of the harvingers?" asked Malchomite.

"We deal with that as it comes Malchomite," replied Theodonus.

"Well, it's just not that easy," said Ecclesias. "We did well last night, but we planned...we were ready."

"Well, we'll just have to make do, won't we," said Bolios, "we have no choice but to move. We've been here too long already, and if we did well last night, we'll do even better today if necessary."

"If we can avoid another encounter with the harvingers, it would be recommended," said Elmahigh.

"Let's be on our way," said Bolios.

The soldiers finished packing and moved through the dense forest as silent as possible. The thick bushes numbered thousands and the tall trees overhead covered much of the light from above. They seemed to be in constant nightfall, leaving them struggling to find good footing. Bolios led, cutting through the bush with his sword, slashing it from side to side. The others followed just behind. The Nymphs brought up the rear, whispering in their language.

"Where are we going?" asked Prince Adinor.

"Continuing east, my Prince," replied Bolios.

"Do we know the Witch is there?" asked Prince Adinor.

"There's no way to know fully, sire," replied Bolios, "but it seems to be the only place left we haven't looked."

The bush seemed endless, a tangled mess of interwoven trees, moss, and vines. The green and brown thorns made for impassable walls in certain areas, forcing the heroes to seek alternate routes. The continued trek forward taking twice as long.

"Are we sure we have not been here already?" asked Ecclesias.

Elmahigh looked up toward the canopy of trees above.

"Yes, I'm sure," said Bolios, "take rest for a moment."

"Bolios, with the dense cover overhead it seems impossible to discern what direction we're going," said Elmahigh.

"It's true, Bolios," replied Theodonus.

Isilmoire looked at the three, waiting to hear of their decision.

"Have you something to say as well?" asked Bolios.

"Although I agree it is difficult, we must continue on," said Isilmoire.

"I'm beginning to like you, Nymph," said Bolios, "let's move."

The giant tree trunks throughout their path seemed beyond measure. The roots of the trees sprawled all over the ground. Giant immovable logs often decreased the speed of their travels as they needed to assist one another in going over them. The fallen branches made loud crunching noises as they took steps forward.

"Quiet," commanded Bolios.

They carefully moved forward, but the dim light made it hard to see whether or not harvingers were nesting above. They walked for what seemed like days.

"Keep going, men," said Bolios, "be careful here. There's a big drop-off ahead. Mind your footing."

A steep descent forced them to change their approach. They arrived at a massive cliff covered in wild plants, vines, and short shrubs. The drop was too high to jump down. Falling from this height would kill any of them. They would have to climb down carefully. Bolios walked toward the edge and lowered his feet over the fall. He gripped the ledge in his hands and lowered his body over the side as his feet dug into the side of the cliff below. He continued to lower himself slowly and moved down. He used all his strength to move carefully as the sweat poured from his hairline. Elmahigh and Prince Adinor spoke for a moment before beginning their climb.

"This reminds me of a particular challenge during my triped trials, Elmahigh," said Prince Adinor.

"Does it now?" replied Elmahigh.

"Yes," said Prince Adinor, "did my father share with you my successes?"

"He mentioned your exploits, young Prince," replied Elmahigh, "he was noticeably proud of you."

The others began the descent.

Elmahigh and Prince Adinor were just ahead of them.

"I set records throughout my triped trials," said Prince Adinor, "many of which I hope stand for a long time."

"Your time with us has not been triped trials though, your majesty," said Elmahigh.

"No, far from it."

"And do you prefer the triped trials to this?" asked Elmahigh.

Prince Adinor stopped his climb down as he held a large vine while he hung in the middle of the cliff.

"The triped trials were much easier," said the Prince.

"Careful on this next part, young sire," said Elmahigh, "there are some loose weeds."

"Thank you," replied the Prince, "as for your question, although my strengths and skills helped me surpass all those I competed against, the challenges we've had and successes we've achieved outweigh any record I set."

"Ah, so you are no longer a child?" asked Elmahigh.

They were more than halfway down. They continued climbing down.

"Well, don't the triped trials make it official?" asked Prince Adinor.

"What do you think?"

"Well, they are the last proving ground for education for young Mastadans. One is exposed to the most important aspects of understanding.

"That's true," replied Elmahigh, "is that all?"

"And although Bolios would never admit it, I didn't completely embarrass myself against him."

With a puzzled look, Elmahigh asked. "You fought Bolios?"

"Well, it wasn't a true fight. In earnest, he was probably taking it easy on me."

They jumped the last remaining few feet. They were finished the climb. Elmahigh smiled and rubbed the Prince's long hair.

"I didn't enjoy learning about our kingdoms laws or history, but I did complete it," continued Prince Adinor.

"I see."

"With all the aspects of the triped trials complete, yes," said Prince Adinor, "I'd say I am no longer a child."

Elmahigh looked at him and waited to hear more.

"That's it then?" asked Elmahigh, "nothing more to add?"

"Although this experience has been difficult in ways I never imagined," said Prince Adinor, "it's far different than the trials."

"Go on," replied Elmahigh.

"Well, the triped trials were tough and I found some challenging, but in the end, they are only exercises. Out here, it's different."

Elmahigh observed the others descending overhead. "I'm listening, Prince Adinor."

"Well, out here if something bad happens, it costs a lot more than punishment by a teacher. For instance, we still haven't found Litovic. What happened to him?"

"I'm unsure, but I believe we'll have our answers soon," said Elmahigh. "Finding the Black Witch will clear up all of our questions."

"I hope so. I've taken so many things for granted before making this journey. There are so many things that teachers and especially my parents tried so often to teach me," said Prince Adinor.

"Curious," said Elmahigh, "what do you mean?"

"When I was younger, I ran around playing all day, something I still miss," said Prince Adinor, "I wandered the castle halls without fear. Whenever I left my parents' vigilance, the royal guard always accompanied me. I recall so often my trips to the market centers. I enjoyed running and weaving in and out of the rows of merchants selling and buying goods from one another. I often challenged my friends to see which of us could steal a fruit without getting caught. It was fun. I recall my long rides with Mother and Father. We ventured out to the Mastadan farmlands to speak with members of the agriculture guild. The waves of fresh air smelled of corn and maltsen berries as well as vegetables. I still taste them whenever I close my eyes. The bright sun beamed down upon us, baking us, encouraging Father to stop often for rest in consideration for Mother and I. At no time was I without drink. I never went without wanting. I never felt unsupported, unprotected, fearful, or hungry. I can't recall a moment when I didn't have someone giving me everything I needed. I miss my friends from the triped trails. I miss the warm food."

Elmahigh looked at the Prince and smiled.

"Most of all, I miss my parents, Elmahigh," continued the Prince. "I've not gone this long without seeing them. It's new to me. It's difficult to be away from them."

"Careful, men," said Bolios.

The two remaining men, Friedrich and Ecclesias, continued descending from above. The Prince walked closer to Elmahigh and continued wondering about his parents.

"I miss conversations with my father or my mother's caress," said Prince Adinor, "mostly I miss their company."

"You will see them again," replied Elmahigh, "in due time, sire."

Prince Adinor nodded and walked toward Dolamite, Theodonus, and the others. Bolios and Elmahigh were fixated on Friedrich and Ecclesias.

"Bolios, we've used far too much time," said Isilmoire.

"I fear she's correct," replied Elmahigh, "the harvingers may return."

Bolios looked east toward the path ahead and back up toward his two remaining soldiers, hoping for their immediate descent.

"Theodonus," he called.

He neared and said, "Yes, my lord."

"Take the men ahead," said Bolios. "I will remain behind with Elmahigh and wait for the last two."

"My lord…" said Theodonus.

"Friedrich and Ecclesias will be down soon enough," replied Bolios. "We will be just behind you. Go on ahead. You, Isilmoire, and the others can find food. We will be just behind you."

"Very well," said Theodonus.

Isilmoire, Theodonus, Prince Adinor, and the rest of the soldiers continued on as Bolios and Elmahigh waited for the remaining two. They were halfway down when suddenly they stopped. Friedrich was having a difficult time with the climb.

"I'm not sure I can continue, Ecclesias," said Friedrich.

"Don't start," said Ecclesias.

"I'm serious," said Friedrich.

"And why is that?" asked Ecclesias.

"My body is weary," replied Friedrich. "I need rest."

"Well, you picked a hell of a place to try and rest," replied Ecclesias, "in case you didn't notice, we're on the side of a mountain."

Friedrich remained paralyzed. His arms continued to shake. His legs began to bend as his weight seemed too much to hold.

"Something is wrong," said Bolios, "they've been up there far too long."

Elmahigh looked up toward the men, trying to hear the conversation between them, but they were too high up.

"That's it," replied Bolios, "I'm going up."

In an instant, Bolios climbed up toward the men. His strength and speed were on display as he reached his large hands up toward the shrubs above him, lifting his body up as he dug his boots into the side of the mountain, climbing up to his other soldiers. Ecclesias looked down as Bolios was ascending.

"Friedrich, it's Bolios," said Ecclesias.

"Where?"

"He's coming up to us," answered Ecclesias.

Friedrich only continued clinging to the mountain with the little strength he had left. His eyes clenched shut. He began to slip from his position. Bolios was within reach below them.

"I'm so very happy to see you," said Ecclesias.

"What is the problem?" asked Bolios.

"Friedrich hasn't moved," replied Ecclesias, "he's too weary and can't continue. I didn't want to leave him up here alone."

"Hello, sire," said Friedrich.

"Ecclesias, get down to Elmahigh," said Bolios, "I'll make sure to help Friedrich down."

"Yes, sire, right away," replied Ecclesias.

Ecclesias continued on, leaving Bolios to deal with Friedrich. Down below, Elmahigh looked on happy to see one of the two coming down.

"What's wrong, Friedrich?" asked Bolios.

"Sire, I would be quite content to stay right here if it's all the same to you," replied Friedrich.

"I can't let you do that," replied Bolios, "you know, I won't let you stay up here. We need to get moving now."

"I can't seem to get going again," responded Friedrich.

"The distance gets smaller as you keep moving," replied Bolios.

"I just can't do it anymore," replied Friedrich.

"If you stay up here, two things are bound to happen," said Bolios, "either you will certainly fall, most likely to your death. The other option is you will be taken by the harvingers, likely to find you soon and kill you."

Friedrich opened his eyes and looked over to his leader. He then glanced down at the ground below. Ecclesias moved toward Elmahigh. The distance seemed so large.

"Friedrich, you can do it," said Bolios, "only focus on the next step down."

Friedrich didn't respond, choosing only to grip the rock and secure himself even more to the position he held. His grip began to loosen.

"Do you hear me, Friedrich?" asked Bolios.

"Yes, sire," replied Friedrich, "I can hear you. It's just that…"

"It's okay to be afraid," said Bolios, "but the most difficult step you already took. You took the first one,"

Friedrich looked down again, seeing Ecclesias nearly at the bottom.

"Just take one more step, Friedrich," said Bolios.

Friedrich paused and closed his eyes. Upon opening them, he looked down and saw a small rock below his foot.

"That's right, Friedrich, just below your right foot is a good spot," said Bolios, "now step down with me."

Bolios lowered himself to another position and waited for Friedrich's next move.

"See," said Bolios, "you are that much closer to the bottom."

Friedrich looked down and continued to sweat. His entire shirt was drenched and his legs were shaking more than ever.

"Take one more step with me, my friend," said Bolios.

Friedrich looked down for another secure spot for his feet. He found one and again shifted his weight, carefully placed his right foot down, then the left. He gripped another tree root in his hand and a vine with the other.

"You are doing it, Friedrich," said Bolios. "Let's try to go a bit further."

The pair continued down. Ecclesias reached Elmahigh below.

"Glad you could join us," said Elmahigh.

"You're right about that," said Ecclesias, "where are the others?"

"Just ahead," replied Elmahigh, "we'll be with them soon."

"I don't think Friedrich is going to make it," said Ecclesias.

"Of course he will," replied Elmahigh, "they are already farther along."

Up above, Bolios and Friedrich were making progress.

"Excellent, Friedrich, keep going," said Bolios, "follow me and keep up."

"Elmahigh, what is that?" asked Ecclesias.

Elmahigh closed his eyes and listened to hear what Ecclesias was referring to. He opened them and looked in the direction for the departed members of the company and only shook his head.

"Oh no," he said.

He looked up toward Bolios and Friedrich.

"Bolios, you must come down immediately," screamed Elmahigh.

"Why are you yelling?" replied Ecclesias. "The harvingers will hear."

Elmahigh turned and gripped Ecclesias' arm.

"They already have," he said.

Bolios and Friedrich, unaware of the new development, continued climbing at the slow pace. They made progress, but were only halfway down. Friedrich stopped for a short rest.

"Thank you, Bolios," he said.

"It's nothing, my friend," replied Bolios, "you are my brother, there's nothing I wouldn't do to help you all."

Elmahigh yelled again from down below.

"Bolios! Friedrich! You must come down immediately!"

"Elmahigh, they'll surely be killed exposed up there like that," said Ecclesias. "What do we do?"

Elmahigh looked around the grass and bushes nearby, hoping to find something useful to get their attention, but found nothing. He ran toward a tree and again heard the faint sounds of the harvingers. They were coming. He put his hand inside his robe and found some leftover herb. He gathered every morsel of purple grain he could and held it in his hand.

"What is that?" asked Ecclesias.

"Pumpersty," replied Elmahigh, "something that may prove useful. Come quickly, perhaps it's not too late."

They ran over to a nearby group of flowers, and Elmahigh touched and smelled all of them, searching for just the right one.

"What the bloody hell is pumpersty?" asked Ecclesias.

"It's a potent magical powder for conjuring," replied Elmahigh as he continued to smell more plants. "If I find just the right flower, I may come up with something."

"Conjuring?" replied Ecclesias. "Have you lost your mind?"

"Ecclesias, you know nothing about what my order truly does and I have no desire to explain it," said Elmahigh, "however if you want to help me save our friends, I could use your help."

"What can I do?" replied Ecclesias.

"We need a biltley flower," said Elmahigh, "find one and we may be able to help Bolios and Friedrich."

They searched, hoping to find the rare small pink petal flower with the blue center. As they looked, Bolios and Friedrich still remained unaware of the danger that was on its way. They continued descending.

"Keep going, Friedrich," said Bolios, "we'll be back with the others soon."

"It will be nice to be finished with this mountain," said Friedrich.

"You will be a true climber when this is done," said Bolios.

"Bolios," said Friedrich, "I don't see Elmahigh or Ecclesias."

Bolios confirmed the observation. "Let's keep moving, Friedrich," said Bolios. "They're surely waiting for us or perhaps gone ahead to meet the group."

The familiar piercing shrieks of the harvingers announced their proximity.

"Oh no," said Friedrich.

"Go, Friedrich, quickly!" said Bolios. "We have to get down from here right away."

They doubled their speed and raced down as the harvingers closed the distance, apparent by the loud screams.

"We're nearly there, Friedrich, keep going."

"I don't want to die," replied Friedrich.

High above them appeared dozens of harvingers. They walked toward the edge of the cliff and flew out overhead.

"I can't believe it," said Friedrich, "they're here."

"Never mind that, keep moving," said Bolios.

The harvingers circled high. Their piercing shrieks swept through the forest. The loud grinding of their beaks revealed their frenzied state. They were wild over the possibility of fresh food. They circled and looked down toward Bolios and Friedrich, shrieking as they communicated about their position.

"Elmahigh, I've found it," said Ecclesias.

Elmahigh ran over to Ecclesias and grabbed the delicate biltley flower and held it carefully in his hand.

"Isn't that it?" asked Ecclesias.

"Let's hope so," said Elmahigh, "let's go."

The two raced back toward the grassy mountain base staying under the cover of trees as the growing harvinger noise was almost deafening.

"Where are Friedrich and Bolios?" asked Ecclesias.

"There," replied Elmahigh, "look up just below the bare spot on the mountain's face."

"They're almost at the bottom."

"That's not what I'm worried about," said Elmahigh.

Bolios and Friedrich continued dropping further to the ground, making sure to keep an eye on the harvingers above. Then two harvingers dove down toward them at maximum speed, their beaks open and the large sharp talons of their feet wide open.

"Look out," said Bolios.

He drew his sword and swiped at the menacing monsters, discouraging them just enough, affording him and Friedrich a bit more time to descend further.

"I'm sorry I put you in this situation, Bolios," said Friedrich.

"I don't want to hear that from you, Friedrich. This isn't over."

"There's too many of them. The next attack, we will not be so lucky."

"Keep moving," said Bolios.

The harvingers flew about in a circle. The largest of them flew in the middle. It looked down with its menacing yellow and black eyes. It let out a long and wretched high-pitched shriek. Down it dove with the rest of the pack behind it.

Elmahigh ran out from under the cover of the trees, Ecclesias joined alongside him.

"What do we do?" asked Ecclesias.

Elmahigh continued pulling apart the flower in his hands, turning it into as many tiny pieces as possible.

"What are you doing?" asked Ecclesias.

Elmahigh then mixed the tiny pieces of flowers together with the pumpersty he had and clenched it in his hand tightly. He grabbed his staff and drove it deep into the ground in front of him and recited some words in a soft voice over and over again.

"Elmahigh, there's no time," said Ecclesias.

The harvingers were speeding down toward Bolios and Friedrich who tried to cling to the rocks. They drew their swords in defense. Elmahigh continued whispering a spell below them as Ecclesias looked on, frightened.

"Daluum Dalaa," Elmahigh shouted.

A large fireball on top of his staff appeared. It was a mix of dark and light blue.

"Elmahigh," Ecclesias gasped.

Elmahigh threw the mix of tiny pieces of biltley flower and pumpersty into the blue flame. Out of it flew a giant dark blue mouth made up of scales. The mouth opened wide and revealed teeth twice the size of Bolios.

Elmahigh continued chanting quicker.

The blue flame was transforming into a dragon's mouth. What followed was its long neck and torso. It was immense. Its long wings seemed far greater in size than even the largest harvinger. The dragon's eyes were pure white light. Its four round legs also made of blue scales similar to snakes emerged from the flame.

"Elmahigh, what's happening?" said Ecclesias.

Elmahigh continued chanting louder and louder as the blue and white creature's tale emerged.

"Maitona Dailoda," said Elmahigh.

With those words, the dragon flew up overhead. It raced toward the harvingers. The harvingers stopped midair, bewildered by the strange being flying toward them. They made more piercing noises as they flapped their wings repeatedly. Confused, they were unsure what to do. They looked at one another, opening their beaks, letting out more loud high-pitched shrieks. The dragon continued flying up toward them with its burning white eyes. It flapped its wings and increased its speed, closing the distance between them. The harvingers forgot about Bolios and Friedrich below.

"What is that, Bolios?" asked Friedrich.

"I don't believe what I'm seeing. It's a dragon."

The two of them jumped off the mountain as they finally reached the bottom. They stood there as the dragon raced toward the harvingers with its mouth wide open, revealing its sharp teeth.

"Bolios! Friedrich! Over here!" called Ecclesias.

"Come on, let's go," said Bolios.

The two ran toward Ecclesias and Elmahigh.

"Some weather tonight?" said Elmahigh.

"That's no weather, monk," said Bolios. "What did you do?"

The harvingers screamed. The dragon opened its mouth and breathed a giant ball of white and blue fire. With that, the harvingers sped out of its reach.

"What I did, my friend, is to simply buy us some time," replied Elmahigh. "Come quickly, we must catch up with the others. It will not fool them much longer."

The four began to run through the large bushes and rotted trees toward their friends ahead. They put more distance between them and the harvingers. They jumped over roots and ducked under tree branches, cutting through the dense bush.

The harvingers were evading the dragon's fire. They turned left and swooped right, dove down, and rose high.

Free of immediate distress, Bolios couldn't help ask Elmahigh.

"What was that, Elmahigh?"

"Just a bit of help," he replied.

Bewildered, his brow raised, again Bolios spoke, "It did help, but what is it?"

They began to trot. Soon Prince Adinor, Isilmoire, and the rest of the group appeared.

"Hurry," Elmahigh said.

"It looked like a dragon to me," said Ecclesias, who was now panting.

"It looked like a dragon to me too," said Friedrich.

Meanwhile back at the grass mountain cliff, the harvinger leader changed its behavior. It stopped flying away and floated high. It watched the dragon chase all the other harvingers menacing them all. Finding its opportunity, it chose an angle of attack, flapped its black wings, and sped toward the dragon's neck.

"Keep moving, all of you," said Elmahigh.

"Come now, Elmahigh," said Bolios, "the dragon; what is it?"

They all paused a moment, gathering what breath they could from the blistering pace. Friedrich and Ecclesias hunched over as Elmahigh leaned on his staff for support.

Back at the cliff, the largest of the harvingers continued toward the dragon. With all its might, it opened his feet, revealing the sharp talons. He approached the dragon at full speed. The dragon continued spewing its fire toward the smaller harvingers, but failing to torch any of them.

The soldiers regained their breath several hundred yards away.

"If you all must have an explanation," said Elmahigh, "it's a phantom."

"What?" said Bolios.

"An apparition," replied Elmahigh, "it's not real."

At the same moment, the harvinger leader buried its talons into the dragon's back, and instantly, the mirage disappeared. All of the other harvingers looked at one another confused. They shrieked and ground their beaks. The leader led out the loudest piercing cry. It was heard all over the forest.

"And now they've discovered it too," said Elmahigh, "run!"

The harvingers screams echoed throughout the entire forest.

Prince Adinor and the group ahead of Elmahigh looked puzzled.

"Did you all hear that?" asked Prince Adinor.

"Yes, it's the harvingers," said Isilmoire, "wherever they are, they're angry."

Elmahigh and Bolios ran even faster. Flustered, they reached their friends and stormed the camp. Everyone was again accounted for.

"Bolios, we must continue north to the Goulen Mountains," Isilmoire exclaimed. "It's the only way we can survive the harvingers."

"Why not continue further east?" asked Bolios.

"We have. It's the end of the forest," replied Prince Adinor.

"What did you find?" asked Bolios.

"Nothing. It's only barren ground, made of pure rock."

"We must hurry to maintain the element of surprise on the Witch," said Isilmoire.

"I don't disagree, but—"

Elmahigh cleared his throat. "But what, Bolios? We don't have a choice. The harvingers are returning for us, there is nothing left to do. Quickly, hurry all of you. We must cross the edge of the wastelands and move to higher ground."

All of the men began running. The bloodcurdling shrieks of the angered monster grew.

"Run," said Bolios.

They reached the edge of the forest and continued onto the dry rock lands of Furion. It was void of water, plants, and life as a whole. It was extremely hot and dangerous. They raced over the area, hoping to reach the higher altitude of the Goulen Mountains ahead in the distance. It would not be easy. The shifting black rock beneath their feet revealed hot lava flowing beneath the surface. As they ran upon it, tall plumes of smoke and red-hot lava shot up from below.

"Quickly, men," said Bolios, "stay together. Elmahigh, lead the way with Isilmoire."

Dolamite and Prince Adinor, together with a couple of others, struggled to keep up.

"Come, Prince Adinor, we're nearly there," said Bolios.

Elmahigh and Isilmoire ran, hoping to arrive at the foot of the Goulen Mountains before the harvingers returned. The cracks between the separated plates spewed hot steam, preventing anyone from passing it, causing constant changes in course.

"This way, follow me," said Elmahigh.

They moved around the latest wall of hot gas and ran right as they moved across the Furion wasteland. The massive expanse of rock ground was between the forest and the Goulen Mountains, leaving no other option for cover. Then they heard the cries and shrieks of the harvingers. The deafening high-pitched noises grew louder.

"Keep moving," said Elmahigh.

A few of them fell down, tripping over the cracks. Friedrich and Dolamite both smashed their faces upon the black dust below.

"Hurry, come on, Dolamite," said Bolios.

"Lautner, Teinmar, help them," said Isilmoire.

They all leaped over another large deep hole. A river of glowing red and yellow lava flowed below the chasm. The heat was exasperating.

"We need to stop," said Theodonus.

"We can't," said Bolios, "we're nearly there."

The harvingers were within seeing distance.

"Quickly," said Elmahigh.

They all darted toward the Goulen Mountain base. It was close.

"Elmahigh, you and the Nymphs together with Ecclesias and Theodonus, go on ahead," said Bolios, "we'll occupy them with a wave of arrows."

"No, just keep moving," replied Elmahigh. "I'll go ahead with the Nymphs, we'll rain down arrows from the mountain above, but you can't stop."

"Very well," said Bolios.

The group split for a short time as the faster runners increased their speed, leaving some behind. The trailing group continued advancing as fast as they could. The harvingers closed the distance behind them. Prince Adinor glanced back as he ran toward the mountain ahead, seeing what they all feared.

"They are nearly upon us," said Prince Adinor

"Keep going, my Prince," said Bolios.

Bolios turned and sent three arrows back toward the lead harvinger who evaded them. Elmahigh, the Nymphs, and Theodonus, together with Ecclesias, reached the mountain and began climbing.

"Go on," said Bolios.

His group continued running toward the mountain. The harvingers dove down toward Bolios, attacking him in pairs. He stood before them, swinging his sword wildly as he clipped one of them then another. They continued attacking him.

Prince Adinor turned and fired an arrow up toward the two attackers, hitting one in the neck.

"Come on, Bolios," said the Prince.

Bolios turned and ran toward the mountain as the Prince provided protection.

"We're nearly there," shouted the Prince.

Bolios was running as fast as he could, catching up with the Prince.

"Bolios, you're bleeding," said the Prince.

"It's just a small cut. Keep moving, Prince Adinor."

They arrived at the mountain and began climbing. The rest of the group found cover behind large boulders making up parts of the mountain.

"Keep climbing," said Isilmoire from up above.

"We're here behind the rocks," said Elmahigh.

"When do we release our arrows?" asked Theodonus.

"Just wait until the rest of the harvingers come closer," said Elmahigh. "Hold your position and take aim."

Bolios and Prince Adinor were nearly to them, when the dozens of harvingers attacked.

"Now," said Elmahigh.

The warriors unleashed as many arrows as possible, repeatedly striking some the harvingers. The monsters shrieked as they dove and flew higher, attempting to avoid being struck. Some succeeded, but most weren't so lucky.

"Everything you have," said Elmahigh.

Bolios turned just below them and also unleashed the few remaining arrows he had left, striking a harvinger just above him. Prince Adinor aimed well and hit some as well. Dozens of arrows flew through the air. The Mastadans and Nymphs ran out and proceeded to pick up stones, launching them toward the harvingers as well.

They inflicted whatever harm they could. It was not without reward, for the flying beasts were driven away, choosing instead to return to their nests in the forests. As they flew away, they let out additional shrieks, howls, and cries, announcing their return someday.

CHAPTER 18

"Is everyone all right?" asked Bolios.

Dolamite was collapsed on the ground, his large belly moved up and down as he struggled to regain his breath. "This is just too much," he said.

Ecclesias, Marcus, and Friedrich collapsed to their knees.

"Well, let's not do that again," said Theodonus.

Bolios only nodded in reply as his attentions were on the rest of his men. Prince Adinor was sitting on the ground as he clenched the bow in front of him. His eyes fixed on the Petruchani Forest, the home of those dreaded harvingers.

Elmahigh walked toward the Prince and said, "We're rid of them for quite some time."

"How can you be so sure?" asked the Prince.

"We're far from the forest. It's too great a distance for them to venture from their nests. We won't be seeing them again."

Isilmoire stepped away from Teinmar and Lautner.

"Bolios, would you prefer to camp here among these rock formations or perhaps somewhere a bit less exposed?" asked Isilmoire

"I'm unfamiliar with these lands," said Bolios, "what more do they offer?"

"There may be a cave nearby," said Elmahigh.

"That's what we have concluded as well," said Isilmoire.

"Then we keep moving through the mountain," said Bolios, "upon finding something more secure, we make camp and rest."

The mountain seemed to go on forever. The grey and white stones making it up came in all shapes and sizes. A path going up to higher ground helped them reach greater altitudes with ease. The rocky terrain was still better than the dreadful Furion Wasteland. The path seemed unnatural, as though a corridor was cut through the mountain, as a road for easy travel. On either side was flat rock that rose high alongside them. Overhead was nothing except the clouds above. Darkness slowly crept in.

"Who could have made this?" asked Bolios.

"Impossible for this to be done by men," said Elmahigh. "I'm unsure, but we should be careful as we travel through here."

They continued along the path as it turned and twisted through the mountain. There wasn't any sound except the wind wrapping around the mountain, making a whistling sound. The crunching of small pebbles beneath their feet and their small chatter were the only other comforts for them as they travelled. Clouds surrounded them as they scaled higher, seemingly within arm's reach. They came across some strange writings on both sides of the paths.

"What does it say?" asked Prince Adinor.

"The carvings tell a story," Elmahigh said, "observe the different figures on either side."

They continued walking and observing more of the large drawings. Elmahigh stopped, spoke a few words into his staff, and ignited it with light. The entire walls on either side became visible. He continued analyzing them. The shadows of the warriors grew larger as they continued walking away from him. The drawings were figures resembling man.

"Over here," said Prince Adinor.

They found him walking into a dark opening ahead.

"Be careful, young Prince," said Bolios. "Elmahigh, we'll need light."

Elmahigh remained just behind studying the drawings. He ran his hands upon the carvings.

"Yes, of course," he replied.

He rejoined the others. He walked inside, and soon realized how large the cave was. His staff couldn't illuminate the whole cave ahead.

"Is there anyone in here?" said Bolios.

Only the echo of his voice reverberated. Teinmar and Dolamite both drew their swords. Isilmoire and Prince Adinor laughed.

"There's no one here," said Prince Adinor.

"This will do," said Bolios. "Theodonus and Ecclesias, find something to burn, we need a fire. Malchomite and Dolamite, together with Marcus, secure the rest of this cave. I'll take the first watch at the entrance."

"Teinmar, accompany the men searching for tinder," said Isilmoire, "Lautner."

"Yes," he replied.

"You go with the others," said Isilmoire.

Prince Adinor stayed with Isilmoire and Elmahigh as they pondered it all.

"What great fortune," said Prince Adinor.

"This will help," said Isilmoire.

"It would appear that way," replied Elmahigh.

"What do the carvings you were observing mean, Elmahigh?" asked Isilmoire.

"I'm unsure," replied Elmahigh. "I would like to study them more."

"It's getting late," replied Bolios, "we've lost much time evading the harvingers. Perhaps it's best we remain inside the cave. We rest and start anew tomorrow."

"Yes of course," replied Elmahigh.

Theodonus and Ecclesias and Teinmar returned with a large amount of dried branches. They began working on a fire.

"I'm going to sleep like a fatted calf nursed by its mother," said Prince Adinor.

"I don't see how that's possible," said Dolamite who walked back to the cave's entrance, accompanied by Lautner and Malchomite.

"Did you find anything else in here?" asked Bolios.

"No, sire," said Malchomite, "we found nothing but rock formations and a shallow spring of water."

"Is it drinkable?" asked Bolios.

"Yes," answered Malchomite.

"Very well," answered Bolios, "make sure everyone drinks. It's been a long day. We all could use some."

"Yes, my lord," replied Malchomite.

"I can't imagine us sleeping so soundly, young Prince," said Dolamite, "unlike a fattened calf, my belly craves food."

"You and your eating. Is that all you every worry about?" asked Ecclesias.

Dolamite chided, "Well, it's been known to make almost any man happier. What I wouldn't do for a charred piece of buffalo tongue or salted pork."

"Or a warm plate of Mastadan wild rice with pecan sauce and buttermilk-fed goat," said Prince Adinor.

"Yes, Prince Adinor," said Dolamite, "now that is more like it."

"Calm down, you two. You'll only make it worse," said Theodonus.

The men settled around the fire, coping with the fatigue from battle. As the fire flickered, their shadows were cast upon the cave wall behind them. Darkness shrouded them as the fire slowly died. All of the men fell asleep. Only Bolios remained vigilant at the cave's entrance.

He paced back and forth. Fatigure set it. The fire went out. His only source of light was the moon high above. It shone down upon the rocks around him. A couple of slaps and repeated shaked of his head were his best attempts to stay awake. He continued pacing and remembered back to the similar moon flying overhead which accompanied him on the night he trained Prince Adinor. Bolios walked a few paces into the cave and noticed the young Prince was sound asleep as were the other soldiers and Nymphs.

He thought deeply on the losses his warrior company incurred. Two soldiers were already victim to the cause; how many more would be required? He returned back to the cave's entrance and sat down resting his sword upon his lap as he stared out contemplating his decisions. The moon shone down on him. He sat and rested for a moment as he listened for any intruders or threats. The silence was mind numbing as nothing could be heard except the gentle whooshing breeze blowing around the mountain, brushing his face. Bolios closed his eyes for a moment, but fought to open them as he worried of his men's safety.

"No," he said aloud.

He shook himself once more, clamoring for energy to stay awake. He looked over at his troops and immediately rose. He paced back and forth. He looked back toward the moonlight; morning would soon be upon them again.

CHAPTER 19

The bright hot sun rose, bathing the rocks in light and burningw away the evening's chill. The sunshine fell upon Bolios' foot and began spreading up to his legs and body, reaching his face. He stayed motionless as the morning baked him. He'd fallen asleep at the front the cave entrance. His sword rested on his lap.

Off in the distance, there was a small noise and then another.

Bolios remained asleep.

The sound of crunching pebbles continued growing.

The battle-weary soldiers inside the cave remained still too.

Crunch.

Bolios shifted a bit, adjusting his position in an attempt to get more comfortable. He began stirring a bit. Slowly, his awareness returned.

Suddenly, the steps sped up.

Bolios struggled to open his eyes. He detected a faint sound in the distance, but his battle weary eyes felt heavy like anvils. Someone was approaching. "I hear you," he whispered.

Still dazed from the lack of sleep, he rose and grabbed his sword, preparing for battle. The noise was now more pronounced. It quickened.

The high rock walls of the path channelled the noise, making it difficult to discern the direction the intruder's origin. The sound could be coming from the left or right side, making it difficult to defend their position.

"Men," said Bolios.

No one moved. The source of the steps would soon be upon him.

"Show yourself," Bolios commanded.

The surprised look of Elmahigh appeared around the corner. "You're awake."

"Yes, of course," replied Bolios as he put his sword away. "In a moment, I would have skewered you like a pig."

"Well, for my sake, I'm glad you didn't. There is however a much more troubling circumstance which requires our urgent departure."

"What is it?" asked Bolios.

"Come, my friend," said Elmahigh, "let's wake the others. We must leave this place at once."

They walked inside the cave and saw Isilmoire standing just in front.

"I heard you calling," she said.

"It was only Elmahigh," replied Bolios.

"Is everything all right, Elmahigh?" she asked.

Bolios began tugging at each of the sleeping men and gathering the belongings scattered about.

"Rise, men, it's time to leave," said Bolios.

"Just when I was really getting some good sleep," Ecclesias said jokingly.

Elmahigh looked out toward the entrance.

"Elmahigh, what were you doing when you came upon Bolios?" asked Isilmoire.

"I have studied the carvings in the walls," he said.

"The drawings we saw?" asked Isilmoire.

"Yes, the very ones," replied Elmahigh.

The men and Nymphs were awake and continued gathering their things for their impending departure while Elmahigh spoke to Isilmoire.

"The carvings alongside the path tell a story," continued Elmahigh. "It talks of a group of farmers long ago. These farmers tasked with providing the entire kingdom with produce sufficient in quantities to sustain everyone apparently encountered difficulty. There was a drought one year. Consequently, the kingdom suffered famine, sickness, and other problems stemming from it. These farmers sought a means of solving the problem. A select group of farmers traveled to these very mountains seeking a rumored sorcerer capable of ending the drought. Upon arriving here, they climbed and searched throughout the mountain, with no such luck. They surrendered the idea of a potential solution. As it turns out, they were surprised to stumble upon a frail old woman walking in the mountain seemingly disoriented and lost. The farmers greeted her and welcomed her to join them for some food and rest before their journey back to their farmlands. They spoke about the rumored sorcerer and asked the woman whether she knew of the sorcerer's whereabouts. They mentioned their desperate situation and their willingness to do anything to solve the problem. They spoke of their willingness to give their lives in exchange for a solution. The old woman parted from the farmers and continued on. The farmers fell asleep briefly in an attempt to rest after the shared meal with the old woman. Upon awaking, they were forever changed."

"What do you mean?" asked Isilmoire.

All the soldiers and Nymphs followed Elmahigh over to the carvings on the wall. He pointed toward them.

Twelve squares measuring four feet by four feet depicted scenes. Each scene explained a different aspect of Elmahigh's story. The scenes clearly showed human figures. A vertical carved groove in the stone resembled a torso while two perpendicular grooves from each vertical groove resembled arms and two at the bottom of the vertical groove represented legs. A large circle above the vertical groove represented a head.

"That's incredible," Prince Adinor said.

In their hands were a rake represented by three smaller grooves carved into the stone at the top near the end of the arms. Even the old lady showed up in the scene just as Elmahigh explained via a smaller torso and shorter arms and legs. The artist added some hair on the circle drawn above her torso representing a female.

"See the large carvings show the farmers were no longer men."

"I don't understand," Prince Adinor said.

"Something happened to them," replied Elmahigh. He pointed to a scene on the wall with his staff.

"The etchings representing humans are gone," exclaimed Dolamite.

Bolios walked directly next to Elmahigh and Isilmoire. All the Mastadans and Nymphs stood in silence.

"What were they changed into?" asked Prince Adinor.

They all stared at the last four foot by four foot scene at the bottom right hand corner of the cave wall.

"That's difficult to say," said Elmahigh, "as you can see there's only a large circle carved directly in the middle of the scene. The story is unclear."

"You can't be serious," said Bolios.

"It is possible," said Prince Adinor.

The rest of the men contemplated the information.

"Whether or not you choose to believe it," said Elmahigh, "there's more to the story."

"What does it all mean?" asked Ecclesias.

Elmahigh breathed a heavy sigh. "I believe whatever became of those men was the work of darkness in these mountains, and that darkness is still here somewhere. We are not safe. We must leave."

A violent eruption began as the ground below them shook. Large rocks began tumbling down from high above, rolling ahead of them. The sound of the rock crashing upon rock thundered in their ears as the ground became unstable.

"Not more problems!" yelled Prince Adinor.

Again, the ground shook, freeing big rocks from above, causing debris to fall down upon them.

Maddened with fright, Theodonus screamed, "The entire earth is breaking."

Again, the rumble below their feet progressed as the dust falling made seeing difficult. The warriors shook as the vibration increased, knocking some of them down.

"What do we do?" asked Ecclesias.

"Run," said Elmahigh.

They all ran and passed the cave, struggling to maintain their balance from the repeated shaking. Elmahigh led them forward, avoiding the falling rocks from overhead.

"Come on," said Elmahigh.

The men twisted and turned, jumping and ducking the constant barrage of rocks falling from high above them. They moved, hoping not to be crushed.

Prince Adinor and the rest of the Mastadans ran closely behind him as the Nymphs and Bolios brought up the rear. They ran between the rock wall corridors.

"Keep the pace, young Prince," Elmahigh yelled.

The hundreds of rocks and boulders descending from above covered the daylight.

"Hurry," said Bolios..

Elmahigh evaded another boulder from up above, only to realize a huge problem ahead. A giant gorge split the mountain in two. "Be careful ahead," he said.

He stopped just shy of the divide as his foot slid atop the numerous small pebbles. So close was he to the edge that some fell down the gorge far beyond sight.

Prince Adinor arrived after Elmahigh.

"It seems too far a jump," said Prince Adinor.

Elmahigh looked over to the other side. There was no way to climb down. The ledge made for an impossible climb to the bottom. Elmahigh looked back to the falling rocks. In moments, they would fall upon them. Isilmoire and Teinmar arrived next as did Lautner. They all gasped for air and studied the problem.

"Where are the others?" asked Elmahigh.

"They are coming just behind us," said Isilmoire.

Just then, Theodonus appeared followed by Malchomite. They were breathless. The stones and rocks continued falling from high above. The mountain continued to shake.

"We cannot remain here much longer," said Isilmoire. "It's only a matter of moments before one of those giant stones fall upon us."

"What if we climb down?" asked Prince Adinor

"Too dangerous," said Elmahigh.

"We have to jump across," said Isilmoire.

"It seems too far," said Theodonus.

Bolios could see the men up ahead as he helped the fallen Dolamite to his feet.

"Come on, Dolamite, I won't leave you," said Bolios.

"Thank you, sire," replied Dolamite.

The two continued running. Bolios ran faster, noticing the group standing around despite the danger of the falling rocks from above.

Theodonus saw Bolios running toward them and yelled, "Bolios, there is a giant gorge. Stop, sire."

He showed no signs of slowing.

"Bolios, slow down. The path ends here," yelled Isilmoire.

Bolios ran even faster, passing up Friedrich and Marcus who were slowing up as they neared the rest of the group.

"Bolios!" yelled Theodonus.

Bolios pounded his feet down upon the grey arid rock of the path as though he sought to launch himself. Each inch of his foot gripped the ground harder, vaulting him forward faster. He pumped his arms like pistons, clenched his fist and grimaced. With a locked jaw he studied the other side across the divide. Running past all of them, he stepped just before the edge of the path and leaped toward the other side. He came crashing down and rolled to a stop, but not before sending his sword and dagger flying. He was across.

The others were still in awe as they remained eight feet across from him.

"Well, that is the only way," said Elmahigh.

Bolios dusted himself off, picked up his sword, and looked back toward the others.

"What are you all waiting for?" he said. "Keep moving."

"He's right," said Isilmoire.

"I'll go last," said Dolamite.

They moved back away from the edge and ran as fast as possible, mimicking Bolios.

"Jump," said Bolios.

Prince Adinor and Elmahigh ran next to each other, jumping at the very last moment. Pebbles from the path flew down to the bottom of the massive gorge below as they made it across into Bolios' welcoming arms.

"Well done," he said.

Rocks continued tumbling from above landing closer to the group. They all moved back from the edge, ran fast, gathering momentum, jumping at the very last moment, reaching the other side.

"Come on, there's not much time," said Bolios.

Only Dolamite remained.

"He's not going to make it," said Bolios.

Bolios threw himself on the ground near the edge, reached his arm out, and held his hands wide open.

"Hold my legs," he yelled.

Dolamite ran and leaped. He soared over the giant gorge, but seemed to be falling short of the opposite edge. His face was pale white as he began to plummet. He reached out with both arms, hands wide open, trying to grip something on the other side.

Elmahigh, Isilmoire, Prince Adinor, and Theodonus all gripped Bolios' legs and dropped him over the edge of the ledge.

Bolios reached and caught Dolamite's outstretched hand.

"Got you," Bolios said.

Bolios continued clutching one of Dolamite's arms while still hanging upside down toward the precipice below. Bolios strained. His arm began to shake as he pulled Dolamite up.

"Hold on, Dolamite," said Bolios.

Dolamite reached with his other arm and clutched Bolios' arm with all his might. His feet continued dangling over the black drop beneath him. The grains of dry rock began to fall on his face. He was covered in grey powder.

"Pull, men," said Bolios.

Prince Adinor, Elmahigh, and the rest of began pulling Bolios from his legs. Dolamite came up too.

"Keep pulling," said Bolios.

They brought Bolios' entire body back onto solid ground as he continued holding Dolamite.

Now over the edge, Dolamite gripped the ground with his own hands and received assistance from the others to finish getting up.

"I told you I would not leave you, my friend," said Bolios.

Two large tears flowed from Dolamite's eyes. His arms still shaking, he extended them and embraced his leader.

"Let's get off this mountain," said Bolios.

Behind them was the gorge and loud crashing sounds of the falling rocks. They moved farther into the new mountain and were greeted by crisp cold air swirling all around them. They searched for a way down. The mountain revealed no easy way off. The peak was just over their shoulders. They looked down and saw nothing. The temperature reached forty degrees.

"Is everyone all right?" asked Bolios.

Their head nodded up and down, but they remained silent. It began to snow. The temperature dropped another twenty degrees. Their teeth began to chatter. Icicles formed beneath their beards from solid saliva. They struggled to walk.

"We must find shelter," said Isilmoire.

Bolios observed the men struggling to maintain their balance. Some even leaned forward into the fierce storm. The thin metal armor and wool under layers was no match for the cold.

"Very well," replied Bolios, "but where?"

"We continue on," said Elmahigh, "something will present itself."

The snow was beginning to build on the ground. Their feet were soon wet and cold. As they progressed forward atop the mountain, the snowfall increased. Bolios held both hands over his eyes, shielding the massive snow fall, hoping to see shelter ahead. His vision was blanketed by the snow now a few inches deep. A few of the soldiers stopped walking altogether, feeling temporary paralysis as the cold pierced their bones. Their hair turned into hardened ice. All feeling in their toes or fingers was gone. The snowfall continued.

"What is that?" asked Dolamite.

The Mastadans and Nymphs remained stiff in the cold.

"What are you referring to?" Prince Adinor finally said.

"There ahead," replied Dolamite.

"I see nothing," answered Bolios.

"The cold is taking hold of his mind," said Isilmoire, "we must get off this mountain."

"No, wait, he's right," said Elmahigh, "something approaches."

In the distance, giant shadows forty feet tall moved in the blizzard.

"I can't move," said Ecclesias.

"Nor can I," said Theodonus.

"We're all trapped," Prince Adinor cried out.

The dark figures, unbothered by the snowfall, continued approaching.

The Mastadans tried moving, shifting in place but none could break free. Their legs remained buried in snow which was now up to their thighs.

"The shadows are coming toward us," said Isilmoire.

"What are they?" yelled Bolios.

Prince Adinor's vision began fading in and out as his eyes closed. Bolios saw the Prince struggling and clenched his fist closed. He opened and closed them repeatedly hoping to draw blood to his fingertips. Then a shadow appeared to approach. His hands regained some feeling and he reached for his sword. He struggled to draw the blade from its sheath as the frost locked it in. The blade was stuck.

"They're nearly upon us," said Elmahigh.

"Can you conjure anything?" asked Bolios.

"Everything I have is frozen and of no use," replied Elmahigh.

Ecclesias, Malchomite, and Theodonus lost consciousness as the cold began overtaking them.

"Oh no," said Prince Adinor.

"It's too late," said Isilmoire.

The forty-foot figures were directly over them as their identity was finally revealed.

"They're stone giants," said Elmahigh.

Before them stood giants ten times larger than any of them. They were faceless monsters composed completely of dry and hard unbreakable stone. There were four in total.

"What do they want?" asked Prince Adinor.

"I don't know, but I can't imagine it's good," replied Isilmoire.

"Can they understand you?" said Bolios.

"The writings," said Elmahigh.

"They want writings?" asked Bolios. "What writings?"

"No, fool," replied Elmahigh, "the writings near the cave we stayed in. Everything I read, the writings are true."

The stone giants moved closer. They were carrying something.

All of the soldiers' paralysis further amplified their dread. They were immobile.

They were intimidating creatures. Their legs alone were bigger than any of them. Their bodies were one giant boulder and their arms were longer than their legs. Their fingers were a collection of small stones, their faces blank, void of anything at all. With every step the stone giants took, the ground began to shake. Small rocks from the mountain began to fall down toward the Mastadans.

"Look out," said Bolios.

Then each of the stone giants revealed what they carried. They had large nets. The stone giants pulled the Mastadans and Nymphs out of the snow and placed them into the nets as easy as a child throws a rag doll.

The Mastadans and Nymphs were captured.

"This is not good," said Prince Adinor.

"Try and stay calm," said Bolios.

The stone giants gathered them into two different groups.

"I can't move a thing," said Prince Adinor.

"Neither can I," said Isilmoire.

They began traveling toward an unknown destination. Two giants draped the group of soldiers over their shoulders. The other two walked without any prisoners.

"Where are you taking us?" asked Malchomite.

"It's pointless, they can't understand you," replied Theodonus.

"Let us go," said Prince Adinor from inside the first net.

The stone giants continued walking alongside the mountain. The path continued winding around it. They headed higher up. The temperature dropped to freezing. It was dark as night descending upon them, plunging the soldiers into greater cold and harsher suffering.

"This is unbearable," said Prince Adinor.

"Hold on, young Prince," said Bolios.

Suddenly, the stone giants stopped.

The mastadans now discovered that they were at the very top of the mountain. They could nearly touch the clouds.

Two of the stone giants jumped from the mountain summit and disappeared into the snow fall. The other two swung their cargo around from their shoulders down to their sides.

The Mastadans and Nymphs now dangled close to the mountainside. Their bodies were pinned against each other like squished bread at the bottom of a sack.

"Ouch," yelled Theodonus.

"My rib feels as though its cracked," cried out Prince Adinor.

"Get off me, Bolios," screamed Isilmoire.

Then, one of the stone giants burst into a fast run on the summit. Its heavy footsteps shook the ground and caused the entire mountain to shake.

"The path doesn't continue up ahead," said Elmahigh

The giant continued running faster.

"Let us go," shouted Bolios. "Release us and fight, coward."

The stone giant was near the end of the path.

"We'll not survive this," said Prince Adinor.

"That is yet to be our fate," said Elmahigh.

"If he throws us off the mountain, it will be," said Bolios.

The stone giant reached the end of the mountain path and placed his stone foot deep on edge of the cliff, launching himself out over the edge.

"Oh no," yelled Prince Adinor.

Screams filled the net; their hearts sank into their stomachs. They were in free fall from the high mountain cliff, heading straight down to impending death below. They continued gaining incredible speed, as they flew inside the net still held by the rock giants.

"This is it," said Prince Adinor.

Elmahigh clenched his eyes and began to pray and then everything stopped.

The stone giant came crashing down onto another mountain. Their feet pounded against the new mountain sending a thunderous sound throughout the land. A dust-filled cloud consumed them as the force produced a wave of particles thrown about everywhere.

"That was awful," said Prince Adinor.

All the soldiers were grimacing in pain.

The stone giant gripped the side of the mountain with one hand and continued clenching the net of soldiers with the other. The charcoal black peak was surrounded by a ring of white snow. Patches of black crag looked like eyes staring at the warriors where snow was missing from the stone giant's steps.

"I can feel my limbs again," said Bolios. "Can someone reach my sword?"

The others tried to help Bolios and then another loud thunder and cloud of dust came as the other stone giant crashed onto the mountain near the same spot the first giant landed on. The second giant followed the first as they made their way down the mountain toward more unknown. The two giants not carrying soldiers were down below.

Bolios continued trying to reach his sword. He was pinned against the weight of his own warriors. The others helped as they regained feeling in their extremities. The stone giants descended the mountain.

"Keep trying," said Bolios.

"I think I can feel it," said Prince Adinor.

His fingers were upon the sword's end.

"I got it," said Prince Adinor.

"Great work, young Prince," said Elmahigh.

"Draw the blade out, perhaps you can cut us out of here," said Bolios.

The second giant, climbing just behind them, noticed their efforts and peered into the net as they continued fumbling around trying to free themselves. Its head was so large it could hardly detect their efforts. It moved its head closer into the net's activity and poked into the net with its free hand.

"Look out," said Isilmoire.

The stone giant's finger continued into the net, finding a couple of the soldiers, shoving them within the net from one side to the other.

"Duck," said Bolios.

The warriors crawled and ducked out of the way, desperately avoiding the stone giant's fingers. Their grimacing faces strained as they accidentally kicked and punched each other by accident in a scramble for safety.

The stone giants then stepped off the mountain onto the flat land below.

"Look," said Prince Adinor, "there's something up ahead."

A tower of smoke rose high above, and the bright flickers of fire danced.

"Their home, no doubt," said Bolios.

Evening fell as the stone giant's massive ground-shaking steps came closer to the source of the smoke and fire. As they approached, noise could be heard.

"What is that?" asked Prince Adinor.

"Perhaps the appropriate question is who is that?" replied Elmahigh.

"I fear only more danger awaits us," said Isilmoire.

The stone giants entered a large camp. The warriors from both groups of nets tried to see anything that could explain where they were. Each stone giant lifted its net high above their head, flipping the warriors upside down.

"You better be more careful," said Bolios.

"He'll be more careful with you than I will," replied a deep voice from down below.

All of the warriors looked through the nets, trying to see from who or what the words came from. The two stone giants not carrying soldiers blocked their vision. Only the numerous black boots, seemingly of men, standing near the stone giants could be seen.

"Throw them in the pit," said the same voice.

The stone giants walked away from the camp.

"Who are you?" yelled Bolios. "In the name of the Mastadan kingdom, by command of King Ralphus Dolamaic, I order you to let us go."

Suddenly, the stone giants lowered the net containing Bolios and the others.

"Someone approaches," said Isilmoire.

"Can you see anything?" asked Elmahigh

"Not enough," replied Isilmoire, "only footsteps."

"Silence!" said the unknown voice once more. "You have no authority here, Mastadan. Throw them in the pit."

The two stone giants then walked toward a large black wooden door bearing a heavy iron handle on the ground. One stone giant reached down, grabbed the handle, lifting the wooden cover open. The other then grabbed both nets and threw the Mastadans and Nymphs into a deep dirt pit below the ground, plunging the Mastadans into the darkness. They dropped straight down and crashed on the hard ground below. As they collected themselves and stood, they looked up and saw only hints of light from the camp of their captors. Then, the light began to fade as the stone giants shut the opening close. The Mastadan and Nymph warriors were prisoners.

Bolios reached and removed his sword, cutting his group free.

"There," he said.

He moved to the other net and did the same.

"Is everyone okay?" he asked.

"Everyone from our group is here," said Prince Adinor.

"All within our net are also accounted for, sire," said Theodonus.

"Elmahigh, a light please," said Bolios.

"Of course," replied Elmahigh.

He blew into his staff, saying a prayer, and suddenly there was light. Their prison was a huge deep hole, far below the surface, covered by the heavy wooden door high above their heads. There was no tunnel, no hidden door, no anti-chamber, nothing but space overhead. They looked for a way to climb, and studied the dry and hardened clay on all sides surrounding them.

"Seems like we're stuck," said Ecclesias.

They all nodded in acceptance.

"An opportunity will present itself," said Bolios.

CHAPTER 20

Up above, the stone giants stood on either side of the wooden door covering the pit. The camp nearby was full with activity.

"Prepare the war party," said a short fat man, "we leave for the village tomorrow at midday."

A couple of dozen large animal-like creatures wearing nothing but loin cloth covering half their bodies ran about making preparations. They were ugly and vile things. They stood on two hairy pointed toed feet and were muscular and tall, but disfigured with green veins and bulging deformations randomly jutting out from their bodies. They had few teeth, fangs, pointy and sharp in nature. Most had no hair anywhere, except a couple of strands on their heads.

In a large black hut made of coal and black stone was the man that ordered the stone giants to drop the Mastadan and Nymph warriors into the pit. He was a large man wearing animal hides whose eyes could barely be seen as his long black hair, thick black beard covered almost his entire face. His charcoal-colored eyes looked on to the creatures outside his tent and he smiled. The animal skin clothing that failed to cover his body revealed thick leathery skin, dirty from mud and ash. He walked inside his tent back and forth, from one side to the other. The short fat man entered the black tent and spoke.

"Qualvon," he said, "the preparations for another village attack are underway. We will be ready to strike as you wish."

"Very good, Mesthusula."

Qualvon continued walking back and forth, pacing inside his tent. He looked over to the corner where he kept a large black vat filled with a foul-smelling sludge, also black in color. It spewed steam and had an unpleasant odor.

"Should we change our plans as a result of the Mastadan and Nymph arrival?" asked the short and fat Mesthusula.

Qualvon stopped, turned toward Mesthusula, walked directly in front of him, and said, "I am the darkness that cannot be contained. Those opposed to me will find painful death. The way my darkness rises will soon cover all of Mastada and nothing will stand in my way."

Mesthusula knelt down, cowering before Qualvon.

"Of course, my lord," said Mesthusula. "I only asked in the event you are in danger. The arrival of some Nymph and Mastadan warriors could mean our position is known. Perhaps more of their fellow warriors will follow. What if King Ralphus brings his entire army?"

Qualvon smiled and looked at Mesthusula, grabbed him at the neck forcefully, and dragged him over to the black iron vat.

"You've been as useful as you can be," said Qualvon. "It is time to take your capabilities to another level."

"No, please, Qualvon," said Mesthusula.

Qualvon took some of the black sludge in one hand and forced it down Mesthusula's throat.

"Accept your weakness and unbelief and embrace your true potential," said Qualvon.

Mesthusula couldn't respond as his mouth was covered in the black sludge; as it poured into his throat and flowed out of his mouth, he struggled against Qualvon's tight grip, but was unable to break free. He consumed the sludge. As he swallowed more, his arms relaxed at his sides and his eyes became black like the sludge. Qualvon released him, and there stood Mesthusula before him, quiet. In seconds, Mesthusula began to grow in height and his skin also began changing. His teeth became darker, some fell out completely and others became pointy. His hair fell out. Two large horns protruded from his forehead. Rock-like orange hide replaced his skin. As the change continued, he yelled. His human voice became growls and howls like an animal. His muscles also changed as his body was transformed from fat to solid muscle; the change tore most of his clothes, and only small pieces were left covering his lower body.

Mesthusula resembled the creatures in the camp. He stood before Qualvon transformed.

"Can you hear me?" said Qualvon.

A loud boarlike roar blasted from Mesthusula. "Yes, lord," he replied.

"Finish preparations for the village attack," said Qualvon. "We leave at dawn. I need a new batch of soldiers for my bidding."

"Yes, lord," said Mesthusula.

* * *

Inside the pit, the Mastadans and Nymphs tried to uncover a way out.

"We tried climbing and digging," said Lautner. "What is there left to do?"

"It's unsettling indeed," said Isilmoire.

"You could try singing your way out," said Ecclesias.

"What I wouldn't give for a hot meal," said Dolamite.

"Think," said Bolios, "we need to get free from here before whatever is keeping us down in this pit discovers Prince Adinor is with us."

"The wretchedness within this camp," said Isilmoire, "this is the evil we seek."

"We don't know that for sure, my friend," said Elmahigh.

"What else is there to know?" asked Prince Adinor.

"Unsettling circumstance as we may find ourselves in," replied Elmahigh, "we do not have enough to truly know this is the source of the evil attacks upon the village."

"There's a camp full of soldiers here hidden away from Mastadan lands," replied Bolios.

"They are not Nymphs, Elmahigh," said Isilmoire.

"Yes, both of those statements are true," replied Elmahigh, "however, I don't sense the evil of sorcery here. Something is missing. I need chautruce."

"Well, while you're over in a corner humming and praying, can you be sure to keep it down," said Ecclesias, "some of us are trying to nap."

Elmahigh continued walking away from them, shaking his head.

"Elmahigh, if you're taking requests," said Dolamite, "can you please ask the voices to rain down a hot bucket of stew or perhaps even a barrel of maltsenhop and fresh bread?"

"Does chautruce really work?" asked Prince Adinor.

"Many say it does," replied Theodonus, "some say there are those in Elmahigh's order that are still capable of its highest strength."

"And what is that?" asked Prince Adinor.

"Special abilities like visions, magic, or control over other people's movements and minds," replied Theodonus, "some say powers of lightning and fire."

"That's incredible," said Prince Adinor, "perhaps Elmahigh can rip the heavy wooden cover open overhead and get us out of here. He could try."

"I asked him. He doesn't have any flowers or potions to use," Theodonus replied.

"It's not that easy," replied Isilmoire, "it takes great faith and connection to the environment and deep longstanding practice of the techniques."

"I think he can do it," said Prince Adinor.

"Let's focus on what we can do," said Bolios, "right here in the world of the real. We'll need to figure out something a bit more realistic.

"What do you have in mind?" asked Isilmoire.

"We climb out together," replied Bolios.

"No one can climb to the top, there's nothing to grab on to," replied Isilmoire.

Bolios looked up toward the pit and over to all the men seated on the ground talking.

"We'll make a human ladder," he said.

Prince Adinor and Isilmoire looked at one another, puzzled.

"You can't be serious?" asked Isilmoire.

"Indeed I am," replied Bolios. "Men, it's time to leave this dreaded hole."

The men all stayed seated, turned, and looked at Bolios.

"Bolios, there's no place to go," said Theodonus.

"Malchomite tried and he's our best climber," added Dolamite. "Even he didn't reach halfway up it."

"There's no point," said Malchomite, "there's not enough to hold on to."

"You climbed this, yes?" asked Bolios.

"Aye," replied Malchomite.

"You did it alone, right?"

"Yes, sire," replied Malcomite.

"This time will be different," said Bolios. "Now get on your feet."

The men scrambled up and over to Bolios, now flanked by Prince Adinor and Isilmoire.

"We'll make a link between us all," said Bolios, "starting with Dolamite at the bottom. I will then climb atop Dolamite's shoulders and the next of you will climb upon mine. We will continue to do this until the last of us remains."

"Who will be last?" asked Marcus.

"Malchomite," replied Bolios, "with us all stacked one upon the other, Malchomite will then climb atop us all and climb a shorter distance and reach the top of the pit."

There was silence. Elmahigh walked over from the corner, having completed his chautruce. The group was still quiet.

"Shall we begin?" said Elmahigh.

Bolios smiled and they walked toward the shortest side of the pit.

"Ready yourselves," said Bolios, "this will not be easy. It will take us all working together."

Up above, the stone giants remained on guard, flanking either side of the pit's closed wooden door. The iron handle laid flat upon it. Nightfall was at its peak. The groans, moans, and growls of the monsters lurking in the camp filled the evening. The preparations continued as the wretched monsters armed themselves with iron protective plates and swords as well as axes. They carried large shields decorated with combinations of dirt, blood, and black tar—clear signs of previous fighting against villagers of the outlying communities they attacked previously. A dense fog blanketed all of Qualvon's camp. There was more moaning and yelling from the monsters. They grew impatient as the desire for blood and killing increased as dawn approached. They ran around the campsite, wielding torches and beating one another like rabid dogs. They seemed wild with energy and determined to rain chaos—soon. Out of the largest black tent stepped Qualvon. At the sound of his armor rattling, the monsters stood in formation, awaiting his commands. He walked out toward the large fire in the middle of the collection of tents.

"Mesthusula!"

Mesthusula ran from the far side of the camp and arrived directly in front of Qualvon. He knelt and spoke.

"I am at your service, sire."

"You will lead my diatrite in combat," said Qualvon.

"I will do as you command, my lord."

"Very good," said Qualvon, "I will return in two moons to meet my new warriors and bless them myself, as you have been blessed. Let nothing stand in your way. Be certain to kill anyone that opposes the calling. Do not fail me."

"Consider it done, my king," replied Mesthusula.

"I need another dozen soldiers, bring me nothing less," answered Qualvon. "Should you fail me, ride far from my lands, for I will hunt you until the very day I kill you myself."

"There will be no need," said Mesthusula. "Your desire is my purpose."

"Excellent," replied Qualvon, "continue the stone giants watch over the Mastadans and Nymphs. I want the pleasure of killing them when I return."

"Yes, Qualvon."

Mesthusula remained kneeling while Qualvon walked directly through the middle of the camp. All of the deranged monsters remained still as their leader proceeded away from the central fire toward the darkness away from the camp. In mere moments, he was gone. Suddenly, the monsters erupted in a cry out, a yell so fever pitched that it could be heard in the distance within the bowels of the pit, where the heroes remained.

"What was that?" asked Prince Adinor.

The human ladder failed because of the weight. They now attempted a pyramid. Each of the men struggled to maintain their balance, as the far-fetched plan was working.

"Everyone, hold your position," replied Bolios, "we're nearly there."

"That sound was horrible," said Theodonus.

"It's the wretched cries of evil," said Isilmoire.

The human pyramid of Mastadan upon Nymph totaled nine high, as only Elmahigh and Isilmoire remained at the bottom.

"Well, hurry up already, there's only so much I can hold," said Dolamite.

Elmahigh jumped up and began climbing from Dolamite to Bolios, then scaled Teinmar and Lautner, stepping on Friedrich's head then Marcus. He continued on to Ecclesias and then reached to use Isilmoire's locked arm as a means to continue up and passed her onto Prince Adinor. Before he continued, he stopped and said, "Apologies, young Prince."

"This will not be easily forgotten," replied the Prince as Elmahigh smiled.

"Hurry up," said Dolamite.

Elmahigh reached the top, looked up, and surprised at how close they now were to the top of the pit. Nearly halfway, with a little fortune, the plan could work after all. He shook for a moment, losing his balance, and reached for the dry and hardened wall in front of him to steady himself. As he firmly placed both hands upon the wall, small dust and tiny loose rocks fell down upon all the stacked soldiers below him.

"Steady yourselves men," said Bolios.

With every slight movement from one person everyone was affected. They had only seconds to get Malchomite to the top and hope he could climb the rest of the way.

"Now, Malchomite," said Bolios.

Malchomite began his climb.

"Hurry, Malchomite," said Theodonus, "my shoulders are burning."

"My back feels like it's tearing," said Ecclesias.

"Stay strong, men," replied Bolios. "Quickly, Malchomite, they can't hold on much longer.

"What is he waiting for?" asked Dolamite. "My legs are shaking."

Teinmar whispered something in Nymph to Lautner who immediately began to laugh.

"What's so funny?" asked Ecclesias.

Isilmoire held on to the ankles of Prince Adinor and stared straight ahead, saying only, "Certain things are best not repeated."

"Just a few more seconds, Dolamite," said Bolios.

Malchomite jumped off Elmahigh's soldiers and stabbed his sword onto the wall of the pit.

"He's on," said Elmahigh.

"Good, now get off me," said Dolamite.

One by one, the soldiers all jumped off, crawling to the ground below. They stared up, looking for Malchomite's progress.

"It's too dark," said Ecclesias.

"Forgive me," replied Elmahigh.

He took his staff, whispered a spell into it, breathed, and lit the top, pouring light throughout the pit. High above, nearly three quarters of the way to the top, they saw Malchomite.

"He's almost there," said Theodonus.

"It's terrific," said Isilmoire, "he'll need to keep moving fast, if not he'll tire."

"You're right," said Bolios.

"What can we do to help?" asked Prince Adinor.

"Unfortunately nothing," said Elmahigh.

They were all quiet as Malchomite continued up. He reached up and gripped a small break in the clay and lifted himself higher. Soon, he would reach the top.

* * *

Qualvon was gone, and Mesthusula was now in command.

"March to the village," he said, "we fulfill Lord Qualvon's bidding today."

The monsters yelled, the wretched noise echoed throughout the wastelands and into the forest far away. The devilish creatures marched from the campsite heading toward the pit. The heavy metal they wore rattled and clashed, announcing their travel. They marched two by two, totaling no less than a few dozen. As they approached the pit, the stone giants remained on guard, paying little attention to the monsters. Deep within the bowels of the pit, Malchomite and the others could hear the monsters moving.

"Something's happening up above," he said.

"What did you say?" asked Bolios.

Malchomite reached for the heavy wooden door. His faint words were difficult to discern down below.

"Malchomite," yelled Bolios, "what is it you speak of?"

"My lord," replied Malchomite, "there's movement up above. There seems to be something happening."

Malchomite stepped onto another dry crack of the pit wall and arrived even closer to the wooden door and lifted it. Struggling to maintain his balance, he managed to peer out through the tiny crack of the opening he created.

"Malchomite, move carefully once outside. Do not give your position away," said Isilmoire.

The Mastadans and Nymphs down below could see a bit of light slip in from the break between their trap and the outside above them. Malchomite managed to see, for the first time, the source of all the loud noise.

"Malchomite, what is it?" asked Bolios. "What do you see?"

"Perhaps it would have been better to send someone more inclined to follow orders," said Ecclesias.

"Well, then surely that leaves you out, all the same," said Theodonus.

"He will do what's needed," Elmahigh said.

Malchomite continued peering out as he lifted the wooden hatch more. The stone giants turned occasionally as the noise from the approaching monsters crossed in front of them. Malchomite moved his eyes, following the stone giants' gazes, and saw what distracted them. The troop of monsters marched directly toward him. He lowered the wooden door almost closed, reducing his field of vision, but leaving space to see for the first time the enemy.

"Foul wretched things," he said aloud.

The monsters marched past the stone giants. They carried torches and were so close that Malchomite noticed their large deformed feet and their skin. It was unlike anything he'd ever seen. The two stone giants paid no attention to Malchomite, their concern was instead on the monsters departing. Two giants were missing. Nearly half of the entire group of soldiers passed Malchomite; he looked toward the back of the monster group marching, trying to decide when to leave the pit. The still raging fire directly center of the camp revealed an important treasure, rope. At one hundred yards, it wasn't too far. Malchomite lowered the door closed as the rest of the monsters continued past him. He looked down toward his friends and whispered, "I've found a way to get you all out."

"Excellent, Malchomite," replied Bolios, "be sure you're careful."

"I knew he'd do it all along," replied Ecclesias.

All of the soldiers stared at him. Theodonus smacked him behind the head.

"Thank you," said Bolios.

"Now the worst part," said Elmahigh.

"What is that?" replied Prince Adinor.

Bolios stepped toward the Prince and said, "The wait, young Prince."

Elmahigh folded his arms and tucked his chin to chest, pondering Malchomite's next decision. Up above, Malchomite again lifted the wooden door and noticed all the monsters were gone. Their torches only flickered in the distance as they were almost beyond view. The stone giants remained guard, standing in the same positions as before. Malchomite lifted the wooden door more, a small opening big enough for his hand to grip the dry rocky ground above. With the door resting on the palms of his hands, he dug his fingers deep into a crack between the rocks above. He clenched it and pulled himself up toward the opening. The wooden door now rested on his head. He froze as the stone giants moved. The one on the right reached down toward his foot, poking at it with his rock finger then he returned to his standing position. Malchomite reached his other hand out and pulled his entire upper body from the pit and onto the ground above.

"I can't see him anymore," said Lautner.

"He's almost out," said Isilmoire.

With one last pull from his arms, Malchomite was out. The heels of his boots kept the wooden door from shutting closed. He crawled on his belly, back toward the pit as he maintained watch on the stone giants who remained still, standing on either side of the pit entrance. They were close. Malchomite grabbed the wooden door and lowered it closed. He was out.

He rolled away from the pit, keeping the stone giants in view in front of him. He began crawling backward on the dry rocky ground, increasing the distance between him and the pit. The fire from the center of the camp began to shine on his back as the rock giants remained outside the pit entrance. Now far enough, he rose to one knee, then the other, leaping onto his feet. He ran and hid behind a large black tar-covered hut. His back rested against it as he peered back toward the stone giants who remained guard above the pit. Malchomite stayed in the shadows.

He moved around the tent and listened in to hear for any possible remaining opposition. There was none. He passed two more tents, but both were empty. He peered inside the third, still nothing. Arriving at the fire, he stood in front of it, enjoying its warmth for a moment, and proceeded over to the rope piled nearby.

"Perfect," he said.

Malchomite tied the short pieces together forming one long rope. The fire cast a shadow of him on the ground as he worked. He secured all of the pieces together, stopping only to look up and see the stone giants standing above the pit in the distance.

"That will have to do," he said.

Malchomite wrapped the rope around his shoulders, draping it across his chest, hoping to carry the rest in his arms. He did, but just before he started back toward the pit, he looked over to the stone giants who remained there.

"How do I get those dreaded things away from there?" he said aloud.

He looked for a weapon large enough to inflict damage; there was none. He ran into various tents, hoping to find something of use. In the largest of them all, he found a large black iron pot, with bubbling black sludge. He ignored it and ran back outside, staring into the fire.

Nearby were large tree branches dried up and grey in color. They were stacked near the fire in the center of the camp. Outside a tent on the other side of the camp he spotted some animal hides, perfect for warmth on a frigid night. They were from elk and deer as well as cow and bison. Running around the large fire, he pulled out several and carried them close to the fire. He crouched down and felt the warm embers bake his face. Glancing over his shoulder, the rock giants looked toward the camp, but didn't see him hidden behind the mounds of animal skins. He wrapped three animal skins around one grey branch and did the same with the other. Looking down at his own clothes, he used his dagger to cut off the end of his shirt. He took the other end of his shirt and did the same. He crouched down over the two wrapped branches and tied the animal skins securely around the ends. Pleased, he smiled and stuck them in the fire. Within seconds, both dead branches were set ablaze. He looked over to the stone giants off in the distance who remained standing upon the pit entrance, flanking either side.

He proceeded toward one of the tents and cast one of the torches upon it. He stood back at watched as the tent erupted in flames. The fire spread to a nearby tent and now two tents burned in the camp. The heat coming from the fire was stifling, Malchomite quickly stepped away and ran to the other side of the camp and held the torch close to another tent and watched as it ignited. Smoke rose high into the sky. The crackle and pop of the burning tent announced the destruction. Malchomite raced over to the largest of all of the tents and cast the remaining torch upon it, setting it ablaze as well. In moments, the entire campsite was in jeopardy of being consumed.

The stone giants turned, staring straight at the campsite. Confused, they looked at one another. One raised an arm toward the fires; they both seemed to nod, and they began running toward the fires.

Malchomite hurried and ran behind some tents opposite the flames. He circled behind the camp. The stone giants arrived, their massive pounding steps vibrating the entire ground. Malchomite looked on as they tried putting out the fires out with their hands, destroying a couple of the tents in the process. As one persisted, it set its hand on fire. It began smacking itself, trying to extinguish it with no success. The other assisted and began to smack the struggling stone giant as well. As they searched for a solution, he ran around their position, enabling him to escape toward the pit unnoticed.

Arriving at the pit door, he was out of breath. He looked back toward the camp and noticed one of the stone giants was out of sight. The other stone giant continued trying to extinguish the fires, relying now on kicking up rocks and gravel from the ground toward it with no luck. The only result was damaging the tents further.

Malchomite focused back on the pit. He raised the door just enough to leave a small space between the door and the ground, managing to lodge a piece of wood between the opening.

"Look," said Prince Adinor.

From down below, the Nymphs and Mastadans realized something was happening.

"There's a light coming from up there," continued Prince Adinor.

Malchomite bent down and pulled up on the wood and slowly the door opened higher. He raised it a little more and then propped a short fat tree under the pit door, holding it open. He hurried toward the opening and yelled down toward the men below.

"I'm sending down a rope."

"Excellent work, Malchomite," replied Bolios.

"We'll be here, still," said Ecclesias.

"There's a problem," said Dolamite.

"What might that be?" said Lautner.

"Are you Nymphs blind?" replied Dolamite. "Look at me. How do you suppose I climb up that rope?"

"I suggest carefully," said Isilmoire.

"You'll be fine, Dolamite," said Elmahigh.

Malchomite threw down the rope. It reached the bottom with excess to spare.

"Is it secured at the top?" yelled Bolios.

"Yes, climb up," replied Malchomite.

Bolios jumped and began to climb up. Malchomite looked down into the darkness, hoping to see a friend soon.

Back at the camp, the second stone giant returned carrying with him a small tree, which was torn out of the ground, its roots still dangling below mangled and destroyed. The stone giant smashed it against the burning tents. It was working. The second stone giant ran in search of a similar tree.

"Oh no," said Malchomite.

Bolios reached the top and exited the pit.

"It's good to see you again, Malchomite," he said.

"Bolios, sire, we must hurry."

Bolios looked over to the campsite.

"Yes, we must quicken our escape," he said.

He turned back toward the pit, helping Elmahigh out.

"The fortunes smile upon us," he said.

"Not for too long," said Bolios, "look."

Elmahigh turned and saw both stone giants working successfully on extinguishing the flames of the camp.

"When they put the last tent out, they'll surely return to their post," said Malchomite.

"Then we mustn't be here," said Elmahigh.

Isilmoire appeared and exited the pit. Bolios stuck his head into the pit between the opening and said, "Quickly, men, you must hurry, there's not much time. Climb three at a time if necessary."

"What if the rope doesn't hold?" said Malchomite.

"We'll overcome that challenge if it arises," replied Bolios. "For now, let's get our friends out."

Soon, two more reached the top of the pit as Prince Adinor and Lautner exited. Next were Teinmar and Ecclesias.

The stone giants only had one more burning tent to put out. They both converged on it. They raised the trees in their hands and began smothering the fire.

Theodonus stepped out of the pit, followed behind by Friedrich and Marcus who also reached the rest of their friends, leaving only Dolamite.

"Hurry, Dolamite," said Prince Adinor.

Deep down below in the bowels of the dark pit, Dolamite could not get more than a few feet high. His weight was too much for his arms to bear. They continued shaking from the fatigue, and his hands were burning from the rope, he couldn't do it.

Elmahigh looked back toward the campsite and saw just how close the stone giant duo was to putting out the remaining fire. The giants swatted at the small patch of fire as the large flame weakened, it would soon be out.

"There's no time," said Elmahigh.

Bolios ran toward the pit, sticking his hand just under the propped wooden door, lifting the entire door, and throwing it open. He yelled down to Dolamite.

"Where are you?" he said.

"I'm still at the bottom, sire," replied Dolamite. "I can't make it."

"Nonsense, you will climb that rope at once," said Bolios.

"I'm too heavy for my own good, my lord," said Dolamite. "I can't make the climb."

Isilmoire poked Bolios and gestured toward the camp. The stone giants extinguished the remaining fire. They threw down both trees and began walking back toward the pit. They were heading straight for the Mastadans and Nymphs.

"Here they come," said Isilmoire.

Bolios returned to the pit and yelled again to Dolamite, Tie the rope around your waist."

"What, are you mad?" said Ecclesias. "He weighs a ton, let's go!"

"We will not leave him," said Prince Adinor. "What if it were you? Wouldn't you want us to help?"

"Quiet," said Bolios. "All of you come here at once."

The men huddled together, awaiting Bolios' command.

"Everyone grab some of the rope, we're getting our friend out," said Bolios. "I've lost two of my warriors, I will not lose another."

The men all assumed a position as Bolios again yelled down toward Dolamite, "Are you ready?"

"Yes, sire," Dolamite replied.

"All right, men," said Bolios, "pull."

Both Nymphs and Mastadans alike pulled as hard as possible. They all strained as the rope burned their hands instantly.

"That's it, men, again pull."

"It's working," shouted Dolamite from within the pit.

"Pull now, men, faster," said Bolios, "put your backs into it."

Elmahigh looked toward the camp as the stone giants approached.

"I'm nearly there," said Dolamite, "just a bit further."

"Keep going, men," said Bolios.

"Bolios!" said Isilmoire.

"I know. They're nearly here."

The warriors continued to work; everyone tugged at the rope with what little strength remained, and with one last pull, they succeeded. Dolamite reached his hands up from the pit, gripping Bolios' hands, and climbed out safely.

"Thank you all," he said

"No time for pleasantries, Dolamite," said Elmahigh, "run."

"Elmahigh, you lead them and I'll follow from behind," said Bolios.

"We all stay together," said Prince Adinor.

"We will. I'll be just behind you all," said Bolios. "Go on, my Prince."

Elmahigh ran toward a large group of boulders far from the pit, leaving the camp and their prison behind. All the Nymphs and Mastadans followed. Bolios stayed behind to close the pit and sneak away. He ran toward the others as the sun began to creep into the night, burning up the fog. Bolios reached the group and looked back toward the pit. The stone giants stood outside the wooden entrance as though nothing happened. Some of the Mastadans were collapsed on the ground. Still others were bent over. Everyone struggled for breath as their lungs burned from lack of air following the run. Bolios walked among them and was met by Isilmoire and Elmahigh.

"Why did we leave the camp?" asked Isilmoire. "The enemy was there for us to defeat."

"I wouldn't argue the stone giants mean to do us harm, but there's more to their circumstance," replied Elmahigh.

"I'm sure there is," replied Bolios, "there is always more to your view on things, Elmahigh. However, a more pressing concern vexes me."

"What, Bolios?" asked Isilmoire.

"The voice of our captor," replied Bolios.

"I'm confident you will hear it once more, my friend," replied Elmahigh.

"I intend to, for on the next occasion I do," he said, "it will be to crack the neck from which it originates."

"I saw them," said Malchomite.

"What did you say?" asked Bolios.

"Before climbing out of the pit, I saw them."

"What did you see?" asked Isilmoire.

"I can't describe it," replied Malchomite. "It was dark…I was afraid."

"I understand, Malchomite," replied Bolios. "I need you to try, it's important."

Malchomite remained on the ground, struggling for breath as everyone looked toward him.

"They're not human," he said.

"Are they Nymphs?" asked Isilmoire.

"No, they're not Nymphs either, my lady," said Malchomite, "they're something else, something I've never seen. They have skin of green color stained and deformed. Their feet were large and uncovered. They seemed diseased."

"Well, that's no Nymph," said Isilmoire, "but it sounds much like the corpse my soldiers revealed to you, Bolios."

"Yes, it sounds very much alike," replied Bolios.

"They were monsters vile things," said Malchomite.

"It makes no difference," said Bolios, "now we've found them."

"Our capture was a blessing in disguise," said Elmahigh.

"There's more…" said Malchomite.

Ecclesias and Prince Adinor sat up, as did the others.

"Go on," said Bolios.

"They were marching," said Malchomite. "They donned metal armor and carried swords, axes, and bows. They numbered a few dozen, no less than forty for sure."

"It was a war party," said Isilmoire.

"What direction were they heading to?" asked Bolios.

Malcomite pointed east.

"That is where we must go," said Bolios.

"We still do not know if the source of all this madness travels with them," said Isilmoire. "What if the key to ending this lies elsewhere? Perhaps it's best to split the group: one can follow the monsters and uncover their plot while the other can continue on deeper into these wastelands."

"Continue on to where and to what end?" replied Bolios.

Isilmoire stepped closer to Bolios, looking at the Mastadan soldiers. All remained weary and helpless from the escape and lack of rest.

"Your forces are few and they are weak," said Isilmoire. "Perhaps it's best I take Lautner and Teinmar and pursue another course toward what I believe to be the center of all this."

"Isilmoire, if it's the source you seek, I do as well," said Bolios. "If that source was the Witch, then I want to kill her more than you do. Splitting our forces will not help either of us accomplish that."

"Bolios is right, Isilmoire," said Elmahigh, "a war party of monsters possessing strength, arms, and armor marches toward most certain additional carnage brought upon innocent lives. Those lives could be Nymph or Mastadan alike. It would be unwise, my friend, to divide our forces. If the monsters number in the dozens, we'll need every single warrior to defeat them. Perhaps in doing so, we can learn of who is behind all of this."

"Perhaps the person responsible, the Witch, travels with them," replied Bolios.

"We could dispatch her and all of them together," said Elmahigh.

Isilmoire paused and looked toward Teinmar and Lautner; both awaited her decision.

"Very well, we continue on together," replied Isilmoire.

"I'm hungry," said Dolamite, "we should eat."

"We'll forage, Dolamite," replied Bolios, "we have a war party to hunt. Pick berries or fruits along the way. Men, our pace will be swift, we have much ground to cover. Free yourselves of anything that may hinder your speed, anything heavy. I will set the pace, and Isilmoire will be last. Make sure no one gets lost. Prince Adinor, stay close to me. Let's move."

CHAPTER 21

They traveled nearly all night. After resting for only a couple hours, they resumed their pursuit.

Bolios stopped and gazed upon the gravel and pebbles beneath him. He rested on one knee and reached his hand down to the ground. He ran his fingers gently on the dark pebbles and grabbed a few into his palm. Starring at them for a few moments, he brought them close to his nose and smelled them, then released them. He moved to a different area and did the same.

The rest of the group arrived and stopped behind him. Some looked around for food. Prince Adinor walked toward Elmahigh as they both stared at Bolios.

"What's he doing?" asked the Prince.

"He's trying to find a clue," replied Elmahigh, "anything indicating signs of the war party's travels. He's looking for a direction to go."

Isilmoire and Lautner began to speak in Nymph, and quickly, Teinmar nodded and ran towards Bolios' position. He moved from one side of Bolios to the other, taking quick glances at the ground and then back up toward the various paths ahead. He walked away from Bolios who remained crouched on the ground and examined a pile of rubble just a few paces away.

Bolios rose to his feet and walked forward. He looked back toward the soldiers and then forward to the void ahead. Prince Adinor and Elmahigh stood together with Isilmoire and awaited his findings.

"Farther east," Bolios said, "they travel east just ahead of us. They are moving fast."

Teinmar looked over to Lautner and Isilmoire. Isilmoire said something in Nymph. Teinmar nodded.

"He agrees," said Isilmoire, "we can catch them soon. We should keep going, there's no time to waste."

The Mastadans couldn't stand. Malchomite and Ecclesias rolled to their sides and dug both feet into the ground, attempting to stand, but collapsed back down to the ground. Dolamite lay on his back and others rested on one knee.

"We can't go on, Bolios, not at this pace," said Ecclesias.

"The men are weary," said Theodonus.

"This is madness," said Dolamite.

"Madness?" replied Bolios. "Madness, you say? Madness is the wretched devils that would have you confined to the barren nothingness of that pit. Madness is the monsters disregarding our king and our land's laws. Madness is the evil capable of turning good men evil."

Bolios walked back toward them, kicking Dolamite and Malchomite and lifting Ecclesias and Marcus to their feet. Prince Adinor began toward Bolios, but was stopped by Elmahigh. He grabbed the Prince's arm, looked at him and said, "No."

Bolios reached for his sword, removed it from its sleeve, and drove it down into the dirt ground. The remaining Mastadans not yet on their feet rose and stood in attention.

"Hear my words all of you. There may come a day we cannot claim victory. Perhaps that day may result in our death. If that is so, let anyone bearing witness to that moment champion our memories forever. Failing to answer to such a challenge is something I am incapable of doing. Each of you I call my brother and it is for special reason.

Throughout our various trials, you have each proven worthy of donning the Mastadan shield upon your chest. That crest you wear carries history. Actions of men just like you rose to meet the challenges that would be the downfall of our kingdom. Just as those before us championed that crest courageously, I ask you once again, follow me, one last time. Answer the call that no one else can."

Prince Adinor glanced at the Mastadan soldiers. The air felt thick from the heat. Sweat covered them from head to toe. The white and grey rocks below them reflected the rays of the sun back up toward them, blinding them. Then Prince Adinor took a step forward, slow at first. His legs weighed a ton. His gaze rose toward Bolios as he said, "I will follow you."

Bolios lowered his head, bowing to the Prince.

"I will follow you," said Theodonus.

"And I," said Friedrich who rose.

"I," said Ecclesias.

"I," said Malchomite.

"And I," said Dolamite, struggling to his feet.

"And I," said Marcus.

Bolios then walked over to Elmahigh, who remained silent. The priest's head remained resting upon the top of his staff. His hand gripped the handle of his sword.

"And you, ole friend?" asked Bolios. "Will you fight alongside me once again?"

Bolios extended his arm and awaited an answer.

"My friend, why must you ask questions to which you already know the answer," replied Elmahigh.

The two shook hands.

"Thank you," said Bolios.

"Perhaps it's best we have Teinmar lead as his gifts of tracking are special," said Elmahigh.

"Ironically enough, I agree," said Bolios, "but perhaps in a way you do not imagine."

"I'm curious," said Elmahigh.

"Isilmoire, can you bring Teinmar?" said Bolios.

Isilmoire came with Teinmar as they formed a circle together. The Mastadans and Lautner looked on as the group talked.

"What is it?" replied Isilmoire, "name it and we will do our best."

"Go on, Bolios," said Elmahigh.

"We must divide our forces," said Bolios.

"So you are beginning to listen to wiser beings," said Isilmoire.

Elmahigh smiled and turned to Bolios as he did the same.

"I do believe we need to divide our forces as you mentioned but not to the end you seek, Isilmoire," said Bolios.

"Then if not for pursuit of the root of this evil, then what?" asked Isilmoire.

"Please translate this to Teinmar and you will soon understand," said Bolios.

Bolios spoke to Teinmar as Isilmoire translated the plan. All of the other soldiers paced back and forth, clenching their weapons and awaiting orders. The small huddle of Bolios, Elmahigh, Isilmoire, and Teinmar broke. Isilmoire took one look at the awaiting soldiers, pointing toward Ecclesias and Malchomite as well as Theodonus.

"Very well," said Bolios. "Ecclesias, Malchomite, and Theodonus, you are to go with Isilmoire. The rest of you stay here with me."

Isilmoire's group ran away toward the rocky path, leading to the war party and soon disappeared from sight.

"Where are they going?" asked Prince Adinor.

"We will see them once again," replied Bolios. "For now, there are more pressing things that concern us. Gather around all of you."

Elmahigh, Prince Adinor, Lautner, Friedrich, Marcus, and Dolamite did as told. The sun was directly overhead, and it beat down on the back of their necks; beads of sweat fell from their brows.

"Considering the distance we've traveled from the camp and the direction the enemy's tracks are headed, the war party will have to pass through here on their return back to their provisions and safety. From Malchomite's estimates, we're considerably outnumbered. As such, we'll have to set a trap for them to tilt the disadvantage in our favor. We will continue a little further, find suitable high ground, and begin preparing," said Bolios.

"What are we preparing for?" asked Prince Adinor.

"We have one last stand to make and that is where it will be," said Bolios, "our friends will travel ahead and get behind the monsters' position, flanking them. They will surprise the monsters and meet us in the middle."

Bolios led the men in search of a suitable position. The path they now walked was far too exposed. The wastelands were barren. It was dry, flat, and void of life. Not one tree or bush anywhere nearby. Only dry rock below their feet. They continued forward toward something in the distance.

"Bolios, up ahead," said Elmahigh, "could it be the Petruchani Forest once again?"

"If it is, we'll surely find something better suited there," replied Bolios, "come on."

They jumped from one large rock to another, grinding small loose pebbles beneath their boots. The group continued forward, seeing once again the Petruchani Forest. Ahead was a narrow opening; cut vines and trees signaled something or someone had been through.

"They entered here," said Bolios.

Bolios drew his sword and walked inside. All around were large trees and low-hanging vines. On the ground was thick grass and black dirt. Bolios looked in all directions as he moved deeper inside. He bent down and analyzed the dirt and mud below, touching what seemed to be divots within the ground.

"They marched upon these grounds and continued even further east," said Bolios. "They move leaving much of what they encounter undisturbed. They are clever things."

"Bolios," said Elmahigh, "look ahead."

There on the horizon was a large plume of smoke directly in front of them.

"Let's go," said Bolios.

The men ran, retracing the path of the monsters.

"Bolios," said Prince Adinor in between breaths.

"Yes, my Prince," he replied.

"These markings on the ground are of the monsters, right?"

"Yes, that's right," said Bolios.

The Prince looked down. His fear grew. As he ran toward the hill alongside Bolios, he was alarmed. The footprints on the ground revealed the size of the monsters. They more than doubled the Prince's steps and even dwarfed Bolios'.

They arrived at the hill. Bolios began analyzing everything. Prince Adinor found Elmahigh and stood next to him, observing Bolios from a distance.

"Elmahigh," said the Prince, "did you see the size of the monster feet?"

Elmahigh rested one hand upon his staff and looked down toward the ground. His eyes moved from left to right as he searched. He walked towards a tree, looking for a useful herb or plant.

The Prince followed.

"This concerns you?" asked Elmahigh.

Prince Adinor placed his foot inside the footprint of the enemy they would soon battle and looked toward Elmahigh.

"Shouldn't it concern us all?" asked the Prince.

Elmahigh paused as Bolios began climbing a tree high above the hill. The Prince walked closer to Elmahigh who began to outline the monster footprint with his staff.

"Well, Elmahigh, don't you agree that it should concern us?" asked Prince Adinor.

Elmahigh turned toward the Prince. He bent down toward him and said, "Death comes to us all in time, my Prince. The moments it does are not convenient. Consequently, it is never convenient for those we leave behind. Often times, they are stricken with sorrow, anguish, and pain. But those that leave have no more pain. In truth, the spirit of a person lives on in everyone remaining here for they take pieces of the person inside their own hearts and their own minds."

"I don't think I'm ready to die," said Prince Adinor.

"No one is, my Prince," replied Elmahigh, "all the more reason to make certain we do everything necessary to prolong that for many more days. If today should be the day we are called to give our lives, we go together fighting side by side."

Prince Adinor looked down toward the footprint once more. His chest tightened as the sweat dribbled down his neck. His throat began to close and his mouth dried. The large footprint below him became blurred in his vision, as both his eyes shut as he fought back the tears welling up inside. One large tear formed in the corner of his eyes, dropping down into the monster footprint below. Elmahigh walked closer to the Prince.

"Is dying difficult Elmahigh?"

"It's all in the hands of something greater than anyone of us can conceive of," replied Elmahigh, "there is nothing to fear."

Bolios walked over to the two of them and said, "There's much to do and little time to do it."

"Very well," said Elmahigh, "what do you need of us?"

Prince Adinor walked back toward Lautner, Dolamite, and the others. Elmahigh and Bolios remained behind.

"Is something wrong with the Prince?" asked Bolios.

"No, nothing at all," replied Elmahigh, who looked on as the Prince walked away and then asked, "Do you remember your first battle?"

Bolios stared at his tattered hands filled with cuts, blood, dirt, and bruises.

"It's not something you ever forget," he said.

"It will be his first battle," said Elmahigh.

"It was bound to happen one day," replied Bolios, "come, there's much to do."

They both walked toward the rest of the warriors who were consuming some fruits from a small nearby tree. The men stood stopped eating as Bolios approached. He took out his sword and drew two lines in the dirt below and placed an *x* on top of them, one across from the other. The men continued staring at the image on the ground, sampling the fruit while they had the time. Bolios continued drawing and added a pair of circles toward the lower portion of lines.

"This fight will not be the all-out conflicts we've been accustomed to," he said.

"So not like the time we fought the fire breathers near the farmlands in the south?" asked Dolamite.

"No," replied Bolios, "my intention is to deceive these monsters, confusing them as much as possible throughout the engagement. If this plan works, they will think of us greater in numbers than we possess. Perhaps if we're lucky, they'll scatter, dividing themselves."

"What's the plan?" asked Lautner.

"Yes, please tell us. Bolios," said Friedrich, "I'm looking forward to crushing these bastards."

"As you can see, what's represented in the drawing below is the hill we currently find ourselves on. The path below us widens as the hill goes down. The monsters will be marching toward us, giving us higher ground. We'll place two bowmen in the trees above. They will rain down arrows on the approaching monsters from a distance. We will have one on each side of the path.

"You can have my bow in one of those positions, Bolios," said Marcus.

"I was counting on it, Marcus," replied Bolios, "thank you. On the other side will be Friedrich."

"It will be done, sire," replied Friedrich.

"Rain down as many arrow as possible, forcing them to charge up the hill. If necessary, launch the arrows to the rear of the monster group, killing those to the back first, leaving going up the hill the only option."

"What if they're out of range?" asked Marcus.

"Wait to fire your first arrow until the last line of monsters is within range," said Bolios.

"What if the monsters attack us?" asked Marcus.

"That is where Lautner, Dolamite, and myself will come into the plan," said Bolios.

"I was beginning to worry that you forgot about me," said Dolamite, "wouldn't want all of you to have all the fun."

"It's up to us to keep the short-range combat on the ground," said Bolios, "we cannot allow any of the monsters climb to Marcus' or Friedrich's positions."

"That's a solid plan, Bolios," said Lautner, "what of Isilmoire and the others?"

"With some luck, they'll arrive to support the ground fighting, making sure to take out as many as possible from behind."

"What is this mark you've left here between the circles and X's?" asked Lautner.

"We'll need something special from Elmahigh," replied Bolios.

"I'll not dissapoint," replied Elmahigh.

"Everyone, find your places," said Bolios, "there's not much time. It's likely to be a long night. Try and get some rest until then."

Each of the soldiers parted for their respective places. Bolios remained behind, as did Prince Adinor and Elmahigh.

"You didn't assign anything to me," said Prince Adinor.

Elmahigh walked over to the Prince and placed a hand upon his shoulder, patting him repeatedly.

"I did not, my Prince," replied Bolios, "for good reason."

"You can't take away my chance to fight," replied Prince Adinor.

"My Prince, I can't risk losing our kingdom's sole heir to the throne. You have come this far. You exceeded my expectation. The outcome of what will happen here, I am uncertain of. For that reason, I need you to go back to the City Center and convince your father to send the entire legions. If we fail here, the evil will continue spreading and only your father's full force could stand between our kingdom's destruction.

Prince Adinor's head hung as he continued to listen. "Bolios, I did fine against the harvingers," he replied.

"He did, Bolios," said Elmahigh.

Bolios kicked some dirt on the drawing he made. He did not answer either Elmahigh or the Prince.

"I can help," said Prince Adinor.

Bolios stopped and said, "Not this time."

Elmahigh walked toward Bolios and said, "Perhaps he…"

"No," said Bolios, "the boy is too young to die here. There's far too many things for you to see, too much you haven't done. You haven't loved a woman. You have no children. Your responsibility to this kingdom and to all of us is to ensure our kingdom's stability with your lineage. How can you do that if you're dead?"

"My father will," said Prince Adinor.

"And if he were here, it would be better. I'd gladly have him over you," said Bolios.

"You go too far," said Elmahigh.

"We don't need him," replied Bolios. "One day when he's old and seated on the throne of Mastada with his children and theirs gathered around him, he'll thank me. He'll know those joys would not be possible unless he stayed away from this."

The Prince listened. Perhaps Bolios was right. He was royalty, the son of the king. He was tired and hungry. The Prince looked down at the dirt below his face; all of the memories of overcoming adversity with the soldiers as well as memories of safety and comfort with his family came to him. As the emotions of it all hit, he began to cry. He tried and failed to stop the tears from flowing, making breathing all the more difficult. He gathered what little strength he had and stood between Bolios and Elmahigh. The pain from the blow to his confidence and ego was too much. He decided, out of respect, it would be best to follow the orders of the best warrior of the company, but was torn. He looked toward Elmahigh and asked, "Which direction do I take to return home?"

Elmahigh patted the Prince on his head and pointed toward the southeast direction.

"If you head along the south with a slight eastern inclination," he said, "I believe you'll reach the other side of the forest. Stay far enough south of the road to avoid a direct engagement with the monsters. Keeping the road to your left as a reference. Eat what you can along the way, travel only during the day and rest at night. In three days, you should be out of the forest."

"Thank you," said Prince Adinor.

Bolios reached for something on the left side of his body. He unfastened it and handed it to the Prince.

"If the opportunity presents itself, you may find this useful," said Bolios.

Prince Adinor grabbed a small dagger Bolios carried. It had a silver handle with a black grip. On the handle were distinct marking, two small letters engraved on the bottom. The letters were made of pure gold. They read R and F.

"Your father gave me this dagger long ago on a hunt in the south lands. We prepared meat for our return home. Most of our party left to find wood for our fire when a large pack of wolves attacked us. Their teeth were the size of your fingers. I guess the smell of fresh meat attracted them. I was unarmed. Desperate, I jumped in front of your father and grabbed a log from the fire, waving it in front of the wolves. They approached and threatened to attack us both. One launched itself at me, but I successfully burned it with the firewood. The pack left and your father gave me this as a reward for my victory. It served as a reminder to never be unarmed."

Bolios closed Prince Adinor's hand upon the dagger.

"It's better that it remain in your family. When you see him, be sure to give him a message for me," said Bolios.

Prince Adinor looked at the dagger and listened.

"Tell your father I've won him another battle."

Prince Adinor began walking away from Elmahigh and Bolios and followed the instructions to remain on a southeastern direction. As he walked away, he secured the gift from Bolios while maintaining an attentive eye on what lay ahead. The dense forest and large trees failed to yield an easy path, forcing the Prince to cut his way through. He continued walking further away from his friends, but the hurt from Bolios' words remained. He wasn't needed. The words were the only thing on his mind. Maybe Bolios was right. The Prince continued moving further into the forest. He was alone. After everything he had been through, after all the hardships and challenges, in the end he was still unfamiliar with battle. He was only days removed from his completion of the triped trials. Perhaps it was best for him to go home. He thought of his parents and the warmth and security of their protection. He contemplated the things Bolios mentioned. He was on the journey home—it was time to go back.

CHAPTER 22

Back at the hill, every soldier was in position. Everyone was ready, except Bolios and Elmahigh. They both stood atop the hill looking toward the direction in which the Prince took off to, waiting.

"The boy was ready," said Elmahigh.

"I couldn't risk finding out whether or not that's true," said Bolios, "none of us can."

"That's not for us to decide," said Elmahigh.

"I just did," replied Bolios, "besides, Elmahigh, I've seen too many young men die in war. Boys, younger than even him, leave their parents childless. If I can spare one for all the others I couldn't then I will."

"Perhaps," replied Elmahigh, "was it necessary to wound him as you did?"

"I'm sure he'll live," replied Bolios.

"My concern is not the boy's body but rather his spirit," said Elmahigh.

"He wouldn't listen," replied Bolios, "if making him hate me saves his life then it's something I'd do again."

Bolios walked toward the highest point in the hill to check the preparedness of the rest of the soldiers. Elmahigh turned toward the bottom and then back toward the direction in which Prince Adinor walked. He saw only large green ferns, round tall trees, and big bushes covering the expanse. As he looked out into the dense forest, he bowed his head and reflected on the Prince and his journey home. He began to pray.

"It's in your hands," said Elmahigh aloud.

Then Elmahigh stood on the hill. He moved his staff from one hand to the other when he became distracted by something. A large group of birds flew out of a tree down at the bottom of the hill. There were hundreds of them blanketing the sky in darkness as they rose high above. They moved directly overhead heading west toward the monster camp. A distinct sound in the distance began.

Elmahigh walked toward the noise; it seemed to come from down the hill, forty feet away. Gradually, the noise swelled with each additional step he took toward it. Then there was banging and rattling. Small pebbles and loose dirt shook on the ground. He bent down to look closer and confirmed his suspicion as the vibrations upon the ground was even more noticeable. He placed both hands flat on the red dirt road and the reverberation crawled up his hand through his arm and the rest of his body. There was a large roar and then a yell in the distance beyond the tree from where the birds flew. The monsters had arrived. Elmahigh ran back up the hill, reaching the base of the trees where Friedrich and Marcus remained hidden overhead.

"Our enemy marches toward us," said Elmahigh.

Bolios came out from a bush nearby.

"Let them come," said Bolios.

"I'll assume my position and await the time to strike," said Elmahigh. "I'll be near the halfway point of the hill, just behind the bushes on the left."

"Very well," replied Bolios.

Elmahigh ran back down and hid behind a few large bushes. He crouched down underneath the thousands of leafs covering him and looked down the dirt path in anticipation for the monsters' arrival.

The rest of the soldiers sat quietly in their places as well. They listened for the monsters and looked out into the dirt road. Bolios stood, but saw nothing except empty dirt road.

Then there were noises. The sound similar to swine in search of food filled the air. The noise grew louder. Then there were high-pitched growls frequent in occurrence. The loud noises included pounding lances and axes upon the dirt road. The heavy armor of the monsters and the monsters' weight rattled the ground. As they all moved closer to the hill, the noises continued to grow louder.

For the first time, Bolios saw what Malchomite had described. The monsters were foul beings possessing distorted facial features far different than anything he had seen. Eyes spread wider than any man. Their skin green and blue in color covered in dark patches of black. They were large, bigger than Bolios himself. For the few that had hair, it was merely a couple of strands of dry straight black if anything at all. They all were barefoot, revealing large ugly feet.

Elmahigh stood to see the approaching monsters. As they moved closer, Elmahigh looked toward the rear of the marching pack and for the first time saw Mastadan villagers.

Held captive by tied ropes binding their hands and linking one with the other, they walked behind the monsters powerless against them. They were a dozen in total.

"Oh no," said Elmahigh.

Elmahigh wasted no time rising up from his position and ran toward Bolios. He jumped over the dense bushes and ran around the trees heading uphill.

"What are you doing here?" asked Bolios. "You're supposed to remain in your position."

"We have a problem," replied Elmahigh

"What is it?"

"The monsters have prisoners," replied Elmahigh. "I saw with my own eyes. Innocent Mastadans have been captured and travel behind the monsters. We cannot attack. Doing so would put them at risk. The folly of arrows by Friedrich and Marcus would likely strike some of them."

"How many Mastadans in total?" asked Bolios.

"I counted twelve," replied Elmahigh. "We'll have to free them before we attack."

"Yes, we must," said Bolios, "but how?"

"Leave that to me," he said, "be sure not to send a single arrow until you receive my signal."

Elmahigh left Bolios and began down the hill through the trees and bushes along the path.

"How will I know it's time to attack?" asked Bolios.

There was no answer. Elmahigh was gone. Bolios then ran across the dirt road to Dolamite and Lautner.

"What's wrong?" asked Lautner.

"They have captives," said Bolios, "some of our own people."

"These monsters are really on my last nerve," said Dolamite.

"I couldn't agree more," said Bolios, "warn Marcus to await my command."

Bolios left and ran back across to his original position and yelled up toward Friedrich, who remained high up above in the trees.

"Friedrich!"

"Yes, sire," replied Friedrich.

"Do not fire your arrows. The circumstances have changed," said Bolios. "We must wait for a sign from Elmahigh. I will give the command."

"I understand, my lord," replied Friedrich. "Bolios?"

"Yes, Friedrich, what is it?"

"The monsters are within sight."

Elmahigh was at the bottom of the hill, hiding behind two large trees. He looked out toward the monsters. He observed the first line of them passing him as they were within reach of him. He turned away and threw himself down on the ground below. Covered in the black and red dirt, he crawled along the dirt path far enough from the monsters to avoid detection. The ground continued to shake as the numerous monsters marched toward the hill. Their close proximity left Elmahigh struggling to breathe; the foul monster odor was suffocating him. They smelled worse than dead rotting animals. Elmahigh continued moving toward the rear of the monster troop. He was fixated on how best to free the innocent Mastadans. The monster feet pounding upon the red dirt below sent small billows of dust swirling near the ground.

"That's it," said Elmahigh.

He rolled over a few times, away from the dirt path, and rose to his feet. Racing toward the rear of the herd, he looked for the sole monster leading the Mastadan and stopped alongside him. The monster held a rope connecting all the Mastadan prisoners to him. The rope also remained fastened to the monster's waist. Elmahigh followed alongside the monster group, maintaining his eyes on the single monster guarding the villagers. Up at the top of the hill, the soldiers were growing impatient.

"Bolios," said Friedrich, "the rear of the monster group is within range."

Bolios looked down and saw the first line of monsters approaching the hill. The entire pack would soon arrive, and not a single arrow was released.

"Sire, if we wait any longer, they will be upon us," said Friedrich, "it will be too late."

Bolios looked across the dirt road to Lautner who stood up waving to Bolios with both arms. Bolios did not respond. There was no sign from Elmahigh. Bolios crossed both his arms in front of his chest. He did not give the order to fire.

Elmahigh, meanwhile, was still marching alongside the monsters, following next to the one securing the villagers.

"What are we waiting for?" said Lautner.

"They are nearly upon us," said Dolamite.

The first line of monsters began ascending the hill as the second followed behind. They marched a few at a time, climbing the hill with ease.

Dolamite looked down toward the bottom of the hill. The first two lines of monsters were upon it. Then a third row of monsters began the climb. They were approaching and still no sign from Elmahigh.

Friedrich took an arrow and placed it upon his bow, aiming toward the first line of monsters. At the sight of that, Marcus, seated across from him atop a different tree, on the other side of the road did the same. They pulled back on their bows, holding the arrows upon the tension of their strings. They aimed at the monster's necks.

The monsters continued marching up toward them, unaware of any threat. The groans and moans from them grew louder. As they came closer, the features of their hideous faces became more apparent; it was disturbing. Five rows of monsters, nearly fifty in all, were now on the hill. Elmahigh could see the rows advancing, as he remained hidden alongside them staying behind the bushes and trees.

"Just a bit more," said Elmahigh.

The last row of monsters stepped onto the loose red dirt followed behind by the single monster—the keeper of the villagers and Elmahigh's target. Elmahigh watched each step of the last monster, waiting just for the exact moment to launch his plan.

"Two more steps," he said.

The monster reached forward, pulling the Mastadans behind him. He moved one foot forward, turning to hit those not cooperating and then stepped forward with his other foot.

Elmahigh ran from behind the tree, leaping over small bushes and landing upon the dirt road in front of the monster. He drew his sword from beside him and pierced the monster's chest, driving the sword directly through. The monster yelled and howled, alerting the rest of the horde. Elmahigh cut the rope holding the Mastadans as prisoners as the monsters turned him in pursuit as he said, "Run into the forest, quickly."

A few monsters ran toward Elmahigh who grabbed his staff with both hands overhead as he prepared for battle. The monsters continued at him, Elmahigh swung the staff in their direction, hitting one and forcing the others to dive backward. After stabbing the monster lying on the ground, Elmahigh buried his staff in the ground by a few inches.

Startled, the monsters stopped.

Elmahigh quickly knelt down, whispered softly into the staff, and then grabbed it, ripping it out of the ground and struck the ground with just the top as he gripped the other side with both hands. Suddenly, a great wind came under the monster's feet. Red dirt flew up from the ground in all directions as thrashing winds swirled enveloping the monsters. They were blinded. Confused, the monsters howled and screamed. The thick cloud of dust swallowed them. Elmahigh ran toward the forest in search of all the fleeing Mastadans. Bolios and the others still atop the hill looked down, seeing the large cloud of red envelop the monsters in the back of the marching herd.

"What is that?" asked Friedrich.

"It's our sign," said Bolios, "attack!"

Friedrich began his assault, sending arrows into the red cloud of dust swirling around the monsters. Marcus joined as well, launching arrows from his position.

The arrows whistled in the air, knifing through the cloud, landing upon their targets. The first monster fell followed by another. The bevy of arrows decimated the monsters. Those not enveloped in the dirt cloud moved away from it and ran wildly in every direction confused.

The largest of the monsters, one more hideous than the rest, groaned at them all. Its massive curled horns were a striking uniqueness. He organized them into rows once more and began to yell at those still fumbling about.

"March forward uphill," it yelled.

The monsters ran up toward Bolios and the others atop the hill. The monsters picked up speed and were in an all-out assault. They were coming for the bowmen atop the trees.

"Now," said Bolios.

Lautner and Dolamite sprang from their hiding places, meeting Bolios in the center of the road. The monsters came straight at them. One carried an ax, the other a ball and chain. They both attacked Lautner who avoided the swinging ball from the one monster with a roll onto the ground. He rose to his feet, swinging his sword at the other monster. Having no time to react, the monster was dispatched quickly. Lautner turned to the remaining monster. It launched the heavy iron ball toward him once more. Lautner parried it away, allowing the heavy ball to glance off his sword, thereby giving him the opportunity to land a kill strike. Lautner did and another monster fell.

Dolamite picked up the ball and chain and swung it overhead; faster and faster with every turn of his wrist, it picked up speed. A monster ran toward him holding a sword. Dolamite continued to swing the ball and chain as the monster approached and then released it, sending it toward the monster killing it instantly. The body crashed to the floor, tripping another monster following closely behind allowing Dolamite to finish him as well.

Bolios reached down and grabbed a monster he had just defeated with both hands clenching it in his grip and, in one motion, lifted the beast overhead. Three monsters ran directly at him, each carrying a sword aimed right at his chest. Bolios took one step forward and launched the dead monster toward the three approaching, sending them all rolling back down the hill. He drew his sword once again, gripping it tight, all his muscles flexed as he raised the large sword overhead. A pair of monsters approached. Bolios ran then jumped, spun in mid-air, and sliced both monsters down in one action. The three stood atop the hill waiting for more monsters to approach. Several more did, meeting the same result. Marcus and Friedrich up above continued launching arrows and killed a dozen.

"Keep sending more of these wretched creatures to their demise," said Bolios.

Lautner and Dolamite smiled and awaited the next assault from the remaining monsters. There was none. Instead, they gathered together. They held their shields overhead and hid in the bushes and trees near the dirt road. They quieted and hid into the dense forest, becoming invisible.

"Why don't they attack?" asked Dolamite.

"They've had too much already," said Lautner.

They both laughed.

"Be ready, they will come again soon," said Bolios.

The men and Nymph found cover and maintained a watchful eye on the monsters. They tried watch on the monsters, who remained hidden under the thick forest below. Only the occasional shaking of a bush or sway of a tree proved their presence.

Down the hill, deep in the forest, crowded all together were the Mastadan villagers. Some cried, others sat silent. Elmahigh finally reached them as he now tried comforting them.

"My name is Elmahigh," he said, "I am here to help."

None of the Mastadans spoke. They were simple people, farmers and tradesman, far removed from war. They continued shaking. Their eyes were upon Elmahigh, but there was an empty malaise about them. As though they lost the capacity to comprehend. They were numb.

"It's going to be all right now," said Elmahigh.

He was quick to grab a small flower nearby. It was blue in the middle and had bright green petals with spots of yellow. He sprinkled some dust from inside his pocket on top of it, and in moments, the flower began to double in size. Its petals turned completely yellow and its blue center became brighter. It was now three times its original size and beautiful. He handed it to the youngest of the group, a boy of school age.

"Th-th-thank you," the boy said.

"Thank you very much," said the boy's father.

"You're welcome," said Elmahigh, "what's your name, young squire?"

"My na-name is Du-Du-Duncan," the boy replied.

"And I'm Thomas," said the man.

"Thomas, I can't begin to understand how difficult things have been for you and your son," replied Elmahigh, "but if you want to keep your son safe and away from those diabolical creatures, I am going to need your help."

Thomas was still shaking. He looked toward his son, embraced him, and cried once more.

"Duncan, I need you to lead these people to the large beskat tree over there," said Elmahigh. "Do you see it?"

"There," replied Duncan, "the one with the large roots at the bottom?"

"Yes, that's the right one, Duncan," replied Elmahigh. "Lead the others there and be sure to leave no one behind. Once you arrive, dig as fast as you can and hide yourselves below it. The tree is large, its roots will provide ample room for you all beneath it. You stay there and wait for my return."

Thomas stared back at Elmahigh blankly.

"Your son needs you, Thomas," said Elmahigh.

There was a short pause, Thomas didn't respond.

"Okay, I will," he said finally.

Then, there was noise nearby. A branch cracked.

"Get down everyone," said Elmahigh.

Then another snap as yet another branch cracked beneath the footstep of something. There was movement from a bush behind the Mastadan villagers. They all huddled together. They were surrounded. Elmahigh removed his sword and held his staff in front, keeping himself between the approaching noises and the villagers. There was an additional noise, this time clearly footsteps. The pounding upon the dirt ground was growing louder.

Elmahigh turned toward it, seemingly closer than the others. The bushes nearest to the sound of footsteps shook. The bushes behind the Mastadans also moved. Elmahigh raised his sword in preparation to strike down whatever came through. The steps quickened as the assailant approached full speed. Suddenly, something dove through wall of bushes in front of Elmahigh, revealing the identity of the attacker. It was Isilmoire.

Chapter 23

"Come out," she said.

Malchomite, Theodonus, and Teinmar appeared from behind the bushes behind.

"It's good to see you, Isilmoire," said Elmahigh, "and not a moment later."

"We've been following the monsters for some time now," said Isilmoire.

"Were there many casualties in the village?" asked Elmahigh.

"I don't know," said Isilmoire, "we only encountered them after their attack once they re-entered the forest. These villagers you've just released were all we saw them transport."

"It's a comfort to know none of those captured have been killed along the way," replied Elmahigh.

"Now that you've succeeded in freeing them, we can finish this," said Isilmoire.

"Where are Bolios and the others?" asked Theodonus.

"They wait for us atop the hill where we must now go," said Elmahigh.

"The monsters are still unaware of our presence, Elmahigh," said Isilmoire. "We could still use this to our advantage."

"Yes, a most opportune situation," said Elmahigh. "I will return to Bolios and inform him of your arrival. As we draw the entire monster force out, your group can attack from the rear."

"I will leave now and position ourselves behind them," said Isilmoire.

"Excellent," replied Elmahigh, "did you encounter any monsters in this area?"

"No, it's clear of any fighting," replied Isilmoire.

"Very good," said Elmahigh.

The Mastadan villagers ran toward the beskat tree, but not before Duncan hugged Elmahigh and followed the others.

Thomas turned to Elmahigh and said, "Thank you, my lord."

"Stay hidden under the tree as I have instructed you," said Elmahigh. "We will return and provide you safe passage home."

"Good be with you," replied Thomas.

Elmahigh ran through the dense forest, heading straight toward the hill. He jumped across bushes and fallen trees. He ran through the opening where the villagers had escaped from and was on the dirt road again. It was quiet. The body of the killed monsters lay still upon the ground. Up at the top of the hill, Bolios and the others stood below the trees underneath Friedrich and Marcus.

"Bolios, can you see anything?" asked Dolamite.

"There's some movement just south of the road," he replied. "I see branches moving, but they cover the monsters.

"Why do they wait?" asked Lautner.

"They are clever," replied Bolios.

"I have only two arrows remaining, Bolios," said Friedrich from up above in the tree.

"Stay in position," said Bolios.

"What do I do upon sending my last?" asked Friedrich.

"I'll need you here with me," replied Bolios.

"Lautner," said Bolios.

"Yes."

"Find out from Dolamite what Marcus' inventory of arrows is?" replied Bolios.

The Nymph ran across the dirt road to the tree holding Marcus. Dolamite spoke to Lautner and gave him the news. He returned to Bolios and shared the grim news.

"He has only one," said Lautner.

"Worse than I hoped," said Bolios. "Send word. Upon exhausting the last one, he is to rejoin you and Dolamite on the ground. We'll need him to fight as well.

"Yes, I shall," replied Lautner.

"Lautner," said Bolios, "be sure to remind him to have the last arrow hit its intended target."

Lautner laughed and said something in Nymph Bolios couldn't understand.

The sun was setting.

The temperature began dropping. The air became frigid as a chill stiffened all of the soldiers. Rain began to creep in. Slow at first, just a few drops, then there were hundreds; soon the entire sky let forth a torrential down pour. Darkness of the night together with the heavy rains made seeing difficult. The water began collecting on the ground, forming puddles and mud throughout the hill. The water flowed down the bottom of the hill. The leaves and trees bounced up and down as the rains fell upon them. It was black. No stars were in view. Finding the monsters was impossible. Bolios ran toward Lautner and Dolamite and found them undeterred.

"What do we do?" asked Dolamite.

"We still have the higher ground," replied Bolios, "we wait for them to attack. We will beat them as many times as it takes until they are all wiped away."

"It's dark, Bolios, we can't see anything," said Dolamite.

"Should we move our position elsewhere?" asked Lautner.

"No, we stay here," replied Bolios.

There was movement nearby. A bush to their left began shaking, then another.

"Arm yourselves," said Bolios.

Lautner and Dolamite prepared themselves. Marcus and Friedrich took aim from the trees. Footsteps approaching were close.

"It may be a scout," said Bolios.

"Where?" asked Dolamite.

"To my left, get ready," replied Bolios.

The steps continued, with no light, nothing could be seen. The rain continued falling. Just then, a small light crept through the dense bushes. It came closer and became obvious. It was Elmahigh.

"Good of you to join us once more," said Bolios.

"My sincerest apologies, though the villagers are safe at present," replied Elmahigh.

"Were any lost in the escape?" asked Bolios.

"No, thankfully, all were spared."

"Their safety means we can once more focus all efforts on these dreadful things," said Bolios.

"I bring good tidings," replied Elmahigh. "Isilmoire has arrived. She is positioned behind the monsters and will strike when we are compromised."

"That's excellent, Elmahigh. Perhaps while we wait, we can derive a better form of defense."

As Bolios gathered his force, Isilmoire and her force moved behind the monsters. Teinmar spoke to her in Nymph. Malchomite, Theodonus, and Ecclesias grew impatient.

"Why don't we attack?" said Ecclesias. "The others will join us upon hearing all the fighting."

"We must all strike at the same time," replied Theodonus.

"Well, whatever we do, it needs to happen soon," said Malchomite.

"Mastadans," said Isilmoire.

The three approached Isilmoire from behind.

"What is it?" asked Theodonus.

"Teinmar believes something is wrong," said Isilmoire, "and I'm starting to agree with him."

"What's the problem?" asked Ecclesias.

"There's too little movement," replied Isilmoire.

* * *

Prince Adinor began to settle in for his evening of rest before resuming the journey home in the morning. He traveled away from the battle following Elmahigh's instructions. He settled under a large set of cantamor trees, known for their smooth large trunks. They were often filled with patches of moss, inviting spiders, arachnids, and other insects. These two however did not. They stood out in the forest as no other trees were like them. In fact, it was a bit odd. They bent at the top and their tops kissed one another, a rare sight. They made a perfect arch. Under their shade is where Prince Adinor rested. He lay curled up in a ball. As he slept, his dreams were filled with wild thoughts of extremes.

He dreamt of unicorns racing around the kingdom's competition center. He saw them flying about the dirt grounds as though their hooves were light as feathers; no dust flew up as they sprinted round and round the track. His dreams also included his father and mother. He dreamt of their welcoming him back with a feast unlike any he'd ever seen. The largest of game meats displayed for all to consume. The richest of colors spread throughout the table as the finest produce from all over the kingdom was brought in. There were crimson red peppers and orange sweet potatoes, and so much more. There was maltsenhop and wines and hot breads and mouth-watering sweets. He could hear the music and feel himself dancing. He also saw something else. He dreamt of a clear pond littered with flowers of a vast variety. He saw violets and blues, yellows, and oranges, whites and greens, pinks and also a figure. He walked toward it, but it moved along the pool, just far enough to stay out of sight. He found himself chasing the silhouette of what seemed like a woman, but too vague to know for sure. Whatever it was, it didn't want to be caught by him. It made him want it all the more, motivating him to run around the pond, his boot marks pounding upon the ground as he ran searching for the mysterious woman on the other side. He stopped, leaned down to grab a handful of flowers, and offered them toward the woman, now directly across from him. The woman finally turned, her face still unseen. He felt a hot wave come over him as he was filled with excitement. And yet, the woman walked farther away from him.

The Prince awoke startled.

He wiped the sleep from his eyes and sat up against the cantamor trees. He looked up and it was still night. *How long had he slept for, was his first thought.* The last thing he recalled was his argument with Bolios and his brief conversation with Elmahigh, then his departure. He reached in his waist and found some nuts he stored earlier. It was a welcome treat. He was weak, a result of no food over too long a period of time.

He looked back toward the direction he left behind and thought of his friends. He wondered of the result of the battle.

He began to walk away from the cantamor trees. As he walked, his thoughts drifted to his dreams and he paid little attention to his whereabouts or direction. He looked up, noticing a few stars visible through the heavy leaves overhead and thought of their origins. As he continued, he kicked a few loose rocks, hitting some trees, and even threw some for amusement. He stopped and looked around, hoping to orient himself. He noticed much of the same he saw earlier. He walked a few steps backward, and sure enough, there to his left were the two giant cantamor trees. He approached slowly and stood. Confused, he rubbed his head and chin. Still unsure, he walked toward the trees, and oddly enough, they were bent just as he remembered. He looked up and could see in the starlight streaming down from above, but he also noticed the two treetops kissing just as before. He bent down toward the ground and noticed a couple of nuts, just like the ones he ate moments ago.

"Well, I'll be," said Prince Adinor.

Then there were footsteps. He turned toward them, removing his sword.

"Who goes there?" he said.

There was no answer. The steps were faint. They seemed to be moving away from him. He put his sword away and ran in the direction of the steps. He ran, avoiding fallen trees, pits, or any vines he found along the way. He stopped to listen for the steps once again. Not far from him, again there, in close range behind a group of trees more steps. He raced toward them once more and closed the distance. Directly in front of him, just a few paces away, was the source of the noise.

"Stop there," said Prince Adinor, "or I'll run you through."

Suddenly, there was no movement and no sound. Prince Adinor stepped once toward the dark figure and removed his sword, pointing it at the shadow standing in front of him.

"Turn around," said Prince Adinor.

The figure turned as Prince Adinor continued approaching toward it. It was smaller than he thought. The figure was difficult to discern at first. No light from the stars came through the dense canopy of trees. Then the mystery was revealed as a woman removed the scarf from around her head.

"I'm terribly sorry, madam," said Prince Adinor.

"It's quite all right," replied the lady. "I was too afraid to say or do anything. I thought I was alone out here."

"What are you doing out here?" he asked.

Prince Adinor sheathed his sword, securing it at his side. He walked toward her, realizing her skin was smooth, her lips unblemished, her eyes and nose, all perfect. Her hair was long and flowed past her shoulders. She was older than the Prince, but only by a few years. She was not what the Prince expected.

"Well, it may be improper to say," she replied.

Prince Adinor took out his sword, but left it at his side for the moment.

"It's best you share," he said.

The lady stepped back away from him, scared by his drawn weapon.

"Have you a just reason to consider me a threat?" said the woman.

The Prince looked upon her; she seemed harmless. He thought it odd that a woman be out alone in such a remote place.

"If you do not answer," he said, "I'll be sure to cut that tongue from inside your mouth, perhaps then you'll have no reason to answer. Speak."

The Prince raised his sword toward her and looked into her eyes. They were filled with fright as though perhaps tears were soon to come forth from them.

"I am merely a Mastadan villager, my lord," she replied, "my people live not far from here just beyond those trees over your shoulder."

"That's impossible, we're not near the village," replied the Prince.

"Yes, I'll show you," replied the woman who began to walk.

"Stay there."

He walked closer. He gripped the red boar skin handle in both hands, pointing his sword at the woman's face. It was inches beneath his blade. She began to shake with fear. He looked at her hands as they gripped one another. He noticed her skin, soft and delicate. She continued looking toward him, her mouth shut and beads of sweat beginning to collect upon her brow.

"You haven't answered my question, woman! What is your business out here?"

The woman closed her eyes as she continued clenching her hands together. The Prince's sword hovered over her.

"You'll need to answer me now," he said.

"I'm running away," said the woman.

The Prince paused and looked at her again. He kept his sword fixed on her and continued, "You're what, I beg your pardon?"

"Must you ask it again?" she said, "as embarrassing as it is to admit once, I have to repeat myself?"

"Well, it's just a bit strange," said the Prince.

"Enough with the questions of me, and you?" asked the woman. "Why are you here, young master?"

"I'll be doing the questioning," said the Prince, "of all the stars of the night, my word…"

"Well, it's equally strange, don't you say?" said the woman.

The Prince paused and looked around to see if the woman had a weapon or object in her possession.

"Are you alone?" he asked.

"You could say that."

She observed his attire and noticed the blood upon his clothes and also the strange sword he carried.

"Are you hurt?" she asked.

"Why do you ask?" he replied.

"The blood upon your clothing," she said. "Is it yours?"

"No. Something we came across in our journey."

"So you're not alone."

"I am now," he replied.

The woman unclenched her hands and dropped them at her side. Her clothing was simple enough, much like that of a villager. He raised one arm and lowered his sword down to the woman's waist.

"Do not move," said Prince Adinor, "I am still unsure of what to make of your odd appearance and at such a late time of day."

"And why should it be more odd for a woman to be out at evening?" she replied. "Cannot a man be out without the need for querying or reprisal? Should not a lady endeavor to venture away just as a man, if she should see fit."

"Well, I'm not the decider of those things," he replied, "but for one, you are defenseless."

Looking at his sword, the woman said. "Am I to understand that because you have that tool in your hand, you are safer than me?"

"Well, not entirely but yes…"

"I'll have you know," she said, "I too have weapons and means to defend myself."

"So you are armed," he said, "stay there."

Prince Adinor raised his sword once again, putting it directly in front of the woman. She raised her hand toward it and playfully turned it away. She raised her cloak over her hair, hiding her face, and walked away from the Prince.

"Where are you going?" He asked.

The woman continued walking away from the Prince toward the pair of cantamor trees he couldn't seem to get away from. She walked in a small circle, her long dress twirled as she did. The Prince followed behind her, carefully observing her. She sat underneath the trees just as he did moments ago.

"Where are your friends?" she asked.

"I'm not sure you know what you're talking about."

"You're not from the village. If you were, you wouldn't have blood or even a sword for that matter. Are you one of them?"

"One of whom?" he asked.

"The creatures that attacked the villagers?"

"How do you know of that?" he asked.

"Everyone knows," she said, "they come from the forest and they take whatever they like. They take mostly men, young or old, it does not matter. Do you know why?"

The Prince walked around her as she sat with her legs folded underneath her dress, the large black cloak over her, still hiding her face from his.

"They say it's to kill the men," she said. "People say it's to weaken the village, pure sport."

The woman looked up toward the Prince. Her features were quite nice to the Prince's liking. In truth, he had not seen many women during the time of the triped trials, sure, there were those in the royal court and a few he ceremoniously danced with at functions, but this was different.

"Do you think they do it for amusement?" she asked.

The Prince stood directly in front of her and then knelt down before her.

"I'm not sure why they do it," he replied.

"They must have a reason. Maybe it's a good one."

"What did you say?"

He looked at her curiously. He waited to hear what she'd say next.

"Well, take you. You're not from the village and I take it you're not one of them, are you?"

"No, I'm not one of them," he replied, "you would be dead already."

"So you are not from here. What part of the kingdom do you hail from?"

"It's not important. It's time I get home."

"I'm not eager to go home," she said, "no different than you."

The Prince looked at her.

She smiled.

"How do you know?" he asked.

"It's written on your face. Something troubles you."

The Prince began to scratch the ground with his sword, thinking again of his friends back on the hill and the battle taking place. He also thought of Bolios' words. He looked back toward their direction, wondering what was happening.

"You ran away too?"

"No, it's…well, it's difficult to explain."

The girl lowered her headdress once more and leaned back upon the catamor tree. She folded her hands in her lap and stared at the Prince.

"You can tell me," she said, "you can tell me anything."

The Prince lowered his head and remained in front of her. He tilted his head back up and caught her smiling at him again. He liked it. He sat down, placed his sword at his side, and said, "All right."

The woman smiled from ear to ear.

"My friends and I are trying to find the evil you speak of that is responsible for the disappearances of your fellow villagers."

The woman continued smiling, as Prince Adinor continued.

"We were sent here to end the attacks and rid your fellow villagers of the threat."

He paused for a moment and noticed her staring back at him, but her smile began to fade.

"After a long journey, we've at last found the things responsible, and as it turns out, they're monsters of some kind," he said.

"Monsters?" she replied.

"Horrible and wretched things that were even responsible for holding us prisoners," he said.

The woman's jaw stiffened.

"Thankfully, we escaped and managed to avoid detection leading us to a hill whereby the monsters must return through on route to their encampment on the Furion wastelands."

"You escaped even after they caught you." Her tone more elevated.

The Prince smiled, revealing the victory, and said, "Yes, it was clever of us."

"So it was," she said, "how could you possibly escape if the forces had you imprisoned? What type of stupidity was tasked with the watch?"

"They were stone giants," replied Prince Adinor.

The woman stood up and paced between both cantamor trees.

The Prince continued with the story, which she ignored. As he continued to tell the rest of the story, she gripped her chin with one hand and placed her other hand behind her body. Her pace quickened. She looked concerned and troubled, but the Prince only told his story with more zeal and excitement. He was talking about his dreams under the trees they were now under when the woman interrupted him.

"What did you say?"

"The unicorns running around…"

"No," she said, "not that…before that."

"Were it not for me being Prince, I would have been able to stay and help."

The woman paused and dropped her hands at her side. Her eyes widened. She clasped her hands together as the Prince only looked back toward her.

"You are the Prince?"

He continued sitting in front of her and said, "Yes, I am Prince Adinor."

The woman walked toward him and stopped just in front, her mouth opened wide from the surprise.

"There's no need to be alarmed," he said. "You don't need to kneel or bow."

"How comforting…" she said, "I'd never."

She folded her arms and smiled again.

"So that is why you are here alone," she continued. "They tried to spare you of death."

"Yes."

"And wouldn't you know it. You've now come to me."

"Amazing," said the Prince, "how ironic. You were wandering away from home and we run into each other."

"You have no idea."

She walked over to the Prince, his sword still remained at his side just near his hand. He noticed her eyeing the sword and he moved closer to it.

"So your friends are back atop a hill not far from here?"

"Yes, that's right."

"How many of these so-called monsters will they face?"

"From the estimates of one of our party, a few dozen."

She turned away from him.

"How can you be here while they fight the enemy in your name without you?" she asked.

"Well, it's something that's troubled me since I've left them."

The Prince stood with his sword in hand. The woman looked over to him and bowed her head as she held her hands together.

"I've thought of what to do in service of my father and my kingdom but know not of the best path."

Prince Adinor stared back toward the direction of his friends.

She noticed his sword and its ruby-filled handle.

"From what you shared, you've already come so very far with them," she said.

"Yes," he replied, "I've developed a true appreciation for each of them."

"That's quite touching. Can you imagine the guilt and torture you would feel is something happens to them?"

"I do not want them to be harmed in any way."

"That is out of your control now," replied the woman, "only the monsters have something to say about that."

She walked away for a couple of seconds and came back.

"Or do you?" she said.

The Prince's hands tightened around his sword's handle as the woman twirled around in her dress, stretching her arms out. She danced in the dark shadows of the trees as Prince Adinor thought about her words.

"Do your friends stand a better chance with you at their side?"

Prince Adinor thought of the adventures he shared with the soldiers and the victories they achieved. He thought of the dangers they now faced and how desperate it would be. How stupid he had been to leave them, despite what Bolios had said. It wasn't even his decision to make after all. He was the Prince and the future ruler of the kingdom.

"Aren't you capable of making a decision yourself?" she asked.

The Prince looked toward the line of trees beyond, toward where the village supposedly was.

"There's nothing there for you," she said. "Your friends need you."

He turned toward her.

She stared back at him. The smile she wore faded.

"Thank you," he said. "If I ever see you again, I'll be sure to compensate you for your wisdom."

"Believe me. It is my pleasure."

The Prince began to run in the direction of the hill. He hurried to reach his friends soon. He stopped and turned back toward the woman and yelled, "How will I find you?"

There was no reply. His thoughts were on his fellow warriors. He needed to help them. It couldn't be too late. He began running once more, leaping and jumping through the forest. With every step, he was closer to his friends.

Back at the pair of cantamor trees, the woman in the dress continued to look toward the Prince as he moved toward the battle. She smiled once again and laughed repeatedly over and over. It was a sick laugh, a sinister laugh. Her smile wore off. The dissimulation spell ended and slowly, her dress changed to a coal-like color. Her skin returned to its dry cracked form. Her hair turned grey. She grinned and whispered, "You won't."

CHAPTER 24

Atop the hill, Bolios and the others battled a few monsters that reached them. One in particular pinned down Dolamite and was striking downward with an ax, which Dolamite defended with his sword. The two continued battling. Dolamite rolled over to one side and struggled to get back to his feet. Every time he managed to push the monster away, the dreaded creature returned immediately.

Not too far away, Lautner battled a large monster, easily bigger than him by several inches. The monster was strong and kicked him, sending Lautner rolling down the hill. Lautner stabbed his sword into the earth, holding it, avoiding further rolling. The monster began walking toward him, bearing down upon his position. Lautner looked behind him and saw no help coming. It was only him and the creature. The monster's armor shone in the bright starlight from above, revealing his exact distance. Lautner studied the creature and looked for a weak point in the armor. The creature continued approaching, leaving Lautner little time. The creature opened its arms as it held a sword in one hand and a shield in the other. It smiled and basked in its recent accomplishment of knocking down the Nymph.

"You stand no chance against our force, Nymph," said the monster.

Its voice was raspy and somewhat difficult to understand as though it was choking on its own blood.

Lautner looked up toward the monster as the higher ground boosted his advantage.

"Prepare to die," said the monster.

The creature began raising its sword overhead in preparation for a final strike on Lautner. Lautner noticed an unprotected area, the monster's armpit. The monster's eyes became large; it was thrilled at the idea of killing his Nymph opponent.

Lautner took close aim and concentrated while drawing his sword back. Lautner smiled as the monster quickly jerked his arm forward, but before he did, the Nymph had launched his blade deep into the monster's one vulnerable spot. Instantly, the monster's arm flew off its body. Lautner grabbed the fallen blade and walked toward the monster. The creature began swinging its shield. Lautner continued evading it. Lautner rolled away a couple of times. He picked the best opportunity, then ran, and leaped onto the monster's back. He sliced downward, defeating the monster for good.

Just away from the hill, Elmahigh faced off with a monster who yelled a high-pitched and dreadful noise, painful on the ears. The monster ran swinging its sword from left to right in hopes of landing a crippling blow on the monk. Elmahigh waited for the monster's proximity and then ran, leaping upon a tree with one foot and then vaulted himself behind the monster. The monster was confused as Elmahigh was now behind him. The monster turned, its dreadful voice still trying to deafen him.

"That's quite enough," said Elmahigh.

In one motion, the monk jabbed the monster in the throat, silencing the creature's voice permanently. The monster clenched its throat and dropped its sword and shield upon the ground. Elmahigh shook his head.

Lautner began ascending the hill but was taken to ground. Bolios, noticing this, ran down the hill, holding a large spear in hand. Lautner twisted and rolled away from the monster, kicking it repeatedly. The monster was knocked away temporarily as Lautner crawled uphill. Just when the monster was about to reach for Lautner's foot, it looked up and saw Bolios approaching. Bolios took another step, then launched the spear right into the monster's chest, sending it back down the hill, dead.

"Come, Lautner," said Bolios.

Lautner turned and reached out his hand as Bolios helped him to his feet.

"Thank you," said Lautner.

Dolamite was lying on the ground, a monster corpse draped on top of him. Lautner and Bolios approached him, as Dolamite's wide eyes were the only part of him visible. They moved from left to right. Bolios and Lautner looked around in search of another potential attack while Dolamite still remained trapped.

"Get up, Dolamite," said Bolios.

Dolamite tried to respond, but no words followed.

"What did he say?" asked Bolios.

"I'm unsure," replied Lautner.

"Get him up from there," said Bolios.

Lautner walked over to Dolamite, reaching down to the corpse covering him, and rolled it to one side.

"Finally," said Dolamite, "I couldn't take the stink much longer."

Dolamite rose to his feet and joined Lautner and Bolios. A moment later, Elmahigh arrived. Marcus and Friedrich also came down from the trees overhead.

"Well, I have no arrows," said Marcus.

"Nor do I," added Friedrich.

"You've done what you can," said Bolios, "both of you did well."

"It will be daylight soon," said Elmahigh. "They will know we are not the formidable numbers they fear."

"I'm unsure of their exact position," replied Bolios. "If we attack, we could succumb to their same mistake and be caught by surprise ourselves."

"Perhaps we leave down the hill and gather back together with Isilmoire and the others," said Elmahigh.

"It's a good idea," replied Bolios. "Is anyone hurt?"

"Nothing beyond the usual," replied Dolamite.

"All is well," said Marcus.

"I too am able to move," said Friedrich.

"Let's get off this hill," said Lautner.

"I could lead," said Elmahigh. "I'm familiar with a clear path free of any monsters."

"Very well," said Bolios, "let's begin.

The warriors moved toward the side of the hill and stopped as the leader was down at the bottom of the hill directly in the middle of the road. It was easy to see for it carried a torch in one hand and a sword in the other. It was the largest and strongest by far. It began walking up the hill, still holding its torch and sword. Its large curled horns protruding bounced a bit as he walked. The group looked toward it. They stood shoulder to shoulder and faced the creature together. It showed no signs of stopping, but also did not quicken its pace. One step forward then another, it walked directly at them.

"Perhaps it wants to acquaint itself with one of our blades," said Lautner.

The Nymph began toward it but was stopped by Elmahigh who reached out and grabbed him by the arm.

"It could be a trap," said Elmahigh.

The monk looked around and tried to spot any signs of monsters or even Isilmoire and the others. He saw neither.

"Something is amiss," Elmahigh said.

The monster continued toward them, its eyes fixed upon them as the light from the torch revealed their haunting crimson red color. The monster's sword a jagged piece of metal resembled that of a bolt of lightning.

Others were soon lit. The plot was revealed. The Mastadans and Lautner were surrounded. The ring of fire began to collapse upon the warriors, and just inside the ring was the one monster. The one creature had blood-red eyes thirsting for a fight. It was he that coordinated the monster retreat into the forest in response to the arrow attacked by Marcus and Friedrich.

He continued toward the warriors. The monster, now in a large circle of torches, began closing in upon the warriors. Bolios and the others stepped back toward the large trees behind them as the monsters began to stomp their weapons upon the ground.

"Bolios, do we?" said Lautner.

"There's too many," he replied.

The noise grew louder as the banging of the shields and the stomping of the spears upon the ground swelled in the air. Outnumbered three to one, the warriors continued stepping back, arriving just below the tree Friedrich used.

"We can't risk a fight without Isilmoire and the others," said Elmahigh.

Mesthusula continued forward just inside the circle as he was now halfway up the hill.

"Quickly, everyone, up the tree," said Bolios.

Marcus ran and climbed up. He was followed by Friedrich. The monsters continued stomping upon the ground, inching closer toward the warriors. Lautner was now climbing up followed by Elmahigh. Dolamite and Bolios remained on the ground. Their time for climbing up was cut short; the monsters were upon them. Just as the massive circle approached, one torch disappeared in the darkness, confusing the two monsters next to it. Then in a different part of the circle, another monster was brought down, also disappearing into the dark. The monsters hesitated. They began yelling and roaring over the disappearance of two of their own.

"It's Isilmoire and the others," said Dolamite.

"Quickly, up the tree," said Bolios.

Dolamite used Bolios as a stool and jumped up, finding suitable grip, and began to climb the tree. Bolios remained behind as Mesthusula approached him. Even Bolios was smaller than the giant. Mesthusula was truly formidable.

Bolios, observing Dolamite needed more time, jumped off the tree and ran directly at Mesthusula. The monster plunged its torch deep into the red dirt below, keeping the lit end up just next to him. Bolios raised his sword overhead. Mesthusula did the same. The two combatants met in the middle of the ring of fire. Their swords clashed together, sending loud thunderous sound rippling across the entire forest.

Dolamite finally arrived at the top of the tree. He looked down and saw Bolios' sacrifice.

"Oh no," he said.

Bolios clashed his sword against Mesthusula's. Quickly, the giant demon monster swung his sword, sending Bolios flying back toward the base of the tree. A different monster approached the tree just on the opposite side and began to set it ablaze. Bolios rolled over and attacked the monster, quickly stomping out the fire.

"They intended this all along," said Elmahigh. "We've been led on a fool's errand."

Elmahigh looked down and continued to see as Bolios battled once more with the giant Mesthusula. He looked at the rest of the monsters who remained encircling the combatants, waiting for an opportunity to once again set the tree on fire. In between fighting Mesthusula, Bolios fought off any monster efforts to set the tree on fire.

"Quickly, Dolamite, stand toward the end of the branch of the tree," said Elmahigh.

"Why?" replied Dolamite.

"Do it immediately," replied Elmahigh.

Dolamite tiptoed his way around the others, bringing a noticeable tilt to the branch as it struggled to hold his weight.

"Quickly," said Elmahigh, "the rest of you chop the branch."

"Are you mad?" said Marcus.

"Elmahigh, there must be a better way," said Lautner.

"Unfortunately for us, there is no alternative, my friend," said Elmahigh, "look."

The group of warriors looked down and saw that it was only a matter of time before Mesthusula would have the rest of his forces converge on Bolios, certainly killing him.

"All right," said Friedrich.

They all began to cut the branch, swinging swords and axes upon it. Bolios continued fighting with Mesthusula. The monster was obsessed with taking down the Mastadan leader. At any moment, the other monsters stepped toward the center of the circle in hopes of fighting Bolios, but the hideous and powerful Mesthusula would roar, scaring off any other fighter. He wanted to kill Bolios himself. Bolios was on the ground and noticed his fellow Mastadans overhead as they worked on cutting the large branch they stood upon. He looked under it and saw a collection of a dozen monsters, standing oblivious to anything happening overhead.

Bolios smiled and got up once more, jostling with Mesthusula who tried to slice Bolios with a strike of his sword, but Bolios evaded it with a roll. Bolios stood before Mesthusula as both leaders seemed to have little effect on each other. As Bolios continued to twirl his sword in a display of relaxation, the monster's eyes widened, its ragged pointy teeth clenched together, and then Mesthusula let out a large roar, making even Bolios step back. The devilish monster ran toward him full speed and kicked him across the circle. Bolios landed near a few monsters, which tried to stab him with their swords. Bolios rolled away and cut one of their legs, sending the monster sprawling to the ground. As Bolios stood, he turned back at Mesthusula and noticed Isilmoire hidden on the ground behind two monsters nearby. Isilmoire looked toward Bolios and whipped her head toward his right, attempting to communicate a plan. Bolios shook his head, not understanding the message Isilmoire was trying to convey. Then Isilmoire pointed toward his right. Bolios followed with his eyes and saw Teinmar and Theodonus behind a bush. Bolios nodded in confirmation. The message was received. No sooner did Mesthusula grab Bolios from behind and threw him, smashing him against the large tree in the center of the ring of fire.

Elmahigh and the others continued chopping at the tree when one monster broke rank and set the tree on fire at its base. The monsters nearby, excited by the treachery, roared and yelled in approval. Elmahigh saw the flames beginning to spread.

"Double your efforts," he said. "They have set the tree on fire."

The flames first engulfed the base and crept up gradually, reaching the rest of the trunk.

"Faster!" said Elmahigh.

Down below, Bolios continued exchanging swipes with Mesthusula. They matched strikes, sending sparks flying in the night sky. Bolios pushed Mesthusula back for the first time and struck him in the chest with a heavy kick, sending the menacing monster backward. He looked in the direction Isilmoire indicated and saw nothing. Mesthusula ripped a shield out of a nearby monster's hands and raced toward Bolios once again. Bolios stepped backward, inching closer to the position Isilmoire wanted him on. Mesthusula beared down on Bolios and landed a kick to the stomach, then a punch with the same hand he carried a sword with. Bolios was sent sprawling to the ground; dazed, he misplaced his sword. Mesthusula walked toward it and kicked it far away, beyond Bolios' reach. Bolios struggled to find his footing and remained on his hands and knees. Mesthusula walked toward him, as the Mastadan was unaware of any advance.

Elmahigh now joined the others as he looked down toward Bolios and saw the imminent danger. The tree was nearly completely on fire. Only the branches remained. Bolios crawled away from Mesthusula toward the outer circle of the monsters. One kicked him. Then another punched him. Bolios fell on the ground, depleted of energy. Mesthusula approached from behind, stepping on his leg. The Mastadan leader yelled in pain. Isilmoire gathered the others around him. Teinmar whispered something in Nymph.

"Not yet," replied Isilmoire.

Malchomite and Teinmar stepped toward the ring of monsters as they were within reach of Bolios. Only three monsters stood between them and Bolios. In the large tree back up above, Elmahigh and the others were almost nearly through the branch. It cracked more.

"Move to the end, Dolamite," said Elmahigh.

Dolamite inched out further.

"Hold your balance," said Elmahigh.

"This is going to hurt," said Dolamite.

Elmahigh stepped just beyond the crack next to Dolamite and the others.

"Here we go," said Elmahigh.

He stabbed his sword downward with both hands, slicing the branch clean off the tree, sending it along with them falling downward toward the group of monsters below. Within seconds, a large thud got all the monster's attentions as even Mesthusula turned toward the other side. Elmahigh, Lautner, Marcus, Friedrich, and Dolamite landed the branch right on top of a group of unsuspecting monsters, crushing them instantly. The warriors struggled to their feet, dusted themselves off, and stared toward the rest of the remaining monsters.

"Now what?" said Dolamite.

A large roar from Mesthusula sounded throughout the forest, and instantly, the monsters began to attack the group of crashers. Mesthusula then raised his sword up as he stood over Bolios.

"Now!" said Isilmoire.

Her group ran in, cutting down a couple of unsuspecting monsters heading to battle Elmahigh and the others. Isilmoire raced past the fighting. She went straight for Bolios and dove toward his body, extending her sword out just before Mesthusula's dropped down upon Bolios' neck.

Mesthusula looked down toward Isilmoire who rose fast.

"You'll have to go through me first," she said.

Mesthusula spit on Isilmoire's face. The Nymph stood tall and with one hand, wiped it off onto her shoulder.

"You'll pay for that," she said.

The Nymph lunged toward the monster in hopes of killing it straight away. Mesthusula moved and swung its sword wildly toward

Isilmoire who rolled under it, evading any danger. The Nymph slashed at Mesthusula, cutting the monster's leg.

"Now we're even."

Mesthusula roared once again and continued the fight against Isilmoire. As the two battled, Theodonus ran through a monster and went to help his leader, Bolios. The Mastadan juggernaut was slow to his feet, weary from the long drawn-out battle with Mesthusula.

"Good of you to come, Theodonus," said Bolios.

"My lord."

"Help me," replied Bolios.

Bolios grabbed Theodonus' shoulder for support. He noticed the fighting off toward Elmahigh and the other group.

"They need assistance, go to them," said Bolios.

"My lord, you are still weak," replied Theodonus. "I will stay at your side until you can stand on your own."

Bolios let go of Theodonus and took one step then another. He twisted his body at the waist, first left then right.

"Everything seems in order," replied Bolios, "go."

"Yes, my lord, as you wish."

Theodonus ran toward the massive battle. It was utter chaos. The group of Elmahigh, Dolamite, Marcus, Friedrich, and Lautner battled the entire force a few at a time. Theodonus, Teinmar, Ecclesias, and Malchomite arrived behind the monster forces, killing a few before they were discovered.

Swords clashed, axes flew, punches and kicks were abundant. The monsters fought in a reckless fashion, slashing and stabbing wildly with no true rhythm or design. Although their skills in combat were novice compared to the sophistication of all the Mastadans and Nymphs, their physical strength more than made up for it.

Elmahigh ran his sword into the side of a monster opponent and yet the monster continued fighting, raining punches on him all the while. Dolamite cut off another monster's arm and yet the monster proceeded to swing its ax violently, with the remaining arm. Theodonus and Teinmar fought back to back as several monsters encircled them, attacking all at once. A monster would run in, attempting a spear attack, forcing the Mastadan and Nymph pair to split off. One swung his sword, striking downward, deflecting the spear to ground while the other cut off the monster's head. Friedrich and Marcus bravely fought with only their bows as they stabbed monsters when possible, cleverly using the ends of the bow as blunt weapons. Elmahigh wiped out two more monsters as he swung both sword and staff.

The numbers of the monsters still remained greater; Ecclesias began to struggle as three bared down upon him. One monster landed a small blade in his back, sending the Mastadan to the ground in pain. As the monster continued toward him, Malchomite interceded, leaping between Ecclesias and the monsters.

The monsters slashed toward Malcomite who met the blade with his sword, knocking the small blade to ground. The monster ran toward Malchomite, knocking him over Ecclesias. The two were on their backs. Theodonus ran toward them, shoving the monster from behind by driving his shoulder into the monster's back. The monster fell on its knees directly in front of Ecclesias and Malchomite. The two Mastadans looked on as Theodonus finished it quickly.

"Get up," said Theodonus, "tend to the wound."

Immediately, Malchomite aided Ecclesias who was bleeding badly.

"I'll be all right," said Ecclesias.

"You'll need something to cover the gash, perhaps a plant nearby," said Malchomite.

"Yes, it will help," replied Ecclesias.

The two continued fighting through the mob as they looked for something to relieve the pain.

Isilmoire still faced off with Mesthusula. They crossed blades once more matching strike for strike. The blades rang thunderous clashing sounds and sent sparks flying. Still dazed, Bolios looked around for his sword and found it halfway hidden in the dirt ground. He walked toward it while still holding his side. The Mastadan leader bent down and reached for his sword, but struggled. The throbbing pain was growing. There were a couple of footsteps approaching just ahead of him.

"You may need some help with that," said Prince Adinor, "let me get it."

The Prince stepped forward and lifted the sword from the ground, handing it to Bolios. Bolios stared back at him. He only nodded.

A monster ran toward them both. Bolios prepared lifting his sword overhead, using his one good side as support. The monster continued toward him, but Prince Adinor jumped in front, knocking away the monster's sword to one side, sending the monster after it. The Prince then ran toward the monster as it grabbed its sword. The monster roared.

"I do not fear you," said Prince Adinor.

The monster attacked with an overhead swing of its sword. Prince Adinor met the blade with his and lunged backward as the monster's weight came upon him. The Prince placed his feet in the monster's gut and launched the creature high into the air, behind him. The monster again lost its sword. Prince Adinor rose up from his back, still carrying his, and plunged the sword into the monster's horrid flesh. It flailed wildly. The Prince stomped upon its face, stopping its movement entirely.

"Well done," said Bolios.

"I won't run from a fight again," said Prince Adinor.

"And I'll always be there alongside you to fight them," said Bolios.

Bolios reached out his hand. Prince Adinor did the same as they both shook.

"I'll count on it," said Prince Adinor.

"Come, let's aid our friends," said Bolios.

The two jogged toward the main battle, killing a couple of more monsters along the way. Elmahigh was battling a difficult opponent who successfully injured Friedrich and threatened to do more.

"Wretched creature," said Elmahigh.

The monster roared in response. They crossed swords. The monster gained the advantage over Elmahigh. The wizard held firm, as the monster twisted, sending Elmahigh to the ground. The monster kicked Elmahigh's sword away and then kicked dirt in his eyes, blinding him. The monk only had his staff in hand and could not see. The monster mocked him and began to launch another assault when Elmahigh spoke a prayer into the staff and blew into it, lighting it immediately. The monster covered its eyes, shielding itself from the light. Elmahigh rose to his feet, his eyes still closed. He sensed the monster nearby and turned toward it while the creature shielded its eyes. With two motions, Elmahigh ran the staff into the monster's midsection, bringing it to its knees and then he smacked the monster on its back, defeating it. He wiped off his eyes with this tunic and looked after Friedrich.

"Well done, Elmahigh," said Friedrich.

"I thoroughly dislike a cheat," said Elmahigh. "He learned his lesson. How badly are you injured?"

"My leg is cut," replied Friedrich, "rather well, I may add. I wish I could have beaten one more of them before they got me."

"You will, my friend, in time," said Elmahigh, "let's get you away from here."

Lautner was nearby and said something to Teinmar in Nymph. Teinmar turned and saw Elmahigh struggling to help Friedrich. In an instant, the Nymph ran toward the two, grabbing Friedrich on one side as Elmahigh grabbed the other.

"Thank you," said Elmahigh.

Teinmar nodded. Bolios and Prince Adinor joined in the fight from behind and continued battling as many monsters as possible. The efforts were helping. Monster numbers were shrinking. The accomplishment came at a price. Friedrich and Ecclesias were both injured. Then Lautner too succumbed to a wound, a knife struck him in the chest. He pressed down on the open wound hard, putting as much pressure as possible. The monster was shocked that one of the Nymphs could be hurt. They all roared and found a renewed motivation to fight harder than ever. They continued attacking using their advantage of numbers and overwhelmed the warriors. The injured tried to help but were ineffective. Elmahigh decided instead to remove them from battle.

"Stay here, we will return for you all," he said. "Do what you can to protect yourselves."

They held on to their weapons in the event any monsters approached. Elmahigh rushed back to the battle. He noticed the slowing ebbing sun rising.

"Dawn," he said. "We live to see another day."

He ran toward Bolios and Prince Adinor who continued fighting off monsters. They fought alongside Dolamite and Theodonus. The five slashed and kicked the monsters back, hurling shields at them together with small blades found on the ground.

"We can't continue to hold them much longer," said Elmahigh.

Off to their right, forming the other half of the defense against the monsters was Teinmar, Marcus, Theodonus, and Malchomite.

"They are beginning to break free," said Theodonus.

Elmahigh ran over to support that side of the defense, stabbing whatever poked through.

At the same time, Isilmoire was beginning to win against Mesthusula. The Nymph spun and slashed down upon the monster, sending Mesthusula to ground. The demon monster picked up dirt and threw it toward Isilmoire who evaded it by jumping over the small cloud of debris.

The monster rose once again and tried to kick the Nymph, but Isilmoire blocked the kick with her own foot. The monster was starting to tire. Isilmoire twirled her sword and began to strike the monster once more, which Mesthusula defended with its crooked blade. Anticipating this, Isilmoire struck the beast with the opposite hand, sending it reeling. For the first time, it was dazed.

The warriors continued to hold their line as the monsters continued to try to break them.

"Keep fighting," said Bolios.

Prince Adinor swung his sword, hitting another monster upon the head, killing it. Another immediately barreled through. Dolamite held a shield with two hands stiffening his position with a firm plant of his foot. Theodonus and Malchomite employed spears and thrusted them at the monsters who ducked and dodged in response. Elmahigh used both staff and sword to inflict damage as best he could, but the monsters protected themselves with shields.

The sun continued to rise. Both forces were arriving at the end. Just one key moment remained to tip the scales of battle in favor of one group over the other.

Isilmoire looked over to the scene as her friends could use help. The Mastadan and Nymph efforts focused on the protection of those injured. Isilmoire continued toward Mesthusula who was up once more. The monster drew back its sword and launched it toward Isilmoire in a reckless attack. Isilmoire raised her sword, knocking Mesthusula's down. Just as she bent down to grab it, Mesthusula was upon her and punched her in the gut. The Nymph received a kick from the powerful monster lord and was sent a few feet away. Her sword still in hand, Isilmoire turned as Mesthusula approached directly at her. The Nymph swung her sword, slicing off Mesthusula's hand. The monster roared and punched the Nymph's arm, forcing Isilmoire to drop her sword. As a response, Isilmoire punched the monster in the head, then kicked him in the gut and ran toward him launching herself with both hands clenched and arms extended, like a projectile. The monster was knocked back from the force of the impact. Mesthusula fell to both his knees and roared in response. Isilmoire grabbed her and Mesthusula's sword. She walked toward the monster. Mesthusula remained stunned. He grit his teeth and snarled. In a quick motion, Isilmoire beheaded him using both swords. She looked back at the rest of the monster party, bearing down on her Mastadan and Nymph friends. They would not hold much longer.

"And now the rest of you," she said.

She ran toward the monsters, slicing two dead as she used both her sword and Mesthusula's.

"I am here to help," yelled Isilmoire.

"God smiles upon us once more," said Elmahigh.

Isilmoire dispatched another monster, a couple turned toward her, freeing Bolios and Prince Adinor to fight a different group. The Nymphs and Mastadans were able to continue dividing the monsters, spreading their numbers equally. Within moments, they successfully dropped the several remaining monsters to only a few. Then the final remaining few became two. The Nymphs and Mastadans surrounded the remaining two. They dropped their swords in surrender.

"A wise decision," said Elmahigh.

"If you cooperate," said Bolios, "you may live out the rest of your days in the comforts of a Mastadan dungeon tower in the city center. Perhaps you both may serve another use."

One monster opened his mouth to speak, but the other monster punched him in the mouth.

"Do not do that again," said Prince Adinor. "Let him speak."

The first monster began once again.

"There is not much to say, but whatever I can share, I will."

"Very well," said Bolios, "was this all the monster forces? Are there other monster battalions elsewhere?"

The second monster looked at the first and shoved him.

"There is no point in lying," said the monster. "Yes, these were all our forces."

Elmahigh walked over to the injured and attended to their needs. Ecclesias, Lautner, and Friedrich each exhibited different pain.

"Hold still," said Elmahigh.

Theodonus and Dolamite joined Elmahigh. The three moved the wounded closer to the shade of the giant tree near the Bolios, Prince Adinor, and Isilmoire.

"Perhaps some water may help," said Elmahigh.

"Yes, it would be most welcomed," replied Ecclesias.

"Well deserved," said Theodonus.

"There may be a stream nearby," said Dolamite.

"I will stay with them," said Elmahigh. "Both of you do what's necessary to find water. If you find yourself too far from us, be sure to return here."

"Very well," replied Theodonus, "come, let us depart."

And so Dolamite and Theodonus walked away.

Back atop the hill, Bolios, Prince Adinor, Isilmoire, and the others continued the interrogation.

"Are there any other Mastadan villagers still prisoners or in danger?" asked Prince Adinor.

"None," replied the monster, "aside from those you've freed here."

"That is encouraging," said Bolios.

"Indeed," replied Isilmoire, "perhaps the decision to battle these creatures helped stave off future attacks on the villagers and maybe, too, my people."

Elmahigh returned from seeing the wounded and walked to Bolios.

"The wounded will heal," said Elmahigh, "however, the men must be tended to. There are no herbs or potions nearby. I have no medicines to help slow the bleeding. We must get them to the village. There we will find bandages, fresh water, and the necessary ointments and provisions to treat them. They require needle and thread to close the wounds and a powerful agent to reduce the swelling and eliminate the poison resulting from the monster blades."

"Is there no water nearby?" asked Bolios.

"Theodonus and Dolamite have already left to find it, if there is, it will be ours," replied Elmahigh.

Teinmar said something in Nymph. Isilmoire responded and then turned to Elmahigh and Bolios.

"Teinmar will search out some as well. If there is water nearby, he will surely be able to find it. In which direction did they go?"

"They moved south by southwest," replied Elmahigh. "They have strict instructions not to venture too far."

Isilmoire spoke to Teinmar and pointed in the direction the Mastadan pair ventured to. He then said a few words and left in an opposite direction.

"He will try another option."

Elmahigh knocked the first monster on the head, returning Bolios' and Isilmoire's attentions to the two prisoners.

"Surely, there are yet to be discovered answers these two can still provide," said Elmahigh.

Bolios, the Prince, and Isilmoire looked at one another and smiled. Elmahigh returned to attend to the wounded soldiers nearby.

"Where is your leader?" asked Bolios.

The second monster turned toward the first, hissing at him. The first monster recoiled and did not speak. He instead stared toward the ground.

"I do not like you much, monster," said Prince Adinor. "Let your wiser friend speak, he knows what is better for him."

The first monster continued staring down at the ground as the second hissed at him and flicked its tongue in spite.

"Speak to us, monster," said Bolios, "your forces are gone. Here lay these bodies spoiling upon the ground. There will not be escape for you or your friend. Cooperate and come to terms with your fate and the rest of your days may be more pleasant."

"I am Prince Adinor, son of Ralphus Dolamaic, King of the Mastadan people. Do as he says, and I ensure you it will be as Bolios offers."

Isilmoire, Bolios, and Prince Adinor paused and waited. The monsters were silent. The second looked at the first. The first began to lift its head. It wanted to say something, but stopped.

"Do what is right, you fool," said Bolios, "speak."

"This is fruitless," said Isilmoire, "perhaps it's time we leave."

"Perhaps you're right," said Bolios.

"Qualvon…" said the monster.

"Yes, go on," said Prince Adinor.

"Qualvon would not go back to the camp," continued the monster.

The second monster jumped on top of the first and began punching him repeatedly. Isilmoire and Prince Adinor removed him and separated the two with added distance. The second monster was livid and continued wrenching himself left and right as it tried to break free of the Nymph and the Prince to resume its attack upon its fellow monster. The first monster wiped its face from the black blood flowing out of its nose and mouth.

"Speak," said Bolios.

"Qualvon would not return to our encampment," said the monster.

Prince Adinor and Isilmoire held the rebellious monster down.

"What is the other option?" asked Bolios.

The second monster jumped again, forcing Isilmoire and Prince Adinor to pin it to the ground.

"Who is he? Where can we find him" said Bolios.

"He is the one who gave us our way, the one who opened our worlds to the other vision."

The second monster was uncontrollable. Isilmoire hit it with the back of her sword, stunning the creature.

"What vision?" asked Bolios.

"A vision of darkness," replied the monster, "pure and utter perfect darkness. This darkness is embodied in the source of our strength and power. It is the change within us that makes us what we are."

Elmahigh approached, clutching his staff to the side.

"The one Qualvon is the cause of it all," said the monster. The first monster looked toward the heroes and said, "He is not of this world."

Elmahigh looked toward the monster. The creature's eyes widened and it began to shake.

"What is it you say?" asked Elmahigh.

"Our creator is much more powerful than Mesthusula. Mesthusula was nothing, a mere agent of his. Nothing compares to the mastery of evil which he possesses."

"How do you come to know of this?" asked Elmahigh.

"I have seen it," replied the monster.

Bolios looked at Elmahigh and then Isilmoire.

"Neither of you actually believe this, do you?" asked Bolios.

"There is nothing to reveal one way or another, but these creatures are unnatural," replied Isilmoire, "their presence does prove something foul is at work in all this. The extent of the power that has created these things we will only know upon facing it. It must be dealt with now."

"And you, Elmahigh?" asked Bolios. "These ravings of madness from this wretched thing, are these not just ramblings of a zealot? A twisted soul no more human than the bark of that tree."

Elmahigh looked down toward the monster, its eyes filled with fear and panic. It was still shaking and sweating.

"I know where to find him," said the monster.

The warriors all looked at the creature.

"You know where?" asked Bolios.

"Yes," it replied.

Bolios walked closer to the monster and said, "Tell us."

"For blood," said Prince Adinor. "Look at the death around you. Look at the hurt you've caused here. My friends are wounded and bleeding. The lives you've taken and what you've done affects innocent lives everywhere. Children are left fatherless and mothers lose husbands. I met a young woman fleeing the same carnage I speak of, the carnage you and your leader have caused. That is no way. You are lost."

"Where is he?" asked Bolios.

"If you are not prepared to give your lives, you should not seek him for that is what he will demand," replied the monster.

"Enough of your antics," said Bolios, "where?"

"He's gone to the mountain," replied the monster.

Without notice, the other monster jumped and freed himself from Isilmoire and Prince Adinor, kicking Isilmoire and grabbing Prince Adinor's small blade. It rushed past Bolios and struck the talkative monster in the throat, killing it. Bolios responded with a swift slash of his sword, dropping the monster assassin to his knees. The only remaining two monsters were both dead.

"And so the adventure continues," said Elmahigh, "the Mountains of Citerac, a void of life, its barren black rock spewing hot vapors from the burning fire red magma below. Its steep climb will be challenging for anyone, let alone weary and weakened travelers. Bolios, we cannot continue on this journey having so many wounded in our party. There are too many risks we expose ourselves to."

"I agree," said Isilmoire.

"So what do we do?" asked Prince Adinor.

Dolamite and Theodonus returned followed behind by Teinmar.

"Have you found any water?" asked Bolios.

"None," replied Theodonus.

Isilmoire spoke to Teinmar in Nymph asking the same thing. Teinmar shook his.

"That complicates things," said Elmahigh.

"How so?" asked Isilmoire.

"We have another dilemma which requires our attentions. The Mastadan villagers are still hiding in the forest not far from here. They too will need safe protection. We must return them home."

"How many?" asked Bolios.

"If memory serves me, ten or so," replied Elmahigh. "There are young ones among them. They will slow our speed."

"Dolamite and Theodonus prepare the wounded for travel," said Bolios, "Isilmoire, if you can spare Teinmar, perhaps he can go on ahead and assure the path back to the villagers is a safe one."

"I will speak to him."

Dolamite and Theodonus went to the wounded and continued to monitor their condition. Each of the Mastadans' skin was cold and covered in sweat.

"Do you take the monster's words as truth?" asked Bolios.

Elmahigh and Isilmoire looked at one another. Prince Adinor walked over to the murdered monster that spoke about Mesthusula and Qualvon. He took one knee near the creature's corpse. He noticed on either side of its head, tiny deformed ears. In its skull, it had two eyes, a half-deformed boney structure of a nose, and the discernible couple of hairs atop its head.

"These creatures are not natural," said Prince Adinor, "they are not born into this world like this. Something made them like this. Whatever is the source of evil capable of doing this to someone needs to be destroyed. I think in a way, this creature knew that."

"At best, he wanted to keep its life," said Isilmoire.

"Perhaps you are right," said Bolios.

"They both are," said Elmahigh, "undoubtedly, the worst-case scenario may be true. And in seeking out the source of these heinous situations, we will indeed be tested. For nothing dealing in absolutes gives way to diplomacy."

Bolios stepped away from the monster corpses and looked out toward the dirt path leading toward the village. He glanced toward the grimacing soldiers wounded at the hands of the monsters.

"I will not risk more Mastadan lives," said Bolios. "This evil made us shed the blood of our own people. I will not allow anyone else to die for this. We will get the villagers back to their homes and make sure all the wounded receive treatment and then I will meet Qualvon alone."

* * *

The group moved slow and tried not to shift the wounded too much. Ecclesias, Lautner, and Friedrich struggled to stay conscious.

"How far to the villagers?" asked Bolios.

"We're nearly there," replied Elmahigh.

"At this pace, it will take too long," replied Isilmoire.

"She's right," said Bolios.

"We have no choice," replied Elmahigh

Elmahigh led the soldiers through the dense bushes ahead and arrived at the beskat tree hiding the villagers.

"Hello once again," said Elmahigh.

The villagers were missing.

"Duncan, Thomas," said Elmahigh, "It's all right. It is I, Elmahigh."

There was silence.

"You can come out, you will not be harmed," said Elmahigh.

There was movement. A branch wiggled, then another. The moss began to peel away, and in moments, the warriors began to peer through the foliage, revealing the hidden villagers underneath. A young boy crawled out from underneath the tree.

"It's quite good to see you, young squire," said Elmahigh.

Duncan smiled and embraced Elmahigh. Behind him, his father Thomas and the rest of the Mastadan villagers emerged.

"Help them out," said Bolios.

Theodonus and the rest of the uninjured attended to the rescued Mastadans. In short time, everyone was accounted for.

"Thomas, is it?" asked Bolios.

"Yes, my lord," replied Thomas.

"Understanding you and the rest of your group are ill equipped for battle and are incapable of any defense en route back to the village, I ask of your favor in a matter," said Bolios.

"You brave people have saved us," said Thomas, "anything."

"Perhaps your eldest and able-bodied members of the group can assist my wounded in travel," replied Bolios.

"It will be done, my lord," replied Thomas.

A few villagers walked toward the injured members of the party and attended to them. They tore off pieces of their own clothing and dressed their wounds. They formed pairs and organized themselves to carry the wounded warriors.

"Blessings continue to smile upon us," said Elmahigh.

"The additional help can speed our return to the village," said Isilmoire.

"Yes, a much needed change of fortune," said Bolios, "the rest of us will surround the group, ensuring any surprise attacks are defended against."

Running through the bushes and stumbling upon the entire group was Teinmar who had returned from scouting the path ahead. He spoke to Isilmoire in Nymph.

"He says he has found a safe path to return us to the village," said Isilmoire.

"Very well, have him take us through," said Bolios.

The group now made of villagers, Nymphs, and Mastadan warriors moved toward the open road once again. They gained a steady pace thanks to the extra bodies now able to share the load of those injured and unable to move. Teinmar maintained vigilant eyes in all directions as they headed toward the village.

"How long until we're back in the village?" asked Prince Adinor.

"I'm unsure," replied Elmahigh, "I've not travelled this path. Ignorance has a way of clouding things, like a haze over a calm lake. The haze makes it difficult to see where the lake begins and ends."

"At least we're moving forward," said Prince Adinor.

"It appears that way," replied Elmahigh.

"Elmahigh, when I left all of you, many thoughts plagued me," said the Prince.

"Oh, and what were those thoughts?"

"Well, I thought of home and the possibility of seeing my mother and father once more. I thought of everything we've experienced and the challenges we've overcome."

"I see," said Elmahigh, "go on."

"The journey has been something I never anticipated, and even from its beginning, I underestimated it."

Elmahigh continued walking together with all the others.

"Please don't misunderstand me," said Prince Adinor. "I knew the challenges would be difficult and I feared what I may encounter before taking one step from the city center. But the hardships faced in our time together overshadowed even my biggest concern initially felt when my father first told me of my task to accompany you all."

"Looking back, do you think yourself arrogant for underestimating?" asked Elmahigh.

The Prince continued walking for a few paces.

"Maybe a little, but mostly…"

"Yes, mostly what, young Prince?" asked Elmahigh.

"I look at who I was in the outset and realize how little I knew then. It's a wildly large adventure stepping out into the unknown, and with every added step taken, there's more to learn."

"Have you found the experience you've undergone similar to what you learned in your triped trials?"

"Far different," said Prince Adinor, "wildly different. Out here for you, Bolios, Isilmoire, and everyone else, I am still my father's son. I am Prince over our kingdom, but it has no impact in every situation we've experienced so far."

"I wouldn't be so hard on yourself, young Prince."

"What I mean to say is I've seen so much and learned so much and have been tested so much and yet…"

The Prince paused and looked out toward the group ahead. Elmahigh listened.

"And yet I still know so little," finished the Prince.

Elmahigh placed his hand upon the Prince's chest, stopping him from advancing. The group continued walking forward. Elmahigh and the Prince remained behind. Elmahigh leaned in toward the Prince and said, "Look to the bushes on the ground or even the trees surrounding us, young Prince. See the smallest of creatures or the largest of seas surrounding us, each start from small beginnings. Take this flower."

Elmahigh tore a small flower from the ground and presented it to the Prince.

"Even this flower began from a tiny seed deep within the dirt below us requiring sunlight, water, nourishment, it's grown and found its own path among all the other flowers," he said. "It journeyed toward this very moment by a multitude of different circumstances. It faced days bathed in rains or others of dryness baked by the sun's powerful rays. Each circumstance and situation has contributed something to its formation. You too are much like this particular flower, young Prince. Your journey isn't marked by a singular event of one particular success or failure, but rather a collection of all things you come to know. In your admission of knowing so little, perhaps you've freed yourself to explore so much."

The Prince grabbed the flower and stared at it in the palm of his hand.

"So not knowing a lot isn't a bad thing?" asked the Prince.

"In a way, it can be," replied Elmahigh. "Staying clouded in the lack of knowledge on something could be. You reaching conclusions without experiencing it for yourself could be a form of ignorance in a way, could it not?"

"Well, I had some information and stories based on what I learned in the triped trials," replied the Prince.

"Yes, but had you experienced it, seen it, battled it yourself?" asked Elmahigh

"The little I experienced was in school and that was far different," replied Prince Adinor.

"Indeed and in so doing, you've opened yourself to learn in a deeper sense, through your own experience," said Elmahigh. "Never forget how important that will always be. Let's catch up with the others."

Prince Adinor walked alongside Elmahigh. He continued to think of the words shared as he held the flower in his hand.

"When did you finally decide to come back?" asked Elmahigh.

"It was a curious situation," replied the Prince, "I came to rest between two cantamor trees. I do not recall for how long I travelled. I remember waking in the middle of the night from the strangest dream."

"Some say dreams can be glimpses into the future," said Elmahigh. "What did you dream?"

"I recall three," said the Prince, "one featured unicorns racing about wildly in my view. They were in plain sight, strong, innocent, and beautiful."

"How many unicorns did you see?" asked Elmahigh.

"Three."

"What color were they?" asked Elmahigh.

"A pure white," replied the Prince.

"Interesting."

"Do you know of its meaning?"

"Were there other dreams?"

"Yes, two others," replied the Prince, "I dreamt of a banquet of the largest I've ever seen. A celebration of sorts. I saw my parents. The finest of foods and most delicious of produce and most succulent game meats."

"I see," replied Elmahigh, "was it the last one?"

"There was another."

"Go on."

"I saw an image a silhouette of what I thought was a woman. She walked away from me. She kept a pond between us. There were flowers of all different colors and sizes throughout."

"Could you recognize the woman?"

"No, her face was never discernible. I didn't recognize her."

"The dreams you've had say much, young Prince."

"Do I want to know?"

"In my order, we believe dreams to be visions into the future or perhaps for others, the present," said Elmahigh. "I myself tend to disagree."

"What part do you disagree with?" asked Prince Adinor.

"For me, nothing is written. Our actions determine outcomes which are but choices within us."

"And my dreams, Elmahigh? Is there any meaning in them?"

Elmahigh looked at the eager Prince.

"Some would say the dreams of the unicorns represent your children in the future," said Elmahigh. "You say you saw them clearly and they were strong, innocent, and pure. Mankind's infancy is most pristine, and it's a strong correlation to what you have seen. The woman you pursued in the pond, indiscernible, her face remained hidden from you."

"Yes, that's correct," said Prince Adinor.

"She may have been your wife," said Elmahigh, "you pursued her throughout. The flowers around the pond may have been signs of a wedding one day."

"I really did want to catch her."

"Whoever it will be, the dream speaks to her strength and independence," replied Elmahigh. "It would not surprise me if she would have those qualities. In earnest, those are good qualities to have in her."

"And the dream of my parents, what of the feast?"

"It could have been a celebration of your past, my Prince or perhaps a banquet celebrating your return from this journey."

The Prince was confused and took a couple of more steps forward.

"It could have just been your appetite," said Elmahigh.

The monk chuckled and continued catching up to the others.

"Come, we're nearly there," said Elmahigh.

CHAPTER 25

Bolios and Isilmoire followed closely behind Teinmar. They were within seeing distance was the end of the forest.

"Theodonus and Malchomite," called Bolios.

The two came running to the front to join Bolios and Isilmoire.

"Yes, my lord," said Theodonus.

"Run ahead to the village and make ready the necessary supplies to treat the injured," said Bolios, "clean implements, hot water, herbs, and powerful elixirs. You know what we'll need. Go along with him, Malchomite."

"Right away, Bolios," said Malchomite.

The two ran ahead, passing Teinmar, in search of everything their leader demanded. Bolios walked toward the back of the group as the Mastadan villagers continued carrying the wounded. He examined Ecclesias, Friedrich, and Lautner. A villager spoke.

"They have not spoken for some time," said the villager.

Isilmoire joined Bolios near the wounded. The two Mastadans looked dreadful.

"Bolios," said Isilmoire, "your people cannot help Lautner. I will need to take him to my people, only they can treat him. We have ocean-derived medicines."

Elmahigh reached out and placed his hand on Ecclesias and Friedrich's wrists. Their pulse was faint. Isilmoire spoke to Lautner in Nymph. With a nod from his head, Lautner agreed. Isilmoire embraced his Nymph friend and yelled to Teinmar who came running. Both Isilmoire and Teinmar reached down toward Lautner, wrapping their arms beneath their friend and holding him up between them. Prince Adinor approached.

"You can't leave," said Prince Adinor, "we can help, there's food and medicine just ahead. Let us help you.

"They need their own medicine, Prince Adinor," said Elmahigh.

"But you have too long a journey," said Prince Adinor, "you are only three."

Teinmar spoke in Nymph. He let go of Lautner, leaving Isilmoire to hold him. Teinmar walked toward the Prince and embraced him. He returned back to help hold Lautner. The Prince began to cry.

"We merely have a small walk to a river not far from here," said Isilmoire. "Once we reach it, we'll return to the grotto shortly thereafter. Before dark, Lautner will receive the necessary care. He will be okay."

"I've come too far to die before any man," said Lautner.

Both Mastadans and Nymphs alike laughed. The three Nymphs began their short walk to the nearby river when Bolios walked toward them.

"Isilmoire," he said.

The three Nymphs turned.

"I almost forgot to thank you," said Bolios.

"It's nothing," said Isilmoire.

"It's everything," replied Bolios.

They both shook hands and parted company.

"Will we see them again?" asked Prince Adinor.

"I'm sure we will, my Prince," said Elmahigh.

The Mastadan warriors and villagers neared the village. High rising smoke from the chimneys of the village homes meant they were close. Two women in the streets dropped their berry-filled baskets and ran toward the group. They shouted, alerting other villagers to the sight of the returning warriors. A crowd swelled. Malchomite and Theodonus pushed through them, returning to Bolios.

"Everything has been prepared, my lord," said Theodonus, "bring them this way."

Theodonus led the group into the village. Villagers looked on amazed and tear filled from seeing their fellow villagers returned. Theodonus led them down a narrow street, then turned a corner arriving at the healer's home.

"Come inside, they are expecting us," said Theodonus.

Bolios motioned to the others and the wounded were carried through the door.

"Greetings, my lord," said the healer.

A prune-faced older bald man with a wispy white beard welcomed them in. His home was small and dark. It had little inside except two small slabs, each covered with a variety of animal skins for warmth. Upon a wall nearby, he had dozens of jars filled with different colored liquids and on another shelf were herbs and plants of various types. He dressed strange, wearing something similar to a court jester.

"Are you certain he can help?" asked Bolios.

"Yes, my lord," replied Malchomite.

"His reputation is quite well known among those here in the village," said Theodonus, "he's most highly recommended."

"The old man has even been known to perform removal of limbs and assisted in births when needed," said Malchomite.

"Very well," said Bolios, "place them down upon the beds there. We'll learn soon enough of his skills."

Bolios walked toward the old man standing in the doorway and said, "Harm my friends and it will cost your life."

"No, my lord, never," said the healer, "here they get good care."

Bolios walked out of the home and saw dozens of villagers encircling the soldiers outside. They asked questions and provided hugs and kisses in a display of gratitude for their friends' safe return. Thomas and his son Duncan together with the others gradually left. One villager walked up to Bolios and asked, "Are we safe, my lord? Will they return?"

Bolios looked on as all those present listened intently. Dozens of sets of eyes looked back at him, their faces pale, weary, and malnourished.

"Yes, you are safe," he said, "no harm shall come upon you. Live your lives."

The villagers shouted and embraced one another. Some cried and others kissed. The mob of villagers dispersed and moved into their respective homes and trades.

"Now what?" asked Prince Adinor.

"We wait, young Prince," said Elmahigh. "Our friends need much care. Our time perhaps can be best spent in thought and meditation, keeping them in our wishes."

"I could eat an entire horse myself," said Dolamite. "We're starved, Bolios."

"Eating is a terrific idea," said Prince Adinor.

"Very well," said Bolios, "I will find you all in time."

"And you, Bolios, where will you go?" asked Prince Adinor.

"I will remain here and make certain Ecclesias and Friedrich's conditions improve," replied Bolios. "Be sure to mind your behavior. Keep them under control, Theodonus."

"Yes, my lord," replied Theodonus.

The men raced around the corner as Dolamite said, "I will drink all the maltsenhop within this entire village."

"Not if I beat you to it," replied Prince Adinor.

"Get back here, confounded boy," said Dolamite. The Prince continued to run toward the inn, leaving Dolamite behind. The soldiers slapped one another's arms and hugged.

"I can almost taste it," said Malcomite.

"I as well," said Marcus.

Only Elmahigh and Bolios were left standing outside the healer's home.

"They have earned some spoils," said Elmahigh.

"Yes, they've fought bravely," replied Bolios, "you've done well too, old friend."

"The times have carved us both into steadfast pillars of this kingdom," said Elmahigh, "though even pillars fall eventually."

"We have won a great victory, Elmahigh," said Bolios.

"Yes, you are right, Bolios," said Elmahigh. "As the days go by, it seems all the more rare to have victories. And so I shall relish it."

"Where will you go?"

Elmahigh revealed his custom carved wooden pipe; it was shaped in the likeness of a falcon. A memento he carried with him always.

"Perhaps the local farmer may be kind enough to exchange some of this season's herb for me to sample."

Bolios laughed as he turned back into the healer's home. Just before he walked in, he said, "Will you join them later at the inn?"

Elmahigh lifted his pipe and said, "Most certainly."

And with that, the monk walked away. Bolios walked into the healer's home and noticed a strange odor.

"What is that smell?" he asked.

"A potent tea I've made, my lord," replied the healer, "A mix of fruit and herbs with a touch of a special leaf that sprouts from a rare mountain flower. I call it urquell. Both of your friends had some, it helps speed up recovery. It gives much needed nutrients and aids in healing wounds."

"Is that so?" said Bolios.

"Yes, my lord," replied the healer, "I've left some for you on the table there. I suggest you rest and have some. It will help with the fracture you have in your side."

Bolios walked over to the table and sat down. He reached for the small wooden cup and took a generous sip.

"How did you know?" he asked.

"You favor one side in your posture," replied the healer, "a natural response to the injury."

Bolios stared at his two fellow warriors. "Will my friends be all right?"

"Yes, they arrived just in time," replied the healer, "you should rest, the body calls for it. I assure you, under my care, the wounds of both your friends will be closed in due time. Even their fever will subside too. Their bodies are merely fighting the poison within their blood. Some of which I have released. The rest will be dealt with shortly. First I must get them stronger. More teas and elixirs will do them good. Clean food and rest will be their ally."

Bolios continued drinking the tea. The earthy flavor of the leaves together with fresh fruit juices served warm was comforting. Gradually, his eyes became heavier. Within moments, his hands and feet lost feeling and his head fell toward his chest. He was asleep. The healer continued sewing up the wounds of the two, working tirelessly to also clean them and continue feeding them with elixirs and food.

Back at the inn, Dolamite, Malchomite, Marcus, Theodonus, and Prince Adinor began to eat and drink to their enjoyment's fill. The maltsenhop was delicious as mug after mug was served. Fresh bison and hot elk stew were served with baked breads. The men sat near the fire eating and joking. They talked of their past tales and the memories just made. Throughout the evening, it seemed to be a combination of zeal mixed with a touch of competition. Each turn saw one Mastadan embellish his account just a bit more than the other. At the first sign of an empty glass, the innkeeper sent his attendants to replenish it with more maltsenhop. The men tore into the hot and spicy bison, a delicacy this time of year. It was slightly charred, a preference for Dolamite who ordered all the food.

"Must you always ask for it overcooked?" said Marcus.

"It is just right," replied Dolamite.

Prince Adinor ripped the meat of the bone and ate wildly.

"Where are your manners, boy?" asked Dolamite.

The meat continued to be savored by them all as they laughed repeatedly as Prince Adinor mistook Dolamite's joke for seriousness. The enjoyment deepened as the hot pourage was placed on their table. The soft potatoes and carrots, onions and cabbage, stewed together with rabbit and hen, made for a rich and savory stock. A villager at the inn pulled out a small flute and played a Mastadan classic. The warriors began to sing along. Another villager began to clap his hands in melody, and a boy from the kitchen banged atop an empty keg to form a jovial song.

"Is Bolios coming?" asked Prince Adinor.

"He won't leave Ecclesias or Friedrich until they're well," said Theodonus. "He always stays at his men's side."

The Prince put his drink down as a couple of soldiers began to dance.

"Has he always been that way?" asked the Prince.

"Since I can recall," replied Theodonus, "you don't know why, do you, young Prince?"

"He's such a good leader," said the Prince.

"It's not only that, sire," replied Theodonus. "When Bolios was a boy, he lived in a remote village much like this one. His family was of humble beginnings. Farming was their trade. He was an only child. His father was a quiet man and his mother known by most in the village as a skilled dressmaker. They lived honest lives and never bothered anyone. One day, when Bolios was but a child, no more than four or five years at most, a vagrant came upon his home. The man, for no apparent reason, killed both of Bolios' parents. Bolios, away in the field playing, returned to his home to see his parents lying lifeless before him."

Prince Adinor sat staring at Theodonus, who took a drink from his mug.

"When he was old enough at eleven years of age, he began his service to the kingdom's forces," continued Theodonus, "not much is known about his time in between, but don't you see? He has nothing except his men. He has no family. He keeps no company of friends. All his life, he's known battles and fighting. Everything he has is his fellow warrior. We are his only family."

He felt guilty.

"The maltsenhop has taken hold of me. I should not have shared this, young Prince. Please assure me what I speak of this evening remains here and that is all. Never speak of it to him or anyone."

The Prince nodded and returned to his maltsenhop. Theodonus rose from the table and joined the others dancing.

"Come, young Prince," said Theodonus. "It is a time to rejoice."

Theodonus grabbed the Prince as they swelled in the excitement. Together with Dolamite, Marcus, and Malchomite, the Prince and Theodonus joined in a terrific night of jubilation. For the few inside the inn, it was a terrific moment. As the last of the evening's enjoyment wound down, the warriors found the nearest space and collapsed in surrender to the fatigue built up from the long embattled journey.

Chapter 26

The next morning, Prince Adinor walked over Dolamite and Theodonus and the others still fast asleep. He stepped out from the inn and into the village square. He raised a hand to his brow, shielding the bright sunlight. Feeling the heat, he tied his hair and began to wander around the village. Drifting down different roads, he noticed a pleasing friendliness from the people. As he walked, he received greetings in the form of nods of the head, bows, or even hugs.

Prince Adinor observed a carpenter and his apprentice. They worked on a small wooden chair. It had a round seat and large spiral legs. The two hammered and carved, measured and evaluated, then resumed once again. The Prince continued on and found a couple of farmers selling apples and turnips as well as sweet peas and pomegranates. Their large stand's baskets were filled to the top with bright colored fruits and vegetables. Upon seeing the Prince approach, they offered him the best of their crop. The Prince continued to refuse them. They all but stuffed the fruit into his mouth, finally, the Prince relinquished and the fresh fruit was his. They made for a perfect meal while walking through the village. The roads he walked on were nothing but dirt, sparsely covered by grass. He wondered of the possibility of a stone road connecting the city center to the village and perhaps extending toward the other areas of high population throughout the kingdom. Doing so could unify all regions of the kingdom making trade and travel easier. He would surely mention it to his father upon returning. Next, he walked past a blacksmith and then a group of children in the middle of the street. They were embarrassed and stopped.

"No, it's fine," said the Prince, "go on, continue as though I am not here."

He winked at them and the children continued playing, jumping, and messing about. Up above in the openings overhead of the homes, he could see a couple of girls his age staring down toward him. They waved, which he answered in kind by doing the same. They swooned and hid inside, disappearing from sight. He bit into an apple; its crisp outer shell revealed its freshness. His tongue burst with flavor from the juicy white. The sweetness of each bite invigorated him with energy, and he continued bouncing along the street, eager to see more of the villagers.

He made his way to the outskirts of the village and found a church just ahead. It had white shiny clay walls. A three-foot steeple was directly in the front.

The Prince approached, still engrossed in his fruit meal. As he entered, it was nothing more than a few columns and bare walls. Upon entering, he realized it was abandoned. Weeds, more than a foot high sprang from the ground and hardly any light entered from the dirt caked windows in the walls. From the ceiling hung webs and small spiders. As the Prince walked throughout the small chamber, he recognized something in the corner, a symbol similar to that of a pendant his mother wore. He moved closer to it and realized it was the mirror image of it, except this one was larger.

"You've seen it before," said a voice from the temple's entrance.

"Hello, Elmahigh," replied Prince Adinor, "yes, my mother wears this symbol in a pendant around her neck."

"Spend much time in prayer, young Prince?" asked Elmahigh.

Prince Adinor hung his head a bit. "Never really got into it, but my mom often does."

Elmahigh exited the temple. He took several deep breaths and exhaled mouthfuls of the fresh crisp air outside.

"A gorgeous day," he said, "and a beautiful landscape."

"This village is a wonderful simple place," said Prince Adinor, "so much happiness and goodness. Everyone is friendly and kind."

"It is a beautiful way of life," said Elmahigh.

"I could live in a place like this," said the Prince. "Care for an apple or pomegranate?"

"Very kind of you, young Prince," said Elmahigh, "I think I'll accept your offer. I'd love to try a pomegranate and some of the dates you carry."

"Whatever you like, Elmahigh. I couldn't possibly eat them all. My pouch is full of a few."

"Have you been up long?" asked Elmahigh.

"Yes, after last night's enjoyment, I thought a walk would suit me."

"Care if I join you for what's left of it, young Prince?" asked Elmahigh.

"Not at all."

They continued walking further away from the temple toward the outlying farmlands nearby. They saw children helping their parents work the fields and even witnessed ox and mules used to tend the land. In gardens, women and small girls alike cut and trimmed where necessary to keep vegetables growing. As both Elmahigh and Prince Adinor walked back toward the village, birds of various types flew overhead. First, some crows, then doves, but the best sights of all were hawks. Often, Prince Adinor tried impressing Elmahigh with his knowledge of nature by calling out both animal and plants by name as he came across them. It was a peaceful relaxing walk, as Prince Adinor's mentor posed questions and listened to the young Prince's responses.

The two walked through the entrance of the village, their long discussions continued. They arrived to the large well near the village center where a few of the villagers gathered to collect water. The crowd ran to Elmahigh and the Prince, hugging and thanking them as champions. The Prince and Elmahigh smiled as they slipped out of the embraces and parted again. They returned to their conversation, but were again interrupted as Theodonus approached.

"Good morning," he said.

"It is a glorious one, dear friend," said Elmahigh.

"How did you fare last night, young Prince?" asked Theodonus.

"I lost count of how many mugs of maltsenhop I had if that's a telling sign," replied the Prince.

"The others are beginning to rub off on you," said Theodonus.

They all laughed, enjoying some small talk as stories from the morning's events included Dolamite running within the inn, searching for more bison or pourage.

"It was legendary," said Theodonus.

"I can imagine," said Elmahigh, "although perhaps I shouldn't as we all know of Dolamite's temper when his appetite gets the best of him."

"Yes, if only enemies took the form of food, there would be no better warrior than he," replied Theodonus.

The three broke out in laughter once more.

"In seriousness, I must depart and check on the others," said Theodonus.

"Very well," said Elmahigh, "a most appropriate decision."

"Before I do, did you both hear?" asked Theodonus.

"Nothing of particular interest, what news?" asked Elmahigh.

"There's talk among the villagers of a celebration tonight," answered Theodonus. "They want to honor us for the safe return of those freed from the monsters. The preparations are already underway. Everyone from the village will be there. Goat, beef, stew, soups, the finest crops and fruits will be served. There's even talk of a ceremony and music."

"Well that sounds lovely," replied Elmahigh.

"That's incredibly generous of them," said Prince Adinor.

"I wonder if Bolios will allow it," asked Theodonus.

"See to the others and be sure to keep them out of trouble," replied Elmahigh. "The young Prince and I will go to the healer's place. It is a good time for us to check on their progress. In doing so, we will speak to Bolios."

"Very well, until later," said Theodonus.

"Godspeed," said Elmahigh.

Theodonus left and turned a corner, searching for the warriors while Elmahigh and Prince Adinor walked toward the healer's residence. The entire village seemed consumed in a myriad of tasks for the evening's celebration. Some ran holding large baskets of corn and potatoes. Others carried wood for fire. Everyone teemed with enthusiasm. Elmahigh and Prince Adinor approached the doorway of the healer. Bolios was standing outside.

"Greetings, Bolios," said Elmahigh, "you look well."

"Good morning to you both," he replied.

He wore a different shirt, a gift from a villager most likely. His hair and skin were clean, a sign he'd bathed recently.

"Hello, Bolios," said Prince Adinor.

"How are Ecclesias and Friedrich?" asked Elmahigh.

"They struggled through the night, a normal result from the strong herbs and pumices employed by the healer," said Bolios, "so he says. They did however wake a few moments ago and were both lucid and in good spirits. They are resting once again."

"A good sign, I take it," said Elmahigh.

"Thankfully, everyone's high opinion of this old man was correct and he will cure them in the end," said Bolios.

"Can I go inside and see them?" asked Prince Adinor.

"Of course, young Prince," replied Bolios, "they will be grateful for the visit."

The Prince walked under Bolios' outstretched arm and entered the small doorway.

"Have you rested?" asked Elmahigh.

"Yes, a powerful elixir helped settle me in for an unusually long amount of sleep," replied Bolios. "The evening seemed to fly by."

"And your injury?" asked Elmahigh.

"It will heal," said Bolios. "I take it by now you've heard of the village plans to honor us?"

"Yes, we've just learned of it from Theodonus on our way here."

Bolios watched as the villagers continued running about in the streets.

"I imagine the men deserve some rest for the heroic deeds they've done," replied Bolios, "In truth, I wouldn't want to be the one to tell any of these villagers we wouldn't stay. They don't seem to take no as an answer for their generosity."

"I take it you've already witnessed it firsthand?" asked Elmahigh.

Bolios revealed his abdomen and showed fresh bandages in addition to fine thread and sheep's wool.

"A fresh wrap applied just this morning by the healer who insisted I use one to help support me and speed the healing in my ribs," said Bolios. "Even this awful shirt was a gift from a village woman that insisted I put it on in front of her."

"I did find it remarkable that you are not favoring the injured side at all," said Elmahigh.

"I tried everything to stop them, but they wouldn't relent," said Bolios.

Elmahigh started laughing.

"As for the celebration, given Ecclesias and Friedrich still require attention, tell the men we will stay for the celebration this evening," said Bolios. "I will remain here with Ecclesias and Friedrich."

Prince Adinor walked out of the house and stopped next to Bolios.

"You be sure to enjoy yourself, young Prince," said Bolios.

"You should join us tonight," replied Prince Adinor.

"Given all the commotion of the villagers flocking here and there and everywhere," said Bolios, "I'll be better off resting and avoiding tonight's debauchery."

Bolios stepped inside and joined Friedrich and Ecclesias.

"Let's share the news with the others, Elmahigh," said Prince Adinor.

Prince Adinor and Elmahigh walked past dozens of meandering villagers. Many were so focused they didn't notice the Prince or Elmahigh. The two headed to the inn.

Upon entering, they found it empty. Not even the attendants or workers were inside. It was quiet. Elmahigh and Prince Adinor walked over to the fireplace and observed the absence of heat.

"Where did everyone go?" asked Prince Adinor.

"A curious question," replied Elmahigh.

There were creaks from the dry wooden stairs leading to the top floor. Footsteps descended, revealing the innkeeper.

"Pardon the lack of attentions, my lords," he said, "there won't be supper this evening. There's a large celebration tonight, and I fancy it will be a momentous occasion, so I've decided to close and enjoy as well. Everyone will be welcomed to secure a room if need be, but no food is all. If you's understand."

"That will be fine," replied Elmahigh.

"If you're looking for the others, they've gone out to the wood," said the innkeeper, "They fancied the idea of hunting for the evening's procession to be a warranted decision. I reckon I agree. Can't ever have too much food. I tell you, I'll be the first to admit, learned that lesson all too well myself. See, you'd be surprised how often a travelling man can eat in a day."

Elmahigh chuckled.

"At first glance, I thought it nice to detect any a man's appetite," said the innkeeper, "but to my surprise, those conceived by me to be heavy eaters merely would consume a plate of food, I tell you. And just as wildly confusing. A man seemingly tested by a mere strong breeze could surprisingly eat all day. I can't begin to tell you how many guests I lost to heated arguments over the food shortages. No sir, I'd think it unwise to succumb to that mistake again."

"Do you know where in the wood they decided to hunt?" asked Prince Adinor.

"This time of year, there would be only one worthy area. The best game is found there. If I had to wager my wife's recipe for our cow stomach stew, I'd say they went to Beaver's Creek."

"Would you be so kind as to direct us there?" asked Prince Adinor.

"Plan on hunting it again, masters?" asked the innkeeper.

"No, we'd just like to find our friends," said Prince Adinor.

"We will not tell a soul," said Elmahigh.

"Well, certainly it would be unfortunate," replied the innkeeper, "the best fowl in all the village is served right here, and that area is most often where I've amassed my finest hunts. Listen carefully. Go to the edge of town near the stable past the baker's house. As you near the stable, you'll notice a small bog ahead. Most wouldn't think it crossable, but just nearby is a narrow mound you must find. Look behind the mound to a spot of darkness just below the surface of the water. There is where you'll find the stones marking the path I've made. It will seem as though you'd fall into the water if you decided to step into it, but I assure you no such thing will happen. After the first stone, all the others will become visible. Follow the stones and you will certainly arrive at the other side of the bog, placing you within the Beaver Creek hunting grounds."

The Prince and Elmahigh walked toward the end of the village as instructed.

"Quite the curious fellow," said Elmahigh.

"I take it the fowl are untouchable then," said Prince Adinor.

"Heavens yes, Prince Adinor," replied Elmahigh, "we'd be chased out of the inn perhaps for good."

Prince Adinor laughed and continued walking, arriving at the bog. They followed the innkeeper's exact instructions and crossed the bog without issue.

"Quite ingenious," said Elmahigh.

"No doubt other villagers would be envious of our fortunes for the way he spoke of this area gives the impression of sure successes."

"Let's hope so," replied Elmahigh.

The two moved into the wood, stepping upon the dry ground with care.

"Look up above," said Prince Adinor.

"Well, isn't that something."

In the large round treetops were countless fat birds of all kinds.

"That's amazing," said Prince Adinor, "let's keep going further."

The two moved closer and saw a variety of other animals moving. Small brown- and cream-colored rabbits raced across the ground. Squirrels ran up the trees holding nuts and seeds from the ground. The animals seemed unfettered by the pair, a rare circumstance for both Elmahigh and Prince Adinor.

"Perhaps we'll find the others nearby," said Prince Adinor.

"I agree they should be nearby," said Elmahigh, "let's move further."

And so they continued on seeing bushes littered with fresh berries. There were deep rich reds and blues and also purples, a wealth of smells present. The area's black soil cushioned their steps, helping them move silently. Leaves fell upon the ground creating a gentle path leading toward the creek ahead.

"Have you seen deer or elk?" asked Prince Adinor.

"None," replied Elmahigh.

"Nor have I," said the Prince.

"Let's move toward the water, perhaps they'll be there."

The two approached a calm, clear, narrow creek. Its icy waters and its gentle rolling current bathed the smooth rocks peeking up from below creating a peaceful sound.

"Can we stay here a bit?" asked Prince Adinor.

"A terrific idea, young Prince," said Elmahigh.

The Prince sat neat the creek, watching its beauty and obsessing over the many rocks throughout it. He reached for small pebbles and began tossing them into the creek, trying to skip them across. Elmahigh walked away, heading to a tree nearby. He leaned up against it and soaked up the shade it provided. He folded his arms and legs, covered his head with his hood, and slipped into a peaceful sleep.

Prince Adinor continued playing with the pebbles and felt the warmth of the sun hitting his skin, baking it. Small beads of sweat collected on his brow, and he felt the heat around his neck swell. He bent down toward the creek and drank from the cool water below. He splashed his face with water and soaked his head, dunking it in the water. The cool icy water sent thousands of tiny sensations shooting throughout his body. He immersed his head once more and enjoyed the sensation again. He stopped and looked over to Elmahigh who remained still.

"Elmahigh, come try the water," said Prince Adinor.

The wizard slowly lifted his head, opening only one eye, but chose instead to remain seated under the tree.

"It's quite all right, young Prince," replied Elmahigh. "I'm enjoying a wonderful breeze at the moment."

The Prince looked up and down the creek and remembered his Nymph friends. He reflected on his times with them and hoped Lautner was safely treated and healed. How fortunate it was to have met them and how incredible of a tale it would make back home.

The Prince, now satisfied with his fill of water, stepped back from the creek and walked toward a set of trees not far from Elmahigh. He looked for a spot mirroring Elmahigh's. Frustrated by his inability to find one, he chose instead to lean up against the same one Elmahigh was using. As he lowered himself onto the tree, opposite the side Elmahigh used, he discovered just how smooth the trunk of the tree was. Together with the shade and soft ground below, it was a perfect resting spot.

The Prince sat up, however, unable to sleep. He whipped his head around the tree and checked to see if Elmahigh was also awake. He was not. The Prince looked up at the sky and wondered about his parents. What happiness they would feel in knowing he was representing the name of their line so well. In truth, the Prince recalled travelling to various areas of the kingdom but doubted King Ralphus ever came to this particular village. The Prince looked down toward the dagger on his side, the shiny unmistakable gift from Bolios was still there. He thought of how to give it back to him.

The afternoon's heat subsided, and more of the cool breeze from the creek continued dancing off the water. As it continued swirling around him, the Prince began to fade. In a few moments, he fell asleep.

CHAPTER 27

"Prince Adinor sure is out," said Dolamite.

"It's a lot for a young one to experience," said Theodonus.

"He's done well, wouldn't you say?" asked Elmahigh.

"He's surprised me," said Malchomite.

"I can say the same," added Marcus.

"It's nearly dusk," said Elmahigh, "let's wake him."

Theodonus walked toward the young Prince who remained oblivious to their arrival. Theodonus slowly patted the Prince's shoulder and gently shook him.

"There, young Prince," said Theodonus, "up you go."

"Theodonus, when did you arrive?" asked Prince Adinor.

"It's not been long," replied Theodonus, "myself and the others saw Elmahigh from across the creek. We had already concluded our hunt and were returning to the village."

"Was it a success?" asked Prince Adinor.

"You be the judge of that, my Prince," replied Theodonus.

The Prince looked and dDraped around Dolamite's neck was a healthy elk. Marcus carried some large fat hares in one hand and a couple of baskets of wild berries and figs. Malchomite had several fish and some wild mushrooms as well.

The Prince's mouth watered; he was delighted at the sight.

"It's unfortunate, Prince Adino." said Dolamite. "Those that do not help in the kill cannot partake in the eating."

"Yes, it is a rather troubling matter," said Elmahigh.

"But, Elmahigh, you didn't partake in the hunt," said Prince Adinor.

"I'll have you know, young Prince, that of the fish in Malchomite's possession, the majority are my catch."

"You will have to show me that technique one day," said Theodonus.

"Of course," said Elmahigh.

The Prince sulked. Troubled, he looked around to see what he could figure out from things nearby.

"We're only having some fun with you, young Prince," said Theodonus.

"Did you see the look on him?" asked Dolamite.

"I thought he may take a fish right from my grasp," said Malchomite.

"Terribly funny," said the Prince with a blank look.

"Come, let us return to the village," said Elmahigh, "the celebration is soon to begin and this food will need some able hands to prepare it."

The group returned via the innkeeper's hidden path and entered into a bustling village. As they neared the village, a more densely packed street greeted them. Up ahead, there was a large fire. It raged high into the sky as sparks flew from it. The crackle and pop of the burning logs of wood raged. Atop smaller fires nearby, villagers cooked a number of dishes. The warriors approached a few villagers standing near the cooks who accepted the contributions to the feast.

"Let the celebration begin," said a voice in the distance.

Behind the fire was a small stage where several villagers sat atop empty barrels and crates. Others stood forming what seemed like the evening's entertainment. They soon began to clap their hands and stomp their feet. They burst into song. On the stage was the same boy who played the flute at the inn the evening prior. The group was full of spirit, and soon, dozens of villagers spun around and moved in delight and pure joy. In addition to the hot bubbling soups and stews was a giant spit featuring a seasoned boar roasting over a fire.

"I think I'll find my way to that boar, just over there," said Dolamite. "One can never be too careful to not overcook a boar."

All of the barrels of wine were opposite the cooks and fresh breads and sweets were on a table alongside. There was freshly made maltsenhop and fruits. The ladies and men alike enjoyed some immediately. Elmahigh ventured over to the farmer who graciously offered him a sweet herb, different than the one he tried before. He lit his pipe and was soon invited to dance by two young girls in their twenties.

"You really should corral the Prince," Elmahigh said.

The other warriors also enjoyed the celebration. Every which way they turned, they received countless hugs, thanks, and plenty of food and drink. As the music and food and wine continued to flow, more villagers reveled in its enjoyment. Prince Adinor smiled and savored the stews as well as the charred fish. An added joy came in the form of two faces not seen by the Prince in quite some time. Through the crowd, seated near the healer was Ecclesias and Friedrich. Overcome with excitement, Prince Adinor leapt from his seat, abandoning his food, and ran through the crowd to hug them both.

"You've made it," said Prince Adinor.

"Yes, what a joy to be here among you all again," said Friedrich.

"Is there maltsenhop?" asked Ecclesias.

"Of course," said Prince Adinor, "I'll get you both some."

The Prince ran over to the table, grabbing two freshly poured mugs and returned to them in moments.

"Here a toast to you both," said Prince Adinor.

The piercing watchful gaze of the healer from across the way, glaring at their choice, but ignored it, concentrating instead on their mugs.

"Where's Bolios?" asked Prince Adinor.

"I'm uncertain," said Friedrich. "He said he would come."

"He's not much for good tidings," said Ecclesias.

Just then, Theodonus, Marcus, and Malchomite approached. They hugged the two injured warriors. Dolamite also arrived, and they all raised their glasses and drank. They conversed and laughed from jokes Ecclesias and Dolamite shared. It was the best medicine for a low spirit, and so the group enjoyed the evening together. They drank, ate, and danced.

Prince Adinor was convinced by some of the ladies of the village to join them in the merriment. He saw one of the two girls from his walk earlier. Theodonus wasted no time and forced him over to them both.

"This is madness," said Prince Adinor.

"Madness is you not speaking to these lovely girls, and I just won't have it," said Theodonus.

The rest of the soldiers watched as the Prince and Theodonus approached the girls.

"Evening to you, madams," said Theodonus.

The two twenty-something girls bowed and recoiled a bit.

"May I say, the two of you are looking lovely," said Theodonus. "Is that a new dress?"

"Yes, a gift from my mother," said the shorter of the two.

"And you?" said Theodonus.

"Yes, my lord?" replied the other girl.

"Do you enjoy dancing?" asked Theodonus.

"Well, of course, I do," said the girl.

"Excellent!" said Theodonus. "Away you go all of you."

"No, Theodonus," said Prince Adinor, "But I—"

"Nonsense," said Theodonus.

Theodonus pushed the three onto the dance floor, and they were all swept up by the music. The Prince stopped for a second, but the two girls grabbed his hand and spun him around once again. They didn't let him leave. The music quickened and the young trio continued to move to the beat. They were not alone; dozens of villagers enjoyed the pleasantry and spun near them as well. Even the innkeeper and his wife danced alongside them.

"That's it, Prince Adinor," yelled Elmahigh.

The Prince turned and found Elmahigh dancing together with several more people. Theodonus walked over to the Mastadan warriors. They laughed wildly from the jokes and teasing among themselves.

"How's our boy doing?" asked Dolamite.

"I think my work is done," said Theodonus.

They all laughed once more.

"More maltsenhop!" yelled Dolamite.

They all filled their glasses and made a toast once again.

"To Prince Adinor," they said.

"The future of our kingdom," said Theodonus.

"May he always remain in safe keeping," said Dolamite.

Some of the women of the village found their way to the warriors and began to enjoy their company. They talked and danced too, washing any thoughts of battle and threats away, even if just for a while. The married ones like Friedrich and Dolamite began sharing comparisons of their wives, bragging about which was the better cook. Failing to decide it, they moved on to the subject of which of the two had the better offspring. It was a harmless conversation until they began to speak of which son was a better rider.

"That's enough, you two," said Theodonus.

"Let's just say I will gladly have my son at my side on a long ride across country, as long as his mother is nearby to help feed him," said Friedrich.

"Well, finally something we can't argue on," said Dolamite. "I bet you your boy eats just as much as my son."

"Oh, I don't doubt it," said Friedrich.

And just like that, the two made peace once more.

"I'll drink to your son," said Dolamite.

"And I'll drink to yours," replied Friedrich.

"Cheers," they both said.

As the night went on, every villager journeyed to the celebration. There was not a single person missing except Bolios.

* * *

Just outside the healer's house, Bolios stared up to the thousands of stars overhead. He was alone but could easily hear the music shouting and laughter from the celebration in the village center. He began walking toward it, but as he approached, he thought mostly about the battle with the monster. The scenes replayed in his head. The constant repelled monster attacks upon the hill. He recalled the forays with the various monsters he dispatched. The majority of his thoughts and memories of the battle were of Mesthusula. The heavy blows inflicted by the demon monster, the blood-red eyes, the unrelenting determination to inflict harm and punishment. Bolios obsessed over it.

He was reminded of the fear he felt then of losing his friends. He thought of that final moment Mesthusula nearly defeated him were it not for Isilmoire.

Bolios turned away from the celebration and walked back toward the healer's home. He shoved the door open and grabbed his sword near the corner of the room. He raced away from the celebration and made his way to the other side of the village. Carrying only his sword, he walked toward the entrance of the Petruchani Forest. He removed his sword and stepped toward it once again.

"Just where do you think you are going?" asked Elmahigh.

Bolios took another step into the forest. The other remained out.

Elmahigh walked toward the Mastadan leader and blew another small cloud of smoke from his pipe.

"Have you decided to go off again?" asked Elmahigh.

"Yes," replied Bolios.

"Alone?"

Bolios turned and now faced Elmahigh.

"Those men celebrating right now would follow me back into the forest if needed," said Bolios.

"They would follow you to the end of existence," Elmahigh said.

"Which is why I must leave without them," said Bolios. "I've seen too many lives lost in my life, Elmahigh. Too many battles fought. Too many victims left behind to count and the madness never ends. This last battle only requires one sword, and it shall be mine."

"Oh, come now, Bolios."

"Every moment wasted is an opportunity Qualvon strengthens and exacts more carnage on innocent lives like that of these villagers here. There is no need to subject my men to further risk. I will go alone."

"You blame yourself for Ecclesias and Friedrich's suffering?" asked Elmahigh.

"With every fiber of my being, yes," replied Bolios, "lest we forget, Elmahigh, I've lost two of my warriors already to this horrid disease. You saw what became of Litovic? Have you forgotten Salazar? His life was lost due to this evil spreading across our lands. What more will it take from me? What more do we have to give?"

"Come, my friend, you already know the answer to that."

"Yes, and that is why I will not ask of anyone else to follow me. Where I go, I must go alone."

"I cannot stop you, Bolios. If you proceed on this course, you and you alone will determine where it leads. The fate of your journey will be an uncertain one. I would be remiss if I did not share this."

"What might that be?" asked Bolios.

"If you pursue Qualvon alone, as adept as you are at traveling undetected, no one would know how to find you. You may even find him and vindicate yourself entirely, but at what cost?"

Bolios stepped forward once more, now facing the Petruchani Forest once again.

"Think not of your own needs but rather of your men," said Elmahigh, "perhaps you do not need to be followed, but others need to be led. If you leave your men now, how will they respond? Understand this, my friend, some things there is no coming back from."

Elmahigh turned from Bolios and walked back toward the village center, enjoying a few more puffs from his cherished wooden pipe. Bolios thought for a moment of Elmahigh's words. He looked at his side. The evening fog covered the forest entrance and the night grew cold. Bolios looked back toward the village once more and thought about Elmahigh's words.

CHAPTER 28

Back at the party, the villagers were beginning to leave. The center of the village emptied. Only the fire and the Mastadan warriors sitting around it remained. They continued laughing and drinking as only they could.

Friedrich and Malchomite were asleep. They leaned against each other, the perfect remedy for no bed. Theodonus and Dolamite, together with Ecclesias and Marcus, talked of past exploits and encouraged each other to share scary stories of enemies met along the way. Walking around the fire toward them was Elmahigh puffing from his pipe.

"Where have you been all this time, Elmahigh?" asked Ecclesias.

"Oh, I've just gone for a brisk walk."

"I take it you didn't find yourself a pretty young maiden to enjoy that walk with?" asked Theodonus.

"That is one such enjoyment that escapes me," replied Elmahigh.

"I don't know how you forego that?" said Theodonus.

"Is it true?" asked Ecclesias.

"Is what true?"

"You're not allowed to well…you know," said Dolamite, "women."

"It is a part of my order," said Elmahigh, "it's also forbidden to wield weapons. As you know, I do not prescribe to that particular aspect of my order. If I should choose to find a woman, it is my choice, but it's thought to weaken my possibility of gaining further strengthening and enhanced abilities."

"So you could have a woman?" asked Dolamite.

"Hush now," said Theodonus, "leave our friend alone. After all, tonight our dear Prince conquers for us all."

"You don't say," said Elmahigh.

"He left joined by the two lovely young maidens dancing with him throughout the night," said Ecclesias.

"They all looked rather chummy if I do say myself," said Marcus.

"I say good for him," said Dolamite, "a toast for Prince Adinor."

"We already toasted for him, you fool," said Ecclesias,

"Enough," said Theodonus, "you all banter and gossip like a couple of old maids. Besides we're out of maltsenhop."

They all laughed wildly. Then from under the table nearby, crawled Prince Adinor.

"Look, men, he's so far worn, he can't even walk," said Theodonus.

They all erupted in laughs once again.

"Tell us, Prince Adinor, how was it?" asked Ecclesias.

"Give the boy some space, he's only just returned," said Theodonus.

"Well, it's probably best I keep things to myself," said the Prince.

"Spoken like a gentleman," said Elmahigh.

"What's the fun in that?" said Dolamite.

"Well, if we're not to get any details on the young Prince's escapades, I think it a better investment of my time to stir up the innkeeper and find some more maltsenhop," said Dolamite.

"I wholeheartedly agree," said Ecclesias.

"Wake those two and bring them along," said Theodonus.

Friedrich and Malchomite awoke and followed the others to the inn. Elmahigh and Prince Adinor stayed.

"Don't let them get to you, Prince Adinor," said Elmahigh. "You were right to keep those things to yourself. Respect for a lady is of the utmost importance."

"There wasn't much to share anyway," replied the Prince. "I was so dizzy from all the eating, drinking, and dancing that they mostly just talked to me as I lay on the floor sick. The room kept spinning around as if I were a toy top."

Elmahigh erupted in laughter.

"Besides, there's no proof I'd ever see either of them again," said the Prince. "I wonder if one of those girls is the ones from my dream."

"It's said that the right woman is known in an instant," said Elmahigh, "the very world becomes revealed in her and life ceases to be the same from that moment forward."

"Have you ever been in love, Elmahigh?" asked the Prince.

"Yes, of course, young Prince," replied Elmahigh. "It is unfortunate that a life with the woman I loved was not possible, but I was meant for a different path."

The Prince stumbled toward the maltsenhop, discovering only a couple of drops remained.

"I wish I would have seen the girl I met a few days ago," said Prince Adinor.

"Fancied a girl not of the two you met this evening?"

"I was curious about her is all," replied Prince Adinor.

"That's how it starts. Prince Adinor, care to join the others at the inn?"

"No, Elmahigh, I think I'll sit here for a moment," replied Prince Adinor. "The fire is starting to spin around just like in the girls' room. I don't think I could make it to the inn."

"Rest, young Prince," said Elmahigh, "I believe it to be the best idea at the moment. Once the spinning subsides, we will get back to the others. Perhaps one too many maltsenhops?"

The Prince lay near the fire. Its gradual weakening flames helped provide the perfect balance of mild warmth to ease him into relaxation.

Prince Adinor folded his arms across his body. Elmahigh sat nearby on a bench, staring into the fire. He looked up at the stars.

"Prince Adinor, if I may," said Elmahigh.

"Yes, Elmahigh."

"There's a question you've yet to answer."

The Prince struggled to stay awake. He curled up closer to the dying fire and assumed a fetal position.

"What question?" said Prince Adinor.

"What made you return to the battle?" asked Elmahigh.

The Prince rolled on the ground, fighting the drunkenness and fatigue.

"The woman convinced me," said Prince Adinor.

Elmahigh laughed.

"The woman this evening, young Prince?"

"No, the woman that evening," replied Prince Adinor.

"The woman from the dream you spoke of. She spoke to you?"

"No, not that woman, Elmahigh," said Prince Adinor, "another woman."

Elmahigh paused as his smile disappeared.

"Pardon me, your highness, I hate to disturb your rest, but I am a bit confused. What woman?"

Elmahigh stood up and walked toward the Prince who was curled up in a ball like an infant child. He was asleep.

"Prince Adinor."

"Yes, Elmahigh, what did you ask?"

"The woman you speak of," he said, "the woman you say convinced you to return to the battle..."

"Yes, she did."

"Who is she?"

"Oh, Elmahigh, she was a woman, a village woman running away. She startled me that night for I was lost in my effort to leave the forest."

"It was evening when you traveled?" asked Elmahigh.

"Why, yes, it was, now that you mention it," replied Prince Adinor. "I twas just moments after waking from the strange dreams when I stumbled upon her or more like she surprised me. I was startled for I was convinced I was alone. She was difficult to see. She wore dark colors so she blended well in the night."

Prince Adinor sat up and stared at the fire.

"Go on, young Prince," said Elmahigh.

"I heard footsteps and so I walked out to her. We talked for a while, and eventually, it was she that convinced me to return to you all."

"Did she reveal her name?" asked Elmahigh.

The Prince yawned and rose to his feet. He thought of finding his room and sleeping.

"As I think about it now, I don't recall a name. No, I don't believe she gave me her name at all."

Elmahigh began to walk around the fire, holding his hands behind his back. He studied the Prince.

"What was she running from?" asked Elmahigh.

"I'm not sure something was troubling her," said Prince Adinor.

"And she was out in the forest, so far removed from anyone, completely alone?"

"Yes, I found that strange."

"And of all those present here this evening, she was not among them?" asked Elmahigh.

"No. I would have liked to see her once again. Perhaps I could have danced with her."

"I think it to be very odd," said Elmahigh. "Every villager made their way to this gathering at some point or another. No man, woman or child would have missed such a unique moment. There was no mention of any villagers still missing. No talk of any sad news, nothing. Not one person expressed any concerns for an aloof young girl and yet she found you in the forest on her own. Where were you heading when she did?"

"I was heading in the direction of this village," said Prince Adinor, "I was going home."

"Curious," said Elmahigh, "a matter I will have to illuminate further in the morning. Come, young Prince, the fire is nearly out, let's get you to the others."

They gathered Elmahigh's staff and Prince Adinor's sword nearby and walked around the dwindling fire, nothing more than the tiny glow of the last lit piece of wood remained. As the pair walked toward the inn, the fire went out. The little light that remained was extinguished. The two walked down the street led by the howling laughs and full belly shouts of the inn not far away. Though not much, the Mastadan warriors had uncovered the innkeeper's final remaining barrel of malt-senhop. To Elmahigh's surprise, Dolamite, Theodonus, and the others were still enjoying the spirits.

As Prince Adinor and Elmahigh entered, the inn continued the revelry. Prince Adinor walked around them, careful not to alert anyone of his arrival. He went up the stairs to his quarters. Elmahigh instead found the innkeeper and began conversing with him. Soon after, the warriors decided to end the party; feeling exhausted, they too found their way to their quarters. The celebration was over.

CHAPTER 29

The next day, they awoke to the smell of hot bread and links of pork and carrots coming from the kitchen below. They all descended and began enjoying the delicacies, wasting no time at all. Prince Adinor sat next to Theodonus.

"Do we go after Qualvon today?"

"Yes, my Prince," replied Theodonus.

"Finally," said Dolamite.

'The celebrating has been long enough," said Malchomite.

They finished their meals and thanked those responsible for showing them such wonderful generosity throughout their stay. The innkeeper and his wife both cried upon their departure and so too did the attendants that constantly filled their mugs and served them food.

"Perhaps you will see us once again," said the innkeeper, "for all that you have done for us, we thank you."

The warriors waved and left the inn, stepping out into the street where other gathered to wish them well. They hugged and shook hands with as many as possible. Riding up on horse was Elmahigh who surprised them all with a serious look.

"Good morning, Elmahigh," said Theodonus, "I see you've already found yourself to the stable."

"Yes, do the same," replied Elmahigh. "I will be waiting up ahead at the village entrance. There is someone I must see before we go."

"Well, be sure to have some breakfast," replied Dolamite, "you wouldn't want a ride on an empty stomach."

"Hurry, you fools, get to the stable. I'll meet you soon."

Elmahigh rode off, racing through the streets of the village.

"Well, what's gotten into him this morning?" asked Dolamite.

"Maybe he's still mad he didn't enjoy the last of the innkeeper's maltsenhop with us," said Ecclesias.

"Come," said Theodonus, "let's get mounted and be on our way."

The soldiers walked toward the stables, waving to everyone along the way. The villagers celebrated the warriors once again. Some ran into the street hugging them. Others waved. Still, others presented gifts like bread, fruits, or other small items like a leather pouch. Another Mastadan warrior received a necklace.

"They give even though they have so little," said Prince Adinor.

"Is it not incredible?" asked Theodonus.

"Yes, it is," said Prince Adinor.

They arrived at the stables. Each chose a horse. They mounted and began toward the road which would take them to the Mountain of Citerac. "Where is Bolios?" asked Prince Adinor.

"I'm sure he will be meeting us together with Elmahigh," replied Theodonus, "perhaps he was working on some sword skills or archery this morning. He just can't get enough of it."

The group passed the small temple, reminding Prince Adinor of his mother and the symbol she so often used, inside.

"Wait," said Prince Adinor

"What is it, young Prince?" said Theodonus.

"I will only be a moment."

Leaping off his horse, the Prince ran inside the small temple and walked toward the symbol displayed near the front. He closed his eyes for a couple of moments and then kissed it and returned to the others still waiting. The Prince remounted his horse.

"We can go now," said Prince Adinor.

"Yes, my lord," replied Theodonus.

The group rode further, and soon saw Elmahigh seated atop his horse. The sun rose almost directly behind him. They looked around and did not see Bolios.

"Come closer," said Elmahigh, "there is much to discuss."

"Where is Bolios?" asked Dolamite.

"Will he be here soon?" asked Theodonus.

Elmahigh did not speak and instead looked at each of them.

"Elmahigh, where is Bolios?" asked Prince Adinor.

"I'm not sure," replied Elmahigh.

"He would not have left us," replied Dolamite.

"Where did he go?" asked Prince Adinor.

Elmahigh sat on his horse, thinking of what words to choose. He hadn't seen or heard from their leader since the night prior. A pit in his stomach grew.

The warriors looked around, hoping to see Bolios appear beyond the horizon.

"There comes a time when all must make decisions and choose a path to walk, Prince Adinor," replied Elmahigh. "The path we choose and the reasons we choose it are unique to each of us. Perhaps Bolios has gone, and where he goes, we cannot follow."

"But we could find him," said Prince Adinor.

"Perhaps he didn't want to be found," said Elmahigh, "and so we must let him go."

"I don't understand," said Prince Adinor.

"It's not your path," replied Elmahigh, "therefore, you wouldn't. What Bolios needs of us, is to continue on."

"He'll be back right, Elmahigh?" asked Dolamite.

"God willing in his time," replied Elmahigh. "Nevertheless, there is work yet to be done."

A galloping horse approached. The entire group shielded their eyes from the glaring sun light. It was Bolios.

Applause and yells rang out.

"You worried us," Prince Adinor said.

Bolios shook hands with all his men. He patted Prince Adinor on the back.

"Elmahigh sai—"

"Elmahigh offered some very useful words to me just last night, Prince Adinor," replied Bolios. "There is work to be done."

"What do we do?" asked Theodonus.

"It's time we end this," replied Bolios. "We go after Qualvon, together."

"What of the villagers?" asked Malchomite.

"If Qualvon returns, there may be further loss," said Theodonus.

"Perhaps its best a few of us stay behind," said Prince Adinor, "they will be responsible for protecting the village and ensuring the safe keeping of the people."

"A wise decision, Prince Adinor," said Bolios.

"Who of you will stay?" asked Elmahigh.

The men looked around at one another, but most hung their heads. Then both Ecclesias and Friedrich moved forward.

"We have already been injured, some additional rest and attentions from the healer will help us return to the city center eventually," said Ecclesias.

"Perhaps in such an important time, we can remain behind to ensure some opposition to anything or anyone that comes will be dealt with," said Friedrich.

The other Mastadans smiled.

"I have lost my brother not far from here," said Marcus. "I too will stay in hopes of assuring no one else has to do the same."

"I too will stay," said Malchomite, "I will ensure Friedrich's healing and make him return to his family. I would like to remain as long-term protector together with Ecclesias and Marcus."

"Very well," said Elmahigh, "and so it shall be. Dismount your horses. Prince Adinor, I will need your assistance."

The four warriors stood before Elmahigh, Bolios, and Prince Adinor.

"Kneel," said Elmahigh. "By witness of us here present, with the authority of Prince Adinor, son of King Ralphus Dolamiac, you four: Ecclesias, Friedrich, Marcus, and Malchomite, are hereby knighted and are henceforth protectors of this fine village. This voluntary responsibility is of great importance for you are to keep those here in safety and justice. Ensuring at all times no less than three of you remains here present to defend your people. You are also to keep the king's commands in the highest regards. Stand and be recognized."

All the others yelled and congratulated them for their bravery. Prince Adinor thanked them personally with a handshake and a hug, accepting their service on behalf of his father.

The village protectors departed.

"I follow you sire," said Theodonus.

"We're here with you, Bolios," said Dolamite.

"Yes, my lord," replied Theodonus.

"Let's get on with it," said Dolamite.

They all laughed once again.

Bolios mounted his horse as did the others. They trodded to the road leading to Mount Citerac.

"Strange this darkness," said Prince Adinor, "not a single cloud nor is it evening, yet the light is gone."

"The work of evil," said Elmahigh, "we must be careful, all of us."

"We will," said Bolios, "I will lead the way. Our ride will be swift. Do not fall behind. Prince Adinor, follow me, Dolamite behind him, with Elmahigh and Theodonus last."

"To victory," said Theodonus.

The men took off, leaving the village southof them as they raced toward the large black mountain ahead. Plumes of smoke rose from the highest peak. The massive cloud of gases seemed to pour out of the summit with more frequency as they approached.

"Keep riding," said Bolios.

The soldiers raced across the Mastadan lands. Not a single person was seen along the way. It was only the five of them. The mountain became larger as they neared, which made the difficult climb ahead evident.

"We're nearly there," said Bolios, "push forward."

The base of the mountain was within eyesight, and high above them, the massive white gas continued to rise into the dark sky.

"It's unbearably hot," said Theodonus.

"I fear this is nothing compared to what awaits," said Elmahigh.

"Come on," said Bolios.

CHAPTER 30

The men arrived at the base of the mountain. Its dry black rock formed jagged outcroppings. Each was sharp enough to cut metal and rip apart flesh. The heat coming from the mountain was exasperating as waves of thick breeze pelted them.

"From here we climb on foot," said Bolios.

They leapt off their horses and freed them. The animals raced away from the Mountain of Citerac.

"The rock is dangerous," said Elmahigh. "Be mindful of your footing."

Bolios took one step onto the black dry rock, and immediately, a massive shaking rippled through him and all the others.

Theodonus and Dolamite stood up as Prince Adinor also regained his footing. They once again resumed their climb.

"We must hurry," said Elmahigh. "Exposed out here, we will surely suffer severe injury or death."

"Quickly, men," said Bolios.

Bolios stepped forward as the unstable ground beneath his feet continued to vibrate. He took his sword and stabbed down into the ground in an attempt to support himself as he climbed. The others followed his example and did the same. They moved up the mountain, making certain not to fall for they would not survive.

"What if there's nothing up above?" asked Dolamite. "Maybe it's nothing but a waste of our time."

Prince Adinor looked toward Elmahigh and Bolios.

"We could just turn around," said Theodonus. "No one could survive these conditions. There can't be someone up here."

"There is," said Bolios, "I know it."

"I feel it too," said Elmahigh.

"We continue on," said Bolios.

The men continued on foot, but the path ended. Bolios arrived at the black dry rock rising high toward the top and noticed small pockets of hot steam spewing from the mountain. Nearby was a smaller plume of smoke, also coming from inside the mountain. He moved his sword over it, then lifted his sword toward him and touched the blade.

"Do not touch the steam, it's incredibly hot," said Bolios.

They all gathered around him. Dolamite was struggling to breathe.

"The air is too thick to breathe," said Dolamite. "I don't think I can make it."

"Calm your mind," said Elmahigh.

Bolios walked over to Dolamite and patted him on the shoulder.

"We're nearly there," said Bolios.

"Bolios, where do we enter?" asked Theodonus.

Prince Adinor and Elmahigh looked around and noticed how far from the bottom they already were.

"We also have to get back down, Elmahigh," said the Prince.

"One thing at a time, Prince Adinor," replied Elmahigh.

"There," said Bolios.

Bolios pointed up to a stream of red light coming out from inside the mountain.

"There is where we will enter," said Bolios. "I'll lead the way."

The men began to climb, as the hot black rock warmed them. They were covered in sweat. The heat of the mountain drained them of energy, making them feel faint. Bolios neared a plume of smoke coming from the mountain, forcing him to climb around it.

"Be careful here," he said. "There is an opening with hot gas here. Do not go near it."

As he climbed around it, all the others began to approach also. Prince Adinor was nearly to it when the mountain shook once again.

"Hold on," said Bolios.

The vibration caused loose rocks to fall from up above. Small pebbles and large rocks the size of barrels tumbled down.

"Look out," said Bolios.

Small pebbles and dust hit them as the shaking continued. Just then, a massive rock came down, bouncing off the mountain repeatedly, heading straight for Bolios. The Mastadan leader jumped onto a different part of the mountain, evading it.

"I can't hold on," said Dolamite.

"Secure him," said Elmahigh.

Theodonus climbed down to Dolamite and helped him up during the quakes. They all pressed their bodies as close to the rock as the heat permitted, clutching the rocks with all their strength. All of their muscles contracted as they fought with all their power not to fall off.

"It's almost over," said Bolios.

The vibration continued for another moment and then stopped. The men began to relax. Dolamite, Theodonus, and Prince Adinor again opened their eyes.

"We're alive," said Dolamite, "we're still alive."

Prince Adinor and Theodonus laughed.

"If we don't get to that entrance soon, we won't be," said Elmahigh. "Move your big rear end."

Prince Adinor reached up toward a rock above, and as he did, the rock shot out from the mountain as a large thick plume of smoke erupted from behind it. The heat from the gas burned the Prince's hand, sending shooting pain through his whole body. The Prince fell a couple of feet. He caught himself on a large rock with his right hand. His feet dangled below.

"Help him," said Bolios.

Theodonus and Dolamite both climbed up to the Prince and supported him from below.

"We have you, young Prince," said Theodonus.

The Prince was in terrible pain, and his hand had no feeling.

"I'll be all right," he said. "The gas did not hit me directly."

"Can you reach the opening?" asked Bolios. "We're nearly there."

"I believe so," answered the Prince.

The group continued to climb. Bolios was only a few feet above them. He reached up once again, lifting himself higher, and could now feel the heat from inside the volcano spewing from the opening overhead. The hot wave overwhelmed him. It seemed as if the mountain was trying to cook them alive. Bolios reached up for one last grip and felt the edge of the opening. He pulled himself up. He climbed into the opening and stood up turning to help the others.

"You're almost there, young Prince," he said.

The Prince reached up with one hand, grabbing a large rock, as he pulled himself up and then outstretched his other. Bolios grabbed his hand and hauled him up. The Prince's face was hit with the strong vapors from within the mountain's core, as he set foot on the ledge where Bolios also stood.

"We made it," said Prince Adinor.

"Yes, we did," replied Bolios. "Let's help the others."

Dolamite arrived next, followed by Theodonus and then Elmahigh. The five gathered on the opening. The small lights from the city center fires off in the distance.

"If only everyone could see us now," said Dolamite.

"Let's give thanks they do not have to," said Elmahigh. "Let's hope they never see this view."

"It's time we learn of what brought us here," said Bolios. "Let's go."

Bolios led the men through the narrow opening into the inside of the mountain. As they walked forward, the heat increased, forcing each of them to shield their eyes. The gas ahead rose from deep within the bowels of the mountain down below where the bubbling hot red and yellow lava flowed. Up ahead was a figure, a shadow, standing near the inside rock ledge above the flowing lava. They continued toward it and were now in the bowels of the Mountain of Citerac. The gas continued rising all around them, making them feel more faint and weary. The figure seemed unfettered by it.

"You will regret your decision to face me," said the shadowy figure.

Bolios stopped as Elmahigh and Prince Adinor stood alongside him, Theodonus and Dolamite behind them. The figure turned and faced them all.

"Now you will face evil unlike any you have known. For I am Qualvon and none of you can stop me from my destiny."

"And what destiny might that be?" asked Elmahigh.

Qualvon stepped toward the center of the mountain and said, "I will show you."

He raised his sword high into the sky and a flash of black lightning fell from the sky hitting his sword, causing it to glow red. The warriors shielded their eyes.

* * *

Even from the city center, onlookers could see the giant bolt of black lightning descending from the sky down into the mountain's core.

"Look," said Mastadan citizens. "Lightning falls into the heart of the mountain."

People ran scared in every direction, shoving one another. They were frightened.

* * *

Back in the mountain, Bolios and the others looked on as Qualvon's sword continued flashing red from the bolt of lightning from above. The black lightning stopped, but his sword remained red in his hand. He walked toward the edge of the rock ground he was on and pointed his sword toward the bubbling red and yellow lava below. Out from the sword spewed forth the black lightning as it shot into the hot flowing magma below. The mountain shook and the warriors fell to their knees as the familiar vibration rippled throughout the land once again. The lighting from his sword stopped, and Qualvon lifted his sword, saying, "Witness my power."

* * *

Giant red balls of lava flew from the mountain's core up through the top and out into the sky toward the city center. The Mastadans standing outside saw as the glowing red and yellow balls flew through the dark sky and headed toward them.

"What is that?" asked a little boy.

His father and mother looked up, concerned.

"It's coming this way," said the mother. "Run."

The giant ball of lava plummeted toward a small home below, engulfing it in flames. There was another ball of fire flying through the sky and a third. Both fell upon the city center, destroying two more homes. The Mastadans all panicked, running in every direction away from the flames. King Ralphus looked on from the courtyard high above in the city center royal grounds. He called his military leaders.

"Send aid to those people down there," he said. "See to it all those injured have attention."

* * *

"All of you have ruined the spread of my way throughout the kingdom," said Qualvon, "you meddled in my plans with the villagers and stopped their conversion. Since you will not allow me to carry out the kingdom's transformation, then all of your people will be wiped out."

The group of warriors looked on as Qualvon's eyes began burning yellow. He threw off the animal hides he wore and tossed them into the fires below. Again, he raised his sword, which became engulfed in red once more from the black lightning dropping down onto it from high above in the sky.

* * *

The Mastadans looked on from the city center.

"The lightning from high above comes again," said a warrior standing outside in the courtyard near King Ralphus.

They all turned toward the Mountain of Citerac and saw once again the lightning pouring down into the mountain.

* * *

Bolios and Elmahigh looked on as Qualvon again sent the balls of fiery lava out from the volcanic mountain.

* * *

One hit the warrior quarters at the top of the city center grounds, igniting a section on fire. Another hit the royal gardens, setting some of the flowers and grass ablaze.

"Help those people there," ordered the King.

The final ball of fire plummeted down upon the marketplace, destroying produce and shops alike.

"Run," the people yelled.

* * *

Inside the mountain, Elmahigh turned to the others.

"He will see the entire kingdom destroyed if we do not stop him."

"Our chance is while he raises his sword," said Bolios, "this is when we must attack."

Qualvon ignored them, choosing instead to brand himself with the still burning red sword by placing it to his chest. He erupted in pain.

"I am one with the darkness," he said.

"We must all attack at the same time," said Bolios. "Free the sword from his grip by any means necessary. In the event we cannot get it away from him, I am prepared to take him into the fire myself."

"But you'll die," said Prince Adinor.

Bolios looked at the Prince and touched him on the shoulder.

"A small cost in exchange for the lives of the rest of Mastada," said Bolios.

"The moment approaches," said Elmahigh.

Once again, Qualvon reached his sword into the sky. The black lightning ripped through the sky, once again igniting his sword.

"Now," said Elmahigh.

All of the warriors ran toward Qualvon who stared up toward the sky. Bolios arrived first, knocking Qualvon to the ground. The lightning stopped, but the sword still remained in his hand.

"You can't stop me," said Qualvon.

"It seems I just did."

"I will destroy you all and then the rest of your beloved Mastada as well," said Qualvon.

The group of warriors ran toward him, but Qualvon swung his sword in their direction sending a massive wave of energy toward them. It knocked them to the ground.

"What was that?" asked Dolamite.

"There is sorcery beyond our understanding at play here," said Elmahigh.

Qualvon started laughing at the sight of all of them flung about. His black beard and long dark hair covering his whole head together with his bright yellow eyes evoked how twisted he was. He laughed as he stood before them. "Is this the best warriors your people could offer?" he said. "I will kill you all slowly and make you suffer before you die." He walked toward them.

Bolios rose to fight him.

Qualvon raised his sword as it still burned red and swung it toward Bolios, sending a stream of fire toward him.

Bolios evaded it completely by ducking underneath it. Bolios rolled toward him, jumped to his feet, and swung his sword toward Qualvon, hoping to land a blow, but his blade was met by Qualvon's blade. Upon impact, Bolios' sword was sent flying back behind his opponent.

"Nothing can stop me," said Qualvon.

The enemy punched Bolios and pushed him aside, sending Bolios to his knees. The evil leader continued toward the others when Dolamite and Theodonus decided to attack. The pair swung their swords down toward Qualvon, but he stabbed the ground, sending them both flying backward. The two crashed hard on the ground and grimaced in pain.

"That didn't work," said Dolamite.

Theodonus only looked at him and grimaced

"Understand this," said Qualvon, "the hatred that fuels me is like the fiery magma below which cannot be extinguished."

Elmahigh grabbed his staff and twirled it once overhead, sweeping it down to the ground, sending a thick cloud of dust at Qualvon, blinding him momentarily. The madman wiped his eyes. Elmahigh helped Dolamite and Theodonus up.

"Foolish monk," said Qualvon.

Qualvon blew into the sword and sent a ball of fire down toward them.

"Move," said Elmahigh.

The three scrambled to their feet and dove out of the way just in time. Qualvon laughed once again. Prince Adinor ran toward him, jumped, launching a kick, successfully knocking Qualvon back toward the edge of the cliff.

"Brave boy," said Qualvon, "you will die for it but brave nonetheless."

Prince Adinor crawled backward.

Qualvon was now over him and smiled. "Goodbye, boy." He dropped his sword down upon Prince Adinor, but just as he did, Prince Adinor raised his sword in defense. Qualvon's sword, still glowing red, descended down upon the Prince's sword with all his force, and Prince Adinor held his sword firmly, hoping to defend the blow. As the two swords met, the red glow upon Qualvon's sword extinguished. The two blades locked against one another. Prince Adinor was still alive. Stunned, Qualvon looked befuddled as his sword returned to its regular metal form.

"It's not possible," said Qualvon. "How can this be?" His brow wrinkled, revealing his confusion. "No matter," he said.

Qualvon kicked Prince Adinor who remained on his back, sending the Prince's sword flying. The Prince was inches from the edge of the cliff. Singeing vapor from the hot lava rose from below.

"Whoever you are, now you die," said Qualvon.

With another kick, Qualvon sent the Prince over the edge. Theodonus, Dolamite, Bolios, and Elmahigh looked on as the Prince spilled over the edge out of their view.

"No!" yelled Bolios.

Elmahigh fell to his knees.

Theodonus and Dolamite gasped.

"You animal," yelled Bolios.

Qualvon laughed and raised his arms in delight. The four remaining soldiers rose to their feet.

"You will pay," said Dolamite.

All the men rushed toward him, simultaneously attacking.

Dolamite swung his sword at Qualvon who parried the attack away. Theodonus attempted to stab Qualvon as well, but missed as the warlord jumped aside. Elmahigh swung his staff overhead, forcing his opponent to duck below it. Elmahigh followed the attempt with a swing of his blade. Qualvon met it with his own bringing both of them to a standstill. He was unnaturally strong and fast.

"Hold him," said Bolios.

Qualvon noticed Bolios and jumped away from Elmahigh. He ran towards the entrance they all came in from.

"He's getting away," said Theodonus.

"He will do no such thing," said Elmahigh.

He grabbed his sword from one end and launched it toward Qualvon who ducked, dodging the sword all together.

"You missed," said Dolamite.

The sword was now stuck in the black rock above the entrance.

"It wasn't my intention to hit him," said Elmahigh.

Elmahigh took two steps and launched his staff toward his embedded blade, cracking loose dozens of volcanic rocks, closing the entrance. Qualvon was trapped with them. The evil menace turned and looked back toward them, his eyes still burning yellow.

"No more games," he said.

Qualvon ran toward them once again and began to battle them all, exchanging clashes of swords with each of them. Just as they seemed to be gaining an advantage, Qualvon sliced Dolamite in the leg, forcing the warrior to collapse in pain.

"Help him," said Bolios.

Theodonus grabbed his friend and dragged him away from the struggle.

"I'll be all right," said Dolamite.

He tore Dolamite's shirt and tied it above the wound. "Put pressure on it here," Theodonus instructed Dolamite. Then he placed another small cloth on the wound itself, hoping to slow the bleeding.

"Help," said a voice.

"What was that?" asked Dolamite.

"Help!"

"There it is again," said Dolamite.

Theodonus went over to the edge of the cliff and saw Prince Adinor dangling from the rock below.

"Prince Adinor, you're alive," said Theodonus. "It's Prince Adinor, Dolamite!"

Dolamite smiled as he struggled to stay conscious.

"Hang on, young Prince," said Theodonus.

Theodonus ran behind Elmahigh and Bolios, who both fought Qualvon simultaneously. Theodonus picked up Elmahigh's staff lying on the ground. He grabbed it and returned to the Prince and lowered it down to him.

"Grab it, sire," said Theodonus, "I will pull you up."

Prince Adinor nodded. He reached toward the staff only his fingers could touch it. "It's too far," said Prince Adinor.

Theodonus stretched as far as he could desperate to reach the Prince. "Just a little more," he said.

The Prince reached once again and gripped the staff with his entire hand.

"I got it," said Prince Adinor.

"Hold on tight," replied Theodonus, "I'll pull you up."

Prince Adinor reached them climbing back to his feet.

"Where are Bolios and Elmahigh?" he asked.

Theodonus pointed behind the rising gases.

"Stay here and help Dolamite stop the bleeding," said the Prince.

The Prince walked in the direction of Qualvon, but stopped noticing the semi-visible reflection of his sword not far from him. He ran to it and picked it up. He rubbed off some of the black ash and could once again see his reflection on the handle. His face was covered in black soot and sweat. He was bleeding across his forehead and cheek. He gripped the sword's handle and ran toward the fight where Bolios and Elmahigh continued battling Qualvon. They managed to cut him across the arm and midsection, but both Bolios and Elmahigh had wounds to their head and back, respectively. Qualvon kicked Elmahigh sending him flying toward some rocks, knocking his head. He was unconscious.

"Just you and me," said Qualvon.

The warlord swung his sword toward but Bolios rolled away from it. The Prince ran toward Bolios as Qualvon began to strike again. This time he aimed for Bolios' head. Just as Qualvon's blade was about to chop at Bolios, Prince Adinor stopped it with his own blade.

"I already killed you, boy," said Qualvon.

Prince Adinor lifted his blade, sending Qualvon's away from Bolios who remained on his knees. Weak and out of breath, he collapsed.

"Your best warriors couldn't defeat me," said Qualvon. "What makes you think you can?"

"I will always stand up against evil like you," said Prince Adinor. "You have no place in my kingdom."

"Hahaha," Qualvon laughed.

The Prince ran toward his enemy and swung his sword at Qualvon parried the blade. They jostled back and forth as the Prince held his ground. Qualvon head butted the Prince. The Prince was dazzed momentarily, but steadied himself after wiping his brow. Qualvon laughed again and awaited the Prince's attack. Adinor noticed the gas just over Qualvon's right shoulder. The Prince stepped to his own right several times, maintaining Qualvon in front of him.

"Are you trying a dance with me?" asked Qualvon.

Prince Adinor dug his foot down into the ground and ran at Qualvon, slicing left then right, up and down repeatedly. Qualvon defended each attack. As he did, he backed up toward the gas.

"I admire your spirit," said Qualvon.

The Prince again attacked.

Qualvon continued defending, but inched closer to the gas.

"You can't continue much longer, boy," said Qualvon.

"I don't intend to," said Prince Adinor.

Prince Adinor swung his sword as hard as possible, hitting against Qualvon's. The impact was so great, Qualvon's arm was sent back toward the hot gas. It burned his hand instantly, forcing him to drop the sword down through the gas and into the fiery hot lava below. Qualvon's hand swelled from the skin curdling burns. His sword was engulfed in the hot lava below. He dropped to his knees, grimacing in pain.

"Agh!" he yelled.

"You are beaten," said Prince Adinor as he stood over him.

Qualvon smiled and said, "You're just a boy." The madman spit in his face.

"You won't kill me," said Qualvon. "Watch as I show you how."

Qualvon threw a handful of black ash toward the Prince and ran toward Bolios.

The Prince wiped his eyes.

"No," said Prince Adinor.

The Prince raced toward Qualvon who was pulling Bolios toward the edge of the cliff overlooking the hot lava below. Qualvon showed no signs of stopping and continued dragging the unconscious Bolios closer.

The Mastadan warrior's head now hung over the edge; he inched closer to the end. Qualvon's laugh echoed throughout the volcano.

The Prince stepped closer to Qualvon who continued laughing as he had half of Bolios' body over the edge. The Prince gripped his sword and Qualvon's laughter continued. It pierced the Prince's ears and seemed to grow louder. The Prince looked at Bolios who was almost over the edge of the cliff.

The meniacal laughter continued.

Prince Adinor took a step toward him and then there was silence. Prince Adinor dropped his sword and reached down, pulling Bolios' body back over to safety. He remained unconscious but alive.

"Elmahigh," said Prince Adinor.

"My head is pounding," said Elmahigh.

The wizard rose and walked toward the Prince who was in tears.

"Bolios will be fine," said Elmahigh.

"I know," said the Prince as he wiped the tears from his eyes. Elmahigh walked over to the ledge, seeing nothing below.

"Absolutes cannot be bargained or reasoned with," said Elmahigh. "You've done well, Prince Adinor. You had no other choice."

The Prince stood up alongside his mentor and said, "It's still not enjoyable."

Elmahigh looked over to the Prince and placed his hands upon his shoulders.

"That is why you will be a great king," said Elmahigh. "Come, Prince Adinor. Let's go home."

Elmahigh and Prince Adinor lifted Bolios, who remained unconscious. They moved him toward Theodonus and Dolamite.

"Is it over?" asked Dolamite.

"It is," said Prince Adinor. "We're going home."

EPILOGUE

The company returned to the city center. In the next days began the rebuilding of the damaged areas in the kingdom's capitol. King Ralphus and Queen Sarah held the biggest celebration ever seen in Mastada. Citizens from all over the kingdom arrived in the city center as a large banquet was served in the royal garden. Warriors, monks, royal members, farmers, villagers, artisans, and tradesmen enjoyed the largest gathering ever held.

Bolios made a full recovery. He joined Dolamite and Theodonus as the entire warrior class celebrated the historic victory with barrels of maltsenhop, beer, and wine together with everyone. Monks conducted classes and prayer services for those interested in attending the temple. Villagers and farmers alike walked throughout the warrior grounds and religious grounds, learning of all the uniqueness within their respective areas. Even the King's council joined the festivities and ate and drank together with all those in attendance. The entire capitol mountaintop was covered with Mastadans enjoying the unified celebration of safety in the kingdom. Music from traditional flutes to drums and even singing filled the air.

King Ralphus and Queen Sarah smiled and laughed, drunk with joy from their son's accomplishments. They embraced Adinor and recognized him and all of the warriors present before the Mastadan people. Prince Adinor embraced Theodonus, Dolamite, and Bolios. The new friendships were his reward. The crowd cheered and clapped as the warriors waved to their fellow countrymen. They all went to the warrior grounds and continued the celebration.

Deep within the monk temple, Elmahigh met with the elders. The blue fire before them grew larger. The water from the fountain in the corner began to bubble. The tree opposite the fountain began to sway. The elders began to speak in different languages. Elmahigh remained quiet. A swift wind swept through the room; the torches along the walls went out. The white sand beneath them cooled, and they were in complete darkness. Altinuis and Potreaus stepped inside the room and looked at the growing blue flame in the middle of the elder circle. Elmahigh opened his eyes and noticed a black haze emerge in the flame. He walked toward it, but it was small. It appeared, then faded and reappeared. The elders continued chanting. Elmahigh looked closer, squinting, hoping to discern what it was. He reached a hand out into the flame, hoping to touch it. The elder chanting increased. The blue flame rose covering the entire room. Then the small black haze deep within the blue flame disappeared. There was nothing. The elders fell silent, and Elmahigh opened his eyes, discovering he was still seated in the circle and the elders were quietly next to him.

"There is no definitive indication that the Witch has returned," said an elder.

"The evil cast into the Citerac Mountain was as we foresaw," said another.

"The kingdom is safe, Elmahigh," said the bearded elder. "Unburden yourself and let it be."

Elmahigh remained silent for no question was asked of him. His legs crossed beneath him and arms folded across his chest, the monk awaited an opportunity for a question. There was none. The torches on the walls remained lit, and the tranquil sound of the fountain continued in the corner. The tree opposite it remained unchanged and the sand on his feet was normal.

"Thank you," said Elmahigh.

The monk rose and walked out of the elder entrance. He passed the two familiar guards, Altinuis and Potreaus, saying, "Until next time, my friends."

"Be well, Elmahigh," said Altinuis.

Back at the celebration, Prince Adinor escaped the crowds and walked through the royal palace arriving at a large balcony facing the Citerac Mountain. He walked toward the marble banister and leaned against it, staring at the massive black peak in the distance.

"Your father said you'd be out here,"

Prince Adinor turned and saw Elmahigh.

"I was getting tired of all the hugs and congratulations," said Prince Adinor.

The two looked out toward the mountain range.

"A beautiful day for celebration, my lord," said Elmahigh, "you should be enjoying the company of your warriors and parents."

"I can't," said Prince Adinor.

"That's most unfortunate."

"I can't stop thinking about how I did that."

"Young Prince, you've done nothing wrong."

"I understand that I had to kill Qualvon," he said. "I just don't understand how I stopped his sorcery. He wielded lightning and sent fireballs flying through the air. I know nothing of magic or abilities like that. How did that happen? How was I able to do that? Dolamite said it's because he's rubbing off on me and I'm getting as strong as he is."

Elmahigh smiled.

Prince Adinor continued, "Theodonus keeps telling me to forget about it and just concentrate on the girls.

"Ha," said Elmahigh, "and what does Bolios say?"

"Bolios doesn't say much," replied Prince Adinor. "I think he's just glad it's over."

Elmahigh reached into his pouch and removed something from it.

"What is that?" asked Prince Adinor.

"The sword you wield," said Elmahigh, "where did you get it?"

Prince Adinor looked down at his waist, the red handle of his father's gift remained safely next to him.

"My father gave it to me before I left on our journey," said Prince Adinor.

Elmahigh opened his hand, revealing a wooden token inside it. He placed the token face down on the marble banister in front of the Prince.

"We all witnessed power greater than we had ever seen," said Elmahigh. "Similarly in our journey of life, there will always be challenges and difficulties faced, Prince Adinor, some seemingly insurmountable. But those challenges and even Qualvon's sorcery stand no chance against the greatest of forces."

"And what is that?" asked Prince Adinor.

Elmahigh flipped the wooden token over, revealing one of the four symbols representing the tenants of the monk order. It was the two interconnected rings.

"Despite all the sorcery born of hate and evil wielded by Qualvon, his power had no chance against the good embodied in the sword you carry. That sword is a symbol of the love between father and son and your actions on the mountain were of a friend protecting another. There is no greater love than to give one's life for another. You broke Qualvon's sorcery because of it."

The Prince reached down and took the wooden token in his hand. He examined it and placed it back down on the banister. He removed his sword and placed it next to the token.

"As long as there are Mastadans in this world that act from love, evil can never win, Prince Adinor," said Elmahigh.

Several small clouds moved overhead as the crimson sun streamed light in wide rays of gold.

"It is a beautiful day," said Prince Adinor.

"Come, young Prince," said Elmahigh, "your family, friends, and countrymen await tales of your victory."

The End

GLOSSARY

Beskat Tree—giant orange-brown tree with spindled roots that rise above ground beneath the tree's trunk. Raised roots hold the tree trunk resembling the likes of an octopus.

Biltley flower—pink petals and very small blue pod. When mixed with pumpersty and fire can create mirages or appearances. The mirages and appearances can take different forms, depending on the conjurer.

Bittabottom—herbs used for pain.

Canatamor Tree—large and smooth trunked tree always covered in patches of moss inviting spiders and other crawling insects.

Chautruce—is the meditation skill practiced by many of the monk order to connect with the environment and surrounding energies revealing visions, hints, clues, and past events.

Dendlmen—yellow-and-brown-striped bipedal bird twice as big as an ostrich.

Diatrite—menacing hoard of evil monsters.

Elkan—similar to a deer combined with elk animal, having large horns like a ram.

Farrowers—beautiful exotic birds twice the size of the largest Mastadan. They have multicolored rainbow feathers. They live near the coasts of land, eating large fish and nesting in high trees. They only produce one egg in a lifetime. The male and female birds mate for life.

Furion Wastelands—barren area of nothing but stone, extreme dryness, and smoke rising from the earth due to the magma just below the surface. Said to have shifting plates resulting in quakes, heat, hot plates, and incredibly hot fire spurts from below.

Goulen Mountains—this mountain is a range of high, arid, and rounded boulder-shaped mountains extremely large in size and having no trees or plant life whatsoever. They wrap to the northwest of the Nunavot Pits and wrap north of the pits. The range is the northermost point of the Petruchani Forest, indeed it is the range of mountains ending the land side to the north.

Harvingers—a flesh-eating creature, bigger than most men. These detestable nuisances were often the cause of disappearances of small Nymph or human children alike. They had large powerful wings allowing them to fly for long distances. Their bodies are covered with slimy fur, often a sign of its most recently eaten meal. Its sharp claws dangling below its bodies helped provide an excellent weapon for damaging its prey or holding on to heavy objects. At rest, they usually stand upright.

Maltsenhop—delicious and frothy berry-infused alcoholic drink that is sustenance and also fun to enjoy.

Master members—are Mastadan citizens that undergo a battery of tests to achieve distinction bearing the chance to teach the different arts and serve as standard bearers for the Triped. Only those titled in the areas can give instruction, and it serves as a mentoring journey to truly empower the students in the area of study.

Mountains of Citerac—a giant collection of black molten rock. Legend speaks of housing the most precious rubies and emeralds in existence. It is rocky, rigid, and extremely unstable, and boasts of the most dreadful heat known to man near the center.

Nymph Sea—west of the Petruchani Forest, this unexplored body of water is the western boundary of the Mastadan kingdom.

Petruchani Forrest—the westernmost border said to be the most dangerous and treacherous place for anyone to step foot it. No living member in the entire Kingdom that has ever entered has lived to tell about it. Rumors and legends speak of its inhabitants consisting of everything from witches to trolls and dragons. Mastadan law forbids entry for the kingdom's citizenry's safety.

Pionard—village near the Petruchani Forest. Farthest Mastadan village west of the capitol.

Pumble prat—game of rope on the ground. Kids jump in and hop constantly, and when the "magician" elected by the children yells "pumble prey," you have to leap out of the circle; if the magician yells "pumble pawn," you're "tricked," and if you leap out, you die. If pumble prey and you're last, you die. If you leap out and you're supposed to stay in, you die. Last one alive wins and becomes the "magician."

Pumpersty—a magical powder used over fire or water to create desired conjurings or magic.

Rivers of Ire—three gorgeous rivers to the eastern border of the Kingdom which flow south all the way to Ocean of Despair. Also known as the Trident Rivers, the three rivers are made up of the West, the North, and the East. They flow south and at the point which the river splits in three, from which the north drains to two separate flows, it's also known as the Trident of Ire. Its water source is the Mountains of Citerac.

Sacred Lilliet Garden—a Nymph garden filled with the finest and ripest fruits and vegetables in all of the land, greater than the finest harvest of Mastada. It was originally tended by the First Nymph Queen in the ancient Nymph Empire and is maintained always by the Nymph people.

The Falanx—Prince Adinor's sword gifted to him by his father, King Dolamaic. It is fashioned from the most precious steel in the entire kingdom and forged by the most knowledgeable swordsmiths of the Mountains of Citerac. Its handle is wrapped with tightly sewn bright red board skin and the rubies on the gold base are the precious stones of the kingdom, hammersmede, idorac, tactocite, and zinfeld. It is light and cunningly effective.

The Mercurial—a shipwrecked relic of a time long before. This once fast and gorgeous ship made of finest woods of the Petruchani Forest. A collaboration between Nymph and man, this served as a joint exploration and mapping of the Mastadan kingdom. The descendants of King Nemus and Queen Lilliet, together with the grandsons of the first king of Mastada, lead the efforts.

Triped Trials—the final examination consisting of trials in which boys are actually tested in each area of the triped to determine if they obtained the necessary level of skill from the Triped education. The youngest age a student can be tried (tested) is thirteen, but the majority of students manage the level of achievement necessary at eighteen.

Triped—the three-prong phase of education of old: the academic (reading, writing, and the understanding of morality and law), the natural (resource gathering, understanding the land, using it in congruence with nature's existence and man's dominion as a partner with nature), and the final aspect is military (to understand individual combat, military engagement, and use of weaponry and skills). Each of these areas of study is taught by master members of the kingdom.

Tuckle flutes—warm flaky crust of spiraled usually warm dough interwoven with chocolate or varied fillings.

Urquell—a powerful tea mix of fruit, mountain flower, and herbs with healing capabilities.